CUPCAKE DIARIES

Catch up on all the Cupcake Diaries!

CUPCAKE DIARIES

Katie, batter up!

Mia's baker's dozen

Emma all stirred up!

Alexis cool as a cupcake

by coco simon

Simon Spotlight

New York   London   Toronto   Sydney   New Delhi

Simon Spotlight
An imprint of Simon & Schuster Children's Publishing Division
1230 Avenue of the Americas, New York, New York 10020
This Simon Spotlight bind-up edition June 2015
Katie, Batter Up!; *Mia's Baker's Dozen*; *Emma All Stirred Up*; and *Alexis Cool as a Cupcake* copyright © 2012 by Simon & Schuster, Inc.
All rights reserved, including the right of reproduction in whole or in part in any form.
Text by Tracey West and Elizabeth Doyle Carey
Chapter header illustrations and design by Laura Roode
All rights reserved, including the right of reproduction in whole or in part in any form. SIMON SPOTLIGHT and colophon are registered trademarks of Simon & Schuster, Inc. For information about special discounts for bulk purchases, please contact Simon & Schuster Special Sales at 1-866-506-1949 or business@simonandschuster.com.
Manufactured in the United States of America 0515 FFG
2 4 6 8 10 9 7 5 3 1
ISBN 978-1-4814-6020-0
These titles were previously published individually by Simon Spotlight.

CUPCAKE DIARIES

Katie,
batter
up!

CHAPTER 1

My Cupcake Obsession

$\mathcal{M}$y name is Katie Brown, and I am crazy about cupcakes. I'm not kidding. I think about cupcakes every day. I even dream about them when I sleep. The other night I was dreaming that I was eating a giant cupcake, and when I woke up I was chewing on my pillow!

Okay, now I *am* kidding. But I do dream about cupcakes, I swear. There must be a name for this condition. Cupcake-itis? That's got to be it. I am stricken with cupcake-itis, and there isn't any cure.

My three best friends and I formed the Cupcake Club, and we bake cupcakes for parties and events and things, and sell them. We're all different in our own way. Mia has long black hair and loves fashion. Emma has blond hair and blue eyes and lots of brothers. Alexis has wavy red hair and loves math.

I have light brown hair, and I mostly wear jeans and T-shirts. I'm an only child. And I hate math. But I have one big thing in common with all my friends: We love cupcakes.

That's why we were in my kitchen on a Tuesday afternoon, baking cupcakes on a beautiful spring day. We were having an official meeting to discuss our next big job: baking a cupcake cake for my grandma Carole's seventy-fifth birthday bash. But while we were thinking about that, we were also trying to perfect a new chocolate-coconut-almond cupcake, specially created for my friend Mia's stepdad and based on his favorite candy bar.

We had tried two different combinations already: a chocolate cupcake with coconut frosting and almonds on top and then a coconut cupcake with chocolate-almond frosting, but none of them matched the taste of the candy bar enough. Now we were working on a third batch: a chocolate-almond cupcake with coconut frosting and lots of shredded coconut on top.

I carefully poured a teaspoon of almond extract into the batter. "Mmm, smells almondy," I said.

"I hope this batch is the one," said Mia. "Eddie finally started taking down that gross flowery wallpaper in my bedroom, and I have to find some way to thank him. I would have paid someone a million dollars to do that!"

"You realize you could buy a whole new house for a million dollars, right?" Alexis asked. "Probably two or three."

"You know what I mean," Mia replied. "Besides, you know how ugly that wallpaper is. It looks like something you'd find in an old lady's room."

"Hey, my grandma Carole's an old lady, and she doesn't have ugly wallpaper in *her* house," I protested.

Emma picked up the ice-cream scoop and started scooping up the batter and putting it into the cupcake pans.

"We need to find out more about your grandma," Emma said. "That way we can figure out what kind of cupcake cake to make for the party."

"Right!" Alexis agreed. She flipped open her notebook and took out the pen that was tucked behind her ear. Sometimes I think Alexis must have a secret stash of notebooks in her house somewhere. I've never seen her without one.

"First things first," Alexis said. "How many people are coming to the party?"

I wrinkled my nose, thinking. "Not sure," I said.

Then I yelled as loud as I could. "Mom! How many people are coming to Grandma Carole's party?"

My mom appeared in the kitchen doorway. "Katie, you know how I feel about yelling," she said.

"Sorry, Mom," I said in my best apology voice.

"The answer is about thirty people," Mom said. "So I think if the cupcake cake has three dozen cupcakes, that would be fine."

"What exactly is a cupcake cake, anyway?" Mia asked. "Do you mean like one of those giant cupcakes that you bake with a special pan?"

"I was thinking more like a bunch of cupcakes arranged in tiers to look like a cake," Mom replied.

Mia nodded to Alexis's pen and notebook. "Can I?"

"Sure," Alexis replied, handing them to her. Mia began to sketch. She's a great artist and wants to be a fashion designer someday.

"Like this?" Mia asked, showing Mom the drawing. I looked over Mia's shoulder and saw the plan: three round tiers, one on top of the other, with cupcakes on each.

"Exactly!" Mom said, smiling and showing off a mouth full of perfect white teeth. (She *is* a dentist, after all.)

4

Alexis took back her notebook. "Excellent," she said, jotting something down. "Now we just need to decide what flavor to make and how to decorate it."

"What do you think, Mom?" I asked.

"Oh, I'm staying out of this. This is your project," Mom replied. "I think I'll let you girls come up with something. You always come up with such wonderful ideas, and I know Grandma Carole will love whatever you do."

"All done!" Emma announced, putting down the ice-cream scoop.

"Mom, oven, please?" I asked.

"Sure thing," Mom said, slipping on an oven mitt. She put the chocolate-almond cupcakes into the preheated oven, and I set the cupcake-shaped timer on the counter for twenty minutes.

Mom left the kitchen, and the four of us sat down at the kitchen table to work out the details.

"So what kind of flavors does your grandmother like?" Alexis asked.

I shrugged. "I don't know. She likes all kinds of things. Blueberry pie in the summer, and chocolate cake, and maple-walnut ice cream . . ."

"So we can make blueberry-chocolate-maple cupcakes with walnuts on top!" Mia joked.

5

"Hey, we thought bacon flavor was weird and that worked out well!" said Emma. It was true. Bacon flavor was a really big seller for us.

"You know, we don't know anything about your grandma," Emma said. "Maybe if you tell us something about her, we can get some ideas."

"Sure," I said. "Hold on a minute."

I went into the den where Mom and I keep all our books and picked up a photo album. We have lots of them, and there were pictures of Grandma Carole in almost all of them. I turned to a photo of me and my mom with Grandma Carole and Grandpa Chuck at Christmas. Grandma Carole looked nice in a red sweater and the beaded necklace I made her as a present at camp. Her hair used to be brown like mine, but now it's white.

"That's her," I said. "And that's my grandpa Chuck. They got married, like, forever ago, and they have three kids: my mom and my uncle Mike and my uncle Jimmy. She used to be a librarian."

"Just like my mom!" Emma said, smiling.

I flipped the pages in the photo album and found a picture of Grandma Carole in her white tennis outfit, holding her racquet.

6

"Mostly she loves sports and stuff," I said. "She runs, like, every day, and she won track medals in high school. She goes swimming and plays tennis, and skis in the winter, and she likes golf even though she says there's not enough running."

"Do sports have a flavor?" Mia mused.

"Um, sports-drink-flavored cupcakes?" Alexis offered.

"Or sweat-flavored cupcakes," I said, then burst out giggling.

"Or smelly sneaker-flavored cupcakes," Mia said, laughing.

"Ew, sweat and sneakers . . . those are so gross!" Emma squealed.

"But I guess she does like sports most of all," I said. "She's always trying to get me to do stuff with her. Because I am *soooo* good at sports." I said that really sarcastically, because the exact opposite is true. Now it was Emma's turn to giggle.

"Yeah, I've seen you in gym," she said.

"It's even worse than you know," I confessed. "When she tried to teach me to ski, I wiped out on the bunny hill—you know, the one for little kids? I even sprained my ankle."

"Oh, that's terrible!" Emma cried.

"And when I played tennis on a team with

7

Grandpa, I accidentally whacked him in the head with my racquet."

Mia put a hand to her mouth to try to stop from laughing. "Oh, Katie, that would be funny if it weren't so terrible!" she said.

I nodded. "He needed four stitches."

"So I guess you don't take after your grandmother," Alexis said.

"Well, not the sports thing," I admitted. "But everyone says I look exactly like she did when she was younger. And she's a good baker, too. She used to own her own cake baking business."

Alexis stood up. "You're kidding! Why didn't you tell us?"

"I just did," I said.

"But she's a *professional*," Alexis said. "It's not going to be easy to impress her."

"Yes, the pressure is on," Mia agreed.

I hadn't thought of that before. "Well, we'll just have to make a superawesome cupcake cake, then."

Alexis sat back down. "Okay, people, let's start jotting down some ideas."

We tried for the next few minutes, but nobody could think of anything. Then Emma looked at her watch.

"You know, I need to get home," she said. "It's my turn to make dinner tonight."

"We need some more time to come up with ideas, anyway," Alexis said. "Let's schedule another meeting."

"Let's do it tomorrow," I suggested. But Alexis and Mia had whipped out their smartphones, and Emma took out a little notebook with flowers on it—and they were all frowning.

"Alexis and I have soccer practice tomorrow and Thursday, and a game on Friday," Mia reported.

"And I have concert band practice on Wednesdays and Fridays," Emma said. Emma plays the flute, and she's really good at that.

"Sorry, Katie. You know spring is a busy time of year," Alexis said.

"Yeah, sure," I said, but really, I didn't. I don't really do anything besides the Cupcake Club, and it's not just because I have cupcake-itis. I'm no good at sports, and I'm not so great at music, either. When we learned how to play the recorder in fourth grade, I ended up making a sound like a beached whale. My teacher made me practice after school, after everyone went home.

Just then the cake timer rang. I put on a mitt and opened the oven door. All the cupcakes in the pan were flat. They should have gotten nice and puffy as they cooked.

"Mom!" I yelled.

Mom rushed in a few seconds later. "Katie, what did I tell you about—Oh," she said, looking at the deflated cupcakes.

"What happened?" I asked.

"This looks like a baking powder issue to me," she said. She put the pan of flat cupcakes on the counter and picked up the little can of baking powder. "Just as I thought. It's past its expiration date. You need fresh baking powder for your cupcakes to rise."

I felt terrible. "Sorry, guys."

"It's not your fault," Emma said.

"Yeah, and anyway, Eddie's not finished taking down that wallpaper yet," Mia said. "We can try again next time."

"Whenever that is," I mumbled.

Emma, Alexis, and Mia started picking up their things.

"We can talk about your grandma's cupcakes at lunch on Friday," Alexis said. "Everybody come with some ideas, okay?"

Emma saluted. "Yes, General Alexis!" she teased.

"Ooh, if Alexis is the general, can I be the cupcake captain?" I asked, and everyone laughed.

10

When my friends left, the kitchen was pretty quiet. Mom went into the den to do some paper-work, and all that was left was me and a pan of flat cupcakes.

As I cleaned up the mess, I thought of Alexis and Mia and Emma all going off and doing stuff—stuff that I couldn't do. They were all multitalented, and the only thing I was good at was making cupcakes. It made me feel a little bit lonely and a little bit like a loser.

In fact, it made me feel as flat as those cupcakes.

Yummy!

CHAPTER 2

Do I Really Look Like a Deer?

After I cleaned up I did my math homework while Mom made dinner, but that did not exactly improve my mood. In fact, when I sat down to eat I was feeling flatter than ever, even though Mom made tofu and broccoli in sesame sauce, which is superdelicious. (And please don't go hating on tofu. It's got a bad rap, but that stuff is pretty tasty. You should try it sometime.)

But that night even the deliciousness of tofu couldn't get me out of my mood. Mom noticed right away. She always does. I think it's because it's just the two of us in the house most of the time. Dad left when I was little, and I don't have any brothers or sisters, like I said before. If I had a big family, like Emma's, I could probably sulk through dinner without being spotted. But Mom started with the questions right away.

"What's wrong, Katie? Did you get enough sleep last night? You weren't up reading under the covers again, were you?"

"No, Mom, I'm not sleepy," I said.

"Are you feeling sick? Does your throat hurt?"

"No," I said, picking at some tofu with my fork. I didn't look up from the plate.

Then Mom changed her tone. Her voice got softer. "Okay, honey. If there's something you want to talk about, I'm here."

That understanding mom voice always gets me, even when I don't feel like talking. I put down my fork.

"It's kind of hard to explain," I said. "It's just . . . Mia and Alexis and Emma all do other stuff besides the Cupcake Club. Like play soccer and flute, and Emma walks dogs . . . and I don't do anything. Besides the Cupcake Club, I mean."

Mom didn't say anything right away. Then she said, "Well, you do well in school, and the Cupcake Club takes up a lot of your time. But maybe doing a different kind of activity isn't a bad idea. Is there something you're interested in?"

"That's the problem," I said. "I'm not good at

sports. I'm just not. I'm the worst in my whole gym class. And I could never play an instrument like Emma. Remember what happened when I learned the recorder?"

Mom cringed. "Oh dear. I see what you mean," she said. "But sports and music aren't the only things the school offers. I'll tell you what. After dinner let's get on the computer and look at the school website. Okay?"

"Okay," I agreed. It actually sounded like a good idea. Why hadn't I thought of that before? There had to be something that I would like.

So after we ate (I ate every single piece of tofu on my plate) and cleaned up the dishes, Mom set up her laptop in the kitchen. I'm not sure why, but we seem to do everything in the kitchen. It's like if the house had a heart, it would be the kitchen, you know? (Okay, I know that sounds a little weird. Maybe I'm eating too much tofu.)

Anyway, we went on the Park Street Middle School website and clicked on "Activities and Clubs." There was lots of stuff to choose from. We went down the list alphabetically.

"How about the chess club?" Mom asked.

"Boring," I said.

"The drama club?" Mom suggested. "You're

very funny, Katie. You're always entertaining your friends."

That was a pretty nice compliment, I thought. But I had one objection. "I can be funny in front of my friends. But on a stage? No way. I would totally freak out."

"Are you sure?" Mom asked. "You don't know until you try."

I tried picturing myself in front of an auditorium full of people, and I got sweaty just thinking about it. "Nope."

"All right," Mom said. "How about the debate team?"

I shook my head. "If I don't want to be funny in front of people, I certainly don't want to debate in front of them. Plus, I'd have to research topics and gather information. You need to put a lot of work into getting your point across."

"Well you certainly did a good job getting your point across that you don't want to debate," Mom said with a smile. "How about the math club?"

"That would be 'no' with a capital *N*," I said.

Mom sighed. "Well, there must be *something* here you'd like to do," she said. "Why don't you take a look?"

As she turned the laptop to face me, the phone

rang. Mom got up from the table and picked up the phone on the wall.

"Hi, Mom," she said, and I knew she was talking to Grandma Carole. "Yes, the girls met today, but we're going to keep your special dessert a secret. No, I won't give you any hints!"

Then Mom took the phone into the living room, and I knew she was trying to talk to Grandma without me hearing. I strained to listen, but Mom was talking in her low phone voice.

Then she came back in the kitchen. "Katie, Grandma wants to talk to you."

I took the phone. "Hi, Grandma."

"Hello, Katie-kins!" Grandma Carole said. She has called me Katie-kins since I can remember, and she is the *only* one who calls me that—so don't get any ideas. "So, your mom tells me you're trying to find an after-school activity you can try."

"Yeah," I said. "But I'm having a hard time."

"What about sports?" Grandma asked.

"Well, I'm not exactly great at sports," I said. "Remember Grandpa's stitches?"

"Accidents happen," Grandma said. "And you're young—like a baby deer finding her legs."

A baby deer? I thought. This conversation was getting a little weird.

16

"Haven't you ever seen a baby deer on one of those animal shows on TV? At first when they try to walk they are really wobbly. But after just a little while, once they gain confidence, they are frolicking in the woods with all the other deer. You just need practice—and confidence. Maybe you'd feel more comfortable joining a team with your friends. Do your friends play any sports?"

"Mia and Alexis play soccer," I replied. "But I stink at soccer."

"Nonsense!" Grandma Carole said. "Have you ever played before?"

"Well, a couple of times in gym, and—"

"That's all? That's not a true test," she interrupted. "Soccer is a wonderful game. Doesn't it look like fun when you see your friends play?"

"It kind of does," I admitted.

"Life is not worth living if you're always sitting in the stands, Katie," Grandma said. "Go out there and try out for the soccer team. I bet you will surprise yourself."

"Maybe I will," I told her. Grandma Carole was so convincing, I was starting to feel like I could kick a goal from all the way across the field.

"I love you, Katie-kins. Now will you give me a hint about my birthday dessert?"

17

I laughed. "Nice try, Grandma! Not a chance. It's a surprise."

Grandma chuckled. "Okay then. It was worth a shot. Please give me back to your mom."

"Bye, Grandma. Love you, too," I said and then handed the phone to Mom. She was smiling.

I was smiling too. I didn't feel flat anymore. I had a plan. Tomorrow at lunch, I would talk to Mia and Alexis about soccer.

CHAPTER 3

I've Got a Plan

The cafeteria at Park Street Middle School is pretty much like any other cafeteria. Lunch ladies serve food from behind steamy serving tables. It's superloud, and at some point spitballs will be thrown (usually by Eddie Rossi and his friends). And even though the seats aren't marked, everyone sits in the same place every day.

Take the Popular Girls Club (PGC), for example. They have the best table in the cafeteria, the one closest to the lunch line, where you can see everybody who goes by. Sydney Whitman, their blond-haired, blue-eyed leader, always sits in the right corner seat. Her friend Maggie sits next to her, and Bella sits across from Maggie. Callie, my former best friend, sits across from Sydney. The rest of the seats are empty—unless Queen Sydney gives her royal permission for someone to sit there.

Even though Callie's not my best friend anymore, she's still kind of my friend, so I always say hi to her on the way to my table. Callie always says hi back, but Sydney usually rolls her eyes or else she whispers something to Maggie and they laugh. I just ignore them. It makes life easier that way.

Anyway, I think the Cupcake Club table is the best one in the cafeteria even though it's kind of way in the back. But it's a little bit quieter back there, so Mia, Alexis, Emma, and I can talk cupcake business without anybody bothering us. (Well, most of the time. There was that one day when Eddie shot a spitball at us from ten tables away. Gross, but impressive.)

This Wednesday I found Mia at the table. She usually gets there first. Alexis and Emma were in the hot-lunch line, like they always are.

"Hey," I said to Mia, who was opening the lid of her plastic lunch container. I noticed what looked like little pies inside. "Pie for lunch?" I asked.

"They're empanadas," Mia explained. "They're kind of like pies, but they don't have to be sweet. These are chicken and cheese. My dad and I visited my *abuela* last weekend, and she sent me home with a bunch."

Now, I only started taking Spanish this year, but I hang around with Mia enough to know that "*abuela*" means "grandmother."

"Cool. Your grandma bakes too," I said.

"Want a bite?" Mia asked, holding out one of the empanadas.

"Sure," I said. I opened my lunch bag and took out some carrots and some homemade oatmeal cookies. "Only if we can trade."

"Deal," Mia said with a grin.

Alexis and Emma walked up carrying trays of spaghetti and salad.

"I love spaghetti day," Alexis said, sliding into her seat. "It actually tastes like food."

"If the other stuff doesn't taste like food, then what does it taste like?" I asked.

"I'm not sure," Alexis replied. "Alien brains, maybe?"

Emma giggled. "It's not that bad."

Alexis and Emma started to eat their spaghetti. I decided to come right out with my idea. It was all I could think about all morning.

"So, I was talking to my grandma last night," I said.

21

"About cupcakes?" Alexis asked.

"Not exactly," I answered. "We were talking about why I don't participate in activities, like sports. I know I'm terrible at them, but grandma thought maybe it's because I haven't played a lot. You know, just to have fun."

Emma nodded. "That could be it. I've been playing basketball and Wiffle ball with my mom and dad and my brothers since I was little. Maybe that's why I don't stink at it."

"And in Manhattan, I joined my neighborhood soccer league when I was five," Mia added.

"Yeah, so, I was thinking maybe I could try soccer," I said a little shyly. "I mean, I know I'm no good or anything but—"

"Katie, that would be so cool!" Mia said, her dark eyes shining with excitement. "I would love it if you played with us!"

"Definitely," Alexis agreed. "That would be so much fun if you were on the team!"

"And don't worry about not being good," Mia said quickly. "Alexis and I can help you. Right, Alexis?"

"Of course," Alexis said. "We have a game on Saturday, so maybe that afternoon we could practice with you."

"Perfect!" I said happily.

It made me feel good to see Mia and Alexis so excited about me being on the team. And with their help, maybe I could be a halfway decent player. I actually felt a little bit excited about trying out. Maybe this wouldn't be so bad after all.

"You know, you should come to my house tomorrow after school," Emma said. "You could play some basketball with me and my brothers. Just for fun, like you said. Who knows? If you're good, you could try out for the team next winter."

The idea of playing basketball with anybody— especially teenage boys—would normally make me very nervous. But for some reason I felt like I could actually do it. Maybe my friends' enthusiasm was rubbing off on me.

"Okay," I said.

The little voice inside me was saying, *Basketball? Are you crazy? You couldn't make a basket if you climbed on a ladder!*

It's just for fun, I told the little voice. *I've got to try, just like Grandma said.*

CHAPTER 4

It's Supposed to Be *Touch* Football

There was one thing that Grandma Carole hadn't psyched me up for: gym class. There are lots of reasons why I hate gym class more than any other class, even math:

   1. I stink at all sports. (Yes, I'm trying new ones. But right now I stink at most of them.)
   2. The teacher, Ms. Chen, has no heart. She's not mean, exactly, but when you mess up, she doesn't say, "Oh, don't worry about it, honey," like my mom would. Instead she says, "Look sharp, Katie!" or "Get it together, Katie!" If Ms. Chen wasn't a gym teacher, I think she would be an ice princess living

in an ice castle, with her glossy black hair pulled back and a white sparkly dress, and everything she touched would turn to ice.

3. Both Sydney *and* Maggie of the Popular Girls Club are in that class, and I only have one friend in gym with me: Emma.

4. Back in September my friend George Martinez started teasing me by calling me "Silly Arms," after that sprinkler thing with the arms that wiggle all over the place, squirting out water. I guess that's what I look like when I play volleyball. Anyway, I didn't mind when George said it, but now other kids call me that too.

So two periods after lunch I was in the gym, wearing my blue shorts and my blue T-shirt that says PARK STREET MIDDLE SCHOOL in yellow writing on the front. Emma and I were sitting on the bleachers, waiting for class to start.

Sydney and Maggie were the last ones out of the locker room. Maggie has frizzy brown hair that's always in her face, but Sydney always manages to look perfect, even in a gym uniform. Her straight, shiny hair is never out of place. I'm not sure how she does it. I think she must have been born that way. I can just picture Sydney as a little baby in the hospital. All the other babies would be screaming and crying, and little Sydney would be quietly smoothing her perfect hair.

Ms. Chen marched out of the gym teacher's office carrying her clipboard, and Sydney walked up to her with a big smile on her face.

"Ms. Chen, what are we doing today?" she asked.

"Flag football," Ms. Chen replied. She nodded over at George Martinez and Ken Watanabe. "George, Ken, get the flags from the supply closet."

"Flag football! Awesome!" Ken shouted. He and George high-fived as they raced to the supply closet.

I groaned as the boys ran off.

"It won't be so bad," Emma said, but she didn't sound convinced.

"Honestly, I will never figure out how to play that stupid game," I said. "Are you supposed to run around and grab other people's flags? Then why is there a ball involved?"

"It's like football, but instead of tackling the player with the ball, you grab their flag," Emma explained.

26

I shook my head. "You might as well be telling me how to build a rocket right now," I said. "I do not get it. It's too confusing."

"Then just run around and stay away from the ball," Emma suggested.

"Now *that* sounds like a plan," I agreed.

Ms. Chen blew her whistle, and we both jumped up and ran to line up on the black line that goes all around the edges of the gym. Ms. Chen took attendance and then made us warm up with jumping jacks, push-ups, and sit-ups.

I'm pretty good at jumping jacks and sit-ups, but that whole push-up deal is not so easy; maybe because my arms are so skinny. I am usually on my third one while the class is finishing up number ten.

"Look alive there, Katie!" Ms. Chen called out.

Or I will turn you into ice, I thought. *Actually, that wouldn't be so bad. Then I wouldn't have to play flag football.*

Then it was time to choose teams. She made George and Ken captains. George picked me to be on his team, which was nice because he didn't even pick me last. But then he picked Sydney and Maggie, and Ken picked Emma.

"Oh this is great. We're on a team with Katie,"

27

Sydney said loudly, in a supersarcastic voice.

I looked at Emma across the room.

Help me! I mouthed and then frowned, but all Emma could do was make a sad face back.

We were the red team, so we each had to strap this red belt thing around our waists and then stick a red scarf thing, the flag, in it.

Just stay away from the ball, I kept telling myself. *Everything's going to be all right.*

Boy, was I wrong.

It didn't start out too bad. Our team had the ball first, and George threw it to Wes Kinney, and he ran toward the other team, and Ken chased him and pulled his flag. I didn't have to do anything.

Then the other team had the ball, and Ken threw it to Aziz Aboud, and then Aziz threw it back to Ken, and then Wes grabbed Ken's flag and yelled out, "Revenge!"

Then it was our team's turn again, and before Ms. Chen blew the whistle I saw Sydney whispering to George. Then the play started, and George pretended like he was going to throw the ball to Wes again, only he handed it to Sydney.

I was kind of running around in a circle, minding my own business, when I heard Sydney yell, "Katie! Catch!"

The next thing I knew, I saw a football flying toward my head.

"Ow!" I cried as the ball smacked me on top of the head.

Sydney giggled. "Oops! Sorry, Katie. I guess my aim is off today."

Yeah, right, I thought as I rubbed my sore head.

"Shake it off, Katie!" Ms. Chen yelled.

See what I mean? No sympathy.

Ms. Chen blew her whistle again, and I resumed my plan of running around aimlessly.

Emma ran up to me. "Sydney *so* did that on purpose!" she whispered.

"I know!" I hissed back. "And she doesn't even get in trouble!"

For the next few plays I was Sydney's target. She kept getting the ball, and every time she got it she threw it to me no matter where I was.

"Come on, Silly Arms. Try to catch it!" George called out.

"Yeah, Silly Arms!" Sydney repeated, and she and Maggie burst into giggles.

Wes rolled his eyes. "You guys are so dumb," he said, and I thought he was actually standing up for me. But then he said, "Why would you even throw it to Katie? She can't catch anything. She

29

couldn't catch on fire if she wanted to."

I could feel my cheeks getting red. This game was turning into my worst nightmare. When did it suddenly become "Let's Pick on Katie Day"?

Luckily, the next time Sydney had the ball, Eddie ran up to her and grabbed her flag. Eddie is kind of a jerk, but he's the tallest boy in middle school, and I guess he's pretty handsome. He even grew a mustache last summer, but his mom finally made him shave it off.

Anyway, Sydney got all giggly and pushed into Eddie after he got the flag. The next time Eddie had the ball, Sydney and Maggie chased after him, and then instead of grabbing his flag, they kind of fell into him, and all three of them fell onto the floor.

Ms. Chen blew her whistle. "Break it up, people!"

From then on all Sydney and Maggie wanted was to get the boys' attention, which was fine with me. The next time Sydney got the ball she ran right *at* Eddie and Aziz instead of trying to avoid them. The boys started tackling her, and Sydney started shrieking.

"My hair! You're messing up my hair!"

Ms. Chen blew her whistle. "Eddie! Aziz! On the bench!" she yelled.

Grumbling, the two boys walked to the bleachers. I couldn't believe it. Sydney was the one who started everything, and once again, she didn't get in trouble at all! I know Mom says I shouldn't say "hate" about anyone, but I really do hate Sydney Whitman.

The rest of the game was a mess. Even though the blue team had lost Eddie and Aziz, our team couldn't score because Sydney and Maggie kept bumping into George and Wes and the other boys and giggling.

Finally the game ended.

"Blue team wins by two points!" Ms. Chen announced, and the blue team cheered.

Wes punched me in the arm. "Thanks a lot, Skinny Arms," he said in a mean voice.

"Yeah, thanks for making us lose, Skinny Arms," Maggie added, and everybody on the red team laughed.

Well, everybody but George. "Hey, she's Silly Arms, not Skinny Arms!" he yelled. I gave him a look. Then he came up to me and said, "It wasn't your fault, Katie." But I didn't say anything to him. Everybody else thought I made the team lose, and that was so unfair. It was Sydney's fault! But if I said anything, Sydney's crew would back her up

31

and I'd just end up looking like a sore loser.

I felt like crying, but I didn't because I knew that would only make things worse. So I ran into the locker room without looking back.

I was going to have to get good at sports soon or the rest of my life was going to be miserable.

CHAPTER 5

Outshined by a Kindergarten Kid

The next day after school I walked home with Emma. She seemed really excited. As for me, I wasn't as confident as I had been the other day at lunch. My stomach had been in nervous knots all day. Me, play basketball? What was I thinking?

"This is going to be fun, Katie, I promise," Emma said. "Nothing like gym class."

I wanted to believe her, and I knew that Emma's brothers were basically nice. Jake was in kindergarten, and he's really cute and sweet. Her oldest brother, Sam, is in high school, and he plays sports and works at the movie theater, and he's smart and nice, too.

Then there's Matt, who's one grade above us in

middle school. Alexis had a crush on him a few months ago, and I'm not sure why. I guess he's cute, but he's definitely not as handsome as Sam. And he's a total slob. And sometimes he says mean things to Emma. But most of the time he's pretty nice.

"Okay," I said, taking a deep breath. "Just for fun. I can do that. At least Ms. Chen won't be there telling me to look sharp."

"And Sydney won't be there either," Emma promised. Then she started talking in a silly high voice. "Oh, help! Help! My hair!"

I laughed. Emma is one of those people who never says anything bad about anybody, but Sydney was being so ridiculous lately that even Emma couldn't help it.

"Well, I don't care if my hair gets messed up," I said honestly. "I'd just like to make at least one basket for a change."

"I'm sure you'll do great," Emma said confidently.

When we got to Emma's house, her three brothers were already playing in the driveway. Matt was dribbling a basketball between his legs, and Sam was holding up Jake, so he could make a dunk shot. Jake dropped the ball through the hoop and then clapped his hands.

"I did it!" he cheered.

Sam swung Jake around and put him on the ground. Then he saw me and smiled. "Hey, Katie."

"Hey," I said back, and my heart was beating really fast, and my palms started to get sweaty. I didn't mention this before, because it's kind of embarrassing, but I guess I have kind of a crush on Sam. Mia does too. He's got blond hair, like all of the Taylors, and he always smells nice; not sweaty like Matt. And, I know, he's in high school and I'm in middle school, so I couldn't date him or anything. (Actually, the whole idea of dating kind of terrifies me, anyway.) But still, I can't help how I feel when I'm around him sometimes.

Then Matt ran up to the basket and did one of those shots where you jump up and sink the ball from the side. He was showing off, I think.

"So let's get this game started," he said. "Boys against girls, right?"

"Seriously?" I asked, and I suddenly felt cold and clammy. How were Emma and I supposed to play against two older boys who were practically professionals?

"Don't worry, you can have Jake," Matt said with a grin. He tossed the ball to Emma. "Girls first."

Emma took the ball to a chalk line drawn across the driveway.

"This is the foul line," she explained. "Every time we start, we start from here."

"Got it," I said.

"I've got Katie!" Matt called out, and he ran and stood next to me.

Sam stood facing Emma, blocking her. Jake was running around yelling, "Throw it to me! Throw it to me!"

Sam was a lot bigger than Emma, but Emma was fast. She ducked to the left, and before I knew what was happening, she threw the ball to me!

To my surprise, I caught it. And then . . . I stood there.

"Go to the basket, Katie!" Emma called out.

I turned around and started to dribble the ball. One . . . two . . . and then Matt slapped the ball away from me.

"Oh yeah!" he cried, dribbling up to the basket. Then he sank a shot cleanly through the net.

"Two points!" he cheered, and he and Sam high-fived each other. Then Matt took the ball to the foul line.

"Block him, Katie," Emma instructed me. "Don't let him get past you."

I stood in front of Matt, like I had seen Sam stand before, and kind of spread my arms wide and bent my knees.

"Katie, you look like a gorilla!" Matt teased. "Come on, try and get the banana."

He held up the ball, like he was going to throw it, and I jumped up to block it. Then he darted to the left and bounced the ball toward the basket, sinking another shot.

"And he scores again!" Matt congratulated himself.

"Dude, you're hogging the ball," Sam complained.

"I can't help it if I'm awesome," Matt replied, and Sam punched him playfully in the arm.

Then it was my turn to take the ball to the foul line. Matt was guarding me, and I was really stressed out. Sam was so tall that I couldn't even see Emma, and Jake was running in circles again, yelling, "Me! Me!"

I just stood there, trying to decide what to do. Matt started tapping his foot impatiently.

"Sometime this century, please," he said.

I had no choice. I bounced the ball to Jake, and he caught it! Then he ran up to the basket and chucked the ball underhand with all his might.

The ball rolled around and around on the rim—and then it went in!

"Yay, Jake!" Emma cheered.

Jake ran up and high-fived her. "I'm awesome too!" he bragged.

I was happy for Jake, but even more embarrassed than ever—a kindergarten kid was better than me!

Still, it was kind of fun, even though I was terrible at it. The next time our team got the ball, Emma threw it to me, and Matt accidentally knocked into me while he tried to block me.

"Foul!" Sam yelled. "Katie, you get a free shot from the foul line."

Matt tossed the ball to me, and I stood on the chalk line, facing the basket. Everyone was staring at me, and I could feel my palms getting sweaty again. I wasn't sure if I was holding the ball right or how to shoot. I swung the ball underhand and then let go. The ball soared through the air and . . . crashed into the garbage cans on the other side of the driveway.

"Wrong basket, Katie!" Matt teased, and my face went red.

Sam ran and got the ball. "She gets a do over," he said.

"No fair!" Matt cried. "Why?"

"Because I said so," Sam told him. (Didn't I tell you he was nice?)

Sam stood behind me and reached over my head and put the ball in my hands. I could feel my heart getting all fluttery again. He placed my hands on the right spots on the ball and then he grabbed my arms.

"Pull back, then push up," he said, moving my arms the right way as he talked. "Let go when you're at the top. Don't aim for the basket, aim for the spot on the backboard just above the basket."

What I heard was "Blah, blah, blah, blah, blah" because I couldn't concentrate with Sam so close to me. Then he stepped back.

"Okay, give it a try, Katie," he said. "You can do it!"

I took a deep breath and tried to throw the ball the way Sam showed me. The ball soared through the air . . . and dropped down at least three feet below the basket.

"Painful!" Matt called out. "Better luck next time, Katie."

Sam tried to cheer me up. "Don't worry about it, Katie," he said. "Anybody who can make cupcakes like you can shouldn't worry about whether they can make a basket or not."

"Thanks," I said, but it didn't make me feel much better.

Making cupcakes was not going to help me solve my problem!

CHAPTER 6

What's the Point?

Even though I was terrible at basketball, I didn't give up. I didn't make any baskets at all during the game, but Emma and Jake made some. In the end Sam and Matt beat us by six points.

"Good game, Katie," Matt said, giving me a fist bump. "You looked better the more we played." That's when I figured that his teasing was part of the game, like what my friend George does. He didn't give me a hard time about losing or playing badly, and I was grateful for that.

Then Sam had to leave for work, and Matt had to go to a practice, so Emma and I did our homework in her kitchen while Jake colored next to us.

"So, what did you think?" Emma asked.

"Well, it was kind of fun," I admitted. "But I definitely stink at basketball. There's no way I can try out for the basketball team."

"Oh, you weren't so bad, Katie," Emma said kindly.

I shook my head. "Emma, I tried to make a basket in your garbage cans," I said, laughing. "I'm bad."

Emma started to smile. "Well, maybe you wouldn't be a good fit for the basketball team," she said. "But I hope you'll play with us again sometime."

I thought about Jake being so cute when he made a basket, and Matt goofing around, and Sam showing me how to shoot the ball. . . .

"Sure," I said. "That would be fun."

Then my cell phone rang, and it was my mom calling to tell me she had pulled up outside. I packed up my books in my backpack and said good-bye to Emma and Jake.

I climbed into the car with Mom. Even though she wasn't wearing her dentist jacket, she still smelled a little bit like a dentist's office—a mix of mint and . . . teeth. "Did you have fun?" she asked.

"Yes," I said. "But I stink at basketball. Everything

is still the same. I have no other talent, and I will always be a loser in gym. I don't even know why I'm trying. What's the point?"

"Well, sometimes the point is just to have fun," Mom said. "And I wouldn't give up yet. There are still lots of other things you can try."

"I guess," I said, and I sank down into my seat.

When we got home I helped Mom make dinner—a big salad with chicken and avocadoes and tomatoes and lots of other good stuff in it. Before we sat down to eat, I saw that I had a text from Grandma Carole on my phone.

How is your sports quest going?

I quickly wrote her back.

Terrible. Played basketball today. Couldn't make a basket.

Then I got another text from her.

Keep trying! I am sure you will find your talent.

Maybe. I just hoped I'd find one soon.

Tx Grandma. ♥ you.

She texted me back.

♥ you too Katie-kins!

But even Grandma's texts didn't make me feel better. During dinner I didn't feel like talking much, and so most of the time all you could hear was me and Mom crunching on lettuce. But then Mom had an idea.

"I was thinking of going for a run after dinner," she said. "Do you want to join me?"

I didn't. I was still bruised and sweaty from playing basketball, and besides that I was cranky.

"I just don't get the idea of running," I said. "You run and run and then you end up in the same place where you started. What's the point?"

"The point is that running is really good for your cardiovascular system," Mom said in her I'm-going-to-teach-you-something voice and then she proceeded to tell me how great running is for your health and stuff. It still didn't make me feel like running. "Plus, you just feel great after."

"Not now," I said. "Maybe some other time, okay?"

"Okay," Mom said, and her voice changed. I could tell she knew something was bothering me. "How about when I get back we make some cupcakes? I've got this green-tea recipe I want to try. And if you say 'What's the point?' I'll probably scream."

I had to smile. "There is always a point to making cupcakes," I said, and I realized I meant it. Even if baking cupcakes didn't help me be good at sports, at least it was something I was good at. And that was something to be proud of, right?

Even Sam thought so.

CHAPTER 7

I Hate to Admit It, but Sydney Is Right

$\mathcal{M}$om and I made a batch of green-tea cupcakes with cinnamon and other stuff in the icing. The green tea tasted weird and good at the same time, and the sweet cinnamon icing tasted really good with it. I brought four cupcakes into school the next day—Cupcake Friday.

I decided to have some fun with the cupcakes. When we were done eating lunch, I handed one to each of my friends.

"Okay, welcome to everyone's favorite game show, *Guess That Cupcake!*" I said, using the banana from my lunch as a microphone. "Take a bite and see if you can guess what flavor it is!"

Alexis answered first. "No idea, but it's green, so . . . cucumber?"

I shook my head. "Nope! Emma?"

"Um, maple?" Emma answered.

"Not maple," I told her. I turned to Mia. She was taking a second bite, and she had a thoughtful look on her face.

"Hmm," she said, thinking out loud. "I think this is . . . green tea."

"You are correct!" I cried. "How did you know?"

"My dad and I get green tea when we go out for sushi," Mia replied. "So what do I win?"

Whoops! I hadn't thought of that. I handed her the banana. "You win this delicious banana!"

"A banana? I've always dreamed of owning a banana," Mia joked, and I laughed with her.

"So is this a flavor your grandma likes?" Alexis asked, opening her notebook.

"No, that's just something my mom wanted to try," I replied. I reached into my lunch bag and pulled out a piece of paper. "I made a list of Grandma Carole's favorite flavors last night."

Alexis took the list from me. She looked impressed. "Thanks."

"Maybe Alexis is rubbing off on you," Emma suggested.

Alexis turned over the list. "Katie, this is written

on the back of your math quiz," she said.

I shrugged. "I'm recycling. Anyway, check it out. There're some good flavors in there."

"Blueberry, chocolate, raspberry, lime, and . . . chubby?" Alexis asked.

"That's *cherry*," I said. "Although chubby cupcakes would be awfully cute, wouldn't they?"

Alexis sighed. "I think there are some good flavor combinations here," she said. "We need a baking session. How about Sunday?"

"That's perfect," Mia said. "Because tomorrow we'll be teaching Katie how to play soccer before our game."

I had almost forgotten about that. "Oh yeah, sure."

Then I heard a loud voice behind me.

"Watch out for Silly Arms, Mia." It was Sydney, of course. "She'll spill her lunch all over that designer sweater you're wearing."

I turned and saw that Sydney was standing with the whole PGC—Maggie and Bella, who were giggling, and Callie, who looked like she wanted to sink into the floor.

"I'm not worried, Sydney," Mia said. She's one of the only girls in school who can stand up to Sydney. They were kind of friends, once, but I don't think that worked out too well.

Sydney rolled her eyes. "Have you seen this girl in gym? Loser! She's a safety hazard. The school should make her wear a helmet just to walk down the hall."

"There are no losers at this table," Mia said, and she looked angry. "I think you need to apologize to my friend."

Mia is so brave! I love her so much. I wanted to hug her. Then Callie spoke up, and I thought she was going to defend me too. After all, we were best friends for, like, twelve years. But instead she just tried to distract Sydney.

"Hey, Syd, Eddie Rossi told me he wanted to talk to you before," she said.

Sydney took the bait. "Really?"

"Yeah, I think we should go see him now," Callie told her.

"Bye, Mia," Sydney said, as if she had just been talking about tuna fish instead of insulting me.

Sydney marched off across the lunchroom and Callie and the rest of the PGC followed her. Callie kind of glanced over her shoulder at me with a worried look, but I just turned away. I guess by distracting Sydney she was trying to help me out, but frankly it just didn't seem like enough.

"Oh, Katie, Sydney is just awful!" Emma cried.

"Don't worry," Alexis said. "One day, when we're all cupcake millionaires, we'll buy a big billboard that says 'Sydney Is a Loser.'"

I turned to Mia. "You are awesome for standing up for me. Thanks."

"It's okay, Katie," Mia said. "You're the one who's awesome. Don't listen to her. She doesn't know what she's talking about."

"Actually, she does," I pointed out. "She's right. I'm a total spaz. I probably should wear a helmet."

"You're letting her psych you out," Mia said. "You'll see. Tomorrow, when we play soccer, you'll see you're not a spaz."

"I really hope so," I said. "You know, I started out just wanting to be good at something besides cupcakes. But now I feel like I've got something to prove. I'll never get through middle school and high school if I can't get through gym. I'm tired of being teased, you know?"

My friends nodded sympathetically. Alexis was punching in numbers on a calculator with a serious expression on her face. Then she looked up and smiled.

"The way I see it, there's about an eighty percent

chance that you'll be good in at least one sport," she said. "Maybe it will be soccer. I haven't worked out the numbers for that yet."

"Those odds sound pretty good to me," I said. "Just keep your fingers crossed. Or else the next six years of my life will be totally miserable!"

CHAPTER 8

I Discover My Secret Skill

You can do it, Katie-kins!

I tried to imagine Grandma Carole's voice cheering me on as Mom drove me to Mia's house for my soccer lesson.

"I'll pick you up at four, okay?" Mom asked as we pulled up in front of the big white house.

"Okay," I replied. "Hopefully I won't have some freak soccer ball accident and end up in the hospital or anything."

"Don't worry. I'm sure you'll do fine," Mom said. "Just remember to have fun! And don't forget to wear your mouth guard!" With a mom as a dentist, I practically have to wear a mouth guard to walk down the hall.

Remember to have fun. Who says that? Moms,

that's who. Why on Earth would someone have to remind you to have fun? Shouldn't fun just . . . happen?

I heard noises coming from Mia's backyard, and when I walked back there, I saw Mia and Alexis. Alexis was setting up orange cones all over the biggest part of the yard. In the side yard next to the garage, Mia's stepbrother, Dan, and some other guy were playing catch with a softball.

Alexis marched up to me. Like Mia, she was wearing her red soccer shorts and her practice T-shirt. But Alexis had a whistle around her neck and a clipboard in her hand.

"Okay, so we're going to start with some drills," she said crisply.

I had to laugh. Alexis sure loves being in charge— no matter what is going on.

"Um, hi, Alexis, nice to see you, too," I said.

She gave a slightly embarrassed smile. "Sorry, Katie, don't mean to get carried away. It's just kind of fun getting to be a coach instead of listening to a coach, you know?"

"Anyway, drills are a good idea," Mia chimed in. "That's how we start all our practices."

I looked at the cones, which were arranged in a kind of zigzag pattern all the way across the lawn. "So what do I have to do exactly?"

"You just kick the ball around the cones," Mia said. "Like this."

She started dribbling the ball, kicking it a short way and then running after it and kicking it some more. She wove around all of the cones perfectly. The way she did it, it looked kind of easy.

"Okay," I said. "I'll try it."

Mia kicked the ball to me, and I gave it a kick. It went skidding across the grass, nowhere near the cones.

"Just small kicks," Alexis said. "And kick with the inside of your foot, not the toe."

She ran after the ball and dribbled it back. I saw what she was talking about.

"Cool," I said. "Here we go."

I kicked the ball like Alexis had shown me, and it didn't go sailing away this time. I kicked it toward the first cone—and knocked the cone right over.

"That's okay, Katie!" Mia called out. "Keep going."

I made my way to the second cone, but this time I tripped when I was trying to kick the ball. I stumbled into the cone and knocked that one down too.

I was starting to get discouraged, but I could hear Grandma Carole inside my head.

Keep trying!

So I gave it my best. I promise you. But I barely made it through the course. By the time I got to the last cone, I had knocked over almost every one.

"If this was a game where you got points for knocking down cones, I'd be an all-star," I joked.

"Don't worry, Katie," Mia said, trying to keep me from being too discouraged. "Nobody gets it the very first time they try."

"It just takes practice," Alexis said. "I would recommend going through the course four or five more times."

Mia must have seen the look of horror on my face. "Or how about a kicking lesson?" she said. "We can practice passing. We'll kick the ball back and forth to each other as we make our way down the field."

"Okay," I said. "As long as there are no cones involved, I should be fine."

Once again Mia and Alexis demonstrated for me. They each got on opposite sides of the yard, and Mia kicked the ball hard. It skidded across the grass in an almost perfect straight line to Alexis.

"Okay, now I'll kick it to you, Katie," Alexis said. "And you can kick it to Mia."

"I'm ready!" I called out, trying to sound confident.

Alexis kicked the ball, and I ran to meet it. Then I kicked it as hard as I could in Mia's direction.

Only the ball did not go in Mia's direction. Instead it sailed backward, over my head, and bounced into the side yard where Dan and his friend were playing catch. Dan's friend ran to get the ball.

"Sorry!" I called out.

"Hey!" Dan called out in a teasing voice. "Now we're going to throw our ball at you!"

He lobbed the softball right at me, and I reached up and something amazing happened: I caught it!

Then something even more amazing happened. Without even thinking I threw the ball back to Dan. The ball did not fly backward over my head. It did not knock over any cones or garbage cans. Instead the ball soared in a beautiful arc and landed right in Dan's glove!

"Hey, you've got a pretty good arm," Dan said, and he sounded impressed. "Are you on the softball team?"

"Um, no," I answered shyly. "I've actually never played softball before."

"Really?" Mia asked, running up next to me.

I thought about it. "Well, sometimes we play Wiffle ball in gym. But I always stand way, way back in the outfield. And usually the guys think I can't catch the ball, so if it comes to me, they jump in front of me and catch it."

Alexis looked confused. "I don't get it, Katie. You can't catch or throw a football like that. So why did you catch that softball?"

I shrugged. "I don't know. Footballs are kind of . . . wobbly," I guessed. "They confuse me."

"Maybe it's because a softball is more cupcake-size," Mia teased. "It's got to be cupcake related somehow."

"It doesn't really matter *why* you can do it," Alexis said, and she sounded excited. "You *can* do it! And it's spring, which means that softball tryouts start soon. Katie, I think you've found your talent."

It seemed too good to be true that I could actually be good at a sport. Maybe my catching and

57

throwing the ball perfectly was a fluke, a one-time thing.

"Let's make sure," I said. I called out to the guys. "Dan! Over here!"

Dan threw the ball to me again, and once again, I caught it. I grinned.

I had finally found my secret skill.

CHAPTER 9

So Running Isn't So Bad After All

The first thing I did when I got home was call Grandma Carole.

"Hi, Grandma. It's me, Katie," I said.

"Katie-kins! What a nice surprise. Is everything all right?" Grandma asked.

"More than all right, Grandma," I said. "I found a sport I'm actually good at! I'm going to try out for the softball team!"

"Good for you, Katie-kins! I love softball. I bet you'll be hitting home runs out of the park in no time!" Grandma said. I could hear the excitement in her voice.

"Oh . . . ," I said.

"What's the matter?" Grandma asked.

"Well, you just reminded me of something.

I might be good at catching and throwing the ball, but I didn't really think about the hitting part."

"You'll be fine," Grandma said. "You just need a little practice, that's all."

"You sound so sure," I said.

"That's because I *am* sure. I can't wait to see you and hear all about it in person."

"Thanks, Grandma!" I said. "I can't wait to see you too! Love you!"

"Love you, too," Grandma said. "See you soon. Bye!"

I hung up the phone and tried to think positive, the way Grandma always did. But what I was actually thinking about was whiffle ball. Whenever we played whiffle ball at school, I always struck out. I started to feel nervous, but I knew I couldn't back out now.

"I'm very excited for you, Katie," Mom said as we ate our usual Saturday night pizza with mushrooms-and-sausage topping.

"But what if I don't make the team?" I worried. "Everyone's expecting me to become this great softball player. You should have seen the way everybody reacted when I caught and threw the ball."

"I don't think that's the case," Mom said. "Everyone's happy that you found something you're good at and that you like to do. If you don't make the team, at least you know you did your best."

I know Mom was trying to make me feel better, but a slow feeling of panic kept creeping up on me. "I need to start training, like, now," I said. "Can we play catch after dinner?"

"We could, but we don't have any balls or mitts," Mom pointed out. "I'm sure your friends will help you out. In the meantime why don't you go on a run with me tomorrow morning? That will definitely help you get in shape for the tryout."

Just the idea of running seemed superboring, but I knew Mom was right. And I was anxious to start doing something to help me train.

"All right," I said. "But maybe just a few blocks, okay?"

Mom smiled. "We'll see."

The next morning I was sound asleep when Mom came into my room and pulled open the curtains. The bright spring sunshine hit my face, and I groaned and rolled over.

"Rise and shine, Katie!" Mom sang. "It's time for our run!"

"Seriously?" I asked. "The birds aren't even awake yet."

"This is the best time for a run, trust me," Mom said. "Put on some shorts and your good sneakers, and I'll meet you in the kitchen."

I was still pretty sleepy when Mom and I left the house. Mom started jogging, not too fast, and I could keep up with her easily.

I'm not usually an early riser, but I must say it was nice to be up when most of the neighborhood was still asleep. And the air smelled so nice and clean! The sun had just come up, and everyone's lawn was sparkling with morning dew.

I was wrong about the birds. They were all awake, and I had to admit that all the singing and chirping they were doing was kind of pretty. Otherwise, the streets were pretty quiet, because most people were still sleeping.

We jogged down our street and then made a right and headed for the town park. I used to go on the swings and slide there when I was little, but I never noticed the path that went all around the park, weaving around the trees. I saw two squirrels chasing each other around a tree, and a big yellow butterfly, and then there was this bubbling creek we ran past that I didn't even know was in the park.

When we left the park I was sweating a lot and panting a little.

"Wanna go back?" Mom asked me.

To my surprise I didn't. I was actually liking this.

"No," I said. "Let's keep going."

In the end I had to walk the last few blocks home, but Mom said that was good, because we needed to cool down, anyway. My leg muscles hurt, but at the same time I felt good, like I was ready for anything.

"Thanks for coming out with me," Mom said. "Maybe we can do this again sometime."

"Definitely," I agreed.

Then I took a shower, which felt awesome, and then Mom and I went to Sally's Pancake House where I got a short stack of chocolate-chip pancakes, which tasted superdelicious. In the afternoon Mom drove me to Emma's for our cupcake baking session.

Before we make a cupcake for a client, we always test out the recipe first. We use the money from our profits to buy supplies and stuff, and whatever's left over we split among the four of us. We also take turns doing the baking at one another's houses.

At the end of our Friday meeting we had

decided to test a blueberry cupcake and a choco-late raspberry cupcake. When I entered Emma's kitchen, Alexis was already there, setting out the bowls and measuring spoons on Emma's big kitchen table. Emma was taking ingredients out of the blue plastic tub that we use to store our basic stuff.

I didn't see Sam anywhere, but I figured he was working. (And I would never ask where he was—that would just be too embarrassing.) I did see Jake. He was up on a chair, leaning over the table, so he could grab blueberries from the bowl.

Emma shook her head at him. "No, Jake! Those are for the cupcakes."

"There's plenty here for one batch," I said. I took a few blueberries from the bowl and gave them to Jake. "You can have these, and then you can have a cupcake when they're done."

"Thanks!" Jake said happily, and then he left the kitchen as Mia came in.

"My stepdad got all the really ugly wallpaper off of the walls!" she announced happily. "Now I just have to decide what color to paint my room."

"How about rainbow?" I suggested. "With stripes all across the wall."

"Or pink," Emma said. That's Emma's favorite color.

"I like white or cream walls," Alexis said. "It looks neat, and you can always decorate with posters or pictures."

Mia sat down on one of the stools around the counter. "It's just so hard to decide. I'm thinking maybe pale pink with an accent wall, or some kind of purple." Then she noticed all the cupcake supplies on the counter. "But enough about my room. We have cupcakes to design, right?"

"Right," Alexis agreed, getting down to business. "We're going to do some vanilla cupcakes with blueberry jam centers and vanilla frosting with fresh blueberries on top. Then there's a chocolate raspberry cupcake with chocolate frosting and fresh raspberries."

"They both sound *sooo* good," Mia said. "You know, I've been so busy worrying about my room that I forgot to come up with decorating ideas."

"I had one," Alexis said. "Since Katie's grandma likes sports so much, we could do the blueberry cupcakes, but instead of putting blueberries on top, we could decorate them to look like different kinds of balls. Like a soccer ball cupcake and a baseball cupcake, and we could dye the icing green to make a tennis ball cupcake too."

"That's pretty cool," Emma said.

"Definitely," I agreed. "I'm just wondering if it feels adult enough. Soccer-ball cupcakes and baseball cupcakes sound like something Jake would like, you know?"

"I see what you mean," Mia chimed in. "It's great for a kid's party, but maybe not a seventy-fifth birthday celebration."

Alexis nodded. "Yeah, that makes sense," she said. "But I will definitely put this idea in my kids' party file."

"I thought of something," said Emma shyly. "Your grandma was born right at the start of spring, so maybe we can do a spring theme. We could put birds and flowers on the cupcakes."

"That would be so pretty!" Mia said. "I can just picture it!"

"That does sound really nice," I agreed. "And I think that would go nicely with the blueberry cupcakes."

"And maybe the icing could be blue, like a robin's egg," Emma added.

"That is so perfect because Grandma Carole

always looks for the first robin of spring," I said. "She says it's good luck."

"I like it," Alexis said. "Okay, so let's scrap the chocolate raspberry for now. Mia, do you think you can come up with a flowers and birds design?"

"Sure," Mia said, nodding her head. "Maybe I can play with the icing today. We have blue food coloring, right?"

Alexis grabbed the bottle from the table. "Check," she said, holding it up. "Okay, so we have a plan."

For the next couple of hours we worked on our sample cupcakes. We made some basic vanilla batter, and when the cupcakes cooled, I got to use one of my favorite cupcake tools. It's a special tip you can put on the end of a pastry bag. You fill the bag with jam and then stick the tip into the cupcake. One squeeze, and your cupcake has a delicious jam-filled center.

We tested the cupcakes without frosting first.

"Yummy," Alexis said. "But tell me again why we're not using real blueberries in the batter?"

"We could, but it's tricky," I told her. "Since the blueberries are heavier than the batter, usually they fall to the bottom. You can coat them in flour first, but that doesn't always work."

"The blueberry jam is delicious," Mia remarked. "These kind of remind me of that peanut-butter-and-jelly cupcake your mom made for you on the first day of school."

Emma smiled. "Yeah, that cupcake sort of started everything, didn't it?"

"I guess it did," I said. I looked down at Jake, who had blue jam all over his face. "What do you think, Jake?"

"Awesome!" Jake replied.

"Okay, I've got two icings going," Mia said. "One is vanilla with mashed-up blueberries mixed in. The other just has blue food coloring."

The food coloring one looked pretty, just like a robin's egg. The blueberry one looked a little weird. It was more purple than blue, and there were some big blueberry chunks in it. But it tasted really, really good.

"I can't decide," I said. "One is the perfect color, but the other one tastes superamazing."

"I can't decide either," Emma agreed.

"There must be a way to combine them," Alexis suggested. "Katie, maybe your mom can help us. She is, like, the queen of cupcakes."

"And I am the cupcake captain, don't forget," I joked. "But, yeah, I'll definitely ask her."

Then I remembered something. "I need a favor from you guys," I said. "After we clean up."

"What is it?" Emma asked.

I grinned. "Wanna play catch?"

CHAPTER 10

Callie's Mad at *Me*? Seriously?

*W*ow, it's true, Katie," Mia said as I tossed a softball to her from across Emma's backyard. "You really can play softball."

"Don't sound so surprised," I joked.

"You know what I mean," Mia shot back.

"I know," I said. "But it's not such a big deal. I can throw and catch. I'm not so sure if I can hit the ball."

"I'm sure Matt will help you with that," Emma said. "As long as you bribe him with cupcakes."

I was secretly hoping she would suggest Sam as a softball coach, but Matt would have to do.

"Sure," I said. "We can give him some blueberry cupcakes from today as a down payment."

Alexis looked at her watch. "Hey, I've got to get

home. We're having dinner early, and I want to get a good night's sleep tonight. We have a big game tomorrow."

"Where is it?" I asked. "Maybe I'll come."

Because I'm not good at sports, I have never much liked watching games on TV or in person. But my friends had been helping me so much, I felt like I had to support them.

"Cool!" Mia said. "It's at the middle-school field at six."

Mom said I could go to the game as long as I finished my homework. On Monday my mom had Joanne, who works with her at her office, pick me up after school. Joanne does that a lot because Mom still doesn't like me being home alone all that much. She took me to Mom's office, and I did my homework with the sound of dentists' drills in the background. I shuddered. Honestly I hate going to the dentist even though the dentist is my mom. But nobody was screaming or crying or anything, so I guess Mom was doing a good job. When Mom finished with her patients she dropped me off at the field.

It's a little weird going to a soccer game when you're not playing, because almost everyone watching is a parent or else a little kid who's been dragged to the game. In the stands I saw Mia's stepdad, Eddie, sitting with Alexis's mom, and I waved hi.

Then I heard a voice calling to me.

"Katie! Over here!"

It was Callie's mom. Mrs. Wilson and my mom have been friends since before Callie and I were born. She's almost like a second mom to me, which is why it's extra weird that Callie and I aren't best friends anymore. I kind of miss seeing her all the time.

So I walked over. "Hi, Mrs. Wilson," I said.

"Hi, Katie." She gave me a hug. "Are you here to see Callie play?"

Uh-oh. Tough question. "Well, sure, and I have two other friends on the team too," I said, only lying just a little bit. "Mia and Alexis."

"Oh yes, they're good players," Mrs. Wilson said. "Come here, have a seat. I haven't seen you in so long."

So I ended up sitting next to Mrs. Wilson for the whole game. That was good, I guess, because she explained a lot of the soccer stuff to me. Like how in the spring league the girls played other teams from Maple Grove. And how many points you got for scoring a goal and who could be on what side of the field when and stuff like that. It all sounded pretty complicated. Maybe it was a good thing I wasn't good at soccer!

Still, the game was pretty exciting. The ball kept going up and down the field. I noticed that Alexis was a really good kicker. She could kick the ball really far and fast. And I cheered when Mia made a goal.

I was kind of surprised to realize that Callie was the star of the team. She was superfast, and whenever someone passed her the ball, she was right on it. And she scored four goals! It was amazing. I cheered for her, too, and I think she heard me because she looked up. But mostly she concentrated on the game.

Even though the Rockets rocked, the other team, the Comets, beat them 8–7. At the end of the game the two teams lined up and then slapped hands as they walked past one another. I thought the Rockets would look sad, but when I ran up to Mia and Alexis after the game they looked pretty psyched.

"Alexis, that pass you made was amazing," Mia was saying.

"Thanks!" Alexis said, high-fiving her. "I think

this was our best passing game ever."

"You did great, guys," I told them. "Soccer looks pretty fun."

"It is," Mia said. "I'm glad you came."

Then Callie walked over, and she looked kind of mad. At first I thought it was because of losing the game. But it turned out she was mad at *me*.

"Katie, what are you doing here?" Callie asked. "You hate sports."

"Maybe I used to," I said, getting defensive. "But not now."

Callie shook her head. "I used to ask you to come to my games all the time. . . ." She looked at Mia and Alexis.

I couldn't believe what she was saying. *Yeah, and I was your best friend until you sold me out to be part of the Popular Girls Club,* I wanted to scream. Not to mention how just the other day she stood by while Sydney made fun of me, and she didn't say a thing! She had no right to be mad at me for this, not even a little.

"We all cheer for one another," Mia said, and she smiled at me. "And it's true, she's really good at softball."

"Yeah, she's even trying out for the team," Alexis said proudly.

74

Callie looked surprised and then she didn't look so mad anymore.

"Really? Wow, that's pretty cool, Katie," she said. "Good luck."

"Thanks," I said. "And good game. I can't believe how many goals you made."

Callie actually smiled. "Thanks," she said. She looked around, and I wondered if she was looking for her new friends, but there were just a lot of parents waiting around. "See you!" She waved, and then she ran off to see her mom.

"That is one complicated situation," Mia said, looking after Callie.

I shrugged. "I guess," I said. "But right now I'm a lot more worried about that softball tryout!"

Especially now that Callie knows I'm trying out, I thought. *If I don't make the team, I am going to look like a loser!*

CHAPTER 11

I'm Keeping My Eye on the Ball, I Swear!

*A*ll right, Katie," Matt said. "Like I showed you. Bend your knees and hold the bat just below your shoulders."

"She's holding it too high!" Alexis said directly behind me.

It was Friday afternoon, the day before tryouts, and Emma had finally arranged to have Matt give me a batting lesson. During the week I ran with Mom a few times after work, and Mom got us a ball and gloves so we could practice catching. But so far, no batting.

And in case you're wondering what Alexis was doing there, she offered to come along and help.

"You can't have batting practice without a

catcher," she said, and I know she's right. But sometimes I wonder if she's really over her crush on Matt.

To be fair, though, Alexis seemed a lot more interested in telling me how to bat than she did in flirting with Matt.

"I am *not* holding it too high," I protested.

"She's good," Matt called back. "Okay, Katie, now keep your eye on the ball!"

"Sure," I said, but actually, I have a problem with that advice. Because when the ball comes at me, it's spinning really fast and it's all blurry and it just makes me nervous.

Then Matt pitched the ball to me underhand, like they do in softball, and I kept my eye on it, I swear—both eyes, even. And when it got close to me I freaked out a little and swung the bat way too soon.

Whump! I heard the ball land in Alexis's catcher's mitt.

"Steeeeee–rike!" Alexis cried, like some professional umpire.

"Too soon, Katie!" Matt called out.

"Yeah, too soon, Katie!" Alexis repeated.

"I know!" I said, a little frustrated. "It's hard to know when to swing."

Matt walked up to me and Alexis. "Okay, how about this?" he asked. "When you think you want to swing, don't. Count to two and then swing, okay?"

"Okay," I said, nodding. Then I got back into batting stance.

"Oh, you are holding it a little too high," Matt said. "Here, move your elbows, like this."

Matt got behind me and positioned my arms—sort of like when Sam was showing me how to shoot a basket. But I didn't have any heart palpitations or sweaty palms this time.

Is that all it means to have a crush on someone? I wondered. Sweaty palms? Would Alexis get sweaty palms if she were standing here now?

"Earth to Katie," Matt said. "Are you listening?"

"Oh, sure," I said. I placed my arms in the right position. "Like this, right?"

"Okay, let's give it another try," Matt said. "This time, count to two before you swing."

"Got it," I said.

Matt pitched the ball to me again. I kept my eye on the ball, and when it got close, I freaked out again.

"Strike!" Alexis cried.

"Why is it that it's good to get a strike in bowling

but bad to get one in baseball?" I wondered out loud, trying to distract Alexis and Matt from the fact that I was terrible.

"Well, this isn't bowling," Alexis said. "I know you can do this. Just keep your eye on the ball."

"I am. I swear," I protested. "That's not the problem."

"What happened to counting to two?" Matt called out.

"I get too nervous," I answered. "When the ball starts to get close, I feel like it's going to hit me in the face or something. So I swing."

"I am not going to throw the ball at your face. I promise," Matt said, rolling his eyes. "Geez!" Then he muttered "Girls!" in an exasperated voice.

"Hey, I heard that!" Alexis called out. "Katie's just nervous, that's all. This has nothing to do with her being a girl."

"That's right!" I agreed. Now I had something to prove. "Let's do this."

Matt pitched. I kept my eye on the ball. When the ball got close, I started counting.

One Mississippi, two Mississippi . . .

Thump! The ball landed in Alexis's glove before I could even swing.

"Ball one!" Alexis yelled.

"What does that even mean?" I said.

Matt shook his head. "Katie, I said count to two, not count to two million."

"I *did* count to two," I told him. "I counted by Mississippis."

"Well, no wonder," Alexis said. "That's way too long, Katie."

Matt gave an exasperated sigh. "Forget about counting. Just hit the ball when it gets close to the bat, okay?"

"Got it," I said. I got back into batting stance, more determined than ever.

Do not freak out. Do not freak out, I told myself. *Matt will not hit you in the face.*

Matt pitched. The ball soared through the air. I swung.

Crack! I hit the ball! It went careening to the left, and Alexis ran after it.

I started jumping up and down. "I hit it! I hit it! I hit it!"

"That was a foul ball," Alexis said, running back to me.

"Good job, Katie!" Matt said, and I felt like I was going to burst with pride. "Now next time straighten it out, okay?"

"Okay," I said, even though I had no idea what that meant.

So Matt pitched the ball a bunch more times. And after a while, I sort of got used to the ball coming straight at me. I lost my fear and just concentrated on trying to follow it with my eyes and hit it when it got close. I struck out a few times, and I had a lot more foul balls. But I "straightened out" after Matt showed me how, so I also hit a few good balls. One of them popped up in the air, and Matt caught it. But another one rolled on the grass, and Matt had to chase after it.

Finally Matt called it quits. "You're doing good, Katie. You'll be fine at the tryouts, I think," he said. "Just keep throwing and catching like you do."

"Thanks," I said.

He held out his hand. "And now I believe there was a payment involved?"

I walked over to the Taylors' deck and picked up the box I had brought with me.

"One dozen chocolate peanut-butter cupcakes," I said.

Matt smiled and took the box. "You are the best, Katie."

"Thanks," I said. "You are, too. And so is Alexis. She's a great catcher."

(Did you see what I was doing there? Just trying to help out a friend—just in case Alexis was still getting sweaty palms.)

"Yeah, thanks," Matt said. He turned and smiled at Alexis. "You can play on my team anytime."

Alexis blushed, and I felt like I had done a good deed.

In fact, I was feeling pretty good when Mom took me home. And Mom had a weird smile on her face, like she was keeping a secret.

"A package came for you today," she said as she unlocked the door.

"Really?" I asked. "What is it?"

"I'll let you open it yourself," Mom said, and she handed me a box that looked like a shoebox. I looked at the name on the return address: Carole Hamilton.

"It's from Grandma Carole," I said. Then I ran to the kitchen to get scissors, so I could cut through the tape.

The box was filled with crumpled-up newspaper. I felt around and pulled out a softball. There was a note on a small piece of blue paper.

Dear Katie-kins,

I am so excited that you are going to be on the softball team! I know you're going to do great.

This is a softball I saved from my high school championship team. It's very special to me, and I know it will bring you luck.

Love,

Grandma Carole

"Wow," was all I could say.

Mom read the note over my shoulder. "That's very special," she said.

I tossed the softball from hand to hand, thinking. Grandma Carole was counting on me to get on the team. I didn't want to disappoint her—or Mom or the Cupcake Club or Callie or even Matt.

I *had* to get on that team. Failure was not an option. But first I had to get rid of this nervous energy.

"Hey, Mom," I said. "Want to go for a run?"

CHAPTER 12

I Don't Totally Stink

Tryouts were Saturday morning at ten at the middle-school field. I was so nervous that I woke up at five a.m. Mom was still asleep, so I went down to the living room and stared at the ceiling until she woke up.

"Katie, you're up early," she said, yawning. "I'm going to make some coffee. What would you like for breakfast?"

My stomach felt like it was tied in a knot. "I don't think I can eat," I replied.

"You have to eat something," Mom said. "You need energy for your tryouts."

I groaned. I know she was right. "Then I guess, cereal, please."

I munched on a bowl of Grainy Flakes and

changed into shorts and a T-shirt for the tryouts. When we got to the field, there were a lot of girls and parents there. Most of them were lined up in front of a folding table set up over by the stands with a sign that read PARK STREET SOFTBALL TRYOUTS.

"I guess we should get in line," Mom said, so we did.

When we got to the front of the line, we saw a woman about Mom's age wearing a white polo shirt with a whistle around her neck. She had blond hair pulled back in a ponytail.

"Hi, I'm Coach Kendall," she said. Then she nodded to a young guy with brown hair bringing some equipment out of the locker room. "That's Coach Adani. We'll be running the tryouts today. I just need your name, age, and grade on the form, okay?"

I nodded, too nervous to say anything, and filled out the form. I forgot that anyone at Park Street could try out. There would be girls older than me too. Ones that had been playing longer. I gulped.

"I'll head for the stands," Mom said. "Good luck, Katie."

I'm sure she wanted to give me a hug, but

thank goodness she just waved and started walking away.

I headed for the baseball diamond on the field, where most of the girls seemed to be going. I recognized a few girls from my grade. There were Sophie and Lucy, who are nice but they're best, best friends and pretty much only hang out with each other. I saw Beth Suzuki, a girl from my Spanish class who trades notes with me sometimes. And then I saw Maggie Rodriguez from the Popular Girls Club.

I groaned. Just like gym class! She was going to give me a hard time, I just knew it.

But so far, Maggie didn't seem to notice me. In fact, I thought she looked as nervous as I did. She was kind of hanging off to the side and not talking to anybody, which was fine by me.

Before I could think too much about it, Coach Kendall and Coach Adani walked onto the diamond, and Coach Kendall blew her whistle.

"All right girls, line up!" she called, and we quickly got into a line.

"Coach Adani and I are going to put you through some drills today to see what you can do," she said. "First up, I want to see you run around those bases. Don't stop until I tell you. Let's go!"

I relaxed a little bit. Running—I could do that. Sophie was at the head of the line, and she started leading us around the diamond. For a while we all stayed in line. But then it was obvious that some of us were faster and some of us were slower. Without even realizing it, I was at the front of the line, right next to Beth.

We must have gone around about four times when Coach Kendall finally blew the whistle for us to stop. I stepped on home plate, and my heart was pounding. The run had me feeling good, and it also felt good to know that I was one of the fastest on the team. I couldn't help noticing that Maggie was the last one to finish, and she looked really winded.

"All right," Coach Kendall said. "Now we're going to try some fielding." She pointed to me, Beth, and another girl who I didn't know. "I want you to each take a base."

I started to feel nervous all over again. Beth ran to first base, so I took second, and the other girl took third. Coach Adani stood at home plate, and Coach Kendall stood behind him with a catcher's mitt.

"Here's how it's going to work," he said. "I'm going to hit out a ball. If it comes to you, catch it and throw it home."

This is it, I thought. *This is where I prove myself. Can I do it?*

Then I heard cheers from the stands.

"Go, Katie!"

I looked up and saw Alexis and Emma. I knew Mia was at her dad's in Manhattan or else she would be there too. I had my very own cheering section, and I couldn't let them down.

I put my hands on my knees and focused on Coach Adani. He hit a ground ball to Beth. She scooped it up and threw it back to Coach Kendall. The throw was a little wide, and Coach had to chase after it.

Then Coach Adani hit a pop-up to second base. Easy. I caught it and threw it to Coach Kendall— and it landed right in her glove.

I had aced it! I didn't feel so nervous after that. Coach Adani hit two more balls to each of us, and I caught each one that went to me. Then we left the field and the other girls got a turn.

I sat on the grass and watched the competition. Some of the girls, like Lucy, were really good. But a few girls couldn't catch very well. And Maggie . . .

well, Maggie was pretty terrible. But you could see that she was trying really hard.

Maggie missed the first two balls, and when she threw them back, they didn't go anywhere near home plate. And then when Coach Adani hit the third ball to Maggie, it went way to the left. Maggie actually jumped and then dove to catch it! It was pretty cool, and everybody cheered even though the ball ended up bouncing out of her mitt.

As I watched the rest of the fielding tryouts, I felt more and more nervous each minute. I knew what had to be next: batting.

And that's exactly what happened next. Coach Kendall put me and two other girls on the bases while the first group of girls came up to bat. Lucy went first, and she hit her first pitch way, way out into the outfield, which was awesome—but it only made me more nervous.

All I could think about was when my turn would be next. I was so distracted that I missed an easy pop-up that one girl hit right to me.

And then, before I knew it, I was standing at home plate, a bat in my hand. Coach Kendall was pitching, and Maggie, Sophie, and another girl were on the bases. My hands were shaking, and I felt like I was going to toss my Grainy Flakes all over the field.

"You can do it, Katie!" Alexis called out, and my mind flashed back to our practice session.

Think, I said. *You know what to do. Bend your knees. Don't hold the bat too high. Don't swing too early.*

But when Coach Kendall's first pitch came speeding toward me, I was so scared that I swung before it was even halfway to the plate.

"Just relax, Katie," Coach Adani said behind me. I took a deep breath and tried to focus. When the next pitch came, I forced myself to hold off swinging. Then I swung wildly.

"Foul ball!" Coach Adani called out as the ball veered off sharply to the right. At least I hadn't struck out.

I did strike out on the next turn, though. And then I hit two more fouls before I managed to get one near first base. I ran like crazy, and the only reason I was safe was because poor Maggie dropped the ball three times as she tried to pick it up.

It's over, I thought, my heart pounding. *For better or worse, it's over.*

After all the girls had a turn, Coach Kendall

had us all gather in a circle. "We'll put the team list in the front hall on Monday morning," she told us. "Those of you who don't make the team will be put on our alternate list. But no matter what happens, you should all be proud of how you performed today."

"Thank goodness that's over," I said out loud as the coaches walked away.

"I know, I was so nervous," said a voice behind me. It was Maggie.

"Me too," I agreed. "I almost threw up my breakfast."

Maggie laughed, and we started walking off the field together.

"So, I guess none of your friends are trying out?" I asked, hoping desperately that I would not end up on a team with Sydney.

Maggie shook her head. "Sydney's trying out for cheerleading," she answered. "So is Callie. And Bella is on the swim team."

"How come you're not trying out for cheerleading?" I asked. I thought Maggie did everything that Sydney did.

Maggie looked embarrassed for a second. "I could never do a cartwheel, no matter how hard I tried," she admitted. "Plus, I kind of want to do my own thing, you know? I really like softball. It's fun."

I suddenly realized that talking with Maggie wasn't so bad once she wasn't with the PGC—or making fun of me in gym. But then I heard Sydney's voice.

"Mags! Over here!"

Sydney walked up with Callie and Bella. "Maggie, oh my gosh, you are soooo sweaty!" she said, wrinkling her nose. (Of course, Sydney looked like she just stepped out of a makeup chair on a movie set.) "And, ew, gross, is that grass on your pants?"

Maggie looked flustered. Instead of answering Sydney, she started trying to rub off the grass stain.

"Yeah, you should have seen her," I said. "She dove to make this amazing catch."

Sydney looked at me like she had just noticed I existed.

"And what did you do?" she asked. "Accidentally throw the bat instead of the ball? Or maybe you knocked out the catcher with your silly arms."

Now it was my turn to clam up. I don't know why, but somehow it was easier to stick up for

Maggie than to stand up for myself. Besides, what could I say that would make any difference?

Maggie didn't tell Sydney that I didn't stink at softball, and I couldn't blame her. But I could blame Callie, who just stood there like she did last time and let Sydney be mean to me.

"Come on," Sydney said, nodding to her friends. "We need to get to that sale at Icon. But, Maggie, you definitely need a shower first. And please do not get any gross dirt in my mom's car!"

I really don't get Sydney sometimes. How can someone who looked so pretty and so sweet be so mean? Was she born that way? Did she squirt milk from her baby bottle at the other babies in the hospital? It's a mystery.

"Good luck, Katie," Callie said as she walked away. She said it kind of soft, and it didn't seem like Sydney heard her. She turned back around fast and just then Emma and Alexis ran up to me.

"You did great, Katie!" Emma said.

"I kept a record of how everyone did when they tried out," Alexis said. "I think you're in the top thirty or forty percent."

"So, does that mean I didn't totally stink out there?" I asked.

"Exactly," she answered. "It also means you're

probably good enough to make the team."

"I hope you're right," I said. But now that I was close, I had another reason to get nervous.

If I made the team, I'd actually have to play softball games. In front of people. With rules and winners and losers.

I grabbed my stomach and groaned. "I should never have eaten those Grainy Flakes."

CHAPTER 13

I'm Happy! . . . I Think

So did you have fun at tryouts?" Mom asked as she drove me home.

"Are you kidding? I was so nervous!" I said. "It was fearful, frightening, ferocious, and freaky—but definitely not fun. Why, are they supposed to be?"

"I guess not," Mom said, and she sounded a little worried.

As we drove through town I remembered something that took my mind off of the tryouts.

"Can we make a quick stop at Food City, please?" I asked. "I need to get some blueberries for the cupcakes."

Remember that blueberry frosting? I was going to ask Mom about it, but then I looked online to get some ideas. And I thought I had a way to make the perfect icing.

"Do you think you can help me try out this icing?" I asked Mom when we got home with the blueberries.

"Sure," Mom replied. "But why don't you take a shower first?"

"Good idea," I agreed. "I don't think sweaty cupcakes would taste so good."

A few minutes later I was squeaky clean, and Mom and I were setting up the food processor to begin my icing experiment. First I made a basic buttercream icing with butter, sugar, and vanilla. Normally we add a little bit of milk to make it creamy, but I wanted to hold off on that until I added the blueberries. I didn't want the icing to get too runny.

Then I put the blueberries in the food processor and with Mom's help we pureed them until they were supermushy. Then I put a strainer over the bowl and poured them into the strainer. The blueberry juice went into the bowl and the skins and seeds and stuff stayed in the strainer.

Next I poured the blueberry juice into the icing, a little at a time, and beat it in. It was a pretty, light purpley-blue color. But we were going for robin's-egg blue. So I added a couple of drops of gel color, and the blue became bright and happy—just like a robin's egg.

"What do you think?" I asked Mom.

"I think it's a lovely color," Mom said. "And I also think we need some cupcakes to go with it!"

I thought making cupcakes with my mom would take my mind off of softball, but when I was making the batter, it hit me.

I was making cupcake *batter*—and I was a terrible softball batter. Why could I be good at making batter but not actually be a good batter?

"Batter up!" I said, pouring the cupcakes into the tin, and Mom laughed.

And so I thought about the tryouts for the rest of the weekend. The only thing that cleared my mind was going on a run with Mom.

Monday morning I got on the bus and sat with Mia, like I always do.

"Sorry I missed your tryouts," Mia said. "How did it go?"

"Okay, I think," I said. "Alexis did her magical calculations, and she thinks I'll get in."

"You don't sound happy about that," Mia said, noticing the nervousness in my voice.

"I'm not sure how I feel," I confessed. "If I don't make the team, I'll feel like a loser. Plus, I'll disappoint everybody. But if I make the team, that means I'll have to play in games and that makes me nervous."

Mia nodded. "I get nervous sometimes before a game. But usually it goes away when I start playing."

Then she noticed the cupcake box in my hand. "What's that? It's not Friday."

I opened the lid a little bit. "I tried to get that blueberry icing right. What do you think?"

"It's so pretty!" Mia cried. She reached into her backpack and pulled out a sketchpad. "I did some designs over the weekend."

Mia showed me a sketch in colored pencils of a cupcake cake. On the bottom round layer, the cupcakes had green icing with flowers in pretty spring colors on them. The top two layers of cupcakes had blue icing and little birds on them. It looked absolutely beautiful.

"Oh, Mia, that's perfect!" I cried. "We can leave the blueberries out of the bottom ones and just use green food coloring."

"I found tiny cookie cutters shaped like flowers and birds," Mia said. "We can get different colors of fondant and roll it out and then cut out the shapes."

"Grandma Carole is going to love these cupcakes," I said.

George looked over the back of our seat. "Did somebody say cupcakes?" he said, eyeing the box.

"Sorry, George, these are for my friends," I said.

He made a sad face. "Aw, come on. I'm your friend, aren't I?"

I giggled. "Forget it, George!"

Then the bus pulled up in front of the school, and I started to feel nervous all over again.

"Come on," Mia said. "I'll go with you."

We walked up to the bulletin board in the front hall, and there it was: SOFTBALL TRYOUTS RESULTS. I took a deep breath and stared closer.

The list was alphabetical, so I saw my name right at the top: KATIE BROWN. I couldn't believe that I made it!

"Oh my gosh! I made it!" I said.

"I knew you would, Katie!" Mia said happily, and she gave me a hug.

I scanned the rest of the list and saw that Beth, Lucy, and Sophie had made the team, but Maggie was listed as an alternate. I felt kind of bad for her. I knew how much she wanted to play.

Then the opening bell rang, and I had to run to homeroom. I was dying to text Grandma Carole, but there's no texting allowed in our school.

When I got to the cafeteria later, I saw that Alexis and Emma were at the table already with Mia, instead of in the lunch line. They were all smiling.

"Congratulations!" they cried, and Alexis took her hands out from behind her back and presented me with an open cardboard box with four cupcakes inside. Each one was decorated to look like a softball.

"Thank you!" I cried. "These are so awesome. You didn't have to do that!"

"It's exciting," Alexis said. "Plus, I wanted to test out my cupcake idea."

"But what if I didn't get on the team?" I asked, teasing.

Emma held out another box of cupcakes. These said, "World's Best Friend" on top.

"Alexis had a backup plan," Emma admitted.

"Of course I did," Alexis said.

I held out my cupcake box. "Well, I brought

cupcakes too," I said. "I did a blueberry icing test."

"How are we possibly going to eat all these cupcakes?" Mia wondered aloud.

I had an idea. "I'm going to give one to George."

I picked up one of the blueberry cupcakes and walked across the cafeteria to George's table. On the way I passed the PGC table. Sydney was talking very loudly to Maggie.

"I don't understand why you're upset, Maggie. You're lucky you didn't make the team," Sydney was saying. "Why would you want to wear those ugly uniforms and get all dirty and sweaty just to play that boring game?"

Maggie looked like she might cry. "I—I just like it, that's all," she stammered.

Then Callie spoke up. "Leave her alone, Sydney. Maggie wanted to be on that team really bad."

Well, it's nice that she's standing up for Maggie, I thought as I walked past. *It would be even nicer if she would stick up for me once in a while.*

When I reached George's table, I put down the cupcake in front of him.

"You looked so pitiful before," I teased him.

"Thanks, Katie," George said. "I promise never to call you Silly Arms again."

If I had known that all I had to do was bribe George with cupcakes, I would have done that a long time ago.

"I hope you remember that," I said to George.

Then I walked back to my table, where my friends were waiting to celebrate with me.

CHAPTER 14

Can I Actually Do This?

So practice started on Monday after school and lasted until six thirty. By the time Mom picked me up I was sweaty, starving, and exhausted. And I still had to do my homework!

I have to say that I didn't do too badly in practice. But I still couldn't stop worrying. Every time I was in the field, I kept worrying that I would drop the ball or make a bad throw. And every time I was at bat, all I could think about was striking out. Which I did, a few times, but I got a few hits, too.

I think Coach Kendall knew I was nervous. Whenever I got up to bat, she would say, "Relax, Katie! Just have fun!"

Grandma Carole said the same thing when I called to tell her I made the team.

"You'll do great, Katie! Just have fun!"

Even my Cupcake Club friends had the same idea. One day at lunch, Mia asked me how practice was going.

"It's hard," I said. "And I keep worrying that I'm going to mess up."

"Just have fun," Alexis said. "Like we did when we had batting practice with Matt."

I thought about it. Practicing with Alexis and Matt had been kind of fun. But that's because they're my friends, and it didn't matter if I did good or not.

"I'll try," I said, but I knew I was kidding myself. I mean, how can you "just have fun" if something isn't fun?

Which is exactly what I asked my mom. "Everybody says 'just have fun,'" I said. "But how do I do that? It's not like I can turn on a switch in my brain or anything."

"I think everyone means to just relax and not take it so seriously," Mom said. "It's important to do your best, but in the end, it's just a game."

What Mom said made sense, but it didn't change anything. I still couldn't shut my brain off whenever I was at practice.

I did notice that one person was having a

lot of fun—Maggie. Even though she was an alternate, she came to every practice. Usually she was the first one to arrive. She asked to play different positions, too. One day she was in the outfield, the next day she'd be playing first base or at shortstop.

"You never know when coach will need me to play," Maggie told me. "And I want to be ready."

Maggie messed up a lot on the field, but she didn't let it get her down. She even made friends with the girls on the team really fast. I still didn't know some of their names.

One Tuesday we got our game schedule, and I saw that my first game was just four days away, on Saturday morning. We were playing the team from Fieldstone at their school field.

"Are you sure the game is *this* Saturday?" I asked Coach Kendall. "I mean, we're not actually ready to play another team, are we?"

"Playing another team is the best way to get experience," Coach Kendall said. "And a lot of their players are new, just like you. It'll be fine."

The Friday night before the game I didn't sleep very well. I dreamed that I kept swinging and swinging and striking out, and everyone in the stands was pointing and laughing at me.

The game the next morning was at eleven, but once again I woke up superearly. Thankfully, Mom woke up early too, and we went for a run. The sound of the chirping birds and the gentle breeze blowing through the trees in the park all helped to calm me down a little bit.

When I got home I changed into my softball uniform: gold baseball pants, white socks, black cleats, and a blue shirt that said PARK STREET MIDDLE SCHOOL in gold letters. I put my hair in a low ponytail, so I could fit my hat over it.

I looked at my reflection in the mirror. I looked just like a real softball player.

"This is it, Katie," I whispered to myself.

Even though the game started at eleven, Mom dropped me off at ten, so I could warm up with the team.

"I'll be back later," she promised. "And Katie—"

"Please don't say, 'just have fun,'" I said.

Mom smiled. "I was going to say, just do your best and you won't have anything to worry about."

"Thanks, Mom," I said.

I got out of the car and ran toward my team. On the other side of the field, the Fieldstone girls in their black and gray uniforms were warming up. It might have been my imagination, but I swear they all looked bigger and stronger than all of us.

To warm up, we did some exercises and then practiced throwing and catching. The whole time my head felt like it was full of cotton balls— so full of fear that I pretty much drowned out everything all around me. It was a really weird feeling.

We were walking to our dugout when a loud cheer erupted from the stands, and I looked up. Alexis, Emma, and Mia were holding up a big sign that said, GO, KATIE! Mom was sitting next to Mia, and sitting next to Mom was a lady with white hair, wearing a blue T-shirt and a gold baseball cap.

I couldn't believe it. "Grandma?"

Grandma Carole saw me looking and started waving like crazy. "Surprise, Katie-kins!" she yelled.

I felt like everybody was looking at me, which was embarrassing, but I was still happy to see Grandma. I ran over to the stands, and she climbed down to meet me by the fence.

"I came a week early to surprise you," she said.

"I can't believe it!" I said.

Grandma grinned. "I wouldn't miss this for anything. Go get 'em, Katie-kins!"

I was really happy that Grandma was here, but now I really didn't want to mess up. I gulped hard and ran back to the field.

CHAPTER 15

Are You Sure Those Other Players Aren't Professionals?

It felt good to have my own personal cheering section, but I also felt like it was extra pressure, too. Like everybody would be watching my every move.

They must be wondering, Who is this Katie? I thought. *She must be pretty awesome to have people here holding up such a big sign for her.*

So the game started, and I learned that when you're playing at another field, they have to let you go first. Which meant we were up at bat first.

Luckily, Coach Kendall had me batting sixth.

Maybe I won't have to bat this inning, I thought. *Maybe everybody else will strike out.*

As soon as I had the thought, I felt terrible. Of course I didn't want anyone to strike out. I wanted us to win. Right? Of course I did. Winning was the goal here, wasn't it? Or was it just to have fun, like Mom and everyone kept telling me?

Tanya, the girl who batted first, struck out. I felt really guilty that my first thought was "Good, at least someone else struck out before me." But then Beth got up, and she hit a grounder to left field and made it to first base. Sophie was up next, and she walked, so there was someone on first and second. Then on Lucy's turn she hit a ball way into the outfield. It bounced once, but the fielder got it fast and threw it back to the pitcher, so Beth couldn't make it home and was stuck on third base.

The bases were loaded. My palms were starting to sweat like crazy, and Sam wasn't even around. I held my breath when a girl named Sarah went to bat. She ended up striking out, too.

It was the first inning of my first game, and it was bases loaded with two players out. If you're a superstar hitter, this is your dream situation. But if you're a not so great hitter, like me, it's pretty much your worst nightmare. So you can imagine how I felt.

The fuzziness in my head was worse than ever, and I swear I could have filled a gallon milk jug with all the sweat from my palms. I was so frozen with fear that when the first pitch came at me, I didn't even swing. Unfortunately, it was a perfect pitch.

"Strike!" the umpire called out.

Swing, I willed myself. *Just swing next time!*

So when the next ball came, I swung—way too early, like I do when I'm not focused.

"Strike two!"

When the third ball whizzed at me, I tried to stay focused. But I should have wiped my sweaty palms on my pants, because even though I swung on time, the bat slipped a little in my hands, and I missed the ball.

"Strike three!"

The other team started running off the field, and I was confused for a second until I realized the half was over. We had lost our chance to score, all because of me.

"Good job, girls!" Coach Kendall called out. "Now let's get out there!"

I was still standing at home plate, kind of dazed. "It's okay, Katie!" I heard, and I looked behind me. It was Maggie. "Just shake it off!" Was Maggie pulling a Ms. Chen, telling me to just shake it off? "You're doing great, Katie!" yelled Maggie. Wow, was Maggie actually being nice to me? I was so surprised that I kept standing there.

"C'mon, Katie!" called Coach Kendall.

I put down the bat and helmet, grabbed my glove, and jogged over to my position on second base. I quickly glanced at the stands, where Mom, Grandma, and my friends were still smiling and cheering. Didn't they just see me strike out?

Sarah, the girl who had struck out before me, was pitching. I braced myself as the first Fieldstone batter came up to home plate. She looked about six feet tall and had muscles like a bodybuilder. Okay, maybe that's not exactly true, but that's how she looked in my mind. I was convinced we were playing a team of professionals in disguise.

The Fieldstone batter made contact on the first pitch, whacking the ball way into the outfield. Tanya was out there, and she missed the ball, but Sophie ran and scooped it up. I saw the batter touch first base and figured that was the end of the play.

Then I heard Sophie cry out, "Katie! Katie!"

I turned and saw her throwing the ball to me. To my horror the batter was making her way to second!

My heart was in my throat as I quickly got under the ball and caught it. For a second I stood there, frozen.

"Katie, tag the runner!" Coach Kendall called out.

I had forgotten all about that part. I ran to the Fieldstone player as fast as I could and touched her with my glove about a second before she got to the base.

"Out!" the umpire called, and I almost fainted with relief. Everyone in the stands cheered. Out of the corner of my eye I saw Grandma jump up. Oh boy, I really hope she wasn't yelling "Yay, Katie-kins!" That would be harder to live down than Silly Arms.

I tried to concentrate. Almost messing up the play really bothered me. I kept thinking about it over and over, and so when the next batter hit an easy pop-up, I let it bounce out of my glove. The rest of the inning was brutal. Each Fieldstone batter was stronger than the next, and by the time the inning ended, they had scored two runs.

Lucy tried to psych us up as we ran back to the dugout for the next inning. "It's just the first inning!" she said. "We can come back strong!"

But the game was a total disaster. Every time I was at bat I either fouled out or struck out, and lots of other girls were striking out too. The more runs the other team scored, the worse we played.

We had a chance in the third inning to score some runs. We had a runner on third base. There were two outs. Lucy was up.

"Go get 'em, Lucy!" I cheered. But then the catcher called time out and went to the mound to speak to the pitcher. The pitcher nodded, and the catcher trotted back to her position behind the plate. Then the catcher held her right arm straight out. The pitcher threw the ball to her right hand, far away so the batter couldn't swing. She did this four times; it was an intentional walk. Lucy trotted out to first base.

At first I didn't understand why the pitcher would intentionally want to put another batter on base. And then I understood. They intentionally walked Lucy to get to me because they figured I would be an easy out. Wow, these girls were just as bad as Sydney! Why would they be that mean? I knew it was about winning, but boy that made me even more determined than ever to get a hit. But I was overeager and swung at everything. Three quick strikes, and I was done.

The Fieldstone team didn't even need to go up to bat in the seventh inning, because they had already won the game: 12–2.

We didn't just lose—we lost badly. But I didn't

mind losing as much as I minded how badly I had played. Mom told me to do my best. If that was my best, I was in trouble.

Coach Kendall gave us a pep talk in the dugout. "This was a good first effort, girls," she said. "We're still learning how to play together as a team. You'll see—we'll do better each time we play."

"When's our next game?" someone asked.

"Monday night," Coach Kendall said. "We'll meet an hour early, so we can practice beforehand."

Another game in two days? My stomach hurt just thinking about it. And every time I thought about the pitcher walking Lucy to get to me, my face burned.

But something else was upsetting me even more. Grandma Carole had come out early just to see me play. She had so much confidence in me and was sure I would do well. I felt like I had let her down. She must be so disappointed in me. How could I face her now?

Maggie was trying to cheer everyone up. *Maybe she should have tried out for cheerleading after all,* I thought grumpily.

"Hey, Katie, nice work!" she said. "You really went down swinging!"

I tensed up. Was she making fun of me?

But when I looked at her she looked friendly. "You weren't going down without a fight!" she said.

"Thanks," I mumbled.

Maggie hadn't even played in the game. Maybe that's why she didn't feel so badly. None of the strikeouts were her fault.

"See you on Monday!" she said with a wave.

"See you," I said. Then I turned to face the stands, where my fan club was waiting for me.

CHAPTER 16

I Learn Something New About Grandma

After Coach Kendall finished her speech, I slowly walked to the stands. Mom, Grandma, and my friends were all coming toward me, smiling.

"It's all right, it's okay, you did a great job, anyway!" Mom cheered, and at that moment I wished the ground would open and swallow me up.

"Well, I wouldn't say 'great,' exactly," I told her.

Grandma put her arm around me. "It's just first-game jitters, that's all," she said. "I'm sure you'll do great at your next game."

My next game. The thought made my stomach flip-flop again.

Mom turned to the Cupcake Club. "Can you girls join us for some pizza?"

Vinnie's Pizza was just a few blocks from the

field, so we walked there. We couldn't have all fit in the car, anyway. Mom and Grandma walked ahead of us. Thankfully, we started talking about cupcakes instead of going over that disaster of a game.

"You know, now that your grandma is here early, it will be hard to surprise her with a cupcake cake," Alexis pointed out.

"I didn't think of that," I admitted. "The party's Friday night, so we should bake on Thursday."

"We can probably do it at my house," Mia offered.

"Cool," I said. Then I remembered something. "Mia, aren't you with your dad next weekend?" It made me sad to think she would miss the party.

"Dad said I could come out Saturday morning instead," Mia said with a grin. "So I can bring the cupcake cake with me Friday night."

"Double cool," I said.

We found a big table in the pizza parlor, and Mom ordered one plain pie and one pie loaded with veggies, Grandma's favorite. The pizza was delicious, and of course we ended up talking about softball.

Grandma held up her glass of water. "Cheers to Katie! I'm so proud of you for playing your first game."

Everyone clinked their glasses together.

"I was so nervous," I admitted. "I couldn't focus. And besides, we lost—in a major way."

"You can't win all the time," Alexis said. "Our soccer team lost our last three games. That's just how it is sometimes."

"But don't you get nervous when you play?" I asked.

Alexis shrugged. "Not really. I just play."

I saw Mom and Grandma look at each other. Then Mom got up to pay the bill. Grandma smiled at us.

"I heard you girls are making a cupcake cake for my party," she said. "I can't wait to see it. Maybe you can give me just a little hint about it?"

I shook my head. "Sorry, Grandma. We want it to be a surprise."

"One hint is that it will be delicious!" Mia said.

"Oh, I'm sure it will!" said Grandma.

"Katie told us you used to bake professionally," said Alexis.

"Yes," Grandma said. "But that was a long time ago. And now I'm happy you girls are baking for me. I like eating cupcakes more than I like baking them!"

We left Vinnie's and walked back to the field. Grandma Carole pointed to the grassy lawn, where a gray bird with a black head and a red belly was hopping on the ground.

"There it is! The first robin of spring!" she said. She looked at me. "It always brings me good luck. And I think it's extra lucky that I saw it with you."

Grandma walked ahead, and I looked at the Cupcake Club and smiled. We had definitely designed the perfect cupcake cake for her!

But when we got back home, I wasn't smiling anymore. I kept thinking about Monday's game.

"Katie, come sit down at the kitchen table with us," Mom said.

Uh-oh, I thought. *I must be in trouble for something.* Maybe they were going to tell me all the things I did wrong in the game.

But Mom asked me something I wasn't expecting. "Katie, Grandma Carole and I have noticed that you are not yourself today. Is something bothering you?"

"Well, I guess . . ." I didn't want to disappoint them.

"It's okay, Katie," Grandma Carole said. "We're here to help."

I took a deep breath. "It's like this," I said. "I know I'm okay at softball. And I like playing catch with my friends and even having batting practice

121

with Matt. But being on the team . . . it's so much pressure. I'm not having any fun at all."

"I understand," Grandma Carole said, nodding, and I was kind of surprised.

"You do?" I asked, surprised.

"I do. There's a reason I quit baking professionally," she said. "I love to bake, but once I started doing it as a business, it wasn't fun anymore. I felt all this pressure to make things perfect. One day I was making a cake and I realized that I was hating what I was doing. That's when I knew I had to stop and end the business."

"That's exactly how I feel about softball," I said.

"I figured that because I recognized the look on your face," Grandma said. "I'm sorry if I pushed you into sports at all."

"You didn't, Grandma," I said honestly. "I wanted to try. It wasn't just about making a team. I just don't want to stink at sports anymore. I don't want to be the worst kid at everything in gym class."

"You can be athletic without being on a team," Mom pointed out. "You can still play with your friends for fun. And I'll throw a ball around with you whenever you want."

"And I won't make you play tennis anymore," Grandma said with a grin. "The important thing,

Katie, is that you do things that are good for you and make you happy."

I grinned back. "I just remembered something. There is one sport that I'm good at, and I don't ever need to be on a team. And the two of you are really good at it too."

Mom and Grandma looked at each other, confused.

"Running! Anybody want to go for a run?" I asked.

Mom and Grandma both stood up.

"You bet!" Grandma Carole said. "Let me go get changed."

A few minutes later the three of us were jogging through the park, under the trees.

And I didn't feel nervous at all! In fact, I felt great.

Sydney
me!

CHAPTER 17

My Moment in Gym Class

When I woke up Monday I knew what I had to do, and it wasn't going to be easy. Instead of taking the bus, I asked Mom to drop me off at school a few minutes early. I had practiced what I was going to say with her. "Take a big breath," she said as I opened the car door. "It will be fine."

"I know," I lied.

"I love you, sweetie!" she called out, and I waved and shut the door fast. I love my mom, but you do not want your mom yelling "I love you" in front of the entire middle school, for goodness's sake.

I took a deep breath. Then I went and found Coach Kendall in the gym office.

I knocked on the door. "Coach Kendall?"

"Oh, hi, Katie," she said, looking up at me. "Come on in."

I sat in the metal chair on the other side of her desk. Then I took another deep breath.

"So, I think I need to quit the team," I blurted out. That is not how I planned to say it, but it just came out.

"Is everything okay?" the coach asked.

"Yeah, I'm fine, except that I just get too nervous when I'm playing," I said. "Everybody says to relax and have fun, but I can't."

"But you've just started, and you've got talent, Katie," Coach Kendall said. "I'm sure you'll feel more confident the more you play."

I shook my head. "I don't think so. It's a lot of pressure. I just don't think I can do it. I like playing in the backyard with my friends, but I really hated playing during the game. I got nervous, and I didn't sleep the night before the game. And, honestly, I just kind of hated every minute of it. And I know we just had one game, but I thought about it all weekend, and I don't think softball is for me. Honestly, I almost threw up thinking about playing a game tonight. I'm sorry. I hope I didn't disappoint you."

Whew, well, at least I finally got out what I practiced with Mom.

Coach Kendall frowned a little and nodded her head. "Competitive sports aren't for everybody. I certainly don't want you to be unhappy. But if you change your mind and feel like trying out next year, I'd be happy to have you on the team."

"Thanks," I said. "And thanks for understanding."

Then I left the gym, and even though I felt kind of bad about quitting, I also felt like a big rock had been taken off my shoulders. Like I could float or fly. What a relief!

Now I just had to tell my friends.

At lunch I waited until Alexis and Emma sat down with me and Mia. Then I just spit it out (not my lunch, my news).

"So I quit the softball team this morning," I blurted out.

"Oh no!" Emma said. "But you tried so hard."

"I know," I said. "But I can't take the pressure. I was miserable. I like playing for fun. But for real in a game, it's not for me."

Mia nodded. "Yeah, you looked pretty miserable on Saturday. Like all of your Katie energy was sucked right out of you."

That's why Mia is my new best friend. She totally gets me.

"Exactly," I said. "Anyway, thanks for helping me

out so much, you guys. And I'll still play ball with you and stuff. I just don't want to be on a team."

"So does this mean you're not going to find another after-school activity?" Alexis asked.

"Well, I have one new activity. I am running now," I said. "I go with my mom or grandmother. I really love it. I just put my sneakers on and go, and there's no pressure or anything. And I feel great afterward."

"Hey, you should try out for the track team!" said Alexis.

"I don't think so," I said. "That's the thing about running. It's just me and my legs taking me along. I'm not worried about teammates or letting anyone down or who is watching me. It feels great to just run."

"We do track as a unit in gym," said Emma. "Just think about how great you'll be!"

"And we have softball, too," said Mia. "So that's a bunch of gym classes you should ace!"

"I hadn't thought about that," I said. But it was true. Some worry-free gym classes wouldn't be too bad.

A lot of surprising things had happened in the last few weeks. I had made the softball team. I learned that Grandma Carole and I were more alike than I thought. And then another surprising thing happened, right there at lunch.

Maggie walked up to me as I went to throw out my garbage—and she wasn't following Sydney or the other PGC girls.

"I heard you quit the team," she said. "Why? You were good."

I nodded. "It's kind of hard to explain, but mostly I just wasn't having fun."

Maggie shook her head. "Are you serious? Because I think it's really fun," she said.

I felt my neck get stiff. "Well it wasn't for me," I said a little defensively.

"My mom says there's enough stuff you have to do that you don't like, and that when you can choose, you should always choose the things you love," said Maggie. "So I get that."

I smiled. "Thanks," I said. Maybe I should be giving Maggie more of a break. What she just said sounded like something my mom would say.

"Anyway, I came to thank you. Coach Kendall gave me your spot on the team. I'm so excited. I'm sorry you didn't like it, but I'm hoping I'll be able to catch as well as you."

I was happy then. Maggie deserved it.

Then she leaned close to me. "And I don't care

what Sydney thinks!" she whispered.

I laughed as Maggie walked away. Alexis raised an eyebrow.

"What was that all about?" she asked.

"Maggie's on the team now," I said. "I'm happy for her."

"But doesn't she torture you in gym?" Emma asked.

I shrugged. "Sometimes. But she's not so bad, especially when she's away from Sydney."

That reminded me of my only lasting problem: Sydney. More exactly, Sydney in gym class. We had been playing flag football for a few weeks, and I hadn't gotten any better. Although ever since I gave George that cupcake, he had kept his promise and stopped calling me Silly Arms.

"If only we were done with flag football," I said with a sigh. "I guess I am doomed to be a flag-football spaz forever."

"I'm sorry," Emma said. "But lately Sydney seems more interested in bumping into the boys than bothering you, anyway."

"Good point," I agreed. "Maybe I can practice turning invisible in gym. I heard if you concentrate long enough, it can happen."

"That can't be true," Alexis said.

"Of course not, but I can try," I said.

When I got to gym class later, Ms. Chen had an announcement to make after we did our warm-up exercises.

"The state physical fitness tests are next month," she said. "We're going to start training today. Let's start with some running. Ten times around the gym. Let's move it!"

I can handle that, I thought with relief. Maybe my worry-free gym class was starting sooner than I thought. But as soon as I started running, Sydney started in on me.

"Be careful, Katie, or you'll trip over your own feet!" she said. Then her voice got louder. "Hey, everybody, watch out for Katie! She might crash into you." She smirked and tossed her long, perfect, shiny hair.

This time Sydney's teasing didn't bother me much—maybe because I knew how wrong she was.

"I think I'll be just fine," I told her, and then I ran right past her. I pretended I was in the park with the birds and started flying around the gym, getting ahead of everybody—even the boys.

"Nice hustle, Katie!" Ms. Chen called out. "Sydney, look alive out there! This isn't a funeral march!"

I looked back and saw that Sydney was one of the last runners, and she actually looked a little bit sweaty. I smiled.

"Go, Silly Legs!" called George. "The girl can run!" *I have to start bringing him more cupcakes,* I thought, and sprinted toward the finish.

In a couple of months we'd be playing basketball or volleyball or whatever, and I'd be back to being a spaz again. But for now, all I had to do was run.

CHAPTER 18

I Don't Mean to Brag, but I Am Pretty Talented After All!

𝒯he rest of the week went by very fast. It was nice having Grandma Carole there early, because I didn't have to go to Mom's office after school. She helped me with my homework, and we made dinner together.

Then Thursday was pretty crazy. After school I met Alexis and Emma at Mia's house, and we started on the cupcake cake. Mia's mom was nice and got us Chinese food to eat while the cupcakes cooled down. Then we decorated them with fondant flowers, leaves, and birds in shades of yellow, pink, green, violet, and blue. When we were all done, we boxed them up. Tomorrow, at the party, we would put them on their stands.

Mom picked me up at eight thirty. She had been

decorating the house while we made the cupcakes. Grandma was staying at Uncle Jimmy's tonight. "Everything looks great," she said. "Barbara helped me set it all up. It looks so beautiful."

Barbara is Callie's mom. I knew Callie and her family would be at the party tomorrow, and I wasn't sure how I felt about it. I was still pretty mad at Callie for not sticking up for me.

But I didn't tell my mom that. "I can't wait to see it," I said.

Mom was right about the decorations. The whole house looked like a spring garden, with light green tablecloths and a pretty flower arrangement on each table. The streamers on the ceiling were green and yellow and robin's-egg blue, a perfect match for our cupcake cake.

The next day we got up really early. Mia and her stepdad arrived not long after. Eddie was carrying the cupcake boxes, and Mia had the stands.

"Over there," Mom instructed, pointing to a little round table in a corner of the room. "I can't wait to see them!"

Emma and Alexis arrived next, so all four of us were able to set up the cupcake cake. We started with the green flower cupcakes on the bottom, and the top two tiers were blue with birds on them, just like in Mia's drawing.

"Oh, it's absolutely beautiful!"

Grandma Carole walked in, wearing a blue dress that almost matched the cupcakes. Grandpa Chuck was there too, and he wore a robin's-egg-blue tie with his gray suit.

Grandma walked around the cupcake table, admiring it from every angle.

"This is absolutely perfect!" she cried. "Robin's-egg blue! I love it!"

"And the cupcakes are blueberry, too," I said.

"My favorite!" Grandma said. "You girls are very talented. Your business must be doing very well."

"Our profits are rising every month," Alexis reported proudly.

Then the party guests started streaming in, and Joanne from Mom's office started playing songs from her iPod on a speaker. It really felt like a party.

Then Callie came in with her older sister, Jenna, and her mom and dad. Mr. Wilson gave me a big hug when he saw me.

"Hey there, Katie-did," he said. "My gosh, you must have grown a foot since I last saw you!"

"Not a foot," I said. "But maybe a little."

Then Callie's parents walked off to say hi to my

grandparents, and Callie and I were just standing there, looking at each other. Callie looked kind of embarrassed.

"So, I just wanted to say that I felt kind of bad about the way Sydney's been talking to you," she said. "I wanted to stick up for you, but Sydney . . ."

"It's okay," I said, thinking of gym the other day. "I can take care of myself. Besides, I don't really care what Sydney thinks, anyway."

I didn't believe it until I said it out loud, but it was true. Sydney could say whatever she wanted, but as long as it didn't matter to me, it couldn't hurt me, right?

Callie looked a little surprised. "Um, that's cool, then."

That's when Mia ran up and grabbed me by the arm. "Katie, I looooove this song. Let's dance!"

We all danced and ate a bunch of food, and Mom showed a slideshow of photos of Grandma from when she was a little girl.

"Wow, Katie, you look just like your grandma," Emma remarked.

"I know," I said proudly.

Then Grandpa Chuck walked up to me. "Katie, I hear you're a fine softball player. How about a game outside?"

I hesitated, but then he said, "Just for fun. We won't even keep score."

Then I relaxed. "Sure," I said.

So some of us went outside and played softball for a while, and it *was* fun. And something amazing even happened. I hit a home run!

The ball went way into the outfield, and Alexis ran for it, but couldn't catch it. So I ran around the bases as fast as I could.

"Go, Katie-kins!" Grandma Carole cheered as I crossed home plate. My heart was pounding and I was very sweaty, but not because I was nervous—I was excited.

Finally it was time for cupcakes. After Grandma Carole blew out her candles, everyone dug in.

"Katie, these cupcakes are delicious!" Grandma said. "You could be a professional baker."

"We all made them," I said, blushing.

"Yes, but Katie figured out the frosting," Mia pointed out.

Mom hugged me. "You know what you're great at besides baking cupcakes?" she asked me.

"No, what?"

"You're a good friend," Mom said. "And a wonderful running partner."

"And a pretty good batter," Grandpa added.

"And the best granddaughter ever!" Grandma Carole said, joining me and Mom in a group hug.

I counted in my head—that was one, two, three, four, five talents! Not bad, don't you think? I smiled at everyone around me as they happily ate delicious cupcakes.

Then I remembered to save a cupcake for George. I'd need it—pretty soon in gym we'd be starting basketball!

Mia's
baker's
dozen

CHAPTER 1

I'll Definitely Finish It Tomorrow . . .

Me llamo Mia, y me gusta hornear pastelitos.

That means "My name is Mia, and I like to bake cupcakes" in Spanish. A few months ago, I could never have read that sentence or even written it. Maybe that doesn't sound like a big deal. But for me, it totally was.

Here's the thing: I'm good at a bunch of things, like playing soccer and drawing and decorating cupcakes. Nobody ever *expected* me to be good at them. I just was.

But everyone expected me to be good at Spanish. My whole family is Latino, and my mom and dad both speak Spanish. I've been hearing it since I was a baby, and I can understand a lot of it and speak it pretty well—enough to get my point across. But reading and writing Spanish? That's a whole other thing. And the fact that I was bad at it got me into a big mess. Well, maybe I got myself into a big mess. But Spanish definitely didn't help.

The whole situation kind of blew up this winter. You see, when I started middle school in the fall, they placed me in Advanced Spanish with Señora Delgado because my parents told the school that I was a Spanish speaker. At first I did okay, but after a few weeks it was pretty clear to me that I was in over my head. I could speak it but not write it. The homework kept getting harder and harder, and my test grades were slipping.

One night in February, I was trying really hard to do my Spanish homework. Señora asked us to write an essay about something we planned to do this month. I decided to write about going to see my dad, who lives in Manhattan. I visit him every other weekend, and we always go out to eat sushi.

It sounds simple, but I was having a hard time writing it. I always get mixed up with the verbs, and that was the whole point of the essay—to use future indicative verbs. (Yeah, I'm not sure what those are either.) Anyway, I was trying to write "We will eat sushi," and I couldn't get the verb right.

"*Comemos*? Or is it *comeramos*?" I wondered aloud with a frown while tapping my pencil on my desk. My head was starting to really hurt, and it wasn't just because of the homework.

"Dan, TURN IT DOWN!" I yelled at the wall in front of me. On the other side of the wall, Dan, my stepbrother, was blasting music like he always does. He listens to metal or something, and it sounds like a werewolf screaming in a thunderstorm. He couldn't hear me, so I started banging on the walls.

The music got a little bit softer, and Dan yelled, "Chill, Mia!"

"Thanks," I muttered, even though I knew he couldn't hear me.

I looked back down at my paper, which was only half finished. Where was I again? Oh, right. Sushi. At least that word is the same in any language.

My brain couldn't take any more. I picked up my smartphone and messaged three of my friends at once.

Anyone NOT want to do homework right now? I asked.

Alexis replied first. She's the fastest texter in the Cupcake Club.

Mine is already done!

Of course, I should have known. Alexis is one of those people who actually likes doing homework.

It's better than babysitting my little brother! came the next reply.

That's my friend Emma. I actually think her little brother, Jake, is kind of cute, but I also know that he can be annoying.

The last reply came from my friend Katie.

Let's go on a homework strike!

I laughed. Katie is really funny, and she also feels the same way I do about a lot of things (like homework). That's probably why she's my best friend here in Maple Grove.

Where are we meeting tomorrow? I asked.

I think I mentioned the Cupcake Club already. That's a business I started with Alexis, Emma, and

Katie. We bake cupcakes for parties and other events, and we meet at least once a week.

We can do it at my house, Emma replied.
Works for me! Alexis texted back at light speed.

Alexis always likes going to Emma's house, and it's not just because she and Emma are best friends. She used to have a crush on Emma's brother Matt. He's pretty cute, but Emma's brother Sam is even cuter.

Alexis texted again.

Everyone come with ideas for the Valentine's cupcakes.
Ugh! I hate that holiday! Emma complained.
But there's candy! Katie wrote.
And everything's pink, I reminded Emma since pink is her favorite color.
K, you have a point. But still. We have to watch all the couples in school make a big deal out of it, Emma replied.
And watch all the boys go gaga for Sydney, Alexis chimed in.

Sydney is the president of the Popular Girls Club, and Alexis is right—lots of boys like her.

Any boys who like Sydney have cupcakes for brains, Katie wrote.

I laughed.

Got to go! Twelve more math problems left! Emma wrote.

I have 2 go study, Alexis added.

I thought you were done? Katie wrote.

This is just for fun ☺, Alexis wrote back.

If u want to have fun u can do my homework, Katie typed.

Or mine, I added.

LOL! CU tom, Alexis typed.

I said good night to my friends and put down my phone. I stared at my paper for a few seconds and then I picked up my sketchbook.

My Spanish class isn't until after lunch, so I figured I could finish the essay then. I couldn't concentrate now anyway. Besides, I was dying to finish a sketch I had started earlier.

My mom's a fashion stylist, and she's always taking the train to New York to meet with designers and boutique owners. I guess I take after her because I am totally obsessed with fashion and I love designing my own clothes.

146

Once in a while, Mom takes me to meetings with her and I get to see all the latest fashions before other people do.

Lately I've been trying to design a winter coat that keeps you warm but isn't all puffy. I hate puffy coats. I thought maybe the coat could be lined with a fabric that kept you warm *and* looked streamlined. Maybe cashmere? But that would be really expensive. Flannel might work; and it would be so cozy, like being wrapped up in your bed's flannel sheets!

I opened up my sketchbook, a new one that my dad gave me. It's got this soft leather cover and really good paper inside that makes my drawings look even better. I picked up a purple pencil and started to finish my sketch of a knee-length wraparound style coat.

There was a knock on my door, and then Mom stepped in.

"Hey, sweetie," she said. She nodded to the sketchbook. "Done with your homework?"

"Yes," I lied.

Mom smiled and walked over to look at my sketch. "Very nice, *mija*," she said. "I like the shape of those sleeves. And purple is a very nice color for a winter coat. Most winter coats are black or brown or tan. They're so boring."

147

"Thanks!" I replied, and she kissed me on the head and left the room. I started to feel a little guilty about lying about my homework, but I pushed the feeling aside. I was definitely going to finish it tomorrow, so no problem, right?

Actually, it *was* a problem . . . a big one.

CHAPTER 2

Señora Is Not Happy

"I know how to say all the colors," Katie said helpfully. "Red is *rojo*. Blue is *azul*. Yellow is *amarillo*. I'm not so good at pronouncing that one because I can't do that thing with the two *l*'s."

It was lunchtime, and I was frantically trying to finish my essay while eating the chicken salad sandwich that Eddie, my stepdad, had made for me.

"Thanks, Katie," I said. "But I don't think the colors will help. I need future indicative verbs."

Katie frowned. "That sounds painful. But maybe you could, you know, pad it. Like say the sushi restaurant has red chairs and a blue rug and yellow walls."

I laughed. "Can you imagine if a restaurant was really decorated like that?"

"Rainbow sushi!" Katie exclaimed. "I think it would catch on."

I sighed. "Anyway, I need verbs."

Alexis and Emma walked up to the table carrying trays of spaghetti and salad. Alexis nodded at my notebook.

"Cupcake ideas?" she asked.

"I wish," I replied. "It's my Spanish homework."

Alexis's green eyes widened in horror. "You mean you didn't finish it?" Most people have nightmares about monsters, but Alexis wakes up screaming if she dreams she hasn't done her homework.

"It's hard!" I complained. "I'm supposed to be writing about when I go see my dad. Now I'm trying to say, 'We will visit my grandmother.'"

Alexis frowned. "We haven't done a lot of future tense in our French class yet. Spanish must be a lot harder than French."

I shook my head. "It's because I'm in Advanced Spanish," I said with a moan. "That's why we're already on this."

"But you speak Spanish, Mia," Alexis said. "I've heard you!"

"Yes," I replied. "But I've never taken a Spanish class. I took French in my old school. And when we

150

moved here, my mom thought I should get some formal training in Spanish. She told the guidance counselor that I spoke Spanish at home, and they put me in the advanced class. Without even asking me!"

"So it's not easier because you already speak it?" Katie asked.

"No way," I said. "It's like, when I hear people talking in Spanish, I can understand most of it. And if someone asks me a question, like my *abuela*, I can answer her. But my main language growing up was English."

I took a sip of my water. "And think about it," I said. "You learned how to speak English before you could learn how to properly write it, right? You can say to a baby, 'Show me your nose,' and the baby will point to her nose. But she isn't able to write, 'My nose is on my face.'"

Katie nodded. "You're right," she said. "I can see why it's more difficult to learn how to write a language than to speak it."

I picked up my sandwich, and Katie eyed it. "Did Eddie make you chicken salad again?"

"Uh-huh," I answered, taking a bite.

"He's a really good cook, isn't he?" she asked.

"His chicken salad's pretty good," I admitted.

"But believe me, you do not want to eat his Mystery Meat Loaf."

Katie looked thoughtful. "Maybe he can be my top chef when I open up Katie's Rainbow Restaurant," she said.

"Ooh, that's a great idea," Emma said. "You could divide the menu into seven colors, and people could pick one food from each color."

"That's way too much food," Alexis objected.

"Well, you wouldn't have to order *all* seven," Katie pointed out. "You could order three dishes of your favorite color, if you want."

Did I tell you that my Maple Grove friends are a little bit crazy? They always make me laugh. Maybe "creative" is a better word than "crazy" to describe them. Everybody always has lots of ideas. A rainbow restaurant! Only one of my friends would dream up something like that.

When I look at our lunch table, I sometimes think we are like a rainbow of hair colors. Emma's hair is pale blond, the color most women in Manhattan pay a fortune to try to get. Alexis has gorgeous, curly red hair. Katie's hair is light brown and wavy, and mine is black and really straight.

"We could all be waitresses," I suggested. "We could each wear a different color uniform."

"I'll be violet!" Katie cried. She loves purple.

Emma frowned. "There's no pink in a rainbow."

"You could be red," Alexis suggested.

"Red is *so* not pink," Emma protested.

"I'll be red," I said. Then I took out my sketchbook and started drawing our uniforms.

Before I knew it, the bell rang. Lunch was over, my assignment wasn't done—and I had to go to Spanish class.

"Wish me luck," I said.

"Everybody forgets their homework at least once," Katie said, trying to cheer me up. "It'll be okay."

The problem was, I hadn't forgotten to do it—I just *couldn't* do it. There's a big difference. If you forget to do your homework, it's a one-time thing. But if you don't know how to do it, it's a huge problem. And I didn't expect things to get easier.

I gathered my books together and headed to Señora Delgado's class. The only good thing about that class is that I sit next to Callie, who's pretty nice. She used to be Katie's best friend, but that's kind of a long story. And she hangs out with Sydney and is in the Popular Girls Club. And Sydney doesn't really like me, but that's another long story.

Anyway, I like Callie, and it's nice sitting next to her in class. Especially when things get confusing. She's really helpful.

Callie gave me a smile when I slid into the seat next to her.

"Nice shirt," she said, admiring my boxy blue knit shirt. I had accessorized it with a necklace one of my mom's designer friends had given me—a silver chain with a chunky silver circle pendant.

"Thanks," I said. "I like your scarf." Callie was wearing one of those loopy big infinity scarves in red and black that looked nice with her black sweater.

"Thanks," she said back.

Callie is into fashion too. That's one of the reasons we get along. But our little mutual admiration session was the highlight of my Spanish class.

"Hola, clase," Señora Delgado said when she walked into the room. That means "Hello, class." In advanced class we're supposed to speak Spanish all the time, which is pretty easy for me. (But since you might not speak Spanish, I'll do all the dialogue in this class in English.)

Señora began by asking us each to say a few sentences about what we did the day before. That's so we could practice our past tense. I was able to do that okay.

"I did my homework, talked to my friends, and drew in my sketchbook," I told her, and Señora smiled.

"Perfect pronunciation and accent as usual, Mia," she said. "Good job."

But Señora wasn't smiling at me after she asked us to hand in our assignments. I handed it in and held my breath. Señora went through the pile of papers and then frowned.

"Mia, this is only half finished," she said.

"I know," I said. "I'm sorry."

Señora shook her head. "You are getting lazy these days, Mia. This is not acceptable. See me after class. I'm giving you an extra worksheet for homework tonight."

"Yes, Señora," I said.

Callie gave me a sympathetic look, and I slunk down in my seat. This was just what I needed. More homework that I didn't understand.

I know what you're probably thinking right now. Why didn't I just tell my parents the truth? That I shouldn't be in Advanced Spanish.

Well, I just felt like I couldn't. What would they think? The truth was that their only child,

Mia Vélaz-Cruz, the daughter of proud Spanish-speaking parents, couldn't read or write the language. I didn't think they could handle the truth. It would have to be my secret. Hopefully they would never find out.

CHAPTER 3

Sweet and Spicy

At least I didn't have to face Mom right after school because we had an official Cupcake Club meeting. Emma lives close to the school, on the same street as Alexis, so the four of us walked to her house. It was cold out, and there was still some snow on the lawns from a storm the week before. My red winter jacket kept me nice and warm, though, and for once I didn't mind its general puffiness.

When we got inside, Mrs. Taylor was sitting at the dining room table with Emma's little brother, Jake. He was taking the books out of his backpack.

"Hi, Mom!" Emma called out. "Did you get off early?"

"I'm working story time tomorrow morning, so I had the afternoon off," her mom replied. She's a librarian, and she's got blond hair just like Emma and all her brothers.

Jake ran up to us. "Are you making cupcakes today?" he asked. "I want a blue one with a dinosaur on it!"

"Sorry, Jake, today we're just talking about cupcakes," Emma told him. "But maybe you can help me make some later, okay?"

Jake got a big smile on his face. "Okay!" Then he ran back to the table.

"There's a pot of hot chocolate on the stove, and some oatmeal bars to go with it," Mrs. Taylor said.

"Thank you!" all four of us said at once. Then we headed to the kitchen for our meeting.

You can tell from Emma's kitchen that everyone in her family loves sports. There are sports schedules tacked to the refrigerator, and her brothers' hockey sticks were leaning up next to the back door. The one thing of Emma's that stands out is her pink mixer. Besides being gorgeous, it's great for baking cupcakes.

"Emma, we should use your pink mixer to make our Valentine's cupcakes," Katie suggested as we grabbed our cocoa and snacks. "Maybe they'll add some extra Valentine's magic or something."

Alexis opened up her backpack and took out her notebook.

"So, the bookstore wants four dozen cupcakes for their event," she said, getting right down to business as usual. "And they want them to be Valentine themed. Any ideas?"

"I was thinking we could do a white cupcake," Emma said. "You know, the kind you make with no egg yolks? They're fluffy and light as air. I think they're called angel's food."

Katie nodded. "My mom showed me how to make those." (Katie's mom is, like, the best cupcake baker in the world.)

"And then we could make some light pink strawberry frosting to go with them," Emma finished.

We all made an *ooh* sound.

"That sounds so pretty!" I said. "I had a different kind of idea. I was thinking about something red—maybe a red velvet cupcake, but with red cinnamon frosting and Red Hots candies on the top."

"Spicy romance!" Katie said, and we all laughed.

159

And that was exactly when Emma's brother Sam walked in. How embarrassing!

"Spicy romance?" he repeated. "What are you girls talking about? I thought this was a cupcake meeting."

Sam is a junior in high school, and his blond hair is wavy and sometimes falls over his eyes. And he's just as nice as he is cute.

"This *is* a cupcake meeting," Emma said with a huff. "We're trying to invent some Valentine's cupcakes."

Emma's brother Matt walked in just behind Sam. He opened the refrigerator, took out a carton of milk, and drank right from it.

"Valentine's cupcakes?" he asked. "What, for your boyfriends?"

"We're too young to have boyfriends!" Katie blurted out. "At least, that's what my mom says."

Matt shrugged. "Well, then you can make some for me to give to my girlfriend."

Next to me, Alexis suddenly got a weird look on her face.

"You don't *have* a girlfriend," Emma said. "And stop drinking from the milk carton or I'll tell Mom!"

Matt reached over her shoulder and grabbed

two oatmeal bars from the plate on the table. "Well, maybe I'll get one," he said.

Emma shook her head. "Exactly. You don't have one."

Most of the time, Emma is pretty quiet and shy. But when she's with her brothers, she can totally stand up to them. I think that's cool.

Alexis's face was all pink underneath her freckles. I know she used to like Matt (and maybe she still did, a little), so it must be weird to hear him talking about girlfriends.

Sam took the milk from Matt and poured himself a glass.

"There's too much spicy romance in this room," he said. "I'm getting out of here."

Now it was Katie's turn to blush, only she turned as red as the cupcake I was imagining.

"Can we please get back to our meeting?" Alexis asked impatiently.

"We have two cupcake ideas," I reminded her. "Fluffy and pink, and red and hot."

"We should do both," Katie suggested. "One pink, one red. Sweet and spicy."

"Good idea," Alexis said. "Then people will have a choice."

I started sketching a big heart entirely made of

cupcakes. All the pink ones were in the middle, and the border was made with the spicy red cupcakes. "Here's a fun way to display them," I said. I held up my sketch.

"I love it, Mia!" Emma squealed. Nothing like a big pink heart to make a girlie girl happy.

"That's awesome," Alexis said. "Now we have two cupcake ideas and even a cool way to display them. This was a very productive meeting." She nodded approvingly.

"That was easy!" Katie said, leaning back.

Alexis stood up. "I'd love to stay longer, but I think I should go home," she said.

"Already?" Katie asked.

She nodded. "Tons of homework."

"I think teachers get bored in the winter and give us extra homework so they have something to do at night," Katie mused. "It seems like it's double lately."

Suddenly I remembered the extra homework Señora Delgado had given me.

"I should go soon too," I said. "Let me text Eddie."

"My mom can give you a ride," Katie said.

"That's okay," I told her. "He's expecting me to text him to pick me up."

162

My stepdad, Eddie, is a pretty nice guy. I don't have too many complaints about him, even though it's superweird that my parents are divorced and I have a stepdad in the first place. But one thing that bugs me is that he's way more strict than my dad, and Mom goes along with it.

For example, Mom works at home on her business, but she's out at meetings a lot. And she and Eddie have a rule that I can't be home alone. So if Mom's not home, then Eddie leaves his office, which is here in Maple Grove, and hangs out with me until Mom comes home.

Can you believe that? I mean, I'm in middle school! Emma's mom lets her stay home alone, and she even watches Jake. It's so not fair. When I'm in Manhattan with my dad, sometimes he'll run out to the store or something and *he* lets me stay in the apartment by myself. But not Eddie. And I know Mom's only going along with it because that's what Eddie wants.

I hung out with the Cupcake Club for about fifteen more minutes, and then Eddie called my phone. He doesn't believe in beeping the horn. He says it "disturbs the peace."

I said good-bye to my friends and headed outside. Eddie's car was nice and warm.

163

"Hi, Mia," he said cheerfully. "How did the cupcake meeting go?"

"Good," I replied. Eddie always wants to have these long, chatty conversations, but sometimes I'm not in the mood.

"Do you have a lot of homework tonight?" he asked as we began the drive home.

"Um, some," I said. There was absolutely no way I was going to tell him what happened in Señora Delgado's class.

"You can start that while I start dinner then," he said. "And don't forget to text your mom as soon as we get home."

"Why do I always have to do that?" I asked. "*You* know I'm home! Why do I have to tell both of you?"

Eddie laughed. "Because your mom likes to hear from you."

I rolled my eyes and stared out the window. Back when Mom and Dad were still together, I had a babysitter who picked me up from school when they were both working late. Her name was Natalie, and she was really nice. She would make me mac and cheese for dinner, and I was usually in bed when Mom came home and kissed me good night. Mom never made me text her then.

t there was no use arguing with Eddie.

I ed Mom as soon as I got home, and she
s e'd be home by six thirty. Then I decided
t my dad to see if he wanted to Skype.
ing about those old days in the city was
ig me miss him really bad.

a meeting. We'll Skype after dinner, OK? he
l back.

, I answered, feeling a little sad.

"Guess it's just me and Eddie," I muttered.

There was nothing to do but start my homework. I did my math first and then my vocabulary, and then I started on my Spanish.

Soon a delicious smell filled the air, and I realized that Eddie was making his famous spinach lasagna for dinner. *Yum!*

When I heard the door slam, I knew Dan was home. A little while later, my mom pulled into the driveway.

"I hope I'm not late!" Mom called out.

I ran down the stairs, remembering I should have set the table by now. But when I got into the dining room, Dan was already setting it.

"Hey, thanks," I said.

Dan shrugged. "Dad said you were d_ng_
homework."

Eddie walked into the dining room carryir_
steaming pan of lasagna. He was wearing my mo_
oven mitts with the big red roses on them, and _
looked pretty silly.

"Let Family Time begin!" he announced in _
goofy voice.

A few minutes later I was eating delicious
lasagna and salad and garlic bread, and Mom was
telling me about her new client, and then Dan told
this story about this guy in his chemistry class who
made something explode, and we were all laughing.
It was definitely better than eating mac and cheese
with Natalie. In fact, it was pretty nice.

But you know what would be even better than
that? Having "Family Time" with me and Mom
and Dad all together. It doesn't really feel like
"Family Time" to me completely without my dad
here eating dinner with us. But that's never going
to happen again.

And sometimes knowing that really hurts.

CHAPTER 4

Thank Goodness for Cupcakes

$\mathcal{I}$ felt a little better after I Skyped with my dad; I always do. And I definitely didn't want to disappoint Señora Delgado again, so I made sure to finish all my homework. They were both worksheets, so I ended up guessing a lot. But at least I finished!

Anyway, tomorrow is Friday, which is my favorite day of the week. For one thing, it's the last day before the weekend, and the best things always happen on weekends. But for the Cupcake Club, it's also Cupcake Friday.

We started Cupcake Friday when school started and we all met. I definitely wouldn't mind eating cupcakes every day, but that's not exactly healthy, you know? So every Friday one of us brings in cupcakes to share. Since we started our business, a lot of times the cupcakes are test runs of the cupcakes we're going to make for an order.

The next day in the cafeteria, we all waited eagerly for Emma to arrive. Last night Emma texted everyone and told us she was going to bake the white cupcakes with strawberry frosting. She came to the table with a pink cardboard box and lifted the lid.

"They're a little messy, because I let Jake help me," she said apologetically. "So I added some coconut flakes to cover up the dents in the icing."

"That looks like snow!" I said. I took my sketchbook out of my bag and started sketching with a pink pencil. "I like how it looks on top, but maybe we could test out some other decorations too. Like some white heart–shaped sprinkles, maybe?" I held up my sketch.

Emma's eyes lit up. "Ooh, I like that idea!"

Katie picked up a cupcake. "They look sooo good, Emma," she said, peeling off the wrapper.

We hadn't even eaten our lunch yet, but none of us could resist trying one. I unwrapped one and took a bite. The white cake was superlight and fluffy, and the strawberry icing was perfect—not too sweet.

"It's almost like eating a cloud," Katie remarked, finishing her cupcake in one big bite.

"It is delicious," I agreed.

"It's perfect," Alexis added. "Now we just need to test the spicy ones. Mia, can we do that at the meeting on Sunday?"

"Oh, I almost forgot!" I said. "My friend Ava is coming out to visit this weekend. Is it okay if she's at the meeting?"

"She's nice," Katie said. "Besides, since we're making cupcakes for her birthday party, she can tell us what she wants."

"She's the one we met at your mom's fashion show and wedding, right?" Alexis asked, and I nodded.

"Of course she can be there," Alexis said. She looked down at her notebook. "Oh yeah, I forgot something. I meant to mention this yesterday."

I smiled. "Yeah, it looked like you were a little distracted."

Alexis blushed. "I told you, I don't like Matt anymore! Besides, you and Katie turn bright red whenever Sam walks into the room."

"Ew! You guys are talking about my brothers, remember?" Emma pointed out.

"Sorry," I said. "So what's up, Alexis?"

"The question should really be, 'What's down?'" Alexis said. "And the answer to that would be 'our sales.' They've dropped twelve percent since the fall. We had a little bump during the holidays, but still, we need to pick up business."

"Maybe we can start promoting the business again," Emma suggested. "Remember when we handed out those flyers? They really worked."

Alexis nodded thoughtfully. "True. We haven't done those in a while. But maybe we could put a coupon on them or something. You know, like a special deal."

"We could do a baker's dozen!" Katie said.

"What's that?" Alexis asked.

"It's when you buy a dozen of something and you get an extra for free," Katie explained. "Like they do at the bagel shop. They give you thirteen bagels for the price of twelve, and they call it a baker's dozen."

"I like it!" Alexis said. "Except for one thing. Our cupcake boxes fit twelve cupcakes exactly. Where would we put the extra one?"

Everyone was quiet for a minute. "Maybe we could wrap the extra one in a clear bag with a ribbon," I said. "Then they'd definitely see that they're getting an extra one."

"So cute!" Emma agreed.

"They also make special boxes that fit exactly one cupcake," Katie said. "I've seen them at the store. But they might be too expensive. I can check."

"Either one of those ideas could work," Alexis said. "And you know, maybe we don't have to do flyers. I was doing some research on advertising, and it costs only ten dollars to put an ad on the school's website for parents. Since we need some new customers, we could offer a baker's dozen to everyone who orders for the first time."

"Sounds like a plan!" Katie said.

"I can write something up and show it to you guys on Sunday," Alexis said.

"And I'll get the ingredients together for the cinnamon cupcakes," I added.

And then I realized that I had spent the whole lunch period without even thinking about Spanish class. That's another reason I love being in the Cupcake Club!

CHAPTER 5

Some Advice from Ava

"Why exactly do I have to sweep the basement?" I complained. "Nobody ever goes down there!"

"Would you take a bath and not wash your feet?" Eddie replied. "A truly clean house is clean all over. And we want things to be nice for your friend."

"But she's not even going to see the basement!" I pointed out.

That was when Mom stepped into the kitchen. "Mia, please don't argue with Eddie. It will only take a few minutes to sweep the basement."

I glared at my mom, but I knew I wasn't going to win this argument. So I grabbed the broom from Eddie and went down the stairs.

"No stomping!" Mom called after me.

"I am *not* stomping!" I called back. (Although to be honest, I was stepping pretty hard.)

I couldn't help it. I was feeling pretty cranky. Ava was due any minute, and I was thinking of changing out of my skinny jeans and black sweater into something different. But no—I had to clean the basement.

When we lived in an apartment, we didn't have a basement. In fact, I don't remember cleaning our apartment. I had to keep my room clean, but the kitchen and living room were always neat. I never thought much about how that happened.

But now I lived in a house, and Eddie believes that "a clean house is a happy house." So every Saturday we wake up at the crack of dawn (which to me is any time before ten o'clock) and clean the house, unless I have a soccer game or a cupcake job. It's just one more way that my new life is worse than my old life.

Even though I hate to admit it, Mom was right about the basement. There's not much down there except Dan's and my sports equipment and a metal shelf with some pots and pans and cans of food. The floor is concrete, and it didn't take long to sweep at all.

But by the time I got back upstairs, the doorbell

was ringing. My heart started to beat extra fast. Ava was here!

Ava and I have known each other since pre-school. She was my only best friend in the world until I met Katie. I miss Ava so much! I usually visit her when I spend the weekend with my dad, but she's never been to Eddie's house before—I mean, *my* house. Our house.

I ran to the door and opened it. Ava was there with her mom, Mrs. Monroe. A blast of cold air swept into the room.

"Come in, fast!" I said. "It's cold out there."

Then Mom and Eddie came up, and everybody hugged one another. Ava took off her coat, and I saw she was wearing skinny jeans and a black sweater—just like me.

We pointed at each other and laughed.

"Nice outfit," I said.

"You too," Ava replied.

I've always thought that Ava and I look kind of alike, even though I'm Latina and she's part Korean and part Scottish. We're both the same height, and we both have brown eyes and straight black hair. Oh, and we both have first names that are three letters long. How cool is that?

Eddie took Ava's purple duffel bag from

Mrs. Monroe and brought it over to the stairs.

"Ellie, can you stay for coffee?" my mom asked Ava's mom.

"I wish I could, but I've got to get back for Christopher's hockey game," Mrs. Monroe replied. She hugged Ava and kissed her on the forehead.

"Call me if you need anything, okay? Otherwise I'll see you at the train station tomorrow."

"Okay, Mom," Ava replied.

When Mrs. Monroe left, Eddie said, "Mia, why don't you give your friend a tour of the house?"

"Um, sure," I said. I felt a little awkward. I'd never had to give Ava a "tour" of anything. But everything was different now.

"I'll take you on the grand tour!" I said dramatically, and we both started giggling. "Follow me, madam."

So I showed Ava the kitchen and the dining room, and she kept saying, "Wow! You have so much space!" It's true, I guess. In Manhattan, almost everyone I know has a pretty small apartment.

When we got to the living room, Dan was setting up his video game system.

"Oh, hey, guys," he said, nodding to Ava. "You were at the wedding, right?"

"Right," Ava said, and I saw her cheeks turn pink.

"Ava, you remember my stepbrother, Dan," I said.

Dan nodded and settled down in front of the TV. Then I led Ava upstairs.

"Your brother is so cute!" she whispered when we got to the top.

"He's not cute! He's just . . . regular," I said. Suddenly I knew how Emma must feel with everyone crushing on Matt and Sam. "Besides, he's not my brother. He's my stepbrother."

"Oh yeah, I forgot," Ava said as I opened the door to my room. Then she gasped. "Wow, look at all this space!"

I had been nervous about showing Ava my bedroom. My room in Manhattan has this cool Parisian theme, and it's light pink and black and white. But I haven't decorated my room in this house yet. Right now it has ugly flowered wallpaper on it, but Eddie promised to scrape all that off for me. I still haven't figured out what color to paint it, and none of the furniture matches.

But Ava didn't seem to notice. She went straight for my closet and threw open the door. "Oh wow! This is HUGE!" she exclaimed. "You could fit a whole store in here, Mia!"

My closet isn't really *that* big, but compared to my old one in the city, it definitely is huge. Then Ava frowned.

"Wait! I can't find anything!" she cried. "Where's my favorite top? The one with the butterfly? It used to be next to the red dress!"

"I reorganized it," I told her. "Mom showed me how to do it by color. Look in the blue section."

Ava searched and then pulled out the shirt. She held it in front of her. "You have to let me borrow this again! When it gets warmer, I mean."

"Or you could layer it," I said. I rummaged through the clothes and pulled out a slim-fitting, long-sleeved knit top with purple-and-blue stripes. "See?"

"Cool!" Ava said, grabbing it from me. "Can I borrow them both? I'll give them back next time I see you."

"Of course!" I told her. "You don't even have to ask."

Ava flopped backward on my bed. "Sorry if it was weird that I said Dan was cute. He seems really nice," she said. "It must be fun having an older brother instead of a younger one. Christopher is always getting into my stuff and bugging me!"

"Well, Dan is pretty nice," I admitted. "But wait until you hear the loud music he plays. That's really annoying."

Ava sat up. "So you must like living here, right?"

I shrugged. "It's okay. But I miss not seeing my dad every day. And you and everyone else."

"But you still get to see us," Ava said. "It's kind of like you have the best of both worlds."

"Maybe," I said, a little unsure. "Sometimes I think about what it would be like if things had never changed with my parents. Most of the time I think I would like that. But I'd miss some of this new stuff, like some of my new friends."

"I guess I would be sad if I couldn't see my dad every day," Ava said thoughtfully.

That's what I love about Ava. She gets me, you know?

"So listen to this," I said. "I am failing Spanish class!"

Ava looked surprised, and then she said the same thing everyone else always said: "But don't you speak Spanish?"

"Sí," I replied, and then I explained the situation like I had to Katie and my cupcake friends. Ava nodded.

"It's the same with me," she said. "My dad's a

doctor, and I almost failed science! He was mad at first, but then when he was helping me with my homework, he saw how hard it was, so I had a tutor. It really helped."

I imagined Eddie and Mom sitting in Señora Delgado's class and smiled. "I wonder if Mom and Eddie could even do my homework. It's hard!"

"Just ask for help," Ava said. "They'll understand. I'm sure they'd rather help you than have you fail the class."

"I will," I told her, but I wasn't sure if I meant it. After all, things had been pretty crazy the last few months, with the move and the wedding and everything. Maybe I just needed to catch up, I told myself.

Suddenly a loud screeching came through the bedroom wall, followed by the *thump, thump, thump* of a bass line.

Ava covered her ears. "Oh my gosh! What *is* that?" she yelled over the music.

I grinned. "I told you!" I shouted back.

"DAN! Turn it DOWN!" I yelled, and banged on the wall. "Not so cute now, is he?" I said, and then we both started laughing.

CHAPTER 6

A Different Kind of Cupcake Meeting

Spending Saturday with Ava was awesome. We went to the mall, and after that Mom made spicy chili for dinner. Then we all watched a movie together (well, except for Dan, who was out with his friends). And Ava and I stayed up *way* late talking and talking. I love my cupcake friends, but it's also great to have a friend who knows your history. Someone you don't see all the time, but every time you reconnect, you can pick up right where you left off. Every time I see Ava it's like we just hung out the day before.

In the morning we helped Mom make chocolate chip pancakes, and then we got the kitchen ready for the Cupcake Club meeting. Eddie was making a turkey-and-swiss sandwich on a superlong loaf of bread while I got out the baking stuff.

"I ordered the bread special from the bakery," he told us. "This is a lunch meeting, right? You can't have a lunch meeting without lunch!"

I hadn't even thought about that. Eddie's pretty good that way. I think he likes to take care of people.

To tell the truth, I was a little bit nervous about the meeting. Besides baking the cinnamon-frosted cupcakes, we were also going to talk about the cupcakes we were making for Ava's birthday party in a few weeks. I was invited to the party, but my cupcake friends weren't.

Of course, we bake stuff all the time for events we're not invited to, like that baby shower for our science teacher's sister. So maybe that wasn't such a big deal.

I was also worried that Ava wouldn't get along with my Maple Grove friends. But then I realized that everyone is really nice, so that shouldn't be a problem. At least, I hoped it wouldn't be!

Then the bell rang, and Katie, Alexis, and Emma all arrived at once. It took a few minutes for everyone to take off their coats, hats, gloves, and scarves, but soon we were all around the kitchen table and Eddie was cutting up his giant sandwich for us.

"I like your shirts," Emma said to Ava. She was wearing the striped shirt with the butterfly shirt that she had borrowed from me.

"Thanks! They're Mia's," she replied. "The butterfly one has always been my favorite."

I noticed that Katie suddenly got kind of a weird look on her face. Was she jealous? No, probably not. *Katie's just insecure,* I thought. Her old best friend, Callie, dumped her, so she's always afraid someone else is going to do the same thing.

Then Ava started to talk really fast about stuff, like she does when she's excited or nervous.

"You guys live in such a nice town," she said. "I'm kind of jealous. I sort of wish I had an older brother like Dan too."

Emma rolled her eyes. "You're lucky. They can be *so* annoying."

"More annoying than a little brother?" Ava asked. "'Cause I already have one of those."

Emma nodded. "Worse. At least little brothers do cute things sometimes."

"I tried to tell you, Ava," I said.

"At least none of you have an older sister,"

Alexis chimed in. "She spends hours and hours in the bathroom every day."

"Dan showers longer than any of us," I whispered. "And then he sprays on that cologne for guys that they advertise on TV. Gross!"

I looked at Katie, expecting her to make a joke like she always does, but she was kind of quiet. In fact, she stayed quiet for the rest of the meeting. I decided I'd have to ask her later if everything was okay.

Then Alexis took out her notebook and we got down to business.

"So, Ava, I can show you our most popular cupcake styles," she said.

Ava took her phone from her jeans pocket. "Actually, I have a list of ideas I've been working on," she said. "Mia says you guys can do anything, right?"

Alexis looked flustered—she's used to being the one in charge, and Ava was kind of taking over.

"Well, sure, but sometimes it helps if—"

"Let's hear your idea, Ava!" Emma said, smoothing things over.

"I have a few," Ava replied. "But winter is totally my favorite season, and it almost always snows on my birthday, so I was hoping you could do a snowy cupcake."

Alexis started flipping through her notebook. "Snowy. Hmm, I'm not sure exactly how we'd do that."

All of us were quiet for a minute. A snowy cupcake? That was tough. Then Katie came through, as usual.

"Remember Emma's cupcake from yesterday?" she blurted out. "What if we do coconut flakes on top of vanilla icing? Mia said the coconut looked just like snow."

I nodded. "That could work."

I jumped out of my seat and ran to the kitchen cabinet where I keep all my cupcake supplies. Eddie had cleared out a shelf just for me.

I came back with a big jar of glittery sugar sprinkles.

"How about white icing, coconut flakes, and then some edible glitter, like this?" I suggested. "We could do a silver wrapper."

"That sounds nice," Ava said. "But do I get to see it first?"

"We'll take a photo and send it to you for approval," Alexis said. "But first you need to tell us what flavor of cake you want."

"Would chocolate be okay?" Ava asked. "The brown cake won't show through the vanilla frosting, will it?"

"No way," I said. "Especially if Katie's doing the frosting. She's the best."

"You guys are all just as good," Katie said, smiling a little for the first time.

"We'll do a test run at our next meeting, after we get the ingredients," Alexis said. "Today we've got to do a test batch of Mia's spicy cupcakes."

"I've got the red food coloring and the cinnamon and the Red Hots," I said.

Katie held up the canvas shopping bag she had brought with her. "I was talking to my mom about them, and she thought some other flavors might go nice with the cinnamon frosting instead of the red velvet. Like dark chocolate, maybe, or apple."

"Wow, they both sound good," Ava said.

"I thought we could try a batch of each," Katie suggested. "I brought the dark chocolate, and some applesauce and some extra spices, like ginger and cloves." Everyone agreed to try the two different kinds, and we quickly got to work measuring out the flour and other ingredients for the batter.

185

"Don't you use a recipe?" Ava asked.

"Sometimes," I said. "But mostly we know how to make a basic batter and then add extra flavors to it."

"Ooh, extra spices! *Muy caliente*, right, Mia?" Emma said, and everybody laughed. But that got me thinking about my Spanish class again. How was I ever going to tell my mom and dad and Eddie that I was failing Spanish? Ava was right. They would make sure I got the extra help I needed. And the longer I avoided telling them, the worse it was going to be. But still, the thought of telling them made my stomach feel queasy. Even though I knew it was crazy, I kept hoping that if I avoided the problem, somehow it would magically disappear.

"Earth to Mia!" said Katie, waving something under my nose. She held up an index card. "Mom gave me her recipe for the dark chocolate ones. The measurements are always a little different when there's chocolate," she explained to Ava.

Chocolate. Now that should have caught my attention. But I couldn't get my mind off my Spanish class. This was awful. Baking cupcakes with the Cupcake Club was one of my favorite things to do in the entire world, and now I couldn't even enjoy that. I kept throwing ingredients into the batter and stirring, stirring, stirring, wishing I could make my problems disappear the way the spices were disappearing into the chocolate batter.

Wait—spices in the chocolate batter? I tasted a little bit. *Whoa.* Intense. And not in a good way.

"Um, sorry, guys," I said. "I think I mixed up the two batters. I added the spices to the dark chocolate batter by accident." Alexis frowned at the waste of ingredients, but everyone else was really nice. We've all ruined or burned batches of cupcakes at one time or another, so everyone was pretty forgiving.

"Maybe you should work on something else right now," Alexis suggested.

I agreed, and so I said, "Ava and I will do the icing." Then we made a double batch of vanilla icing dyed red and spiced with cinnamon.

About forty-five minutes later we were staring at two plates of cupcakes with red frosting and dotted with Red Hots candies. They looked great, and both looked the same—although inside, they were both really different.

"Tasting time!" Alexis announced, and we cut

some of the cupcakes in half so we each ate half of one. Everyone got quiet for a few minutes while we ate. Cupcake tasting *is* fun, but it's also serious business.

"They are both so good," Emma said, wiping her mouth with a napkin. "But I think I like the dark chocolate ones best."

"Me too," I agreed.

Alexis shook her head. "I like the spices in the apple cupcakes."

"I vote for apple too," Katie said.

Alexis frowned. "It's a tie."

"Ava can break the tie," I said. "What do you think, Ava?"

"You know me. I love chocolate!" she replied.

I turned to my friends. "What do you think? Should we do the dark chocolate?"

Katie and Alexis looked at each other and shrugged.

"Fine," Alexis said. "Studies show that chocolate is one of the most popular cupcake flavors, anyway. Maybe we'll get some new customers from it."

"And they're Valentine's Day cupcakes," Emma said. "And you know how everybody goes gaga over chocolate on Valentine's Day."

Katie put her arms around the plate of apple

cupcakes. "Then I guess I'll be taking these home," she joked, and we all laughed.

It felt really good to have all my friends together in one place. But I knew it wouldn't last. In a little while, Ava would have to go back to the city. My cupcake friends would be in Maple Grove. And I would still be stuck with Spanish wherever I went.

CHAPTER 7

Tiny Plates and Tiny Lies

After our meeting was over and the kitchen was clean, Ava and I had to hurry and pack up her things. We had a half hour to get to the train station.

Even though Ava was leaving, there was one good thing about that day. You see, I was supposed to see my dad this weekend, but he had to go on a business trip. He was coming back Sunday afternoon, and Mom had to go to the city to style a client for a party, so she and I were going to take the train in with Ava. Mom would go to work, Ava would go home, and I'd get to have a special dinner with my dad.

It sounds complicated, right? Welcome to my life!

Eddie drove us to the train station and dropped us off. He gave Mom a big hug and a kiss. I looked at Ava and winced.

"He's acting like she's going away for a year or something," I said. "We'll be back in a few hours."

Ava laughed. "I don't know. I think it's kind of sweet."

I rolled my eyes. "Seriously?"

Then the train pulled up, and Mom and Ava and I climbed on. It wasn't as crowded as it usually is when I leave on Friday, so we all found a seat near one another. I don't really love the train, though. The seats are an ugly color, and it always smells like stale bread in there. But it's fast and it gets me to my dad, so I don't mind so much.

Mom shopped for accessories on her tablet on the way to Manhattan, and Ava and I talked about her upcoming birthday party. The snowy cupcakes had inspired her.

"I could get silver and white decorations," she was saying. "And sprinkle silver glitter on the cake table, maybe."

I whipped out my sketchbook. "We could put the cupcakes at different heights, like this," I said, quickly drawing my vision for her.

"I love it!" Ava exclaimed.

"And of course you'll need the perfect dress," I said.

I flipped the page and started sketching Ava in a snowy dress—a sleeveless top attached to a flowing, white knee-length skirt.

"The top could be silver," I said, pointing. "But I'm not sure. It kind of looks like an ice skater's outfit."

"No, it's awesome," Ava said sincerely. "You are such a good designer, Mia! You're going to be famous someday."

I blushed a little bit, and Mom leaned over to see my sketch. She smiled. Being a famous fashion designer would be so cool. But I know that takes a lot of hard work, and a lot of luck, too.

Finally the train pulled into Penn Station. It's always crazy when everyone gets off the train, with people running in every direction, but Dad always waits in the same spot for me, by this big pillar by the ticket counter.

When the doors opened up and we walked to the concourse level, I saw him standing there. Dad always looks like a movie star to me. He had on a warm black coat that wasn't puffy at all, and shiny black shoes and an olive green scarf around his neck. Dad wears glasses with black rims, but on him they don't look old-fashioned, they look smart.

I ran up and hugged him.

"Hello, *mija*!" he said. "It's good to see you."

Ava and my mom walked up behind me.

"Hello, Alex," my mom said. Her voice sounded friendly, but a little cold at the same time.

"Hi, Sara," dad replied, and he just sounded uncomfortable.

Ava looked around. "Where's my mom?" she asked.

"She texted me and said she's a little bit late," Mom answered. "But we'll all wait with you until she gets here."

And so we waited, and it was totally awkward. Mom and Dad were talking to me instead of each other.

"Mia, how are you doing in school?"

"Mia, is it colder in New Jersey?"

"Mia, tell your father about your Valentine's Day cupcakes."

I realized that this was probably the longest time my parents had spent in the same place since their divorce. No wonder it was awkward.

Finally, Mrs. Monroe came rushing up. "I'm so sorry! The subways are so slow on Sunday."

193

"That's all right," Mom told her. "Thank you for letting Ava stay with us. She's a pleasure to have around."

"And so is Mia," Mrs. Monroe said. She smiled at me. "We'll see you at the party soon. I can't wait to try your cupcakes!"

Ava gave me a quick hug good-bye. "I'll text you later," I said.

Then Mom kissed me. "I'll meet you back here at seven fifteen, okay?"

"I'll make sure she's on time," my dad promised.

"Thanks," Mom said, and managed a smile. She then rushed off, and it was just me and my dad.

"Sushi?" I asked. That's usually our tradition.

"Well, since this is a special visit, I thought we should mix it up a little bit," Dad said. "Try someplace new."

"Where are we going?" I asked him.

Dad smiled. "I want to surprise you."

So we quickly found a cab outside and traveled downtown for a while. Then the cab stopped in front of a restaurant with a red awning. Painted on the window were the words SABOR TAPAS BAR.

"We're going to a bar?" I asked. "Isn't that kind of inappropriate?"

"It's not that kind of bar," Dad said, paying the cabdriver. "You'll see."

We walked inside, and the place looked warm and cozy. Dark wood panels covered the walls, and the booths were made of wood too, with red cushions. The server showed us to one of the booths, and then Dad handed me a menu.

"In a tapas bar, they serve small plates of food," Dad explained. "And then you share. That way you get to try a little bit of a lot of different things."

The server, a woman with dark hair almost exactly like mine, took our drink orders, and then we looked at the menu. Everything on it looked delicious. I was starting to like this idea.

"This is awesome," I said. "But there's so much to choose from! I can't decide."

"I'll order for us, then," he said.

The server brought our drinks, and then Dad ordered a bunch of tapas from the menu: shrimp with garlic and chilies, a potato omelet, sautéed spinach, and a bowl of Spanish olives.

"Anything else, *mija*?" he asked.

I looked at the menu, and one thing caught my eye.

"Croquetas con pollo y plátanos, por favor," I

ordered. (That means "Croquettes with chicken and plantains, please." I wasn't sure what a croquette was, but I love plantains. They're kind of like bananas, but not sweet.)

"*Bien. Creo que les gustará,*" the server replied in Spanish. That means, "Good. I think you'll like them."

"*Creo que lo haré,*" I replied, which means, "I think that I will."

The server left the table, and when I looked at Dad, he was beaming with pride.

"Such good Spanish, *mija,*" he said. "Your Spanish teacher must love you."

I smiled, but I didn't say a word. I know what you're thinking. This was the perfect time for me to talk to my dad about my problems in Advanced Spanish. I know Ava told me I should ask for help, but I just couldn't bear to disappoint Dad. Not now, anyway. I just wanted to have a nice dinner with him.

And it *was* nice. It turned out that a croquette is a little fried ball-shaped thing, and it was superdelicious. All the stuff Dad ordered tasted good too.

But it went way too fast, and soon it was time to get back to the train. Dad walked me to the platform, and Mom was already waiting there.

"Get home safe," Dad said, giving me a hug.

"I'll text you when I get home," I promised.

Mom got a funny look on her face. After Dad left, I found out why.

"You always complain when I ask you to text *me*," Mom said.

Yikes. She had a point. I had to think about that for a little bit.

"You have me most of the time, plus Eddie and Dan, but Dad is all alone," I explained. "I feel bad for Dad sometimes."

Mom sighed. "It's hard," she admitted, "but please don't worry about your dad, Mia. I know he misses you a lot, but he's still your dad, no matter where we live. And we're all a lot happier this way."

Happier? I had to think about that one.

As the train sped toward Maple Grove, I stared out the window into the dark sky. Mom and Dad fought a *lot* before they got divorced. They tried to do it at night in their room, when they thought I was asleep, but I always heard them. So I guess they weren't too happy then.

But when they got divorced, things still weren't good. Mom moved out and I stayed with

Dad, but it felt weird and I missed her. And Mom and Dad still argued every time they saw each other. Then I moved into Mom's new apartment, but that was extra weird because it was a whole new place.

So was it still weird? I had to think about that. Living in Maple Grove was starting to feel like home. I had good friends. And Eddie and Dan were nice, and Eddie sure tried to make us feel like a "normal" family as much as possible. But happi-*er*? As in, more happy than before, when we were all together?

Like I said, I'd have to think about that.

CHAPTER 8

Can I Start the Week Over Again?

While I was still on the train, I called Katie. I wanted to reach her before it got too late.

"Hey," I said.

"Hey," Katie replied. "Are you home?"

"I'm on the train," I told her. "Is everything okay? You seemed a little quiet at the meeting today."

"Everything's fine," Katie said, but I could tell by the sound of her voice that she was lying.

"Good," I said. I wasn't going to press her about it. "So anyway, we're still going to see *The Emerald Forest* next weekend, right?"

"Of course!" Katie answered, and her voice sounded like the old Katie again. The Emerald Forest is a fantasy book series that we both love, and they finally made a movie out of it!

"Awesome," I said. "I can't wait to see what kind of costumes they're going to do for the emerald fairies. In the books, the description is totally beautiful."

"I can't wait either," Katie agreed. "We're going on Saturday, right?"

"Mom said she'll take us," I promised.

We said good night, and I hung up the phone. When I got home, I was totally exhausted. I fell asleep dreaming of the Emerald Forest. . . .

If only the rest of the week was as peaceful as that forest. But it was anything but. The next day was Monday, my least favorite day of the week.

I was so tired in the morning that I left my gym uniform home by mistake, and I had to sit out of gym. And Señora Delgado gave us pages and pages of notes for our Spanish test the next day—on verbs.

You have to believe me when I tell you that I studied like crazy. I went straight home after school and studied. I ate dinner and then went right back upstairs and studied. I didn't even sketch! (Okay, I did doodle a pair of boots in the margin of my notes, but I didn't open up my sketchbook, I swear.) When I went to sleep that night, I dreamed of verbs instead of emerald fairies.

I even studied at lunch on Tuesday before the test. I was feeling pretty good—until Señora handed me my test paper. The questions looked like Egyptian hieroglyphics to me.

So I took the test, and I did my best. But as I handed it in, I knew I hadn't done well.

That night Mom asked me about it as we were cleaning up from dinner.

"So how did you do on your Spanish test?" she asked. "You really studied hard for that one."

"I think I did okay," I lied. I thought about spilling everything out, right then and there. *Mom, I think I'm failing Spanish. I know I should have told you sooner. The advanced class is so difficult. I'm still having trouble no matter how hard I try.* I opened my mouth to tell her, but I just couldn't bring myself to say the words. I don't know why it was so hard. Usually I could always talk to Mom about anything.

It was then that I realized that Mom really was a lot happier. She smiled a lot, and she seemed more relaxed than ever, even though she was busy. And she really did seem to love Eddie. Then I wondered if my dad was as happy as Mom. Was I?

Mom smiled at me and kissed the top of my head. "I'm so proud of you, Mia," she said.

Ugh. I felt bad about lying, and then something happened that made me feel ten times worse.

"I have a surprise for you," she said. "Come upstairs with me."

I followed Mom to her room. "So you know that Annie Chang has a line out for teens, right?"

I nodded. Annie Chang is a popular fashion designer, and I absolutely love her clothes. I was psyched when I read that she was putting out a teen line. But I know they are kind of expensive, too, so I wasn't holding out much hope that I'd convince Mom to buy me anything.

Mom unzipped a garment bag hanging from her closet. "I met Annie at an event the other day, and I told her all about you," she said. "So today she sent this just for you."

I gasped. Inside the bag was a totally cool mod-looking sweater dress with gray and black stripes.

"That's from her latest winter line!" I shrieked. "Oh, Mom, it's perfect!"

"Wear it with some black tights—or even a jewel-toned color, for that matter—and black boots, and you've got a killer outfit," Mom said.

I slipped the dress off the hanger and ran to my room. "I'm going to try it on!"

I tried the dress with some solid red tights, and it looked awesome. I ran into my mom's room and gave her a big hug.

"Thank you, thank you!" I said.

"You deserve it, with all the hard work you've been doing," Mom said, and I felt a huge pang of guilt.

You should tell her now, a little voice inside me said. But just like Dad and dinner, I didn't want to ruin the moment.

I loved the dress so much that I wanted to sleep in it, but I didn't want to ruin it. So I wore it to school the very next day. At lunchtime, I was walking past the PGC table when Callie called out to me.

"Mia? Is that an Annie Chang?" she asked.

I walked over to her. "Yes, she gave it to my mom to give to me," I said.

"It's really cool," said Maggie, another one of the popular girls. Maggie's actually pretty nice, but she does everything Sydney tells her to do.

Sydney examined my entire outfit from head to toe. I could tell she was trying to find something wrong with it, but she couldn't. So she just made one of her mean comments instead. "It's nice of your mom's friends to give you their castoffs," Sydney said, tossing her perfect blond hair. I knew she was insulting me, but I didn't care.

I smiled sweetly at Sydney. "Yeah, well, Mom says that Annie *is* really nice," I said. "And it's actually not a castoff. It's a sample. Like the kind they give models to wear. See you."

Then I walked away.

My Cupcake Club friends liked my dress too, even though they didn't know who Annie Chang was. Then it was time for Spanish class. Oh boy.

Señora Delgado handed out our tests as soon as we sat down. I already knew how I did, but I was still shocked when I saw the big red F on my paper. I've never gotten an F in anything before.

"Class, please turn to page fifty-seven in your workbooks and start that page," she said in Spanish, as usual. "Ms. Vélaz-Cruz, please come to my desk."

Uh-oh. This wasn't going to be fun. I walked up to her desk as slowly as I could. What was she going to do? Was she going to yell at me in front of everybody?

Señora Delgado is petite, with short black hair, and she wears big eyeglasses. She looks like a very wise owl. And I know from science class that owls are predators. They eat cute little chipmunks and mice.

"Mia, I think you might need some extra help in this class," she said softly, in English. She wasn't mean or angry at all. It seemed like she really wanted to help me. She started to write on a piece of paper. "I know some excellent tutors. Please give this to your parents and tell them to call me if they have any questions."

"Thank you, Señora," I said quietly, and then I walked back to my seat. I couldn't keep my secret any longer now. I'd have to give my parents the note. But I didn't have to give it to them right away.

I'll give it to them, I told myself, *when the time is right! Because they're all too happy now for me to spoil it.*

COOL!

veggie chopper!

CHAPTER 9

Sydney Needs My Help. Really?

Okay, so I technically couldn't give my parents the note that night because my dad was in Manhattan and my mom was working late. It was just me and Eddie and Dan, and Eddie is technically my *step*parent, not my parent. So I left the note in my Spanish book.

We had a Cupcake Club meeting at Katie's house the next day after school. Katie's mom was there. Mrs. Brown has curly brown hair and Katie's smile, and she's really nice. She's the one who taught Katie how to make cupcakes.

"Come on in, girls, I've got it all set up for you," Mrs. Brown said as we went into the kitchen. Katie's kitchen is small, but it's got everything you need to make cupcakes in it. Her mom has every kitchen gadget you've ever heard of—and some you haven't heard of.

We quickly got to work making a test batch of Ava's snowy cupcakes. Katie and I made the chocolate batter, and Emma and Alexis worked on the extra frosting.

"I want to get it extra fluffy," Emma said as they put the ingredients in the mixer bowl. "So it looks like snow."

"Great idea," I said. I opened up my bag. "Good news! My mom found the silver cupcake liners for us."

"She's so nice," Katie said, smiling at me, and I figured that whatever was bothering her wasn't anymore. Maybe she was just uncomfortable around people she didn't know, and that's why she was quiet when Ava was visiting.

As we baked the cupcakes we talked about school and stuff, and then Katie asked me, "So how did you do on that Spanish test?"

I frowned. "I can't bear to say it." Instead, I used the wooden spoon in my hand to draw an *F* in the bowl of batter.

"You failed? No way!" Katie cried. "But you studied so hard."

"I know," I said. "Señora says I need a tutor."

"Will your parents get you one?" Emma asked.

I bit my lower lip. "Well, they kind of don't know yet. I'm waiting for the right moment to tell them."

"That must be so hard," Katie said sympathetically.

"You should tell them soon," said Alexis, always the practical one. "They're going to find out eventually. And the sooner you get some help in Spanish, the better. You've put this off long enough. I thought maybe if you studied a little harder, you'd be okay, but things are obviously getting worse instead of better."

"Just talk to your mom, Mia," Katie said. "I'm sure once you tell her everything, it will be all right."

"I know, I know!" I said crossly. "Can we please talk about cupcakes instead of school?"

Nobody said anything for a while after that, and I felt kind of bad for losing it. But soon we were back in our groove again, and I was decorating our first test cupcake.

"It's perfect!" Alexis said, and I had to admit it looked pretty good. The silver liner was really pretty, the icing was nice and fluffy, and the sparkles looked good on top of the coconut.

"Let me take a picture and I'll send it to Ava," I said.

A minute later Ava texted me back.

It's pretty, but the coconut looks too big or something. Not like snowflakes.

Alexis rolled her eyes. "Great. Another picky client."

"Hey, she's my friend," I reminded her. "Besides, she kind of has a point."

The coconut flakes from the package did look a little big. Luckily for us, Mrs. Brown walked in just then.

"That's beautiful!" she said.

"Except Ava doesn't like it," Katie said, and then explained about the coconut.

Katie's mom looked thoughtful. "I think I have just the thing," she said finally.

She opened up the small pantry closet by the back door and came back with a weird-looking device.

"It's a veggie chopper," she said. "Normally you could use it to chop onions into small pieces. But I bet it will work on the coconut."

She put a pile of coconut on a cutting board,

put the chopper on top of it, and then pressed down a few times. When she picked up the chopper, the coconut underneath was very finely shredded.

"That looks a lot more like snow," Katie remarked. "Let's try another one."

So Katie iced another cupcake, and I sprinkled the coconut flakes and glittery sugar on top.

"Much better," agreed Mrs. Brown. "I'm sure your friend will like it."

"Let's see," I said. I sent another photo to Ava.

This time she was happy. Here was her reply:

♥♥♥♥♥♥♥

"She loves it!" I reported, and we all cheered.

"I think I've got all the details down so we can re-create this for the party," Alexis said. "Otherwise, we're meeting at my house on Saturday morning to do the Valentine's cupcakes, right?"

"Right," Emma said.

"My mom said she'd help us drop them off at the bookstore," I told them.

Alexis shut her notebook. "Just one more thing," she said. She gave each of us a sheet of paper. "Let me know what you think, and then I'll get the ad up on the PTA website next week."

We all read Alexis's ad:

Need a sweet treat for your next party or event? Let us do the baking for you! Click <u>here</u> to contact the Cupcake Club. We can do any flavor or amount you want. And we're having a baker's dozen special for all new customers! Buy a dozen cupcakes and get one free!

"I like the 'sweet treat' part," Katie said.

"It's really good, Alexis," Emma said.

I nodded. "The baker's dozen was a great idea, Katie," I said. "I'll bet we'll get lots of new business from this."

When the meeting was over, Eddie picked me up and brought me home. Mom was home, but she was working in her office. And at dinner she seemed really distracted. So I decided it wouldn't be fair to give her the note while she was so busy.

The next day was Friday, and I was glad it was the last day of the week. No tests, and we had our leftover snowy cupcakes for Cupcake Friday.

But then something really unexpected happened at lunch. Here's how it went down. While I was eating lunch, Sydney Whitman actually came up to our lunch table.

"Mia, can I talk to you a minute?" she asked. "I need a favor."

"Sure," I said. I turned to my friends and raised my eyebrows, giving that *I don't know what she wants* look. Then I followed her over to the wall.

"Thanks," she said. "I got this text from Jackson Montano, and it's in Spanish. Usually I'd ask Callie, but she's home because she's sick today."

What could I say? Should I launch into my entire "I can speak Spanish really well, but I have problems reading and writing it" explanation? Meanwhile, Queen Sydney stood in front of me with her arms crossed, waiting for me to say something.

"Uh, sure," I said, a little nervously. I hoped it wasn't too complicated.

Sydney handed me her phone, and I checked the message.

Te quiero.

Now, if you read Spanish you probably know that this means, "I love you," which is what my parents say to me, and my *abuela* says all the time. But when I saw "*quiero*" I got it mixed up with the word "*queso*," which means "cheese."

Yes, that's right. That's what I thought. And here's what I told Sydney.

"He says you're cheesy," I said.

Honestly, I didn't think that was strange. Jackson is on the football team, and he says mean things to kids all the time. Sydney and Jackson actually would make a perfect couple. Jackson thinks he's supercool just because he's a football player, and Sydney thinks she's supercool because . . . well, because she's Sydney.

Sydney's face turned bright red. "Cheesy? Really? I'll show him!"

Then she stomped away. She went back to her table, and I could see her talking with Maggie. While Sydney talked, she looked shocked and kept glancing down at her phone and looked like she was getting angrier by the minute.

I went back to the table.

"What did she want?" Alexis asked.

I shrugged. "She wanted me to translate some text message for her from Jackson Montano. He

213

told her he thinks she's cheesy."

"Cheesy? That's a weird thing to say," Emma said.

"Hmm. Well, at least that's one less boy drooling over Sydney," Katie said. "So yay for that."

"It figures he's texting her," Alexis said. "Those two think alike."

And then I forgot all about it—for a little while, anyway. In a split second, I had made a terrible mistake—one that would haunt me forever. (I know that sounds totally dramatic, but it's true!)

CHAPTER 10

Katie Is Still Acting Weird

That night at dinner Mom made an announcement.

"I just got the e-mails about the parent-teacher conferences next week," she said. "I can't wait to meet all your teachers!"

I almost choked on my pork chop, and started coughing.

"Mia, are you okay?" Mom asked.

I nodded and took a sip of water.

"Do not believe anything Mrs. Caldwell tells you," Dan said. "She's always accusing me of messing around in class, but it's Joseph, not me."

Eddie raised an eyebrow. "Hmm, we'll see about that," he said. "Any other teachers we should look out for?"

Dan shrugged. "They're all pretty cool, I guess.

Mr. Bender gives us tons of homework, but I always do it all."

"What about you, Mia?" Eddie asked.

I shrugged too. "They're all cool." Normally, I would have told them about how much fun Ms. Biddle's science class is and how strict Mrs. Moore is in math class, but I didn't feel like talking. I couldn't keep my secret about Spanish class much longer. I decided I'd have to tell Mom after dinner.

But then Eddie said something that really made me mad.

"Mia, I'm looking forward to meeting your teachers too," he said.

I almost choked again. Why was Eddie going to my parent-teacher conference? Dad is the one who should be going!

I was too angry to say anything. I kept quiet until the end of dinner. Then after, when Mom and I were cleaning up, I confronted her.

"Why is Eddie going instead of Dad?" I asked her. "Dad's still my parent, right? Shouldn't he be going?"

Mom looked really startled. "Well . . . ," she said, like she was trying to figure out an answer. "I didn't think of it. It might be hard for Dad to get here

216

from the city during the week. I'll ask him. But is there a reason you don't want Eddie to go?"

"Because he's not my dad!" I blurted out.

Mom sat down on the nearest chair. She thought for a minute.

"You're right about that," she said finally. "But he's still your parent. He cares about you very much. And he takes an active role with you. He helps you with your homework and projects. So it's important for him to meet your teachers and know what's going on in your school."

I nodded grudgingly, feeling a little guilty. After all, Eddie did drive me all over the place, and he made me lunch and dinner and snacks. But I was still mad. "Fine. But Dad does those things too. He should be there."

"I promise I'll talk to him," Mom said. "And if he can't go, I'll make sure he gets all the information, okay?"

"Okay," I mumbled. Then I went up to my room. I decided to do some sketching. Sketching always relaxes me and makes me feel better when I'm in a bad mood.

I started to sketch some Valentine's Day outfits. First I drew a really girlie pink dress with a short, full skirt that I knew Emma would love. Then I drew a denim skirt paired with a loose sweater, with a big bold red heart embroidered on the front. It looked very "casual cool." Out of the blue I wondered how I would write "casual cool" in Spanish. I drew a complete blank. I couldn't stop thinking about it, and I found myself getting more and more upset. *Great,* I thought. *Now even my sketch time is ruined by Spanish.* Meanwhile, I had forgotten all about giving Mom the note from Señora Delgado.

The next morning I woke up early, and Mom drove me to Alexis's house. She has the neatest, cleanest kitchen of all of us. We had to get the cupcakes to the bookstore by one o'clock, so we got to work right away.

Katie and I worked on the cinnamon-frosted cupcakes, and Emma and Alexis worked on the pretty pink cupcakes. Emma blasted some music, and we didn't talk much while we worked. Katie calls it "being in the baking zone."

When we were done, we had four dozen perfect, beautiful cupcakes packed neatly into boxes. I had designed labels for us on the computer that said THE CUPCAKE CLUB, and there was a picture of a cupcake on each one. I carefully stuck a label on each box, and we stepped back to admire our hard work.

"Perfect!" Alexis said with satisfaction.

I looked at the clock, and it was ten minutes to noon. "Mom will be here soon. She's going to take Katie and me to lunch, and then we're going to drop off the cupcakes and then see the movie. Are you sure you guys don't want to go?"

"I've got three dog walking clients today," Emma said. "Otherwise I would."

"And we're all going to my grandmother's house today," Alexis said. "But text me when the movie's done! I'm dying to see it."

"Even though I already know how it ends, I still can't wait," Katie said. She looked really excited.

Then Alexis handed me an envelope. "I printed out some business cards on my computer using your label design," she said. "See if you can leave them out on the cupcake table. That way if anyone likes the cupcakes and wants to order some, they know how to reach us."

My mom then came in, and she helped us carry the boxes to the car. We have an organizer in our trunk now, so the boxes don't slide around. The bookstore, Harriet's Hollow, is in downtown Maple Grove. There are a bunch of other stores on Main Street besides Harriet's. There's also a little café where they have the most awesome tuna melts. That's where we went for lunch.

"Mmm, melty!" Katie said when her sandwich came, and we all laughed.

Then it was time to deliver the cupcakes to Harriet's. The owner of the store is named Harriet. She's tall and has long brown hair that she always piles on her head, and she has a very global sense of fashion. Today she was wearing a really flowy purple-and-orange dress that looked like it was made from Indian saris, and she had lots of silver bracelets jangling on her wrists.

"It's the cupcake girls!" she said when she saw us. "And right on time, too. Come here, let me show you the display."

We walked through the store to the place in the back that Harriet called the reading nook. It's filled with comfy couches and beanbag chairs, and Harriet doesn't mind if you sit there and read all day. Today she had decorated it with pink and red flowers on the end tables, and in the middle was a round table with a pink tablecloth on it.

"We'll set them up for you," Katie said, and we started by putting out four round, clear plastic trays that we got from a party store. They don't cost much, and the cupcakes look good on them. Then we carefully placed the cupcakes on them: two trays of my spicy dark chocolate with cinnamon frosting, and two trays of Emma's fluffy pink cupcakes.

"They look too good to eat!" Harriet exclaimed, but then she picked up a spicy one. "But of course I can't resist."

Katie and I held our breath while Harriet took a bite. We always get a little nervous when someone tries our cupcakes for the first time.

Harriet smiled. "Fantastic!" she said. "What's in this?"

Katie and I explained the flavors of the two cupcakes, and Harriet nodded in approval. She walked to the register and came back with an envelope for us.

"Thank you so much, girls," she said. "I'll be sure to recommend you to my friends."

Then I remembered Alexis's cards. "We have some business cards," I said. "Would it be okay if we put some out on the table?"

"Of course!" Harriet said. "My, you girls certainly are professional."

I made a mental note to tell Alexis that later. She would love that compliment!

Next Mom dropped us off at the movie theater, which is in the mall. Now that we're in middle school, our moms have decided that we can go to the movies by ourselves, as long as we don't leave the theater. (Eddie didn't like that idea much, but Mom convinced him.)

Soon Katie and I were sitting in our seats with sodas and a bucket of popcorn between us. They were showing some commercials or something on the screen, so I started to tell Katie about my problems with Mom and Eddie and Spanish.

"It's bad enough that everyone's going to find out that I'm failing, but I don't really get why Eddie needs to go," I said. "My dad should go, right?"

"I guess," Katie answered. She really didn't seem interested, but I kept talking.

"Plus, I have to check in with everyone all the time," I said. "It's like I have three police officers watching my every move or something. I feel like a prisoner sometimes. We're lucky Eddie's not sitting here right now."

"Shh," Katie said. "The previews are coming on."

I have to admit I was a little bit hurt about that. It's like Katie didn't care at all, which isn't like her. Usually she's a great person to talk to.

As the previews played, I tried to figure out what might be bugging her. I know Katie's parents are divorced too, so I figured she'd understand.

Then it hit me—Katie never talks about her dad, ever, and she doesn't visit him the way I do. I don't know why, but she just doesn't. Maybe her dad lives far away or something. I've never really asked her.

So maybe Katie can't understand my problems. Maybe she has some of her own—different ones.

I almost asked her about it but then the lights went dark, and we both got transported to the Emerald Forest.

CHAPTER 11

Sydney's Revenge

*K*atie was like her old self again after the movie, so I didn't bring up anything about her dad. I figured she'd talk to me when she was ready.

Nothing much interesting happened until Monday morning, during my first period math class. Mrs. Moore was explaining a problem on the board when suddenly a note fell onto my desk.

I looked up, alarmed. Mrs. Moore is superstrict, and it takes guts to throw a note in her class. I looked around and saw Bella looking at me.

Bella is in the PGC (Popular Girls Club) with Sydney and Maggie and Callie. She's pretty quiet, but everyone knows she loves vampires—after all, she changed her named from Brenda to Bella because of that series with the sparkly vampires.

She dresses in black a lot and wears pale makeup.

Bella nodded for me to open the note, and I opened it.

Jackson Montano is going bald!
Seriously, it's true!

I gave Bella a strange look. What was that about? But then I saw Mrs. Moore turn away from the board, and I quickly stashed the note in my book.

As Mrs. Moore kept explaining fractions, I suddenly realized what the note was about. Sydney had said that Jackson would be sorry about calling her cheesy, and she meant it.

I showed the note to my friends at lunch, but nobody was surprised.

"There are these texts going around saying that Jackson has foot fungus," Alexis reported.

"I heard it in the hallway," Katie said. "Sydney, Bella, and Maggie were telling everyone who would listen."

"Poor Jackson," Emma said sympathetically.

"I don't feel sorry for him," Alexis said. "He always calls me 'copper top' and asks if my brains are rusting."

"And George says he's mean to the younger kids on the football team," Katie added. George is her friend from elementary school, and Jackson is one grade above us, so I guess he must pick on George.

"Still, nobody deserves the Sydney treatment," I said.

"Well, nobody actually believes this stuff, do they?" Katie asked. "Maggie told me that he has false teeth. I mean, come on."

"It doesn't matter if they believe it or not," Alexis pointed out. "It still looks bad for Jackson. Just imagine if Sydney were spreading those rumors about us."

I shuddered. "That would be awful. But I guess Jackson brought this on himself. He shouldn't have called her cheesy."

I still didn't know that I was the one who was causing Jackson so much trouble. But in the meantime, I still had plenty of other things to worry about—namely, my Spanish.

I had to tell the truth before the parent-teacher conference. It was the only thing to do. And that wasn't going to make anybody happy.

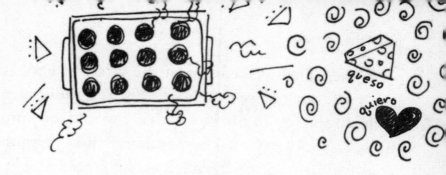

CHAPTER 12

A Really, Really Bad Day

As you can probably guess by now, I like to avoid bad situations. There didn't seem to be a time all week that I could talk to my mom. But that weekend I went to my dad's, and that's when it all came out.

It was after dinner on Friday, and I knew I had to bring up the note from Señora Delgado. But as you know, I love to put things off. So I decided to bake a batch of cupcakes first. My dad loves chocolate, so I made a quick, easy batch of chocolate cupcakes. Soon a delicious, chocolaty aroma was wafting through the entire apartment.

"Something sure smells good, *mija*," Dad said with a smile as he walked past the kitchen.

"They'll be ready soon," I promised.

When Dad walked out of the kitchen, I took the note out of my notebook. For the millionth time, I replayed in my head what I would say and how I would say it. I remembered how proud Dad had been of my Spanish at the tapas bar. He was going to be so disappointed in me. I dreaded giving him this note, and I dreaded telling my mom, too.

As I sat staring forlornly at the note, my dad came running back into the kitchen.

"Mia! Don't you smell that?" he shouted. I looked up, confused, and was shocked to see black smoke coming out of the oven. The cupcakes were burning! My life really was in shambles. Now I couldn't even bake cupcakes anymore. Dad quickly turned off the oven and turned to look at me.

"*Mija,* is something wrong? You've never burned a batch of cupcakes before—especially when you were sitting two feet away from the oven. Is there anything you want to tell me or talk about?" I couldn't put it off any longer. Taking a deep breath, I took the note from Señora Delgado and handed it to him without saying anything.

Dad read it and raised his eyebrows. "Mia, what is this? You're failing Spanish? How is that possible?"

Tears filled my eyes. I couldn't help it.

"You guys put me in Advanced Spanish," I said. "It's really hard. I know I can speak it, but reading and writing it is different. My essays and homework are just too hard for me."

"They can't be that bad," Dad said. "Can you show me?"

I nodded and brought my backpack to the kitchen table, and Dad and I sat down.

"This is the worksheet she gave us for the weekend," I said, handing him the paper. It was another sheet of verbs.

Dad looked it over for a few minutes, and then he frowned. "You're right," he said. "I speak Spanish too, but this looks hard. Have you told Mom about this yet?"

I shook my head. "No," I admitted.

Dad sighed. "Well, I'll have to talk to her about this. We should talk to your teacher and get you one of these tutors she's suggesting."

"You can talk to her at the parent-teacher conference on Wednesday," I said, and Dad looked surprised.

"Wednesday? I don't think Mom mentioned that," he said.

I started to cry again. "Mom's going to be so mad when she finds out."

"*Mija*, we only get upset when you keep things from us. Having trouble in school is nothing to be ashamed of," Dad said, hugging me. "No matter what, *te quiero*."

Te quiero. Dad had said those words to me a million times, and I knew what they meant: I love you. *Te quiero*.

Suddenly it hit me. "Dad, how do you spell *quiero*?" I yelled, breaking away from him.

"*Q-u-i-e-r-o*," Dad answered. "That's one I know. Why?"

My stomach dropped down into my black velvet flats. I had made a terrible mistake.

"And how do you spell 'cheese' in Spanish?" I asked him.

"*Queso. Q-u-e-s-o*," he replied.

"Oh no!" I wailed. "Oh no, no, no!"

I should have *known* that *quiero* meant "love," not "cheesy." Now Sydney thought Jackson had dissed her when actually he liked her. I felt awful! And now she was spreading all those awful rumors about him. So even if Jackson had liked Sydney to begin with, maybe I ruined it for her. I don't like Sydney, but I'd never purposely mess up anybody's budding romance.

"What's wrong, *mija*?" Dad asked.

"I made a terrible mistake." I groaned, and then I told him about Sydney and the note. Dad started to laugh and then stopped himself.

"Sorry. I know it's not funny to you," he said. "And I feel sorry for that boy. Sydney sounds like somebody you don't want to mess with."

"You don't even know," I said, shaking my head.

Dad put his hand over his mouth as he started to laugh again. "Oh, Mia. 'Cheese' instead of 'love'?" Then he saw I wasn't laughing. He put his arm around me again. "Come on, let's watch that movie."

Soon we were settled in the living room with some microwave popcorn, and for a little while I forgot about all my problems while we watched a comedy about talking animals in a zoo. Then I got ready for bed.

Before I fell asleep, I heard Dad call Mom. He was talking in Spanish, but I heard most of it. His voice drifted in and out as he paced across the floor.

"You need to tell me these things, Sara! Just because I'm in Manhattan doesn't mean I don't want to be involved! You're the one who moved away, not me!"

For a second, it reminded me of a few years ago all over again, when Dad and Mom were fighting all the time. I put the pillow over my head, so I wouldn't hear.

See what happens when I tell the truth? It always ends up badly. I told you nobody would be happy.

CHAPTER 13

Just Like Old Times . . . Or Is It?

Saturday was a much better day. Mrs. Monroe took me and Ava to see the Costume Collection at the Metropolitan Museum of Art. Ava and I took lots of pictures, and I spent about an hour sketching shoes from the 1920s. I liked the really cool buttons on them. Saturday night Dad and I went out for sushi, and everything felt like normal.

Then Sunday morning at eleven thirty, Dad said, "Mia, please pack your bag."

"But it's too early for the train," I told him.

"We're not going right to the train," he said. "Mom's meeting us for lunch at Johnny's Pizza."

At first I wasn't sure I'd heard right. Meeting Mom for lunch? Dad and Mom and I hadn't had lunch together since they got divorced.

I must be in big trouble, I thought. So I packed my bag and put on my coat, and then Dad and I headed out to Johnny's.

Johnny's has the best pizza in our neighborhood, and maybe even in the whole city. They cook it in a brick oven with real wood, and the crust gets nice and crispy. Mom and Dad and I ate there a lot when we all lived together.

I shivered the whole walk there, but once we got inside it was warm and toasty. Mom was already sitting at a table, waiting for us. She had her hair pulled back, and she looked kind of tired.

Mom stood up when she saw us. "Hi, Mia," she said, giving me a hug. But she didn't hug Dad.

Dad draped his coat around the chair. "I'll go place our order," he said, and then he got in line.

Mom looked at me and shook her head. "Mia, your father told me about that note from your Spanish teacher. Why didn't you tell me?"

"I don't know," I said, looking down at the table. It was too hard to explain.

"You know can talk to me about these things, Mia," Mom said. "I just don't understand."

Dad sat down. "It should be ready in a few minutes," he said. "So, Mia, I guess you know why we're all here."

I nodded.

"It's like I said the other night," he said. "You can't keep secrets from us. Especially when it's about school and especially when you need help."

"That's right," Mom said, and she sounded angry. "Mia, your only job right now in life is to do well in school. Baking cupcakes, going to fashion shows, that's all good, but school is the most important."

"I know!" I said. "I really do. I'm doing well in my other classes. But you guys put me in Advanced Spanish without asking me. It's not my fault."

Dad and Mom looked at each other.

"I'm sorry about that," Dad said. "We didn't realize we were pushing you into something too hard for you. Sara, can they put her in a different class?"

"I'm not sure," Mom replied. "But I'll ask. I don't know if they can switch her schedule until the spring."

"In the meantime, we can get you a tutor," Dad said. He handed Mom the note. "Her teacher suggested a few."

"We might not need one," Mom said. "Eddie majored in Spanish in college. He's a translator at the company he works for."

I was surprised. "He is?" I asked.

"I thought you knew," Mom said. "What did you think he did?"

I shrugged. I knew Eddie was a lawyer, but I didn't know he also translated. "I don't know. I thought he just went to an office and . . . did stuff." Now I felt kind of silly not asking for help when I had an honest-to-goodness translator living right under the same roof as me.

"Then let's see if Eddie can help," Dad said. "But if not, we'll get you that tutor, okay?"

"Okay," I said.

"And no more secrets," Mom said sternly. "In fact, you can live without screens this week while you think about that. No phone, TV, music, or computer. And if you keep any notes from teachers from us in the future, it will be *two* weeks."

I saw her look at Dad, and Dad gave a little nod.

I didn't even protest. With a sigh, I handed over my music player and earbuds, and my phone.

Luckily, Dad saw our order appear at the counter right then. "Food's ready! I'll be right back."

The rest of the lunch was a lot easier. We ate salads with vinegary dressing and these light green peppers that were sweet and hot at the same time. Then we had our usual—pizza with mushrooms and olives. (I know it sounds weird, but it's really good, trust me.)

For a minute, it almost seemed like old times, like nothing had changed. Except really, everything had. Before, Mom and Dad would have been talking and laughing the whole time. Now they couldn't even look at each other. Just like that other day, they both talked to me instead of each other.

And then, instead of all of us going back home, Mom and I got into a cab and headed to the train station. Back to Maple Grove. Back to our new life.

Things were never going to be the way they'd been before. I knew that. But knowing that didn't make it any easier. Was everyone really happier?

I 🧀 YOU!
(CHEESE)

CHAPTER 14

A Cheesy Problem

When we got home, Mom and I met Eddie in the kitchen, and she told him the whole story.

"I think I can help you," Eddie said. "Let's take a look at your homework together after dinner, okay?"

I nodded, grateful that Eddie didn't give me a hard time about it all. After dinner that night, he and I sat at the kitchen table, and I showed him my worksheet.

"It's verbs I have trouble with," I told him. "There's, like, a million different ways to say and spell each one, and I can't keep them straight in my head."

"Let me see," Eddie said, taking the sheet. He looked it over and then smiled. "I used to have trouble with this too. But let me show you a trick I figured out."

So, I won't bore you with a whole Spanish lesson, but you need to know that by the time Eddie was done helping me, I actually understood what was on the sheet. I answered every question, and Eddie didn't even have to help me with the last two. It was the first time I'd ever felt good about handing in my Spanish homework.

"Thanks, Eddie," I said when we were done.

Even though the tutoring went well, I was still feeling pretty down that night. That's because I knew that tomorrow I'd have to tell Sydney about the *quiero/queso* mistake.

I could keep the Spanish secret for so long because I was only hurting myself. But the *queso* secret was hurting Jackson, and it would be wrong if I didn't say anything.

But I was dreading it. I saw what Sydney did to Jackson when she was mad at him. She was going to destroy me, I just knew it.

So the next day, Monday, I knew what I had to do. As soon as I got off the bus, I walked up to Sydney. She and Maggie were hanging out by the tree in the front school yard, texting.

"Sydney, can I talk to you?" I asked.

"Busy," she said, not even looking up from her phone. "Later, okay?"

I tried again in the hallway, when I ran up to Sydney at her locker. She was talking to Eddie Rossi, but I interrupted her.

"Can I please talk to you?" I asked.

Sydney rolled her eyes. "Excuse me? Talking!"

My face turned red, and I walked away. For a second, I thought I might give up and let her keep torturing Jackson. But I just couldn't do that.

So at lunchtime, I marched up to the PGC table.

"Sydney, I need to tell you something really important," I said.

Sydney turned to Maggie and rolled her eyes. Then she looked at me.

"What's the emergency?" she asked.

"It's about that text message Jackson sent you," I said. "I made a mistake. He didn't say you're cheesy. He said he loves you."

Sydney looked absolutely shocked. "He *what*?" she shrieked.

"*Te quiero* means 'I love you,'" I explained. "I got it mixed up with the word *queso*, which means 'cheese.' I'm sorry."

Sydney stood up. "Are you kidding me?" she

asked, her voice rising. "Are you trying to ruin my life or something? Are you jealous? I bet you did that on purpose."

I shook my head. "No. I wouldn't do that. I'm just bad at Spanish."

Sydney sat down and looked at her friends. She looked kind of embarrassed.

"Can you believe I ever asked Mia to join this club?" she asked in a loud voice. "I must have been crazy!"

"I'm really sorry, and I wanted you to know," I said. Then I turned and walked away. I had one more person to tell.

Jackson Montano sat at a table in a corner with a bunch of other football players. I usually never went near that table, because you always get pelted with spitballs when you walk past. But today I had to go there.

Sydney ran up behind me. "Mia, no!" she hissed. But I ignored her and walked up to him.

"Jackson, a few days ago Sydney asked me to translate that text you sent her," I said, talking fast so I wouldn't chicken out. "I thought *quiero* was *queso*, so I told her that you said she was cheesy. That's why Sydney's been spreading those rumors about you."

Jackson put down his sandwich. "Is she making you say this?"

I shook my head. "No, it's true," I said. "I should have known that *queso* was cheese."

"Yeah, you really stink at Spanish," Jackson said.

"I know," I admitted.

Jackson stared at me for a minute and glanced over at Sydney. He didn't look mad. In fact, he had a little smile on his face, as if he thought the whole thing was sort of funny. At least that's what I hoped. "I'm really, truly sorry," I said again.

Then I quickly walked away, leaving Sydney and Jackson to work things out—or not. I'm not sure what I would do if I were in Jackson's place.

When I finally made it to my regular lunch table, all my friends were staring at me.

"What was *that* all about?" Alexis asked.

I sank into my chair. "You are not going to believe this," I said, and then I told them the story.

For a moment, everybody was quiet. Then we all started laughing at the same time. Katie put her arm around Emma.

"I cheese you, Emma!" she said.

"I cheese you, too, Katie!" Emma said back.

Then Katie picked up her sandwich. "Look! My mom packed me a love sandwich for lunch."

Alexis held up the wrap on her lunch tray. "Mine's turkey and love with a little mayo."

"Really? Yum, I really cheese turkey," Katie said.

"Okay, okay!" I cried. I was laughing so hard, it was starting to hurt. "It was a colossal mistake, I know."

"So I hope you finally got a Spanish tutor," Alexis said. "You can't afford to make this kind of mistake again."

"Eddie's tutoring me, and he's actually pretty good," I said.

"Yeah, I hear he really *cheeses* tutoring Spanish," Katie said, and we collapsed into giggles.

I was embarrassed. I had no idea what kind of revenge Sydney was going to take on me. But for the first time in a long time, I felt . . . free. And pretty happy.

I grinned at my friends. "I cheese you guys so much!"

CHAPTER 15

I Figure Out Some Things

$\mathcal{T}$he next night Eddie helped me with my homework again, and it went really well. Eddie seemed happy.

"I knew you could do it, Mia," he said. "Keep this up and maybe you can stay in that advanced class."

"You're really good at explaining things, that's why," I said. "You should have been a teacher."

Eddie looked really pleased. "I always thought about being a teacher. Who knows? Maybe I'll give it a try someday."

As I was closing my book I heard a little ringing sound from my cell phone, letting me know a text came in. I flipped open the phone and saw a message from Katie.

We're having macaroni and love for dinner tonight. I really cheese that stuff!

I laughed out loud.

"What's so funny?" Eddie asked.

"You're not going to believe this," I said, and then I told him the whole story.

When I was done, Eddie started to laugh, and he didn't hold it in. Soon tears were running down his cheeks from laughing so hard.

"Oh, that poor, poor boy," he said. "I hope you told him what happened."

I nodded. "I did. He seems okay with it. But I'm still worried about what Sydney will do to me."

Eddie nodded. "No wonder, after what she did to Jackson."

Then I found myself talking to Eddie about Sydney—stuff I hadn't even told Mom about. Like how Sydney wanted me to be in the PGC, but I didn't like how she bossed everyone around. And how she's nice to me sometimes and says insulting things at other times.

"I agree that you shouldn't have joined her club, but you might have hurt her feelings when you did that," Eddie said. "Sometimes when people are hurt, they act sad, but other people get angry and lash out."

I might have hurt Sydney's feelings? Now there was a new thought. I realized that Eddie was probably right. I had never really thought about Sydney's feelings before. I guess I figured she didn't have any.

"By the way, don't forget to ask Señora if she wants you to double-space that report that's due Friday," Eddie said as I packed up my homework.

"I don't have Spanish tomorrow because it's a half day," I said. "But you can ask her tomorrow night when you meet her."

Eddie paused. "We can ask your mom to do that," he said. "Your dad's going to go with her."

"Um, okay," I said, and I was remembering what Mom had said before about Eddie and how he should meet my teachers because he helped me with my homework. I realized now that she was right.

"And Mia?" Eddie said.

"Yeah?"

"Turn off your cell phone before your mom sees you. Remember, no screens for a week."

"Oh!" I said. I had forgotten. I turned off my phone. Then I smiled at Eddie. "Thanks," I whispered, and ran up to my room. Eddie has a lot of rules, but he can also be pretty cool, I guess.

After I went up to my room, Mom came in carrying a garment bag.

"I've got another sample for you, Mia," she said. "This one's leftover from Nathan Kermit's fall line, but I think it's pretty timeless. And cute, too."

She opened the bag to reveal a really awesome blue boyfriend-style jacket with rolled-up sleeves, a plaid lining, and what looked like vintage silver buttons.

"I love it!" I exclaimed, trying it on. "I have just the shirt to go with it."

"I knew you would," Mom said, and she turned to leave.

"Hey, Mom," I said, and she stopped. "I wanted to ask you something. I think Eddie should to go the parent-teacher conference tomorrow."

Mom looked surprised. "Instead of Dad?"

I shook my head. "No, *with* Dad," I replied. "Especially since he's tutoring me in Spanish now and everything."

Mom smiled. "Let me make sure it's okay with Dad. But I'm sure he won't mind."

I hadn't even thought that Dad might be

uncomfortable being around Eddie. I guess divorce is weird for everybody involved. And it's definitely complicated! But I had a feeling that Dad would be cool with it.

The next morning I woke up feeling pretty happy about things. I was nervous about what Señora might say to my parents—all three of them—but at least everyone knew the truth now. And I got to wear my awesome new outfit.

When I got to my locker, Sydney and the PGC walked right by me.

Callie stopped. "Mia, I love your jacket," Callie said.

"Thanks," I said.

Sydney kept walking like I didn't exist, and Maggie and Bella followed her. That was just fine with me. Sydney had been totally ignoring me, but at least she wasn't telling everyone that I was going bald.

Then, on my way to homeroom, I passed Jackson Montano. He smiled at me, and I knew that everything was cool between us.

"Hey, Queso!" he said, teasing. But I totally didn't mind.

Since it was a half day, we all went to Alexis's house for lunch and a Cupcake Club meeting.

Alexis's dad took the day off, so he was there when we walked in the door.

"Hope you're hungry!" he called out when he heard us. "I'm making my famous grilled cheese sandwiches and tomato soup."

"Dad, that soup comes from a can," Alexis said, rolling her eyes.

"Hey, you're going to ruin my reputation," Mr. Becker said. "Well, the sandwiches are all mine."

Mr. Becker reminds me of Eddie sometimes. He's really friendly, and he's always joking around. We took off our coats and sat down in Alexis's neat-as-a-pin kitchen. Alexis's dad already had a bowl of soup and a sandwich at each place on the table.

"Nice service, Mr. B.," Katie said. "When I open up a restaurant someday, you can be a waiter."

"I'll do it if I can be *head* waiter," he said.

Katie nodded. "Deal."

We sat down to eat. The grilled cheese was crunchy on the outside and gooey on the inside, just the way I like it. Of course, Alexis opened up her notebook while we were eating.

"I have good news," she reported. "We already have three new orders based on our baker's dozen offer!"

"Woo-hoo!" Katie cheered, and we all started clapping.

Alexis told us about the orders, and we came up with some ideas. Then we just started talking about regular stuff.

"You'll never believe what Jackson Montano called me today," I said. "Queso!"

Everybody laughed.

"I guess there are worse nicknames," Emma said sympathetically.

"Anyway, I'll never forget what that word means," I said. "Plus, Eddie's tutoring is really good. He's even going to the parent-teacher conference tonight. My dad is too. That's kind of weird, isn't it?"

"It sounds kind of nice to have an extra dad," Emma said.

Katie didn't say anything. Remember how she was joking around and cheering just a minute before? Well, she was quiet for the rest of lunch. Just like before. I had a feeling I knew why, but I didn't want to bring it up in front of everybody.

Then my cell phone rang, and it was Dad. (Eddie actually told Mom that I should have my phone on when I was out of the house for emergencies, and Mom totally agreed.)

"I'll be right back," I said, and walked into Alexis's living room.

"Hey, Dad," I said. "What's up?"

"I'm leaving the city now," he said. "I'll be there in plenty of time for the conference."

"Yay!" I said. Then I thought of something. "Did Mom tell you that Eddie was coming too?"

"She did," Dad replied. "It's fine with me if that's what you want, *mija*."

I had to think of a way to explain it without hurting Dad's feelings.

"Well," I began, "you're my dad, and you'll always be my dad. But when you're not here, Eddie's like a spare dad. Kind of like a baker's dozen. Most kids only get two parents. But I have three right now."

Dad laughed. "Baker's dozen, huh?"

I could hear in his voice that he was okay with that. And that was better than anything—even an extra cupcake.

CHAPTER 16

Katie Tells Me What's Wrong

$\mathcal{N}$ow that all three of my parents were going to the conference, and Dan had basketball practice, they didn't want to leave me home alone. At our school, they do the conferences over three nights. Since Katie's mom was going on Thursday, I got to hang with Katie that night.

After we ate chicken tacos and rice with Katie's mom, we went up to Katie's room. There's never a lot of homework when there's a half day, so I was showing Katie sketches I'd made of the *Emerald Forest* costumes.

"These are so cool!" Katie said, looking at a drawing of a fairy in a green sparkly dress. "You have to teach me how to sew sometime. Then we could make awesome costumes for Halloween."

"My mom's a better sewer than I am," I admitted. "Maybe she could teach both of us."

It was nice and quiet in Katie's room, with no distractions—no cupcakes, classrooms, or popular girls to bother us. I figured I might as well talk to Katie about what was bothering her.

I just came right out and said it. "Are you okay?" I asked. "'Cause it seems like something's been bothering you lately. Especially when you're talking to me. And I just hope I'm not doing something to hurt your feelings or anything."

Katie didn't look at me right away. She didn't say anything right away either.

"Don't worry, it's not your fault or anything," she finally said. "It's just . . . hard to talk about, I guess."

"You can talk to me about anything," I told her. "After all, you've been hearing me complain about Mom and Dad and Eddie all the time lately. And I guess . . . I guess I thought maybe something about that was bothering you."

"Kind of," Katie admitted, turning to me. "I never see my dad. He moved away when I was a baby and has this whole other family now."

"Wow," I said. Right away I imagined what it would be like if I never saw Dad anymore. If he spent all his time with other kids, brothers and sisters I didn't even know. "That sounds awful."

"It is," Katie said. She started talking faster, like she couldn't hold in the words. "And every year I used to get a card from him at Christmas, but this year there was no card. Nothing. And it really hurts."

I felt so bad for Katie. "That's horrible."

She took a deep breath. "So when you were complaining about having *two* dads getting into your business, it kind of made me upset. I would give anything just to have one dad in my life. You're really lucky that you have two, you know?"

"I know," I said, nodding, and for the first time I really understood that I was. Having a bunch of parents can be a real pain sometimes, but it's way better than not having any. In a way, I guess I'm very lucky.

"And I know it's hard for you too," Katie told me. "It's just a different kind of situation. So I'm not mad at you at all. I'm mostly just sad for me."

"Hey, if you want, you could borrow one of my dads sometime," I said.

Katie smiled. "It all depends on how I do on my next Spanish test!"

We both laughed, and then everything felt

pretty much normal for us again. It amazes me how Katie can be such a positive person when I know how sad she must be sometimes.

I opened my sketchbook. "Let's design matching costumes for this year. You can be the Emerald Fairy, because you look fantastic in green. And I'll be the Ruby Fairy, because I look great in red."

"Wait, won't we be too old for trick-or-treating next year?" Katie asked.

"Maybe," I said. "So we'll throw a costume party! Then we'll *have* to make costumes."

Before I started sketching, my phone beeped. I jumped, thinking maybe the parent-teacher conferences were over. I was still worried about what would happen with Señora Delgado.

But it was Ava.

Avaroni: Can't wait for the party Saturday!
FabMia: Me 2! Nervous tho. Will everyone remember me?
Avaroni: RU kidding? We all miss u and can't wait to c u.
FabMia: Good!
Avaroni: How r cupcakes coming?
FabMia: We're baking them fresh for Saturday.
Avaroni: Yum!

FabMia: Katie says hi.
Avaroni: Hi Katie!
FabMia: Got to go! Dad's texting.

My text conversation with Dad was much shorter.

Your math teacher really is strict! I love all the others. Let's talk tomorrow.

"Looks like it's all over," I told Katie, after I replied to Dad. "Dad didn't say much, but it sounds like everything's all right."

"Excellent!" Katie said.

A few minutes later Mom and Eddie came to pick me up.

"How did it go?" I asked as soon as I got into the backseat.

Mom turned to talk to me. "We had a long talk with Señora Delgado. She says with the tutoring, you've been doing a lot better lately. So she's going to give you some extra assignments to help you bring up your grade."

I wasn't crazy about getting extra work, but it could have been a lot worse.

"She actually seems very nice," Eddie said. "And

I love your math teacher, Mrs. Moore. She seems like she runs a tight ship."

I shook my head and laughed. "You wouldn't like her so much if you were a student!"

It was pretty much bedtime by the time we got home. After I showered and got into my pj's, I climbed into bed and got out my sketchbook. I just wanted to finish that ruby costume before I fell asleep.

Then there was a knock on the door, and I said, "Come in!" But it wasn't Mom, as usual. It was Eddie.

"Your mom will be up in a minute," he said. "I just wanted to say that I'm glad you wanted me there tonight. I liked getting to know your teachers."

"No problem," I replied.

"Okay, then," Eddie said. "Good night, Queso!"

I groaned and pulled the covers up over my head.

See? I told you that mistake was going to haunt me forever! But like Emma said, I guess there are worse nicknames.

CHAPTER 17

Extra Good

Avaroni: Did you make my cupcakes yet?
FabMia: It's 2 early!
Avaroni: Sooooo excited!
FabMia: Me 2!
Avaroni: Wait till u see my outfit. You'll love it!
FabMia: I bet it's gorgeous. Can't wait to see u!

I yawned and rolled back over in bed. It was only eight a.m.! Ava must be really excited if she was up so early on a Saturday.

I had to get up soon anyway. We were going to make the cupcakes this morning at Emma's house, and then Eddie was going to drive me into the city so the cupcakes wouldn't get bumped around on the train.

That meant I had to pick out two different outfits—one for baking cupcakes and one for the party. What an excellent problem to have! I threw open my closet and stared at it.

Cupcake baking was easy. I pulled out my favorite pair of jeans and a long-sleeved henley top with tiny flowers on it. If I got batter on it, it would be easy to clean.

Then there was Ava's party. That was harder. First, I had to make sure I wore something that went with the party decorations. But also, I wanted to look extra nice. I hadn't seen some of my Manhattan friends in a long time, and I was a little nervous about it.

I changed into my cupcake clothes while I thought about the party outfit. I finally decided to wear my fuzzy white V-neck sweater with a denim skirt, boots, and lots of silver jewelry. My boots are black, but the sweater and jewelry would be very snowy. I put the outfit on my bed to change into later.

After breakfast Mom took me to Emma's house, and pretty soon the Cupcake Club was busy baking. Katie and I made the batter, Emma made the frosting nice and fluffy, and Alexis used the chopper to make the coconut like snow.

We baked two dozen, even though Ava ordered only one dozen. Most recipes make twenty-four cupcakes anyway, and this way we'd have extra if we messed up. (And Emma's brothers will always eat any leftovers we have.)

Matt came into the kitchen while we were all carefully dusting the tops of the cupcakes with coconut and edible glitter.

"More cupcakes for your boyfriends?" he asked, looking over Emma's shoulder.

"No," Emma replied firmly. "These are for a birthday party."

Matt reached to grab one, and Emma pushed his hand away.

"Not yet," she said. "We have to make them all first and pick out the best twelve for the party."

"Thirteen," Alexis corrected her. "This is Ava's first order, so she gets a baker's dozen."

Soon we had a dozen cupcakes carefully stored in a box, and one extra cupcake in a clear bag with a silver ribbon tied around it.

"Now?" Matt asked impatiently.

Emma sighed. "Now."

Matt grabbed one, unwrapped it, and then put the whole thing in his mouth.

"Good!" he said, with his mouth full.

Then Mom picked me up and brought me and the cupcakes back home. I got changed for the party, and then it was time to go into the city.

"Your chauffeur is waiting!" Eddie called up the stairs.

I ran downstairs and put on my coat. We carefully put the cupcakes in the trunk, but I knew the extra one wouldn't be safe there. So I held it in my lap the whole way to the city.

There was a lot of traffic, but Eddie let me pick the music on the radio. Then, before I knew it, we were in my dad's neighborhood.

"Call your dad and let him know we're near," he said. "I don't think I'll be able to park, so I'll drop you off in front of the building."

So I called Dad, and he was waiting outside when Eddie pulled up. He popped up the trunk, and Dad moved to get my bag and the cupcakes. I was about to open the door when I thought of something.

"Thanks for all your help with Spanish," I told Eddie. I handed him the cupcake. "This is the extra baker's dozen cupcake. 'Cause you're kind of like an extra dad for me."

Eddie smiled so wide I could see every one of his teeth.

"Thanks, Mia," he said.

I quickly scooted out of the car and waved good-bye to Eddie, my extra dad. Then I ran to hug my Dad Who Will Always Be My Dad, No Matter What. It wasn't easy because he was holding the cupcakes, but I managed anyway.

I knew Ava wouldn't mind about the extra cupcake, and I was right. I got to her apartment early to help set up, and she practically screamed with happiness when she saw them.

"Mia, they're beautiful!" she cried.

"Thanks. The apartment looks great!" I said.

There were little white lights, those icicle lights, strung all around the living room. Silver snowflakes hung from the ceiling. There was a long, thin table under the window for the food and stuff, and it had a white tablecloth on it with silver glitter dusted over it.

Ava looked just like a decoration herself. She wore a silver tank top with a sequin design and a fluffy white skirt, almost like the one I had drawn for her.

"Ava, you look like a snow princess!" I exclaimed.

Ava smiled and twirled around. "Mom and I looked all over for a dress, but this worked out perfectly. It really reminds me of the dress you drew for me."

By the time I had carefully set up the cupcakes on the table, the buzzer rang and the rest of the party guests started to arrive. Some of my friends from my old soccer team were there, like Jenny and Tamisha. Then there were friends of Ava's that I had never met before— new friends she met after I'd left. Just like my Cupcake Club friends.

I was a little nervous at first, but I fit right in. Tamisha and I were talking and laughing like we had just seen each other yesterday, and Ava's new friends were nice too.

It wasn't exactly like before, when Ava and I were best friends and I lived in Manhattan. But I was starting to think that's maybe just how life is— things keep changing, and there's nothing you can do about it. Sometimes the changes are bad, but mostly they're good, or good things can come out of them. And if something bad happens, sometimes you can learn from your mistakes and start fresh. The way my friends and I do when we make a bad batch of cupcakes.

Take right now, for example. I was having a good time at a party. I had lots of friends. I had three parents who loved me. And I wasn't failing Spanish anymore. In fact, you might say things were very good—*muy bueno*. Just don't ask me to spell that!

Emma
all
stirred
up!

CHAPTER 1

Little Brother, Big Problem

$\mathcal{M}$y name is Emma Taylor, but a few weeks ago I was wishing it was anything but! I was pretending that the little boy who was outside the school bus, wailing that he did not want to go to day camp, was *not* my little brother, Jake Taylor, and that those desperate parents who were bribing and pleading with him were *not* my parents, but rather some poor, misguided souls whom I would never see again.

In fact, I was wishing that I was already an adult and that my three best friends and I—the entire Cupcake Club—had opened our own bakery on a cute little side street in New York City, where none of my three brothers lived. The bakery would be all pink, and it would sell piles of cupcakes in a rainbow of lovely colors and flavors, and would cater mainly to movie stars and little girls' princess birth-day parties. That is my fantasy. Sounds great, right?

But oh, no, this was reality.

"Emmy!" Jake was shrieking as my father gently but firmly manhandled him down the bus aisle to where I was scrunched down on my seat, pretending not to see them. I could literally feel the warmth of all the other eyes on the bus watching us, and I just wanted to melt away. Instead I stared out the window, like there was something really fascinating out there.

"Emma, please look after your brother," said my father. How many times have I heard that one? My older brothers, Matt and Sam, and I take turns babysitting Jake, but somehow the bad stuff always happens on my shift. My dad gave Jake one last kiss, reached to pat me on the head, and then dashed off the bus. I wished I could've dashed with him.

A counselor sat on the end of the seat, scrunching Jake in between us, so he couldn't run away. Jake was wailing, and the counselor—a nice girl named Paige, who is about twenty-one years old and probably wishing she were somewhere else too—was speaking in a soothing voice to him. She looked over his head at me, smiled, and then said, "Don't worry. This happens all the time. We always get one of these guys. He'll settle down within the week."

The week?! I wanted to die, but instead I nodded and looked out the window again. I also wanted to kill Jake that moment, but it was only seconds later that his wails turned to quiet hiccups. Then he slid his clammy, chubby little hand into mine and squeezed, and I felt a little guilty. "It's going to be okay, Jake," I whispered, and squeezed his little hand back. He snuggled into me and looked up at me with these really big eyes that get me every time. It's not the worst thing in the world to have a little someone in your life who looks up to you.

I sighed. "Feeling better, officer?" Jake is big into law enforcement, so it usually cheers him up if we play Precinct. At least he wasn't crying anymore. Paige gave him a pat on the head and then went to help some other kids get on the bus. But Jake wasn't feeling better. I could tell just by looking at him.

"I feel sick," he said.

Oh no. Jake isn't one of those kids who fakes being sick. My mom always says on car trips that if Jake says he feels sick, we pull over, because he *will* throw up, 100 percent of the time.

I jerked the bus window open and quickly flung

Jake over me, so that he was sitting in the window seat. "Put your head out the window, buddy. Take deep breaths—in through your nose, out through your mouth. We're going to start moving soon, so the wind will be in your face. . . . Deep breaths."

I rubbed his back a little and looked up to see if anyone I knew was getting on at this stop. My best friend and co–Cupcake Clubber Alexis Becker was going to the same camp, but her parents were dropping her off on their way to work. I fantasized about them driving me, too, and leaving Jake to his own devices. Ha! As if my parents would let me get away with that! At the very least, I did have our Cupcake Club meeting to look forward to later today. Just quality girl time, planning out the club's summer schedule and reviewing the cupcake jobs we had coming up. Chilling with my best friends— Alexis, Katie, and Mia—and brainstorming. It was definitely going to be fun.

A bunch of little kids streamed on and sat mostly in the front of the bus. Suddenly I spied a familiar shade of very bright blond hair, and my stomach sank. Noooo!!! It couldn't be.

But it was.

Sydney Whitman, mean-girl extraordinaire and head of the imaginatively named Popular Girls

Club at school, came strolling down the aisle, heading straight for the back row, where only the most popular kids dared to sit. I quickly looked out the window and pretended I hadn't seen her. But no luck.

"Oh, that's so cute! You and your little brother sitting together! I guess that's easier than trying to find someone your own age to sit with?" She smiled sweetly, but her remark stung just as it was meant to.

Jake hates Sydney as much as I do, if not more, so when he turned his head to look at her, he began to gag. Sydney's eyes opened wide, and her hand flew up to cover her mouth. "Oh no! He's going to—"

Luckily, Jake turned to the window just in time and hurled the contents of his stomach out onto the road.

"Disgusting!" shrieked Sydney, and she fled to the back of the bus.

I didn't know whether to laugh or cry. It's just one more nail in the coffin of my possible popularity, not that I ever really stood a chance. And not that I really wanted to. But it was also kind of hilarious to have Jake take one look at Sydney and then throw up. Definitely not her desired effect on men. I made a mental note to tell the Cupcake Club later. They'd love this.

Jake barfed a couple more times and then sat back down, looking as white as a sheet. The good news about Jake's car sickness is that after he's done throwing up, he's always fine. I pulled a napkin from my lunch bag and gave it to him to wipe his face. Then I cracked open his thermos and gave him a tiny sip of apple juice. I felt sorry for the poor guy. I hate throwing up.

Jake smiled wanly. "Thanks, Emmy. Sorry."

I laughed. "I feel the same way when I see Sydney Whitman." I wasn't sure I would have been so psyched about going to this camp if I'd known Sydney was going—or at the very least that she'd be on my bus. It definitely put a cramp in my happiness.

Jake rested his head back against the seat and promptly fell asleep. In a minute his head was resting, sweaty and heavy, against my shoulder. First days can be hard for anyone, especially little kids. At least tomorrow we wouldn't have the same problem. I said a silent prayer that Sydney wasn't in my group.

At camp, we got off the bus and a crowd of cheering counselors with painted faces was there to greet us. My mom must've called ahead to tip off someone, because one really pretty counselor was holding up a sign, like people do at the airport. It read OFFICER JAKE TAYLOR. That at least allowed me to peel him off and hand him over to the counselor, so I could go with my group, Team Four, to our rally zone (whatever that was) at the arts-and-crafts center.

The boys and girls have separate areas at camp, so I wouldn't see Jake again all day, thank goodness. And thank goodness again, because Sydney headed off with Team Five in the opposite direction. I didn't have a minute to review who was on whose team. Anyway, I didn't know a lot of the kids, but I did know that wherever Alexis was, she and I would be together. (We requested it, and my mom promised me she had spoken with the camp director.) That's all that matters.

As I headed across the green lawn to the arts-and-crafts center, I heard someone calling my name. I turned, and, of course, it was Alexis! I had never been so happy to see her in all my life.

"Thank goodness!" I cried, and threw my arms around her, like a shipwreck victim who has finally been saved.

Alexis isn't much for big displays of affection, so she patted my back awkwardly, but I didn't mind. In any case, she just saw me a few days ago.

"What's going on?" she asked as we separated and followed our counselor.

"Jake drama. Screaming, puking—the whole deal." I lowered my voice. "And Sydney Whitman saw the whole thing."

Alexis waved her hand in the air, as if to say *whatever!* That is just one of the many things I love about Alexis. She doesn't care at all what other people think. "Too bad he didn't puke *on* her," she said with a laugh. "Or did he?" Her eyes twinkled mischievously.

"No such luck. But the good news is, we aren't on the same team as her."

We'd reached the log cabin that was the head-quarters for our team. On its porch stood two teenage counselors—a guy and a girl. As the crowd amassed in front of them, I counted twelve camp-ers: all girls, of course. Yay! Finally! A break from all the boys in my life!

"Hello, people! Listen up!" The guy counselor was clapping his hands and kind of dancing around in a funny way to get our attention. Everyone started laughing and listening.

He bowed and said, "Thank you, ladies! My name is Raoul Sanchez, and this is my awesome partner, Maryanne Murphy."

Maryanne did a little curtsy, and we all clapped. She was pretty—short and cute with red hair and freckles. Raoul was tall and thin with rubbery arms and legs, and his face had a big goofy smile topped off by black, crew-cut hair. It was obvious neither of them was shy.

"We are going to have the most fun of any team this summer! Raoul and I personally guarantee it!" Maryanne said enthusiastically.

Raoul nodded. "If this isn't the most fun summer of your life, when camp is over I will take you to an all-you-can-eat pizza party, on me."

There were cheers and claps.

"Okay, we have a lot to tell you, so why don't you all grab a seat on the grass and get ready to be pumped!" said Maryanne.

Raoul and Maryanne then proceeded to tell us how we'd get to pick our own team name. ("Team Four" was just a placeholder, they said.) They told us about all the fun activities we'd do: swimming, kayaking, art projects, team sports, field trips, tennis, and more. Then they told us about the special occasions that were scheduled: Tie-Dye Day, Pajama Day, Costume Day, Crazy Hat Day, and finally, the best day of all . . . Camp Olympics, followed by the grand finale: the camp talent show!

Ugh. The camp talent show? Getting onstage in front of more than a hundred people? *So* not up my alley. I made a face at Alexis, but she was listening thoughtfully, her head tilted to the side and her long reddish hair already escaping its headband. She was probably wondering if there was any money to be made here; business was mostly all she thought about. In fact, her parents said if she did an outdoor camp for part of the summer, she could go to business camp for two weeks at the end of the summer. Sometimes I wonder how we are friends at all; our interests are so different!

"Thinking of signing up?" I whispered.

"Myself? No. But you should," she whispered back.

I laughed. "Yeah, right. What's my talent? Baby-sitting?"

Alexis raised her eyebrows at me. "Maybe. But I'm sure you can come up with something more marketable than that."

Right. I can't even keep the kid I babysit for from throwing up.

CHAPTER 2

Meet the Hotcakes!

$\mathscr{F}$irst we played a getting-to-know-you game called Pass the Packet. We had a mystery brown bag filled with something, and we each took turns holding it and telling the group about ourselves and then said what we wished was in the bag. (I told the group I had three brothers and I wished the bag had tickets to a taping of *Top Chef*.) When it was Alexis's turn, she told the group how she, Mia, Katie, and I had a Cupcake Club and about all the business we do, baking cupcakes for special events. The other girls in the group thought it was so cool. I felt great, and Alexis and I promised to bring in cupcakes for the group.

At the end, Maryanne opened the "packet," and it was filled with these awesome friendship bracelets for each of us. We all grabbed for the color we wanted. I, of course, grabbed a pink one.

Then we got down to business, naming our team.

A very pretty girl named Georgia, with light red hair and dark eyes, suggested we be "Rock Stars." I thought it was a great idea, but because it was the first idea, everyone still wanted a chance to make their own suggestions.

A girl named Caroline, who turned out to be Georgia's cousin, said, "How about the 'A-Team,'" which everyone thought was funny. Alexis suggested "Winners," because the power of positive branding would intimidate our competitors. I had to laugh. Then a girl named Charlotte—with bright blue eyes and dark, dark hair—suggested that since we would be having cupcakes a lot (she laughed and looked at me and Alexis when she said it), we should be the "Cupcakes." Right after she said it, a funny girl named Elle said, "No, the 'Hotcakes'!" and that was it.

"The Hotcakes! I love it!" cried Raoul. He and Elle high-fived. "Let's take a vote, girls! All in favor of the 'Hotcakes,' put your hands in the air!"

Everyone screamed and waved their hands high,

and that was that. Maryanne announced it was time for the Hotcakes to change for swimming, then lunchtime.

Alexis and I grabbed our backpacks and headed to the changing rooms.

"This is superfun, don't you think?" I asked as we walked across the central green.

"Yes, *and* I think we have the best group," said Alexis in a sure voice.

I laughed. "How do you know?"

She shrugged. "I counted how many girls we have versus the other two teams in our age group, then I evaluated how many of our girls are nice and smart. As a percentage, we have the nicest team by far. I would also venture that one hundred percent of our team is smart, and with Sydney on Team Five and stupid Bella on Team Three, their intelligence rate is at least ten percent below ours."

"Alexis! You are too much!" I shook my head. "The only bad part is, I wish the others were here."

She knew who I meant. Katie and Mia from our Cupcake Club were doing different things from us this month. Alexis frowned thoughtfully. "Yeah. But we'll see them plenty. And maybe it's good for us to branch out a little. It will generate some new business strategies and connections!"

I swatted her. "Is that all you think about?"

She pushed open the door to the locker room with a grin. "Pretty much!"

"I just hope they don't replace us with new friends."

Alexis shrugged. "Maybe they're thinking the same thing."

I thought back to last fall, when Katie had been dumped by Callie, her old best friend, so that Callie could hang with Sydney and the Popular Girls Club. New friends and old: a tough thing to balance. I sighed after just thinking about it.

When I came to the open house they had in March, one of the things I liked about this camp was that they have private changing rooms in the locker room, so you don't have to strip naked in front of strangers. I could never change in front of other people. Forget about being naked and getting into a bathing suit—I can't even change into pj's at a slumber party or try on clothes at the mall if someone else is in the room. Except for Mom. It's just a personal thing. I am very private about my body. Maybe it comes from being the only girl in a family of boys or from having my own room, but I just like privacy.

Alexis and I changed in rooms next to each other, and were chatting through the opening at the top of the dividers.

"Wait till you see my new suit!" she said. "It's so cute!"

"Me too! My mom brought it home as a surprise!"

We came out and took one look at each other and then started laughing our heads off. We had on the exact same bathing suit! They were tankinis, navy blue with white piping and a cool, yellow lightning bolt down either side. Alexis is kind of muscular from soccer, and I'm kind of thin (I play the flute, but that doesn't exactly build muscles!), so the suit fit us way differently. We couldn't stop giggling, though. We looked like total dork twins.

Georgia and Elle, and Charlotte and Caroline all gathered around, and we admired what everyone was wearing. We all had on new suits. Then one girl named Kira, who was shy and superpretty, came out. She had her towel draped around her shoulders, and she wasn't smiling.

"Let's see!" said Elle, clapping.

Kira shook her head. "Uh-uh." She bit her lip, and we instantly realized we shouldn't push her.

She looked like she might cry at any second.

"Okay!" Alexis said quickly. I could tell she was desperate to make Kira feel better, but couldn't think of how. Suddenly she hoisted her towel across her shoulders, to cover herself like Kira. "Capes it is!" I was so proud of her right then for her idea.

Everyone followed suit. Georgia yelled, "The Hot*capes*!" and we all hooted. I glanced at Kira and saw relief on her face, and we all marched out to meet Maryanne and Raoul, who were waiting outside to walk us to the huge pool. I had to wonder how bad Kira's suit was, though.

We sat for a water safety lecture by the lifeguard and swim director, Mr. Collins, a really nice gym teacher from the elementary school whom I recognized. The safety talk was a little boring (yeah, yeah, don't run, no chicken fights, no diving in the shallow end, swim with a buddy), but then we were in the water for free swim, and it was heavenly! The water wasn't too cold and the pool was huge, with a supershallow end and a superdeep end with a diving board!

In my excitement to get in the water, I had forgotten to check out Kira's suit, but I stole a glance the first chance I could. She was kind of cringing in the shallow end, and her suit was a one piece with Hello Kitty on it, and it was way too small for her. I felt terrible. It was babyish and it looked bad. I wondered why she didn't just swim to the deep end to cover it up.

"Okay, people! Now it's time for some fun!" Mr. Collins blew a whistle and beckoned us all over to the wall in the shallow end. I love to swim and I'm pretty good at it, so I did a loopy backstroke, kind of hamming it up, and Alexis did her old lady breaststroke, where she keeps her head out of the water the whole time. We cracked each other up.

Once everyone had reached the side of the pool, Mr. Collins whistled again to get our attention, then he spoke. He had a very kind voice, and was very quiet and patient.

"Okay, kids, today we're going to just get a feel for skill level and what we need to work on with each of you. One of the great things about Spring Lake Day Camp is that you will all leave here swimming really well by the end of the summer, and you'll have fun learning! So let's break you into four groups of three, and we'll have each of you swim a length of the pool in three heats. Count off by threes, then come down to the shallow end and we'll get started."

Alexis and I swam stood next to each other in the lineup, so we would be on the same team. I was first, and Charlotte was the third in our group. The other girls arranged themselves, and Maryanne and Raoul followed, walking along the edge of the pool. The counselors were in bathing suits, but I guess they didn't have to get in the water since Mr. Collins taught this part of camp.

"Okay, girls. Everyone settled? Any stroke you like, no rush. We're not racing. On your marks, get set . . . *bweeet!*" He blew his whistle hard, and I took off, swimming freestyle, all the way to the deep end. I knew we weren't racing, but it felt good to try hard and swim fast. I hated knowing people were watching me, but at least three other girls were swimming at the same time as me, so the bystanders weren't watching *only* me the whole time, which made it okay.

I got to the deep end and slapped my hand against the wall. First! (Not that we were racing!) I hung on to the wall and watched Georgia, Jesse, and Caroline come in right after me. I was breathing hard, but it felt good. Next up was Alexis, along with a girl named Tricia, a girl named Louise, and Kira in the fourth group. Mr. Collins blew the whistle, and they were off.

Alexis is a great swimmer too. Just what you would expect: efficient; not show-offy; fast, clean strokes. Tricia and Louise were doing fine too. But . . . uh-oh. Kira wasn't.

She had pushed away from the wall fine and was gliding, but then when the water got deeper and her glide wore off, she started to flounder. She put down her feet and tried to push off again, but that only got her into the deeper end, to where she couldn't stand. She started to sink.

Mr. Collins was in the water in a flash, as was Raoul. They both dove from opposite sides of the water and reached her at the exact same moment. I was frozen to the spot, watching as they grabbed her and hauled her toward the side of the pool. *Oh my goodness,* was all I could think. Kira can't swim!

When they reached the wall, Kira was sputtering and coughing. They each had an arm around her, and had towed her to the side in a flash. Mr. Collins lifted her onto the deck and pushed himself up and out of the water. Maryanne came running over with her own towel, and put it over Kira's shoulders. Kira started to cry. Tricia, Alexis, and Louise had reached the deep end's wall (they'd been oblivious to what had happened), and now everyone was just silent, watching.

At first, we were all scared for Kira, and then as it became clear that she was okay, we were all really embarrassed for her.

Mr. Collins quickly established that Kira was not hurt or in danger, then stood and called out to the group, "She's fine! Just a little rusty, like the best of us after a long winter! Everything's okay. Just swim for a minute while we change our plan." He and Maryanne and Raoul chatted in whispers, then Raoul jumped back into the pool and swam to the shallow end.

Mr. Collins called out again, "Now is there anyone else who'd like a little extra practice with Raoul? It's fine! Just raise your hand." He looked around. No one was raising their hand. But then Elle, who was still in the shallow end, raised her hand.

"Great! Go with Raoul to the corner and you'll work on it a little. Kira"—Mr. Collins reached down and patted Kira's head—"just come on over and join Raoul and . . . what's your name, young lady?"

"Elle," called Elle.

"And Elle while they practice at this end, okay? The next group, get ready to swim."

In a few moments Kira was back in the water

with Elle and Raoul. Now, if there is one thing I noticed when we were having free swim, it's that Elle is an amazing swimmer. After what she did for Kira, I knew she'd make an amazing friend, too.

CHAPTER 3

New Friends, Old Friends, and Old Enemies

Sydney Whitman sat at a picnic table next to us at lunch. She must've been bragging to her group that she knew a lot of kids at camp, because she had walked right over to us and acted really chummy. (She was obviously going for quantity over quality since we're not friends.) We weren't falling for it, though, and anyone could see she was really just doing it for show.

"What, no cupcakes?" Sydney asked, with a big fake smile as she inspected our lunch.

Alexis shook her head. "Nope." She continued eating, as though Sydney wasn't even there. The rest of our table (Charlotte, Elle, Georgia, and Kira—Elle's new best friend) just looked blankly at Sydney, probably wondering who she was.

Sydney was floundering. She tried a different topic. "So what's your team name, girls?"

Georgia, who was so sweet, was perplexed. She clearly felt uncomfortable with Alexis's rudeness, while I for one was loving it.

"We're called the Hotcakes," Georgia said politely.

Sydney laughed meanly, but she had a kind of surprised look on her face. "That's so . . . like, young. Like Strawberry Shortcake or something. We're Angels, like *Charlie's Angels*. Gorgeous and powerful, get it?" She flipped her hair.

Georgia and Elle looked at each other, then at me, like *Who is this person?* I just had to shrug.

"I heard someone in your group almost drowned today," Sydney said next, really casually.

I looked at Kira and saw her face turn a deep red. I wanted to throttle Sydney. Instead, I thought about what Elle did earlier and how brave and kind she was. I decided to copy her.

"It was me." I shrugged.

Sydney's hand flew to her mouth, and she started to laugh in surprise. "Really! You can't swim?"

"Actually, it was me," said Alexis.

Sydney looked confused. "Wait, what?"

Georgia was laughing now. "It was me. I fell into the pool and drowned."

"No, me!" said Elle. Now we were all howling. Even Kira was giggling a little.

Sydney looked at us, one to another, then she got a mad look on her face and gave a slight shrug. "Whatever. I'm just trying to be a concerned citizen." And she stalked back to her table. That last line really got us going. While I know it isn't nice to laugh at other people, it felt good to be part of this group and laughing for a good reason. The very idea of Sydney Whitman as a caring, concerned individual was truly hilarious to me. Of course, when we stopped laughing, Alexis and I explained who she was and why she was such a villain. There's nothing like a common enemy to unite a group. That's when Alexis spontaneously promised to start cupcake Fridays for camp, and I wholeheartedly agreed.

The first day of camp seemed to last forever. It was only four o'clock when we all piled back onto the bus, but it seemed like I'd left home weeks, not hours, earlier.

Jake was sticky and muddy and tired when I met him at our bus waiting area. He promptly handed me his grimy, mud-caked towel and wet backpack to hold for him, thereby killing my happy first-day-of-camp glow. At least Alexis was on the bus ride home with me. But as it turned out, Jake wouldn't let her sit with us. He pitched a fit that he wanted to sit with only me, so Alexis sat in front of me so we could chat on the way home. And after all that, Jake fell asleep as soon as the wheels started turning. Apparently he only pukes on the way *to* camp.

Alexis and I spoke in whispers as we reviewed the day, kind of free-associating.

Me: "Mr. Collins is really nice."

Alexis: "Yeah, that was scary."

Me: "Very cool of Elle to pretend she needed help."

Alexis: "I'm psyched for cupcake Fridays at camp, too."

Me: "I wish SW wasn't here."

Alexis: *(Moans. Pretends to puke.)*

We laughed.

But then Alexis grew serious. "You know, I learned more about Kira, because Louisa went to school with her. I feel really bad. Her mom was sick for a few years, and she died about eight months ago. Kira has three much older sisters, but none of them live at home anymore, so she just lives with her dad. He's, like, much older than our dads and kind of clueless and sad about his wife and everything."

"Wow. That is so sad. Poor Kira."

Alexis nodded. "I know. So that kind of explains the lame bathing suit. I guess her dad didn't know which kind to buy her. And maybe her mom just wasn't well enough to teach her to swim, and maybe her dad didn't know you had to know how to swim to go to this camp."

"Bummer. I felt terrible for her."

"Yeah, but at least she's really nice," said Alexis.

"And superpretty," I added, feeling generous. I made a mental note to make an even bigger effort with Kira. Even though my mom isn't around a lot, it would be really hard if she was gone for, like, forever. I couldn't even imagine it.

We had reached Alexis's stop, so she hopped off. We were having a Cupcake Club meeting at her house at five thirty, but I was going to go home and shower first. I'd see her again soon.

Just before our stop, I nudged Jake awake, and when we arrived, I half carried, half dragged him and his disgusting gear off the bus. He was so dirty, I considered hosing him down in the yard, but instead I talked him into a bath by promising him that he could use one of the fizzy blue bath bombs I got for my birthday. His gear I would have to hose off.

I spent a lot of time babysitting Jake earlier in the year, when my mom had to switch jobs for a little while. It was hard work and kind of a bummer because Jake is not the easiest kid to babysit. Also, it cut into a lot of my own activities. Now that my mom is back at her old job, things are a little better. During the summer, I have to take Jake to and from camp, and two days a week I stay with him until 5:15 p.m., when my mom gets home. The other days my older brothers, Matt and Sam, take turns watching him.

After Jake's bath, I got him into his pj's and settled him in front of the TV, and then I showered and cleared out my lunchbox and backpack. At 5:10 I was ready. At 5:20 my mom had not yet appeared. At 5:30 I called Alexis's house to say my mom was running late. At 5:40 she pulled in. I was waiting in the driveway with my arms folded and my bike all ready to go.

"Honey, I'm so sorry," my mom said as she clambered out of the car with all her grocery bags. "The checkout line was horrible, and it took longer than

I'd planned, plus, they were out of the good tortillas for the quesadillas Dad likes, so . . ."

My blood was boiling. I was all ready to start yelling at her about how I'm always left stranded, always ditched with Jake; how no one ever considers my schedule, and so on. But suddenly I thought of Kira and how hard it must have been for her to lose her mom. I took a deep breath; kissed my mom on the cheek; yelled, "See you later!"; and took off.

I was twenty minutes late for the meeting. I needed to be home by six thirty for dinner, so that only gave us forty minutes to meet.

"Mia! Katie! You are a sight for sore eyes!" I said, and it was true. Because even though I saw them yesterday, it felt like a year ago. And it was so exhausting trying to make new friends that it was a great relief to relax with old ones. I just sat and smiled at them like an idiot for a minute.

"Ookaaay . . . ," said Katie, and giggled. "We missed you, too."

Alexis had filled them in on camp, but then I had to give my version and they had to tell me about their day. So it was 6:10 by the time we finished, and we only had ten minutes for club business—fifteen minutes if I biked home really fast.

"First order," said Alexis in her official voice. "I need someone to take over my deliveries to Mona on Saturdays. I now have a summer golf clinic on Saturday mornings."

Every Friday we bake five dozen mini cupcakes for our friend Mona, who owns a bridal store called The Special Day. We met her when Mia's mom got married and we were all bridesmaids in the wedding. We bought our dresses at Mona's store. The store is so beautiful and peaceful and girlie (so unlike my house!), and Mona is so nice. I waved my hand in the air.

"I'll take over!" I said. "I will, I will!"

Everyone laughed.

Alexis beamed. "Great. Thanks. Next, Jake's birthday."

I groaned. "What color cupcake would 'annoying' be?"

Mia loves Jake (it's mutual), so she protested. "No, they have to be really special. Our best work for that little mascot of ours!"

Katie asked, "What about P-B-and-J?"

"Nah, peanut allergies in his class," I said.

"Triple Chocolate Fudge Explosion?" suggested Katie.

"Why don't we just ask him?" asked Mia.

"Fine." I wrote it on my to-do list. (I am all about lists.)

"What else?" asked Alexis.

"Well, I was wondering if we should try to mix things up a little for Mona. Maybe try a different flavor?" asked Katie.

"Yes, but it has to be white," reminded Mia. Right now we baked only white cake cupcakes with white frosting because Mona can't have anything chocolate or, like, raspberry in a store full of white, white, white bridal gowns!

We thought for a minute.

"Cinnamon bun with cream cheese frosting?" I suggested.

"Ooh, I love those!" said Mia enthusiastically.

"Or coconut?" suggested Katie.

Alexis made a face. "Not everyone likes coconut," she said.

"Also maybe allergies, right?" I said.

Katie looked kind of bummed, so I said, "Why don't I ask her on Saturday, okay?"

Alexis made a note in the meeting minutes, and I added it to my to-do list. Sometimes being in this club is about balancing people's feelings as much as it is about baking and making money. It can be hard work.

"So Friday night, we're on, right? My house?" I said.

Alexis and Mia nodded eagerly. They have crushes on my older brothers (Alexis on Matt, Mia on Sam), so they always want to come to my house. And ever since I bought my own pink KitchenAid stand mixer, it's gotten much more efficient to bake at my house too.

I wondered if Alexis and I should mention that we're baking for our new friends on Thursday, too. I glanced at Alexis to see if she was thinking about it, but her face betrayed nothing. I decided to wait.

It's weird having other friends. I wondered if they'd become as close as my old friends. I really couldn't picture it!

CHAPTER 4

A Secret Celebrity!

So, when I thought Jake's crying and barfing were just first-day jitters I was dead wrong! They were *every day* jitters! My mornings were exhausting and mortifying. Seriously, every morning he got himself all worked up, he cried, Dad made me sit with him, and then he puked. It was completely, totally unfair.

I tried to go on strike and get a ride with Alexis, but my parents insisted I take the bus so that I could watch over Jake. The only good thing was that because I did bus duty (and maybe because instead of freaking out at my mom when she was late that time from picking up groceries, I was nice!), my parents declared that I didn't have to babysit Jake anymore when we got home! Now it was all up to

Matt and Sam (and my mom). Yay! Freedom!

Needless to say, the bus was still a major bummer. And Sydney made a big deal of sitting really far away from us and bringing perfume that she sprayed in our direction when she got on. That perfume was probably what was making Jake sick, if you ask me. Either that, or it had just become a bad habit for him. Or maybe the sight of her really did make him gag.

Anyway, besides the bad arrivals and departures, camp was awesome! I loved, loved, loved it! And what's really weird was that I'd grown so close to my Hotcakes teammates so fast. I mean Elle, Georgia, Charlotte, Caroline, and Kira. I felt almost as close to them as I do to Mia, Katie, and Alexis. It's weird. I guess it's because we spent so much intense time together, and we chatted all we wanted (unlike at school, where we actually have to shut up in class and learn!). I think Alexis feels the same way.

Oh, and it was true that we had the best team. We got Raoul and Maryanne to admit it. Sydney's team was the worst because according to her counselors, by way of *our* counselors, every day she made a different girl on her team cry. Can you believe it?

The week seemed really long because of all the newness, so by Thursday night I was pretty wiped out, but Alexis and I had to bake for camp's Cupcake Friday. The other bummer was when Mia called to see if we wanted to go to the movies. (Her stepfather, Eddie, was treating.)

Now, the thing about the four members of the Cupcake Club is that when one of us proposes an activity or a plan, the only thing that really prevents us from doing it is if it's something random, like a sibling's birthday or someone's grandma is visiting. Because we all know one another's schedules so well, we don't even bother proposing plans unless we know all four of us can make it.

So Mia and Katie knew Alexis and I were technically free Thursday night. Except that we weren't. Because we were baking for our new friends. Ugh.

When Mia called I was speechless. Of course I wanted to go, but I also didn't want to let down our new friends, especially when everyone had made such a big deal about our cupcakes. I mean, our team was basically named after our cupcakes! So I ended up kind of lying and telling Mia I was really tired and couldn't go, but that I could do it Friday after we baked. But Mia said we really wouldn't have time to do both. She was kind of bummed and a little annoyed when she hung up. I'd never turned down a plan before.

I wanted to dial Alexis to warn her, but I knew I'd get busted, what with Mia calling at the same time. (I could just picture Alexis: "Oh, hang on, Mia, I have Emma calling on the other line." Yikes!) So I sat by the phone and waited for it to ring, which I knew it would.

"Hi," I said, drumming my fingers on the kitchen counter. I could see from the caller ID that it was Alexis.

"Whoops," she said.

"I know. Major whoops. What did you say?"

"I said we had relays today and I was tired, but I could do it tomorrow."

"Me too! I said basically the same thing!" I love Alexis. She and I have just always been on the same page, ever since we were little.

"Phew," she said. "But I think she was mad."

My heart sank, remembering. "I know."

We were quiet. Finally I said, "Oh well, when are you coming over?"

Alexis said she'd be over soon, so I hung up to await her arrival, and began making bacon for my trademark bacon cupcakes with salted caramel ribbons. It sounds gross, but they're one of our bestsellers. I always make extra for Matt and Sam, because they love them.

I busied myself in the kitchen until, at last, Alexis came in. She took one look at me and flung herself dramatically across the kitchen table.

"What?" I asked. My heart was thumping. Had the others found out?

"They know," she whispered.

"Whaaaaat? How?"

"I confessed," she whispered again. It was almost like she didn't want me to hear her.

I sat down heavily in a chair. "Why? How? When?"

"I called Mia back and said we wanted to bring in cupcakes to camp tomorrow—I didn't say who asked us—and that maybe if they wanted to come to your house tonight, we could all bake them together." She cringed.

"So does Mia know we weren't telling the truth before?"

Alexis nodded.

I put my head in my hands. "We shouldn't have lied."

"I know." Alexis sighed. "Honesty is always the best policy. Especially when it comes to friends. But they are coming. We decided we'd bake the samples and the usual batches for Mona tonight and go to the movies tomorrow instead." She grinned at me.

"Alexis! You tricked me! So they aren't mad?"

Alexis shrugged. "A little, but I think they understand. I offered to let them take some cupcakes with them for tomorrow, too."

Katie was taking an intensive cooking class at the Y (it was actually for older teens but they made an exception for her because of her skill and passion and, I think, the Cupcake Club). Mia was working as an intern for her mom, who was a fashion stylist on photo shoots. Very glamorous. She'd go to sleep-away camp later in the summer.

"Wow, you are some negotiator," I said.

Alexis beamed and did a fake Sydney-esque hair flip.

"I'm not thrilled about delivering two-day-old cupcakes to our best client, though," I said.

"I know, but every once in a while we can make an exception," said Alexis.

"I guess. But let's pinkie promise not to do it again for a really long time, okay?"

Alexis stuck out her pinkie and hooked it with mine, and we shook our hands from side to side. "Okay."

It was a little awkward when Mia and Katie came, but I apologized and explained, telling them why I'd felt nervous to admit our plan. They were mad at first and told me so, but we made up and then it was fine. One of the great things about old friends is they can forgive and forget. Little incidents become tiny in the scheme of longer friendships.

We made new samples for Mona, baked up her minis, and made the frosting, putting each into separate Tupperware containers to keep them fresh. I'd assemble them Saturday morning before I dropped them off. Mia teased me and said it was my punishment for lying.

The cinnamon bun cupcakes turned out delicious, and I knew Mona would love them. I couldn't wait for her to try them.

I was up early Saturday morning, putting the finishing touches on Mona's delivery, even though I was a little tired. The movie the night before had been awesome, and we'd run into a couple of girls from camp. It was actually fun introducing Mia and Katie to Charlotte and Georgia and watching them chat, like two different worlds mixing! Mia and Katie were really pleased when the Hotcakes girls made a big deal about the Cupcake Club and admired how the Cupcakers were such best friends and moguls-in-training. I think then that Mia and

Katie realized Alexis and I will always love them best, even if we have new friends at camp. I would always choose my old friends over my new ones. No matter what.

After Mona's cupcakes were ready, my dad gave me a ride to The Special Day on his way to drop Matt at soccer practice. He was going to round-trip it and then wait for me downstairs. I was looking forward to my trip to Mona's and to some time alone in that all-white plush palace of hers, even if it was for just a half hour.

I was surprised to see that all the assistants were already there. Usually, the few times I'd gone with Alexis to make the delivery (like, if I'd slept over at her house the night before), it was really quiet. The store stayed open late Friday nights to accommodate people with busy work schedules, and Mona didn't open to the public until ten on Saturday mornings.

But today, the store was buzzing, even though it was only nine o'clock. Patricia, Mona's number-one assistant and store manager, came whizzing over to greet me. It was weird. She seemed like she was kind of in a rush to get me out of there. She looked outside the door to make sure no one was behind me, then she locked the door after me. It was like she was nervous other people might be trying to come in.

I said, "Hi, Patricia! I have our delivery, and we also—"

Patricia, who was normally supersweet and patient, interrupted me. "Thanks, Emma. Okay, then, we're all set. Let me just get your money. Wait right here. . . ." She took the carriers from me and headed to the back of the store. Usually we carry them back to the counter, and they pay us out of the register. I stood there in confusion.

"Do you need help?" I called lamely after her.

"Got it!" she kind of whispered back at me.

What on Earth was up?

Just then Mona stepped out of the largest and fanciest of all the salon rooms (called the Bridal Suite) and pulled the door tightly closed behind her. Was there a client in there already? Mona was really dressed up, even for her, and she looked even busier than usual. She strode over to a rack to select something, and then she spied me.

"Emma!" she cried, putting her hand to her chest, like I'd given her a fright.

"Hi," I said, smiling awkwardly.

"Is Patricia helping you?" she asked urgently.

"All under control," Patricia trilled nervously.

"Um, Mona, we brought some new kinds of cupcakes for you today, on the house. We were just thinking you might be tired of the usual order, okay? So just let us know . . ."

Patricia came bustling back to me with the cash. "Okay, then, we're all set. Thanks so much." She took my arm and steered me to the door.

"Patricia, is everything okay?" I suddenly got nervous that maybe they were being held up at gunpoint or something. I'd seen that on a TV show one time, where the robbers made the store employees carry on as usual, even while they were holding one of them hostage in the back of the store. "Are you being robbed or something? Should I call 911?" I asked under my breath.

Patricia stopped in her tracks and took a good look at me, then she collapsed in laughter, her hands on her knees. Mona rushed over.

"What is it, Patricia?" she asked.

Patricia was trying to catch her breath. "Oh my," she said, wiping her eyes with a tissue from one of the many boxes in the store (brides' families always cry when they see the brides in their dresses for the first time). "Just an attack of nerves," she said, still mopping. "Emma, you are too much. No, we are not being robbed. We are fine." She glanced at

309

Mona, seeming to ask a question with her eyes.

Mona stepped in and spoke in a low voice. "We have a very exciting, very private client here this morning. We opened early for her, so she could have the place to herself. It's just a little nerve-racking, but very good. Thank you for your concern, sweetheart." She turned to Patricia. "Isn't this one just divine?" she asked.

"Divine," agreed Patricia.

Just then the door to the Bridal Suite opened, and out walked the biggest surprise of my life.

"Oh my goodness!" I gasped.

CHAPTER 5

Me, Model?

Our town has only ever produced one major celebrity, as far as I know, and it made a doozy. It's like the town saved up its potential star power, and instead of launching a handful of B- or C-list one-hit wonders and soap stars, it stockpiled all its fairy dust for one lucky young lady: a gorgeous, blond Academy Award–, Golden Globe–, *and* Emmy-winning actress named Romaine Ford.

Every girl in America wanted to be her and every guy wanted to date her. Every father wanted his son to marry her, and every mom approved. She was twenty-nine years old, wholesome, smart, beautiful, talented, and reportedly very nice. She did charity work all over the world, recorded hit songs with famous costars, and was a Rhodes Scholar—

whatever that is. I'd only seen Romaine Ford once in real life, when she came to town to be the grand marshal for a parade a few years back. I knew, of course, like the rest of America, that she was now engaged to the devastatingly handsome heartthrob, actor Liam Carey, and that she planned a wedding in a top-secret location for late this summer. She was just about the last person I ever expected to see here this morning.

"Hi!" she said, friendly but a little reserved. She was wearing one of the white velour robes The Special Day gives you to put on in between dresses, and white fluffy slippers.

I was speechless. I think my jaw was actually hanging open.

"Yes, Ms. Ford, what can we do for you?" said Mona, hustling over to her side.

"I just had one thing I forgot to tell you. Um, my niece, who is also my goddaughter, is going to be a junior bridesmaid for me. I'm supposed to find a dress for her, and I wonder if you could help with that, too."

"Of course, we will bring in a selection immediately. Patricia!" Mona all but snapped her fingers at Patricia, who was standing, like me, frozen, like a deer in the headlights. Patricia came alive and started across the store to where the bridesmaids' dresses were.

Romaine was still standing there, actually kind of looking at me. She was so beautiful, I couldn't help staring. Her hair was long and thick and yellow-blond (natural, supposedly), and her eyes were wide and blue. She had a huge, almost goofy smile, and big white teeth, with a big dimple in her left cheek and freckles on her nose. She was tall and thin, in great shape, of course (she climbed Mt. Kilimanjaro last year to get ready for a part, and she did orphan relief work while she was there. Thank you, *People* magazine!), and very graceful.

Mona spoke to Patricia again. "Patricia! Emma!" She gestured at me.

Patricia smacked her forehead hard. "Right. Sorry." She doubled back to let me out of the store first. She went to unlock the door, but Romaine interrupted the silence with one word.

"Wait!" she said.

We all turned to stare at her.

"Sorry, but . . . that girl looks a lot like my niece. And I was wondering, maybe, would it be possible for her . . . I mean, do you have the time, sweetie? Would you be able to try on a dress, so I could see what it actually looks like on a girl?"

Would I? I looked at Patricia, who looked at Mona. Mona seemed to weigh the options, then found herself in favor of the idea. "Certainly. Emma, come."

"Do you have time?" asked Romaine as I started across the expanse of white carpet toward her.

I didn't trust myself to speak, so I nodded, wide-eyed, as if I was in a trance. As if I wouldn't have time for *anything* Romaine Ford asked me to do!

"Oh good!" she said, sighing. "Being a bride is a lot of work. I wouldn't want to fall down on the job and not get the junior bridesmaid's dress right!"

I couldn't imagine Romaine Ford not doing everything perfectly. I also had a hard time picturing any girl not being so happy to be in her wedding that she just wore whatever Romaine told her to. Like a trained puppy, I followed Patricia to the rack, where she selected a few dresses and wordlessly held them up against me to see if they'd fit. Finding four, she led me to a dressing room and gestured that I should go in.

"Call out when you have one on, and I'll come pin it if need be."

I looked at myself in the mirror in the dressing room. Was I dreaming? Had I imagined all this? Was I really going to model dresses for

Romaine Ford because she thought I looked like her niece?

I pinched myself—actually pinched myself—to make sure I wasn't dreaming, then I put on the first dress, quickly but carefully. I know from being a bridesmaid before that these dresses are very fragile and very expensive, but I knew I had to be fast, for Mona's and Patricia's sakes.

"Ready!" I called. Patricia flew into the room and started pinning wildly.

"There!" she declared, taking a long appraising look at me in the mirror. "Let's put up your hair. It will look much neater." Then finally she said, "Okay. Ready."

Patricia led me out into the salon and then knocked on the door of the Bridal Suite.

"Come in!" Mona trilled, and we entered.

Huge fluffy wedding dresses hung from every available rod and pole, and others were draped over the white sofas and chairs. Mona's fanciest silver tea service was laid out on the white lacquer coffee table. There were four women gathered around the table, sipping from fancy china teacups.

"Oh my! You really *do* look like Riley!" said an older blond woman who must've been Romaine's mother.

"I told you!" said Romaine proudly. I smiled shyly.

"Ladies, this is Emma Taylor, our cupcake baker and former client. She has a few dresses to show you, so let's see what you think. This first one is a hand-crocheted lace from Belgium. It truly is one-of-a-kind and, as such, one of our most expensive junior bridesmaids' dresses at eighteen hundred dollars."

Eighteen hundred dollars! I nearly fainted! My bridesmaid dress for Mia's mom's wedding had cost $250, and I thought that was a lot! But Romaine and her group seemed unfazed by the crazy price. I remembered Romaine had earned ten million dollars for her last movie, a big drama where she played a famous queen from the sixteen hundreds. Talk about earning power! *Alexis, eat your heart out,* I thought.

"Very pretty," said Romaine's mother.

Another lady (her grandmother? Her agent?), who was older than the woman who spoke earlier, said, "Yes, and you look lovely in it, dear."

Romaine was looking at me with her head tilted to the side, considering. "Yes, you look fab, and the dress is so pretty. I wonder . . . Would you think I was rude if I asked to see you with your hair down, like it was before? I'm sorry. I just think with the hair up, it's more of a mature look. . . ."

I nodded and looked to Patricia for help. She took right over. "Absolutely. Of course. So right. A natural look is always much better for this age," she said, and she hurriedly undid her previous work and fluffed out my loose hair with her fingers.

"Ahh! So pretty!" said a girl Romaine's age. I think it could have been her sister. According to *Us Weekly* magazine, she has three sisters and a brother.

As the minutes wore on, I thought I'd explode if I had to wait any longer to tell my friends about this. I kept my composure, though, turning this way and that as they admired the dress. A few minutes later they were ready to see the next dress, and I returned to my fitting room to change.

Patricia undid the back of the dress for me and tactfully left the room. I wouldn't be able to do this if I had to change in front of everyone, but as long as I could do it privately, it was okay. I called Patricia back in to help with the buttons, and we did the modeling all over again.

Between dresses number two and three, I rushed to the phone to call my dad to tell him I'd be late. I didn't tell him why. It wasn't that I thought he'd call the paparazzi or anything, but I wanted the experience to be complete before I started blabbing. Maybe it wouldn't end well, or maybe it would. Who knew? It was still just a private event, though.

My dad was fine with a later pickup, and in the meantime, Patricia stood behind the counter and organized the cupcakes on a beautiful silver serving tray to take in to the ladies.

"Remember," I said, "some are different. We included cinnamon bun cupcakes with cream-cheese frosting. Mona hasn't approved them yet."

"Oh, I noticed that some of these looked different than usual," said Patricia. "Well, let's give them a whirl. Maybe they'll be a huge box-office hit!" She popped one into her mouth, and chewed. "Oh, Emma! These are just . . ."

"Divine?" I offered.

We laughed, and she delivered the cupcakes while I changed dresses again.

In dress number three, I took a hard look at myself. This was not such a pretty dress. Even I could see that it was too grown-up for me. The dress was made from a slinky material, with a low-cut front and a slit up the leg. I wasn't comfortable in it at all.

Patricia returned. "Hmm," she said. "It's not right for you. But you know how people dress in Hollywood. I think we should show it, anyway."

She pinned it into place and then led me back into the room.

"NO!" said Romaine as soon as I walked in.

I was taken aback, and it must've shown on my face because she hurried to apologize.

"Oh my gosh, I'm so sorry, sweetie! I scared you!" She jumped up and came over to pat my arm sympathetically. "I just have really strong reactions to young girls dressed inappropriately. I just hate it. I was reacting to the dress, not to you. You poor thing! I forgot for a moment that you're not a professional model! Are you okay? Did I scare you to death?"

I composed myself and laughed a little, but she *had* shaken me. It must be hard for models and actresses to remember that their audiences aren't reacting to them personally, but rather to the outfits or the performances. It would take me a while to get used to that.

In the meantime, Patricia passed around the platter of cupcakes. Romaine scooped one up (from my kitchen to Romaine Ford's mouth! The Cupcakers—not to mention my brothers—would die, just die, when I told them!) and popped it into her mouth.

"Oh my gosh! What are in these cinnamon ones? I love them! They're so insanely delicious!"

Mona looked very pleased. "Emma made them, as I said earlier. She and her friends started their own business baking cupcakes."

"You do?" said Romaine. "That's so entrepreneurial! I was like that at your age." Alexis would love to hear that!

Back in the fitting room, I changed into dress number four. It wasn't much of a hit either. It was kind of *Little House on the Prairie* style, with long sleeves and a smocked front. Kind of country. Romaine didn't like it.

Mona was all business. "We have a trunk show scheduled for next Saturday, with all sorts of new dresses and accessories coming in this week for it. They are absolutely gorgeous and all brand-new, never-before-seen designs. We could arrange for you to come in at the same time and have a private showing, if you're available?"

Romaine's group all consulted their Black-Berrys and iPhones, and agreed. Mona turned to me. "Emma? We'd love for you to return, if you're free?"

I nodded happily. "Sure. No problem. I can come. I'll bring the cupcakes, too."

"Yum! Thanks!" said Romaine. She came and gave me a hug good-bye, careful not to squash the dress. "See you next week," she said. "Thanks for all of your help! You were a doll!"

On my way out, Mona asked me not to mention next weekend's plan to anyone. She said it was fine to say what happened today, but they wouldn't want any gawkers hanging around next weekend if word got out. I felt really privileged to be in on the plan, so I promised I wouldn't tell.

I couldn't believe the morning I'd had.

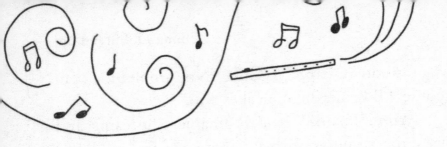

CHAPTER 6

Now *I'm* a Celebrity!

(O)kay, so start again from the beginning, when you first saw her open the door. How did you know it was her?" Katie asked.

Mia, Katie, and Alexis could not get enough of the story.

"No, tell about when she said she was entrepreneurial like us when she was a kid!" begged Alexis.

I had told the story three times already today, and I knew I'd tell it again to a very receptive audience at camp on Monday. I almost wanted to stop now, to keep it fresh for the Hotcakes girls. I just laughed.

"It was amazing," I said, shaking my head. It was like a dream.

"I can't believe you didn't get her autograph!" said Mia morosely.

"I can't believe Mona didn't pay you!" said Alexis.

"Oh my gosh, I probably would have paid her!" I laughed.

"You are so lucky," Katie said with a sigh.

"Do you think you'll ever see her again?" Alexis asked.

"I hope so," I said. I was dying inside since I couldn't tell them about the plan for next weekend.

"If they call you back, maybe we could all go?" asked Katie.

I laughed again. "Let's cross that bridge if we come to it."

"*When* we come to it," said Alexis. "Confidence sells!"

Monday morning at camp was almost more fun than Saturday morning at The Special Day. All the Hotcakes were riveted as I told the story of Romaine Ford. Even Maryanne and Raoul. Raoul kept asking if she was as pretty in person. And Kira was so excited, it was crazy.

"Oh my gosh, she has been my idol ever since I can remember. You are so lucky, Emma. You know, she lived on my block when she was in elementary school. I've always felt like she was my soul sister or something. She's been my role model and my inspiration! She's just an amazing and generous person, and the fact that she is from here, that she went to the same schools as me! I just worship her."

No one noticed Sydney Whitman until it was too late. "What are you Hotcakes yapping about?" Sydney managed to sneer whenever she said the word "Hotcakes."

"Just that Emma modeled for Romaine Ford this weekend," Alexis said.

Sydney's head whipped around. "No way! You? Modeling? That can't be true!"

I nodded, never happier in my life than while seeing this bomb being dropped on Sydney, despite her disbelief that I could ever model.

"Wait, *the* Romaine Ford?" Sydney was still incredulous.

"Uh-huh!"

"Oh, wow! I can't believe it! I'm going to *be* her in the talent show! I'm singing 'Sweet Summer Love,' that duet she had with the country singer, old what's-his-name, you know! I'm singing that!"

"Wow," I said. "Small world." Leave it to Sydney to make it all about her.

"Everyone says I look a lot like her, you know.

324

Everyone says I'll grow up to be just like her." Sydney posed while we all stared at her like she was an alien.

"Really," said Alexis finally, more like a statement than a question.

"Yes!" said Sydney. "Really!"

"Well, good luck with that!" I said cheerfully. I wasn't going to let Sydney "Horrible" Whitman ruin my day by taking over my story and making it about her.

Maryanne came over to tell us it was time for softball, so we ditched Sydney to follow her to the field.

"Listen, what is everyone doing for the talent show?" asked Maryanne as we walked.

"I'm using a Hula-Hoop!" said Elle. She was such a cutup. We all laughed. "No, really! I'm serious. I'm great at it! It's my little-known talent!"

"That will be great!" said Raoul enthusiastically. "I can help you with music and choreography if you like." He was a big dancer. The two of them started scheming and laughing.

Charlotte and Georgia were going to do a gymnastics routine, and Caroline was going to sing. She was in her church choir and, according to Elle, was so good that she regularly sang solos. A few other girls, like Tricia and Louise, told us their plans, and then Maryanne looked at me and Alexis.

"How about you two?" she asked. "What about a bake-off?" Our cupcakes had been a huge hit on Friday. I think she was just angling for more to sample.

"We'll definitely bring some cupcakes, but as for the show, I'm not a talent myself. But I am happy to be a talent manager," said Alexis affirmatively.

"I don't have a talent. Anyway, I'd die of embarrassment up there," I said.

"How about the flute?" Alexis suggested. She turned to Maryanne and the others. "Emma's really great at the flute. She plays in the school orchestra. You should do that, Emma."

"I'm not that good. And, anyway, I don't play alone. It's one thing to be part of a big group when you're onstage, but *alone*? No way."

Alexis turned to Maryanne. "I can see I've found my first client. Don't worry. I'll get her to do something."

It was not going to happen, but I didn't want to embarrass Alexis by not letting her at least pretend she could convince me.

"Just remember," said Maryanne, "there are three qualities they're looking for in the talent show: *Talent*, like how good you are at the thing you're doing. *Presentation*, like, are you confident, is your act polished, and did you think through your moves and your program? And finally, *charm*. This is how appealing the crowd finds you. Do you have that certain charisma audiences love? Each performer is rated in each of the categories on a scale of one to ten. Whoever has the most points wins overall, but there's also a winner in each of the three categories."

Alexis leaned back and whispered, "We're going overall, baby. Shoot for the moon."

She was already talking like a Hollywood agent. I laughed and hit her playfully. "Get real!" I said.

"Oh, I'm real, my friend. I am really real."

The bus ride home was one of the more annoying rides of my life. For starters, Alexis would not back off from the idea that I was going to play the flute in the talent show, and she decided that on this bus ride, she would convince me she was right. In the course of one mile, she moved from asking to demanding I do it, and she was only half joking.

To make matters worse, Sydney asked if I'd brought any baby wipes to sanitize things after Jake threw up. Jake yelled, "I'm not a baby!" and then started to cry, so that was fun. *Not.*

Alexis decided to cheer up Jake by asking him what kind of cupcakes he wanted for his birthday. But he couldn't make up his mind. First he said, "Vanilla, with vanilla icing. That's what my friends and I like."

But, annoyingly, Alexis couldn't leave it at that. She said, "Oh, come on, Jakey, make it a little harder for us. Don't you want a fun topping? Or a cool design? What's your favorite, favorite thing on Earth to eat?"

So Jake moved from one flavor to the next: chocolate, banana, s'mores, cinnamon bun, and caramel. They discussed Oreo topping, marshmallow frosting, SpongeBob colors, police badge designs, and on and on. By the end of the ride, Jake was more confused than when we started. As she stood up to leave the bus, Alexis promised, "Jake, these will be the yummiest, best-looking, coolest Jake Cakes anyone has ever seen. I personally guarantee it," and I wanted to scream at her for setting his expectations so high.

And then, walking backward down the aisle, she called out, "An announcement, everybody: Emma Taylor is playing the flute in the talent show. Emma, practice your piece tonight! Bye!" Then she ran off before I could actually kill her.

All the kids on the bus turned to look at me, and I had to kind of smile and nod and acknowledge what she said. I wanted to die with all those eyes on me.

There was no way I'd play in that talent show!

CHAPTER 7

Shoved into the Spotlight

The weekend couldn't come soon enough! All week I felt butterflies in my stomach every time I pictured going back to The Special Day, but I couldn't tell if they were happy butterflies or nervous butterflies. It was like I dreaded and looked forward to it the same amount. On Friday night at our cupcake meeting/baking session, I couldn't stop thinking that we were baking for Romaine Ford!

We finished the cinnamon bun minis for Mona, and the extra vanilla/vanilla minis. Then it was time to bake samples for Jake.

"I had a great idea for Jake's cupcakes, so I went ahead and brought the supplies," said Mia, pulling a plastic grocery bag out of her tote. "Are you ready?

Dirt with worms!" She held up a package of Oreo cookies and a bag of gummy worm candies.

I groaned. "Gross!"

"He'll love it!" said Katie, clapping.

We had some extra batter from Mona's minis, so we baked up a few full-size cupcakes, and Mia set about crushing the cookies.

Alexis said slyly, "We have a talent show at the end of our camp session, and Emma is going to play her flute!"

I rolled my eyes. "I am not."

"Oh, Emma! You should! You're so good!" said Katie.

"Why wouldn't you?" asked Mia.

I started ticking off reasons on my fingers. "Well, for one thing, I'm not that good. For another, I have nothing to wear. Third, I hate getting up in front of people, and I also hate having people look at me. And fifth, I don't have any 'charm,' which is another thing they score you on, so all in all, I'm not doing it."

My three friends stared at me. Then Mia said, "Wow! You've got it all figured out, I guess. But why are you so down on yourself?"

"I'm not down on myself. I just know what I'm good at and what I'm not good at."

"Well, couldn't you practice a piece? Isn't there anything you know well enough?" Katie asked.

"That's not the point!" I said. I crossed my arms to show I was annoyed. I felt like they were ganging up on me.

"The other reasons are just silly," said Mia. "You could wear the bridesmaid dress from my mom's wedding. That looked amazing on you, and then it wouldn't be just hanging in your closet until you outgrow it."

Annoyingly, she was right. I wished she hadn't solved that problem so easily.

"And you obviously don't hate getting up in front of people that much, since you did it for Romaine Ford last week, for goodness sake!"

"That's different," I said, blushing.

"Why? Wouldn't you think a professional per-former is a tougher critic than a bunch of parents who think you're adorable and little brothers who are just waiting for the show to be over so they can eat some cupcakes?" said Mia, laughing now.

I hadn't thought of that either. "But what about charm? I don't have any charm!" I insisted.

Alexis interrupted. "That is something I can take care of for you. That shouldn't worry you one bit. Anyway, it's not like you'd be trying to win *all three* categories. No one does."

I thought you said we were to "shoot for the moon," I wanted to remind Alexis, even though I didn't want to encourage her. Instead, I huffed and looked away from my friends. They were making it really hard to keep refusing. And now that they'd sort of solved all my qualms, a tiny part of me was starting to problem solve the rest, and think about how I could do it. But . . .

"How can I compete against Sydney Whitman? I know she's going to win, anyway, so why bother?"

Mia pressed her lips into a thin line of disapproval. "That is just a bad attitude right there. You're way more charming than she is, for one thing. Anyway, what is she doing?"

"Singing that Romaine Ford country song," I mumbled.

Katie burst out laughing. "Have you ever heard Sydney *sing*? Wake up, people! I am here to tell you that she was in my music class last year, and the girl cannot sing a note! It was like listening to a dying hyena!" Katie started howling tunelessly, and we all began to roar with laughter.

We finished our samples for Jake, packed up Mona's minis, and cleaned up. By then it was time for the others to go home.

Mia gave me a hug good-bye and said, "You've got to do the talent show, Emma. Even if it's just to beat out Syd the Hyena. Do it for us. Do it for the Cupcake Club!"

"And don't forget to let us know what Jake thinks of the dirty cupcakes!" added Katie.

I laughed and shut the door.

Upstairs, I looked for something to distract me from the butterflies that had returned, and I spied my flute, lying in its case on my desk. I sighed, then crossed the room, picked it up, and set it up to play. I have to admit that as I played, a whole hour passed before I even realized it. I really do love playing the flute. Just not in front of a crowd.

The next morning, I was up at the crack of dawn to shower and blow-dry my hair. Mona had e-mailed to confirm the timing (I had to be there at eight thirty, cupcakes and all), and she reminded me to appear "natural," meaning no makeup, no fancy hairstyles or anything. It was hard to resist the temptation to tinker, but I managed.

Down in the kitchen, I discovered Jake eating worm cupcakes for breakfast. He loved them so much, he tried to hug me, but I dodged him— chocolate crumbs and all.

My mom dropped me off, leaving my dad in charge of the boys. She asked me if I wanted her to wait outside and read a magazine, but I knew I couldn't let Mona down by spilling the beans (not that my mom would call the paparazzi, but still). I told her I had some work to do with Mona, to choose the flavors for the next month, and that she should come back later.

When I reached the store, the door was locked, so I rang the bell. I could see all the attendants bustling around inside. Patricia was putting big vases of white roses on every available surface. The two other ladies were dusting tables and fluffing sofa cushions. Mona heard the bell and made a beeline for me at the door.

"Darling! You look divine! It's so good to see you and your tiny cupcakes! Come in, come in!" She shooed me inside and locked the store's door tightly behind me, just as Patricia had done last week.

I brought the cupcakes to the counter, and she paid me and then led me to an even larger changing room than before.

"Now, a few things before we begin," she said. "First of all, I have this for you." She handed me a full-length nude-colored slip.

335

"Put this on to wear for the whole time. It will give you a clean line under the dresses and make the fabric move right, and it will protect your modesty. This way Patricia can be in the room arranging the next dress as you take one off."

That was a good idea. I wondered how she knew I hated to change in front of other people?

"Everyone hates to change in front of other people, darling," said Mona, reading my mind.

"Next, some tips. Stand up straight, straight, straight. No slouching. Let's see . . . Hmm . . ." She pulled my shoulders back and tipped my chin up into a kind of awkward pose. "I know it feels strange at first, but it looks wonderful. See? Divine!"

I looked in the mirror and saw that she was right. The pose made my neck look longer and kind of elegant.

"Now don't forget to smile, darling. Smile so your eyes sparkle. Let's see it."

I smiled, but she didn't approve.

"No, that's more like a grimace. Think of a princess or a movie star, how their eyes kind of light up. Lift your eyebrows a little. Be happy! Try again. Yes. Better." She turned my face to look in the mirror. Then she did different smiles next to me while I practiced.

336

"Good. Better. Yes, much better. Now, most important of all, don't forget to breathe. Just take deep breaths and think your happiest thoughts. Think about cupcakes and your divine friends and all the fun you'll have this summer. All right?"

I nodded and mentally reviewed her list of directions: stand up straight, shoulders back, chin up, smile with sparkly eyes, breathe, and think happy thoughts. Okay!

I heard the doorbell ring, and Patricia trilled, "They're here!"

Mona and I looked at each other with excitement. "Good luck, darling. You'll be smashing!" And off she ran.

Smashing. Divine. Oh my gosh! Here we go!

CHAPTER 8

Hard Work and a Good Deed

*D*id I mention that modeling is really hard work? You have to do all those things Mona said, plus you're wearing a dress that might be itchy or heavy or too big or too small or loaded with pins that could stab you anytime. You have to get used to people saying they think what you're wearing is ugly or too expensive, that you should take it off immediately. Also you can get hot and hungry and even bored, no matter if your audience is a major star who is beautiful, nice, and interesting.

But I still had a blast!

Romaine was even nicer this time, if that is possible to believe. First of all, she remembered my name. She said, "Hi, Emma!" when I walked in, and jumped up to give me a double kiss, like they do in Europe. Then she ate a bunch of my cupcakes and complimented me on them, even pretending to faint when she took a bite.

Patricia helped me in the dressing room the whole time, and we got to chat about everything. I told her all about the talent show and how the Cupcakers want me to do it and that they told me to wear my bridesmaid dress. She thought I should totally go for it, and was surprised when I said I didn't have the guts.

"But you're so poised doing this! Why wouldn't you just treat it the same way? It's like work. You just go out, you do your little routine, you turn around, and you leave the stage. That's it! It's great practice for real life, because when you're an adult, you do end up having to get up in front of people and perform, for all different occasions and reasons."

I thought about it while I twirled around the Bridal Suite in a tulle-skirted dress that made me look like a ballerina. Romaine tried to get me to do ballet poses, and we started joking around. It was really fun. She'd make a good teacher.

Mona hustled me back to change, though, whispering we were running out of time to keep the store closed to the public. I loved all the dresses I had tried on, so the time had flown. I was sad when I put on the final dress, and I think Patricia could tell.

"It was fun, right, honey? Kind of like being a princess for a day? That's how brides feel when they come in too." She gave me a little pat on the back and sent me into the Bridal Suite for the final time.

Romaine walked over to me to inspect the dress. Meanwhile, in the background, her mom and her aunt were talking. My ears perked up at the word "cupcake."

"Kathy, are you thinking what I'm thinking about these cupcakes?" asked Romaine's aunt.

"Yes, I think I am. They are *so* delicious!" said Romaine's mom.

Turning to me, Romaine's aunt said, "Could we hire your cupcake club to bake some cupcakes for our bridal shower? I'm Romaine's aunt, Maureen Shipley, and I'm the hostess for the event. These would be lovely for the dessert."

Oh my gosh! Could this day get any better? Somehow I found my voice.

"Absolutely. Showers are our specialty! I'll give you my card when I go back to the fitting room," I promised. I silently thanked Alexis for insisting we each have our own business cards made.

340

In the fitting room, I carefully changed back into my now pathetic-looking everyday clothes. I grabbed a business card from my bag and went to say good-bye.

Romaine saw me in the doorway and jumped up. "Oh, Emma, honey, you were the best! Thank you so much for your hard work today and last week. It was such a treat to have you here, and you are just gorgeous. Adorable. Right, Mom?"

Romaine's aunt said, "Honey, let's get a photo, so we can all remember the fun we've had together." She pulled out her camera and had Patricia snap a few shots, including one of just me and Romaine together. Then she double-checked she had my e-mail address and promised to send me the photos.

I was sad to leave—I don't think any of us wanted it to be over—but I knew Mona was eager to open the store, so I said my good-byes and headed out of the Bridal Suite. Before I reached the front of the store, Mona caught up with me. She slipped a white business envelope into my hand.

"Emma, a little something for all your hard work."

"Oh no, Mona, I couldn't. Thank you. It was so much fun and such an incredible experience."

"I insist! From one businesswoman to another.

341

Please take it. Fun or not, it was hard work, and you were divine! Just divine!"

It's hard to argue against a force of nature like Mona, so I laughed and thanked her for the opportunity to model.

Outside, who should I run into walking by but Kira and her oldest sister!

"Hi, Kira!" I said, still flying high after my fun morning.

"Hi, Emma! Oh, Leslie, this is my friend Emma who I was telling you about, who got to meet Romaine Ford! Emma, this is my sister Leslie. She's taking me to get a new bathing suit. What are you doing here?"

I felt funny telling them what I'd been doing. But as it turned out, I didn't need to. Because who should come strolling out of The Special Day but Romaine and her group.

"Oh, look who's still here! Bye, honey!" said Romaine's mom.

I waved, smiling.

"Bye, Emma! Thanks again!" called Romaine with a smile.

"Oh my gosh!" said Kira, her jaw dropping open. "That's her! And she knows your name! Oh my gosh! I think I'm hyperventilating! Oh my gosh!"

She started fanning herself, and tears welled up in her eyes. "I can't believe it's really her."

Romaine and her mom, aunt, and sister were all standing outside The Special Day, as if deciding where they should head to next. Impulsively, I grabbed Kira's arm and quickly dragged her over to Romaine's side.

"Romaine, I'm sorry to interrupt," I said. "But this is my friend Kira. She thinks you are so great, and I wanted you to meet her." I kind of shoved Kira toward Romaine. Kira was in shock, her mouth still wide open and speechless.

Romaine was very friendly. "Hi, Kira! It's nice to meet you! Any friend of Emma's is a friend of mine! Are you in the same class at school?" she asked politely.

Kira couldn't talk. She just shook her head no and continued to stare, wide-eyed at Romaine.

Romaine looked at me and giggled, then looked back to Kira. "How do you two know each other?" she asked.

"Oh, camp. We go to day camp together," I said, since it was clear that Kira wouldn't be able to answer. "Right, Kira?" I prompted.

Kira closed her mouth, and gulped. "Uh-huh. Camp."

"What camp is it?" asked Romaine.

"Spring Lake Day Camp," I said. Kira nodded.

"Oh my gosh! I went there in sixth grade!" cried Romaine. "Mom! Emma and her friend go to Spring Lake Day Camp!"

Romaine's mom smiled. "Oh, what fun! You loved that place!" she said.

"I really did. Well, have a great time there. I have to get going now, but it was nice to meet you, Kira, and thanks again, Emma!" She gave me another hug and then walked away. Kira was still rooted to the spot, speechless.

Leslie came up and showed us a photo she'd snapped on her iPhone of Kira and Romaine chatting.

"Oh wow!" said Kira, coming back to life, as if she'd been in a trance. "I can't believe it! I just met Romaine Ford! Oh, Emma!" She wheeled around to face me. "You're the best. I feel like I dreamed the whole thing."

Leslie was laughing at her now. "Come on, dreamy. Let's go find you a swimsuit. Bye, Emma!"

"Okay, bye! Nice to meet you, Leslie!'

They called their good-byes and strolled off, Kira staring intently at Leslie's iPhone.

I was so glad I'd done what I did. It wasn't the

smoothest thing in the world, but it had obviously meant a lot to Kira, who in general needed a boost. I was just happy to have provided it.

I texted my mom for a ride and sat down to wait. What a great summer this was turning out to be!

CHAPTER 9

Hotcakes and Cupcakes

Camp was out-of-control fun. For starters, because it was separated into boys' and girls' campuses, there wasn't a lot of worrying what boys would think or even, for me, dealing with boys' gross-out behaviors like I did at home. It was a complete break from burping and stinky socks and football. I was in all-girl heaven!

We sang all the time, whatever we were doing. Show tunes, Top 40 songs, camp songs—anything. We braided one another's hair during free time, and one day Georgia brought in a manicure set and gave us all wild, decorative manicures, with tiny flower and star decals and stuff. We also made friendship bracelets like maniacs, taping the embroidery thread to any available surface and twisting, braiding, and tying it into rainbows to wear or give away. We had Tie-Dye Day, when we brought in anything from home that we wanted to tie-dye and made incredible designs with bright colors, like a kaleidoscope. (I brought white drawstring pj pants, plus, the camp gave us each a white cotton T-shirt.)

We had also started to seriously train for the Camp Olympics. There would be events in archery, swimming, diving, track and field, canoeing, not to mention soccer and softball games, four square, tetherball, and relay races (some of them funny, like potato-sack and egg-on-a-spoon races). Not everyone had to participate in every event; you just needed enough people from your team to do it. So Maryanne and Raoul were working on how to divide up everyone and play to their strengths.

Every morning we'd gather at our rally zone and chat about what had happened in the fifteen or so hours since we'd last been together (covering TV shows, celebrity gossip, family news—anything, really). Kira was always there first, her wet hair pulled back into a neat ponytail. Leslie dropped her off way early on her way to work. Alexis was a pretty early arrival too, and Georgia and Charlotte, so they'd all be up to speed by the time I arrived with the the rest of the bus crew.

I was not wild about canoeing or softball, so I didn't plan to participate in those events, but Maryanne and Raoul felt they would have a pretty good team for softball even without me. I volunteered to be the water girl for that game. I was psyched for the running events, because I am fast, and I was feeling really good about the swimming and diving, which I knew I'd ace (not that I'd ever say it out loud). The only bummer was that the swim events required six-person teams, so we could only really field one team from the Hotcakes, with Kira being a noncompeter in that category. We were all really careful not to make her feel responsible, because we didn't want her to feel bad. Alexis and Elle both said early on that they didn't want to do the swim competition (I think they planned it for Kira's sake, because they are both great swimmers), and a few other people said they didn't care either way, so I was on the team that would compete.

The Hotcakes were pretty good athletes, if I do say so myself. Plus, we were training hard. We did warm-ups, calisthenics, drills, and had little mini-competitions within our team. We cheered on everyone's progress all the time. It felt great to be part of a group like this, where everyone was fun and they had your back. Kind of like the Cupcake Club, but all new.

Meanwhile, Sydney was being a nightmare. She was so determined that the Angels would win the whole competition that she was tormenting her teammates to train harder and harder. It would have been funny if she wasn't so awful. Sometimes we Hotcakes just stopped and stared while she lit into one of her teammates. It would only last a moment, until one of her counselors rushed over to put an end to it, but it was still just unbelievable.

One day, after track-and-field training, we were all hot and sweaty, and we jumped in the pool with our clothes on. Maryanne and Raoul were kind of annoyed at us at first, but then they saw how much fun we were having and they jumped in with their clothes on too! It was hilarious. Afterward, we hauled ourselves out and stretched out on the grass, drying off in the sun and talking about our summer plans.

That was when Elle announced that her birthday was coming up, and her plan was to have a party with all the Hotcakes, at her house! It sounded like a blast. She would have us over, we'd eat pizza, and the night she planned to do it, there was an outdoor movie showing in a park downtown, so we'd all go with blankets and watch the outdoor movie and eat treats. Then we'd go back to her house and sleep over. Everyone said they wanted to go. But when she told me the date, my heart sank. It was for a Friday night—the night before the Camp Finale Talent Show, actually—and that was, of course, the Cupcake Club's special baking night for Mona.

Alexis and I looked at each other, knowing what the other person was thinking. It was not going to be easy to tell Mia and Katie that we couldn't make it on a Friday night because we were doing something without them. And we'd pinkie promised not to sell Mona two-day-old cupcakes again.

We tried to discuss it later on the bus home, but Jake was in one of his moods.

"Stop talking, Emmy! I'm trying to sleep!" He moaned, his head against my upper arm.

Alexis and I tried to whisper. "What do we say? Do we tell them the truth?" I asked.

Alexis shot me a look. "Lying didn't do us any good the last time."

I sighed.

"Stop breathing hard, Emmy! It's making my head bounce!" wailed Jake.

Alexis shot me a sympathetic look. I tried to remain calm, but all I wanted to do was chuck him out the window.

That night, while I was practicing my flute piece (I hadn't decided yet whether I'd perform, but I was at least taking care of the talent part by getting a piece in order), my mom tapped on my door. As the only girl in a mostly boy house, I have a strict knocking policy and a big KEEP OUT sign on my door.

"Come in!" I called.

"Oh, honey, I love to hear you play. You're so talented," said my mom. She always says that when she comes in while I'm playing. "Just play a little bit more for me."

She settled into my armchair, which is big and cushy and covered in the prettiest white fabric with sprigs of pink flowers on it. She put her head back, closed her eyes, and smiled.

I played the piece through from beginning to end, and she said, "Again," without lifting her head or opening her eyes. I shook my head and laughed, but I played it again.

My mom's eyes opened and she sat up. "You play the flute beautifully," she said. "I'm so proud of you."

"It's pretty fun," I said, shrugging. "I'm thinking about playing that piece in the camp talent show."

"Oh, you have to!" said my mom. "It would be lovely!"

"I don't know, though. I'd hate to have all those people watch me. And . . . well . . ." I didn't have the dress excuse anymore, or the talent excuse, because the piece was sounding pretty darn good. But how do you tell your own mother that you have no charm and expect her to leave it at that?

She tilted her head to the side. "So?"

"Well, I might play. That's all."

"I suggest you go for it. What do you have to lose? Everyone will be impressed. Is it a competition or just a showcase?"

"Well, there are prizes, so I guess it's a competition."

"What kinds of prizes? Like first, second, third place?"

I shook my head. "No, like categories: talent, presentation, charm, and all-around winner."

My mom put her hand up for a high five. "You could definitely win!"

I high-fived her weakly. "Which category?"

"Any of them! All of them! If I was the judge, you'd take home all the prizes."

We laughed. "Thanks," I said.

"It seems like you're really enjoying camp," said my mom.

"Yeah." I smiled. "I love it. And I've made so many good, new friends. . . ." I bit my lip.

"Wait, why do you suddenly look so sad?" my mom asked with a laugh. "It's like someone just flipped a switch! I thought you were happy!"

"I am. It's just . . ." I proceeded to fill her in on the conflict for Elle's party and the Cupcakers, as well as the incident a couple of weeks ago when Alexis and I had to bake for our camp friends.

"Cupcakes, Hotcakes . . . How do you keep all these people straight?" My mom was smiling. "Seriously, though, I agree with Alexis. Look, the sleepover is a onetime thing. These are new friends; they might not be lifelong friends. Or they might be, who knows? You just need to let Katie and Mia know that they come first, but on this one special occasion, you want to go to this special event. And just make a plan to do something fun with them on a different night. I think it will be fine. Old friends are very important, but you have to have room in your life for new friends, too, right?"

I sighed. "Yeah. I just wish they could all be friends together," I said.

My mom thought for a minute. "Then maybe you should figure out how to make that happen!"

Hmm. Maybe she had a point! I thought about it for a second.

"Wait, maybe I should have them all over—like not *all* the Hotcakes, but maybe just Elle and Kira? Along with the Cupcakers? That could be fun!"

My mom smiled and lifted her hands in the air, palms up. "Why not?" she said enthusiastically.

I reached across and gave her a hug. "Thanks, Mom. Great thinking."

"Oooh! Those words are music to my ears!"

CHAPTER 10

Friendship, Favors, and Flute Practice

A week had passed before I got the e-mail from Mrs. Shipley, Romaine's aunt, but it was a doozy, in good ways and in bad! The good parts were, it had three great photos from The Special Day attached—one group shot and two of me and Romaine that were amazing! (I instantly made it my desktop background!) And it had an order for ten dozen mini cupcakes!

The bad part was that the shower was going to be on a Saturday morning—the morning after Elle's Friday night party *and* the same day as our camp's talent show. Now, it's one thing to bake a day in advance for Mona, a regular customer. But I did not want Romaine Ford's cupcakes to be anything less than fresh and perfect. For starters, it was such a big job, and it might lead to other big jobs. Our cupcakes had to be at their very best that day!

I forwarded the e-mail to Alexis and then called her.

"Hi, Emma," she answered. She also has caller ID, so she knew it was me.

"Hey. Did you see my e-mail?"

"Just opening it. Wow, great photos! Oh, the order! Goody! Oh. Not goody. Hmm."

"I know."

We sat there in silence, thinking.

"Well, we could get up early and bake Saturday morning?" she suggested.

"I guess," I said. "It's cutting it a little close. I mean, ten dozen cupcakes! We'd have to leave Elle's at, like, six in the morning."

"Hmm," said Alexis.

"It's too bad we couldn't have Mia and Katie bake the cupcakes Friday night, then we get together at, like, eight o'clock Saturday morning and do the frosting and delivery."

"That would be kind of mean. Like, 'Hey, we're taking the night off, but why don't you two do this big job for us, and we'll catch up with you later?'" said Alexis in an annoyed voice.

I had to giggle. "But maybe we could ask them.

Maybe we'll just offer them something in return—a night off, or whatever. And we *are* helping Katie for her cooking class's bake-off, remember?"

Alexis sighed. "I guess."

"Honesty is the best policy, remember?"

"I'll call a meeting," said Alexis.

The next afternoon, we had an emergency Cupcake meeting at Mia's house. Alexis hadn't told Mia and Katie exactly why we needed to meet (she just said we had major scheduling issues), so they were a little in the dark.

Alexis wasted no time in calling the meeting to order. "First topic on today's list, Jake's birthday party. Emma, please confirm the details."

"Well . . . Jake loved the dirt with worms cupcakes! He said they were his 'most favoritest ever.'"

I rolled my eyes while Mia and Katie said, "Awww . . ."

I continued, "His party is next Saturday afternoon, so we can bake Friday night and then assemble Saturday morning. They have fourteen boys coming—my worst nightmare—so they'll need four dozen cupcakes, accounting for Matt and Sam and various babysitters and parents."

Alexis interrupted me. "Now, if you'd like, Emma and I can handle the baking on Friday and give you girls the night off. We'll do Mona and Jake all in one marathon session, and you two can, like, go out or something." She tried to look really casual as she said this, but I could see she was nervous.

Mia and Katie were confused. "Where would we go without you guys?" asked Katie, her eyebrows knit together, like she didn't understand.

"Yeah, why wouldn't we want to do the baking for the Jakester?" asked Mia.

"Well, I was just saying. I mean, maybe we don't all need to be there . . . ," said Alexis, shrugging.

Honesty is the best policy, I reminded myself. I took a deep breath and plunged in. "Guys. The weekend after that, Alexis and I were invited to a sleepover on Friday night by our friend Elle from camp. Our whole team is going. But, drumroll, please, Romaine Ford's wedding shower is the next day, and they ordered ten dozen cupcakes!"

Mia and Katie squealed and jumped in the air. They hugged each other, then me, then Alexis, who received them awkwardly. She was still nervous.

"Oh, Emma, that is so awesome! I can't wait to meet Romaine Ford!" said Mia.

"I know." I smiled.

"It's just a bummer that you have to miss your sleepover," said Katie.

Gulp.

"Um . . . well . . ." I looked helplessly at Alexis. She wouldn't meet my eye. "We were actually thinking, maybe . . ."

"Oh! Wait! I get it!" said Mia, who is usually much quicker on the uptake. "You'll give us the Friday before off, so we'll work while you're at the slumber party."

I nodded, feeling like a jerk.

"Wow," said Katie. "Um . . ."

"The other thing is, I'm having a sleepover at my house the night before Jake's party. It's for the Cupcake Club and two of my friends from camp, Elle and Kira. It's going to be really fun, and I won't do it unless you two will come," I said impulsively.

Alexis's head whipped to the side and she stared at me with a question in her eyes.

There was a pause in the room that seemed to drag on forever. Then Mia said, "You know what? We'll do it. Right, Katie? That's what friends are for."

I looked at Katie. She still had kind of a hurt, skeptical look on her face. I knew this would be hardest on her, because of the Callie/Sydney history.

"Katie, we're not going to dump you for our

camp friends. I promise," I said quietly. "They're fun, you'll see, but they're not like the Cupcake Club. It's not at the same level, and it never will be." I knew in my heart that that was true. Once school started again and the Cupcake Club was together every day, I knew I'd drift a little apart from Elle and Kira.

Katie took a deep breath in and then sighed. "Okay. I understand. New friends are great, really. I'm just so cautious ever since Callie."

Mia hugged her. "We know. Don't worry. You'll always have us hanging around, right, Cupcakers?"

"Right!" Alexis and I yelled, then we piled in for a group hug.

It was settled. Now I just had to break the news to my mom about the sleepover.

Okay, that last part didn't go so well.

"Wait, the night before Jake's party you want to have a sleepover for six friends? Are you joking?" said my mother in exasperation.

"Well, actually, it's five friends, plus me. So that's not so—"

She interrupted me. "I'm sorry. I don't care how many friends it's for. There is not going to be a sleepover the night before we're having fifteen

360

six-year-olds running all over this house for the day. You'll have the whole house up all night, you'll have the place a mess, and Jake will be overtired for his party, not to mention me!"

I was starting to fume. The worst part was, I could kind of see what she meant.

"You're the one who had the brilliant idea to get all my friends together from camp and school!"

"Not for a sleepover on that particular night I didn't!" she said firmly.

I knew I wouldn't win this one, but I couldn't face undoing the plan. I'd be so embarrassed. After all, Kira and Elle barely knew me when it came right down to it. They might think I was nuts or that my mom was a mean psycho.

"How am I going to tell everyone they're uninvited, then?" I said. I knew I was being bratty, but I didn't care.

"Just like that. You're uninvited!" said my mom with a toss of her head. "Think of a new plan," she said, and she stormed into her bathroom to take a shower.

I left her room and went into mine, slamming the door behind me. When my anger had cleared, I sat and thought about all the things that were coming up and needed attention.

There was the Camp Olympics, which our team was pretty well set for. There was another superjocky team of girls, the Wolverines, who would probably give us a run for our money, but it wouldn't kill me to lose to them, in that they were so athletic and talented. I just wanted to make sure we beat Sydney's team.

Next, there was Jake's party to bake for and survive. It was going to be hard work.

Then there was Elle's slumber party, my non–slumber party, and Romaine's shower—they were all tied up into one big snarl that needed untangling.

And finally, there was the Camp Finale. Was I in or not? And if I was in, where was I going to find some charm? Time was running out.

CHAPTER II

Cupcakes, Meet the Hotcakes

$\mathscr{R}$aoul passed around an official sign-up sheet the next morning at camp.

"Okay, girls! Everyone needs to sign up and give a description of their act. They're printing the programs this week, so this is final. If you're in, you're in, and if you're out, you're out, but don't make the mistake of being out!" He laughed. "We've got a lot of talent in this group, and I know my Hotcakes are going to bring home the gold!" He pumped his fist in the air, and everyone cheered.

When the clipboard reached me, I stared down at it, unsure and paralyzed. Suddenly, Alexis reached across, grabbed the clipboard, and quickly wrote down my name. Then she wrote "Flute Performance" and passed the pen and clipboard to the next person. She folded her arms across her chest and smiled at me smugly.

I just shook my head slowly from side to side. Finally I said, "But what about charm?"

"Leave it to me," said Alexis, but she didn't look too confident.

I had already e-mailed Alexis, Mia, and Katie the bad news about Friday's sleepover. We'd just have a regular baking session instead, so that was okay. But all morning I had been dreading uninviting Elle and Kira. I had a pit in my stomach and could think of nothing else. Finally, at lunch, Kira said, "I can't wait for Friday night! Should I bring an air mattress?" Alexis and I looked at each other, and sighed.

"Guys, I have bad news. My mom said no sleepover on Friday," I admitted, wincing at the mom reference. (I had been avoiding any mention of mine when I was around Kira.)

"Oh, don't worry about it!" said Elle with a wave of her hand. "No problem." She took a bite out of her sandwich, unfazed. Elle was a trooper, and I loved her for it. She didn't even need an explanation. "You're still coming to mine though, right?" she asked, through a mouthful of turkey.

"Yes," I said. "The problem with my sleepover

plan is, it's my little brother's birthday party at our house the next day, and, well, my mom said we'd all be exhausted if I had a sleepover the night before. I could do it another time, though."

"Bummer," said Kira. I could see that she'd been looking forward to it.

"I know." I wondered if she understood, not having a mom and all that.

"But maybe we could still do something?" Alexis suggested brightly. "Like maybe the girls want to come bake Jake's cupcakes with us!" she said with a smile.

"I'm not sure how much fun that would be, with all that work?" I said, glaring at her. What was she thinking? It would be boring for Elle and Kira, and what would Katie and Mia think about us inviting non-Cupcakers to join us at work? But before I could say anything, in jumped Kira and Elle.

"We'd love to!" said Kira enthusiastically. "That would be so fun!"

"I'm in," said Elle with a grin.

"Ookaaay . . . Great, then!" I said, faking confidence. "You guys can just come home on the bus with me from camp." I'd let Alexis do the explaining to Mia and Katie since it was her idea.

Just as I suspected, Katie was not thrilled. I guess she felt threatened by our new friends and kind of resentful of them and the time they got to spend with us all day while she was with a bunch of strangers down at the Y. I totally understood, but at the same time it couldn't always just be the four of us, could it?

When Friday rolled around and we all showed up in my kitchen, things were a little awkward to say the least, even though everyone had been prepared in advance for the new plan.

Mia was nice, if not all that chatty at first. But Katie was downright cold. I saw Elle and Kira exchange a look of confusion after Katie basically said hi and turned her back on them, but Alexis, bless her heart, kept on chattering away to make up for it. I had brought Jake home from camp and settled him in front of the TV, and my other two brothers would be home soon to look after him.

We set out the ingredients and told the new girls what we were doing. Alexis designated Kira as the Oreo smasher and Elle as the cupcake-liner person, meaning she'd set the papers into the baking tins. Alexis had found awesome camouflage patterned cupcake liners in green, so that's what we were using for the Jake Cakes, as we were calling them.

Katie busied herself at the mixer, and Mia and I were working on the frosting. Alexis was setting out the necessities for Mona's minis, which also needed to be made. It was a regular assembly line!

Elle started telling funny stories about camp, and that kind of broke the ice. Mia offered up some stories from the fashion world, and Kira was really interested in that. But the more they chatted, the more withdrawn Katie became. I knew she was insecure, but it was really annoying me, and rude. Finally, I stood up to talk to her in private, but right then my older brothers came crashing through the door in their usual noisy style.

"Hey, Cupcakers! What's up!" called Sam. Did I mention that Sam is gorgeous? All my friends basically pass out whenever he is around, which makes me feel kind of proud and kind of annoyed. He's a lot older than us (seventeen) and not around that much, but he's tall with blond, wavy hair and bright blue eyes like my dad. Plus, he's superathletic, so he's in really good shape. He also likes to joke around.

"Ooh! Batter!" he said, spying Katie at the mixer.

"Not so fast, mister!" said Katie, covering the mixer with her arms.

Elle and Kira were just watching, speechless. Neither of them had brothers, of course, so these guys were like aliens to them.

Meanwhile, Matt, who, I guess, is also pretty good-looking (according to Alexis, with her on-again off-again crush on him), was talking to Alexis and Mia, teasing them about camp and cupcakes and everything, trying to get them to give him gummy worms and promise him the first cupcakes out of the oven.

It was kind of total boy chaos, but Sam and Matt were making my old friends laugh and making a big deal out of them. I interrupted to introduce Elle and Kira, and although my brothers were polite, they went right back to teasing the Cupcakers.

Finally, I shooed them out, and they went in to take over the TV from Jake. The room was very, very quiet after they left. Katie was standing at the mixer, smiling to herself, Kira and Elle were wide-eyed, and Alexis and Mia were still laughing.

"Phew!" I said. "Those two are a nightmare!" I was kind of embarrassed by all the commotion.

"No, they're not!" whispered Elle, her eyebrows raised up high on her forehead. "They're gorgeous!"

"And they're in love with all the Cupcake girls!" Kira sighed, genuinely wistful. "You're so lucky!"

"Aw, no, they're not," protested Mia and Alexis, but they were pleased.

Katie looked up, unsure if Kira was for real, but when she saw that Kira was serious, she allowed herself to smile at her. My anger at Katie melted a little bit then.

"Seriously," said Elle.

Then Jake came running into the room, crying about how the big boys had taken over the TV and changed *SpongeBob* to *SportsCenter*. He ran straight to Mia, buried his head in her legs, and wailed.

Mia scooped him up and began to soothe him, but he whined that he wanted Katie, too, and wouldn't settle down until the two of them were fawning over him, feeding him gummy worms and setting him up with a little workstation of his own.

I was apologetic and mortified, but Elle and Kira were just bowled over by my brothers and how much the boys loved my Cupcake friends.

"You girls are so lucky," Kira said admiringly. "Especially you, Emma, to have all these boys around all the time."

"Ha! As if!" I laughed.

But I could see Katie smiling out of the corner of my eyes.

Against all odds, my annoying brothers had broken the ice. Hotcakes and Cupcakers united as the afternoon wore on, and by the time my parents got home at six and ordered pizza for everyone, we were well ahead of schedule on both baking jobs. All us girls were sitting around the kitchen table, laughing and talking, as the boys periodically wandered in and out and caused silences and then outbursts of giggles. It was so fun!

At the end of the night, Kira pulled out her phone to call her sister for a ride. I could see Katie looking at her with curiosity. Just as I realized what Katie was thinking, it was too late.

"Why does your sister pick you up instead of your parents?" she asked.

I winced and looked down at my hands. I didn't know what to say.

Kira bit her lip. "Well, my mom died last year, and my dad travels for work all the time. I mean, he has to. That's his job. So, I have three older sisters, and they take turns taking care of me."

"Oh, I'm so sorry. I didn't know," said Katie. And to her credit, she was visibly upset.

"That's okay," said Kira graciously. "Thanks."

"I'd love to have three older sisters!" I said, to change the subject.

Kira groaned. "No, you wouldn't! They are so bossy!"

"It's true!" agreed Alexis. "Older sisters are the worst!"

And just like that, things were back to normal. We chatted as we put the finishing touches on the cupcakes. Too soon, Kira's sister was at the door, and we all hugged good-bye, with Mia and Katie even hugging Elle and Kira!

After they left, it was just the Cupcakers in the kitchen, waiting for Mia's stepdad to come pick them up.

"Wow, those girls are really nice!" said Mia. "I'm proud of you two for going out in the world and finding such nice new friends for us all," she joked.

Katie agreed. "Yeah, and I'm sorry I wasn't very friendly at first. I was just shy, and I felt like, you know, you were kind of replacing us with those two."

"It's okay," I said, putting my arm around her shoulders. "And don't worry. You're irreplaceable!"

That night my mom came to tuck me in.

"Good job, lovebug," she said. "It was really nice

to see all those girls getting along and having such fun. You're a great judge of character, and I love your friends. I'm sorry about the sleepover, but I'm glad you worked something out."

I snuggled under my pink duvet. "I know, Mama," I said, using my baby name for her. "It was really nice. Thanks for the pizza!" I yawned.

"See? Wasn't I right? Aren't you glad you're not lying on the TV room floor in a sleeping bag for the next three hours, giggling?" She gave me a kiss on the forehead.

"Yes. I actually am," I said.

And I was.

CHAPTER 12

Happy Birthday, Jake!

Take fifteen six-year-old boys, add fifteen water guns, two hundred water balloons, mud, tears, and lots of junk food, and what do you get? Total chaos. That was Jake's party.

I had invited Mia, Alexis, and Katie to help with the party. My mom was actually paying us to help wrangle the kids, keep the refreshments going, and stay on top of the garbage and cleanup. We also had to guard the doors, so the kids didn't end up inside watching TV or trashing Jake's room or anything.

For me, the best part was that Mia, Alexis, and Katie got to sample what my life is really all about. There was no time to be squeamish when one kid gashed his foot open. There was nowhere to run when Jake's friend Ben picked up a toad and brought it right up to us to see. Replenishing the snacks and drinks was an endless task. The minute a bowl of Cheetos had been filled, the bowl of chips was empty and needed to be refilled, and so on.

As the party wore on (only two hours had passed!), Mia, Katie, and Alexis began to look more and more bedraggled and overwhelmed. When Jake and another kid got into a fight over whose water gun was whose, my friends were horrified.

"But they're friends!" said Katie, observing the chaos with a hand to her mouth. "Why do they fight like that? Look, that guy is punching Jake!"

"I know," I said. "That's what boys do. They just work it out on the spot and move on. Hey! Guys! No hitting! Use words!" I called, to no real effect. I shrugged.

"Wow, Emma. I had no idea," said Mia.

"Yeah, how cute do you think Jake is now?" I asked.

We all looked at him. He was covered in mud, his hair was soaked and sticking up all over, and he had a scratch on his arm from a tree branch (it was bleeding). He had orange Cheetos dust all over his face and had on ratty clothes. Well, they were ratty now. They didn't start out that way. And he and his buddy Justin were saying horrible things to each other as they yanked a water gun back and forth.

Suddenly, Jake realized we were looking at him. He let go of the water gun, leaving Justin to collapse in a heap, and came over with a big, sweet smile on his face. "Where are my cupcakes, girls?" he asked.

"Awww . . . ," said Mia and Katie, melting all over again.

I rolled my eyes and then looked at my watch. "Five more minutes," I said. "Go back and play, and be a good host! Let your guest have the water gun he wants!" I watched to make sure he did, then I turned to the girls. "Shall we?" I asked.

We went inside to get the cupcakes, candles, and camera, as well as the party plates and napkins. Outside, the boys saw us coming and swarmed us. "Down, boys! We'll call you in just one minute. We're not ready yet!"

"Oh wow!" said Mia, laughing with shock as she held the cupcake platter high above the boys' heads. "They really are savages!"

"See?" I said. "Okay, guys. We have to light the candles and then sing." The boys were busy forming themselves into a straggly line, insisting who was first and second to get cupcakes. I started a rousing rendition of the birthday song, and everyone joined in. Jake looked cute as everyone sang, then he blew out his candle and the crowd surged.

Suddenly, Jake yelled, "STOP!" at the top of his lungs, and miraculously, everyone stopped. Jake smiled, then said, "Let's give a cheer for my big sister, Emma, who is the best! She and her friends all made these cupcakes for us and they are going to be awesome! Yay, Cupcake girls!"

All the little boys cheered and applauded, and there was nothing for us girls to do but take a bow. I turned to smile at Alexis, and I saw she had a funny look on her face, the one she gets when she has an idea. I couldn't begin to imagine what she'd be thinking of now, but I was just glad to see she, Mia, and Katie were happy and Jake was having a ball. All in all, a great party!

It took forever to get the backyard and kitchen back in order. But the Cupcakers were great. They'd stayed late to help clean up, then flopped on the couch to watch TV afterward. We were pooped. They said it gave them new respect for me, living with all those boys.

"See?" I'd said. "I told you so!"

The week after Jake's party, no one at camp could talk about anything but the Camp Olympics and the talent show. We trained for our sporting events like we were in boot camp, and at home I practiced my piece and took out my bridesmaid dress for my mom to press. I was nervous about the charm portion, but Alexis was assuring me she had it all figured out. That kind of scared me, but since I didn't have any better ideas, I had to just let it go.

Sydney was like a slave driver to her team, totally dissatisfied with their performances as the time of the talent show drew near. We watched in horror as she yelled at one girl after another for what she considered their bad performances, and we discussed in whispers the rumor we'd heard that Sydney would not be permitted back at camp for the second session.

Finally, it was Friday!

The Hotcakes got to camp early and warmed up, stretching and dancing to great music. We were pumped. Raoul and Maryanne had brought us granola bars and yogurts to keep up our energy.

The games got off to a great start, with an awesome, three-inning softball game, which we won! Tricia hit an amazing home run, and Louise knocked a double that brought in two runners. I kept the water coming, and before we knew it, the game was over and we were at the track for relays and sprints. This was my moment.

I lined up alongside the other girls my age in the first heat of the first race: a five-hundred-yard sprint. Elle was running too, and so was Charlotte. To my left was Sydney. Nothing could make me run faster than that.

The camp director blew the whistle, and we were off! I didn't look to the left or the right. I just pumped my arms hard and lifted my legs high, and I ran like Sydney Whitman was chasing me. Which she was. After I crossed the finish line (first! Yay!), I looked back, and Sydney was still about twenty yards back. I had beaten her handily and so had one of her teammates, a girl she'd repeatedly yelled at for being slow.

"Nice race, girls!" said the camp director as three of us were given medals for first, second, and third place. Sydney crossed the finish line and then pouted, tossing her hair. I heard her saying to someone that there had been a "false start," and she hadn't been ready, so that race didn't really count. I had to just shake my head.

Our team did well through the track-and-field events, and we had a lead heading into the swimming. We trooped over to the pool as the boys' teams exited, and I saw Sydney trying to chat up a bunch of boys who were clearly having a hard time figuring out what to do or say. Their heads were in the game, but they were interested in her. They just didn't know whether to stay and talk or keep on walking. I almost felt sorry for them.

At the pool, the Hotcakes huddled for a pep talk and a strategy meeting, and Raoul, with a huge smile on his face, asked for our attention.

"Chicas, I have some very exciting news. We will be fielding two swim squads today, after all." He grinned.

Everyone looked around in confusion and chattered while he called for silence.

"One of your teammates has made an extra effort so that everyone would be able to participate in these events. Kira has been coming to camp early all month to work with Mr. Collins, and she is ready to bust out her new moves in the pool today and show you all what she can do!"

I looked at Kira in shock. She was smiling shyly as everyone congratulated her. I thought back to her early morning drop-offs and the wet hair, and was annoyed at myself for not figuring it out sooner.

"Oh, Kira! I am so proud of you!" I cried, and I threw my arms around her in a hug.

We assembled for the relay: two squads, with three swimmers from each at either end of the pool. I noticed Kira was swimming from the deep end, which would be easier for her. If she started to fail, she'd be in the shallow end. But I needn't have worried.

When Mr. Collins blew his whistle, the swimmers dove in and took turns swimming the length of the pool. Kira was in the final heat of the relay, and because her team was a little rusty, she wound up swimming alone, dead last. But she dove into the pool and glided, and the Hotcakes were silent until she surfaced. Then we went wild, screaming and cheering until we were hoarse. We walked the length of the pool with Kira as she swam, encouraging her all the way. Her stroke wasn't perfect and she wasn't that fast, and her team obviously did not win, but it was, for us Hotcakes, the sweetest victory we could ever have imagined. We mobbed her when she got out of the pool, and Maryanne was there with a towel. Kira was crying, and it was the best, best moment of my whole camp experience. It was right then that we all felt we'd won the Camp Olympics, no matter what.

I saw Sydney on the sidelines, looking perplexed, and I was glad she had no idea what was going on. We'd kept this issue private, and we'd celebrate Kira's triumph among ourselves, just the Hotcakes. That was the way it should be. I couldn't have been happier if our team had won every race. Friends were more important than medals, and I was so proud of my new friend Kira. I'd always heard the expression "It's not whether you win or lose; it's how you play the game." But now I finally understood it—and it's true.

CHAPTER 13

Hotcakes to the Rescue!

*W*ell, we didn't win the Camp Olympics overall. The Wolverines did, but that was to be expected. The Angels came in dead last. They were so far behind the rest of us that I had to wonder if Sydney's team mutinied against her and decided to lose on purpose. I would have if I were on the Angels. Still, the Hotcakes came in second, and that was good enough for us. The celebration of Kira's victory continued into Elle's sleepover, and we all toasted her with ginger ale at the movie and again back at Elle's house, when we had a snack before bedtime.

Elle's party was a blast, and for me and Alexis, it cemented our friendships with the summer gang. Even though most of us didn't live in the same part of town—some of us didn't even live in the same town—we knew we'd get together throughout the rest of the year and stay friends forever.

On Saturday morning, Alexis and I were up and packed by seven a.m. Her mom had promised to bring us to Katie's so we could finish frosting the cupcakes. My mom would pick us up from there, after dropping Matt off at soccer, and take the Cupcakers first to Mona's, then to Romaine's aunt's house. *Then* we'd head home to change for the big talent show! I couldn't even think about that last part—I was so nervous. Plus, we had so much to get through before it came time for that.

While we waited for Mrs. Becker, I checked my e-mail on Elle's family computer in her kitchen.

"Oh no!" I said. I couldn't believe the e-mail I'd just received.

"What?" said Alexis, hearing the alarm in my voice.

"Mrs. Shipley e-mailed yesterday, but obviously I didn't get it in time. She wanted to know if we could put daisies on the cupcakes 'cause it's a daisy-themed shower!" I looked at Alexis with horror. "How will we ever have time?"

"Time for what?" Kira yawned, straggling into the room. She was dressed but looked sleepy.

Alexis and I looked at each other in a panic, trying to think. "We need help," she said finally.

"I'll help you!" offered Kira.

"I'll help you with whatever it is too," said Georgia, who'd just come into the kitchen.

Pretty soon we had all of the Hotcakes offering to help us.

"Assembly line?" said Alexis with a smile.

"Totally," I agreed.

With a quick call to Katie and to Mrs. Becker, we rearranged the plan so that Mrs. Becker would pick up Katie, Mia, and all the supplies, and bring them to Elle's, where ten helpers awaited their tasks.

It wasn't an hour before everyone had a spot in Elle's kitchen and dining room, and we were frosting cupcakes and piping flowers onto them, chatting and working hard. Everyone was ecstatic to be working on cupcakes Romaine Ford might eat, so they were taking extra care that things looked perfect.

Mia and Katie were very gracious about the whole change of plan, and Elle even apologized to them, saying, "I'm so sorry I didn't think to invite you two to sleep over, since you're honorary Hotcakes. Next time, you two are at the top of my guest list!" I was so happy to see my friends becoming friends.

Finally, everything was ready and packed to go. My mom was outside in the minivan waiting for us, and the Cupcake Club said our good-byes and thank-yous to everyone. Kira was looking at us so wistfully, and all I could think of was how excited she'd been to meet Romaine at the mall. I whispered a quick question to the Cupcakers, and everyone nodded enthusiastically in reply. So I said, "Hey, Kira, want to come, and we'll drop you off afterward?"

It only took her a nanosecond to process what I meant, but then she cried, "Do I?" and ran to get her things. After all of Kira's hard work for the team, she deserved a special treat like this.

After running Mona's cupcakes to her, we immediately took off for the far side of town and reached Mrs. Shipley's right on time. There was a catering van parked in her driveway, and a few other cars—one of them looked really fancy, like the kind a movie star might drive—so I hoped that meant that Romaine was there.

Nervously, the five of us carried the cupcake bins to the back door. I rang the bell, and Mrs. Shipley herself came to the door.

"Oh, Emma, hello! And this must be the Cupcake Club! Come in, come in!"

I held my breath, waiting for someone to point out that it was the Cupcake Club plus one, but to everyone's credit, they didn't say anything.

"Here we are! Daisy cupcakes!" I said.

"Fabulous! I'm so sorry that was such a last-minute idea, but ooh goody! Let's see!"

We lifted the lid from the cupcake carrier and showed her our work. The cupcakes did look adorable.

"Oooh! Wow! Kathy! Come see!" she called.

Mrs. Ford appeared in the kitchen doorway, decorating supplies in hand. "Hi, girls! I'm Kathy! Hi, Emma, honey, how are you?"

I knew my friends were impressed that these ladies all knew me, and I did feel a little proud, I have to say. But the main thing we were all wondering was, would we get to see Romaine?

And then, "Mom?" I heard her voice!

"In here, honey! Emma's here!"

Mia and Katie nudged me with excitement, their eyes sparkling. I had to smile.

"Emma! And cupcakes! Yay!" Romaine was in the doorway and came over to give me a big hug. I was grinning from ear to ear, and I knew I was blushing. I felt kind of like a dork, but I was proud.

"Hi, girls! Is this the rest of the Cupcake Club?" asked Romaine, superfriendly. "Hi. I've met you before! At the mall, right?" she said to Kira. Kira just about died of happiness.

She nodded.

"That's Kira," I said, taking charge of the introductions. "And this is Mia, Katie, and Alexis."

Everyone said shy hellos, and Alexis congratulated Romaine on her wedding, remembering to mention Liam Carey's name, which I thought was a nice touch.

Then Romaine looked at the cupcakes, and squealed, "I love them! Oh my gosh! They are so pretty!" Then she looked at me with a sneaky expression. "Can I try one?" she asked.

"Go ahead! They're all yours!" I said.

"Mmm! Oh, delicious!" said Romaine through a mouthful of crumbs.

"Speaking of which . . ." Mrs. Shipley handed me a white envelope that said CUPCAKE CLUB on it. "Here's your payment."

I was almost inclined to refuse it, for the honor of baking for Romaine, but Alexis reached out and took the envelope. "Thank you," she said graciously.

"She's our CFO," I said, laughing.

"Good for her! She's doing her job!" said Mrs. Shipley with a smile.

Mrs. Ford suggested a group photo with Romaine, and we all posed with ginormous grins on our faces, Romaine holding up a cupcake like she was about to take a bite.

"Well, we've got to be leaving now," I said.

"Can't you stay a little while longer? Could we get you something to drink?" asked Mrs. Shipley, so gracious.

"Actually, it's our Camp Finale tonight. Our talent show . . . so, we need to get going. . . ."

"Oh, the Camp Finale! I remember that! I did a tap dance for mine!" said Romaine. "Mom, do you remember? That was one of the best nights of my life!"

Mrs. Ford winced and then laughed. "How could I forget?" She put her head in her hands. "Oh, the practicing! I thought I'd never recover!"

We laughed.

"That is so fun. So who's doing what?" Romaine asked.

Alexis and I told Romaine the details, and she asked us what time it was, and what I'd wear and play, and what Kira was singing. Alexis let on that she had a special surprise planned, and while I groaned in dread, Romaine told us how excited she was for us.

Finally, we really did have to go. My mom was waiting in the car, and we knew Mrs. Shipley needed to get back to organizing her party.

With a long good-bye and lots of hugs, we left and tumbled back into the minivan.

We could not stop chattering. "That was so amazing!" and "She's so nice!" and "I can't believe she remembered me!" and on and on. My mom laughed, asking questions as she drove around dropping everyone off. Finally, it was just me and Alexis, who would help me get dressed for the event.

"So what's your surprise?" I asked. "You can tell me now."

"Not yet," said Alexis with a mischievous grin. "Not yet."

CHAPTER 14

Talent and Charm

The butterflies in my stomach had turned into birds by the time we got back to camp. There were so many people milling around—siblings, parents, even grandparents. I could not believe how big a crowd it was.

I had my dress in a garment bag, and I checked in backstage. The camp director handed me a program and told me when I'd go on. Raoul was in charge of props and costumes, and he whisked my flute and dress away for safekeeping while we joined the growing audience.

"Wow. This is major," I said to Alexis, looking around. Because she wasn't performing, her parents hadn't come. She was sitting with me and my parents and brothers. But I noticed she kept

looking around, like she was waiting for someone else.

Finally I said, "Who are you looking for?"

"Oh, just—There they are!" she cried, and I
turned to see Mia and Katie heading right toward
us. Mia had a garment bag too, and I wondered
why until she handed it to Alexis.

"Here's Jake's costume," Mia said. "Hi, Jakey!
Hi, Mr. and Mrs. Taylor." She settled in next to
Alexis and started joking around with Matt and
Sam. Katie smiled.

"You guys are going to be great!" she said.

"Guys?" I looked at Alexis. "Now you have to
tell me."

Alexis sighed and looked at Mia and Katie in
annoyance. They were so busy flirting it up with
my older brothers that they missed the look. "I
guess since *some* people don't know how to keep
a secret," Alexis began loudly, "I will tell you our
plan."

I looked at her expectantly. "This better be
good, or I'm not going up there," I said.

"Oh, you're going! You and Jake, who will introduce you and carry out your chair for you to sit in.
He's the charm."

"Wait, you're having that . . . unpredictable little

slob be the charm in my act?" I said. I couldn't believe this was happening.

"Yes," said Alexis definitely. "And he will not be unpredictable because he has been bribed with a whole dozen Jake Cakes, just for him. And he will not be a slob because"—she unzipped Mia's garment bag—"he will be wearing this!" She pulled out a mini tuxedo and a collapsible top hat.

I began to laugh. "Oh my gosh," I said. "Where did you get that?"

Alexis shrugged and glanced at Mia. "It helps to have connections in the fashion world."

Then everyone started to shush the crowd, and the first act began. It was a bunch of boys who were break dancing, and they were actually pretty good. I had a hard time enjoying it, though, because I was so worried about my own act to come.

Next up was a group of Wolverines who did a rap song about camp that was really funny. Some of it was unintentionally funny because they kept forgetting the words, but in the end they got a lot of applause. Elle and Tricia danced around using Hula-Hoops and were awesome, but it wasn't that much of an act. Just them twirling stuff to music. Caroline sang beautifully, and Charlotte and Georgia did their gymnastics routine, which was pretty impressive.

And then it was Sydney's turn.

The music started up, and she strode out in a cowgirl getup that was waaay too sophisticated for her. She had on piles of makeup—if I could see it from the twentieth row, you had to know it was a lot—and she kind of shimmied in time to the music as she came out. Romaine Ford would have died.

I had to give Sydney a little credit for being brave enough to come out by herself and sing. But then I thought she probably just couldn't find anyone else she thought was good enough to join her.

Until she opened her mouth. Then I realized that probably no one joined her because no one thought she was good enough.

Sydney Whitman can't sing.

At first, it was awkward. People felt bad for her, you could tell. They tipped their heads to the side, as if they were really trying to give her a good listen. But then she started doing these really hammy country dance moves, and people started to giggle. Sydney must've been pleased, seeing all the smiles in the audience. With her ego, she surely thought people were just in awe of how good she was. She began to work the audience, encouraging people to clap along with the song, which they did. And then she sang louder—she was getting progressively worse—and danced more enthusiastically, and people just started to laugh their heads off.

The funny thing was, Sydney was so blindly into herself that she never noticed. When her song ended, she gave a triumphant bow and punched the air with her first, like, "I really nailed that one!" and she skipped off stage.

Alexis, Katie, Mia, and I looked at one another in shock.

"She really doesn't get it, does she?" said Alexis, shaking her head in disbelief.

Katie was smug. "I told you she couldn't sing!"

We didn't have long to marvel over what we'd just witnessed because Alexis was suddenly hustling me backstage. Mia grabbed Jake by the hand (she and Katie were going to be in charge of him), and Alexis led me to my changing area.

"Deep breaths. You are very, very talented," said Alexis as she turned her back to allow me to change privately.

"Ready," I said, even though inside I wasn't. Alexis came to zip me up and help with my hair.

I mentally went through Mona's checklist for modeling, which made me feel more in control. "Chin up, shoulders back, smile, sparkle, and just breathe. . . ."

Mia appeared with Jake all dressed, and I had to admit, he looked absolutely adorable. Alexis hustled me to the curtain and gave last-minute directions as we stood there.

"Jake, you'll carry out the chair, put it down in the center of the stage like you practiced with your mom at home. Then you'll bow and say 'Now presenting, my sister, Emma, who will play . . .'" She looked at Jake.

He nodded and said, "Beethoven's 'Ode to Joy.'"

"Right. Then you turn and hold out your hand, and Emma comes out. Then, Emma, do a little bow, and sit and play. When you're done, stand up, bow, and Jake will come back out to collect the chair, okay? Got it?"

"Got it!" we said.

And then suddenly they were calling my name, and it was all a blur. I remember the crowd clapping for Jake and saying "Awww . . ." when he came out.

I remember sitting to play my piece and that I was amazed that that many people could be so quiet. I caught Sam's eye out in the audience at one point, and he was smiling proudly and nodding, but I had to look away.

Then it was over, and Jake was back out, and this time the crowd roared its approval as we left the stage. I was shaking so hard and smiling and so, so relieved. And most of all, I was so glad Alexis had made me do it! I felt great, like how Kira must've felt when she swam.

Backstage, Alexis grabbed me in a huge hug (so unlike her!), and so did Mia and Katie, and then I was quickly out of my dress and Jake was out of his tux. We were back in the crowd to watch the end of the show with my family. Now I could really relax and enjoy it.

I got to see Kira sing, and she had an amazing voice. I spied what must've been her dad and her sisters in the audience. At the end, her dad gave her a standing ovation and was mopping his eyes with a handkerchief. I was glad he was there for her, and he seemed really proud of her.

And finally, there was a pause at the end while the judge tallied up their results. The crowd chatted quietly among themselves as we waited.

"Cupcakers, thanks for coming," I said to the girls. "And thanks for a great summer so far."

"Don't thank us, thank the Hotcakes!" said Katie really nicely.

"It's been really fun," agreed Mia.

We talked about some of our plans for the rest of the summer and then the camp director was back onstage with the microphone.

"Ladies and gentlemen, we had a wonderful program tonight. All these kids are so talented and worked so hard. All the participants will receive a small silver camp whistle to honor their participation. Now, the winners for tonight are in each of three categories: charm, talent, and presentation. Then we do have one overall winner who nailed all three. But before we announce the winners' names, I would like to introduce a special Spring Lake Day Camp alumna who will be our presenter tonight. Ladies and gentlemen, it gives me great pleasure to introduce to you . . . Romaine Ford!"

There was a shocked silence and then the crowd erupted as Romaine came out, smiling and waving. She was in a pretty white sundress with daisies on it, and the Cupcakers and I exchanged knowing looks. It was the dress she must've worn to the shower. I craned my neck to catch Kira's eye across the crowd, and we smiled at each other and made gestures of surprise.

"Hello, folks, thank you for the warm greeting," began Romaine. "I loved my time here at Spring Lake Day Camp so when my friend Emma Taylor and her Cupcake Club told me that tonight was the Camp Finale, I just couldn't miss it!"

My friends and I all cheered and grabbed one another in excitement that she'd mentioned us. I couldn't believe it! I saw Sydney look around the crowd until she spotted us and scowled in disgust.

"Now there were some really wonderful acts I saw when I got here, and I am impressed by all of your hard work, so congratulations to all of you who performed, and to all the backstage crew who helped the performers. And here we go . . . !" She looked down at a sheet of paper and began reading out the awards.

I was ecstatic when Kira won for talent. She had a lovely voice, and she was thrilled to receive the award from Romaine, who gave her a big hug and a kiss on each cheek. The magic show boys won for presentation—they'd been really organized, with lots of props and stuff—and then Sydney won for charm! I was in shock.

Romaine shook her hand graciously, and maybe I was imagining it, but she didn't seem that friendly toward Sydney. Sydney couldn't tell, though, because she was in heaven. I guess a part of me had to admit that her act *had* had a certain weird, funny charm. And at least this way she did win something, even if she was banned from attending the camp next year.

And finally Romaine said, "The all-around winner is . . . my good friend Emma Taylor!"

I couldn't believe it! It was like I was dreaming. I was up on my feet and on the stage, with Romaine hugging me so hard and rocking me back and forth. I just couldn't believe it! She handed me a big trophy and smiled for a photo Raoul took of us. She called "Good night and good luck!" to the crowd, and we walked offstage together.

Romaine was mobbed afterward, but she managed to sneak over to my family before she left. I introduced her to my parents and my brothers, and she said hi to all the Cupcakers, remembering everyone's name!

"You should be really proud of your sister, boys," she said to Matt, Sam, and Jake. "She's a very talented young woman—in the kitchen, on the runway, and onstage! Watch out, world!"

I never wanted this night to end, but it all went so fast in the end. We dropped off all the Cupcakers and headed home, just the six of us, where we sat and ate some of the dozen Jake Cakes (baked today and dropped off by Mia and Katie) at the kitchen table. (Even though the Cupcakers told Jake all twelve cupcakes were for him, he said we could share them with him.)

"Great job, honey," said my dad. "As usual."

"Yeah, honey, great job introducing us to the hot celeb!" said Sam through a mouthful of cupcake.

I rolled my eyes as the crumbs spilled out of his mouth and onto the table.

"We're proud of you, lovebug," said my mom.

"So am I!" said Jake, with a big Oreo-covered smile.

"Thanks, guys," I said. "You're the best."

I looked at my family and then thought about the Cupcakers and the Hotcakes, and meeting Romaine and all the wonderful things that happened over the summer. I had worried about fitting everyone and everything into my plans, but like a great cupcake recipe, the more things I added to the mix, the more delicious and fun everything became.

Sam, Matt, and Jake were gobbling up all the cupcakes.

"Boys!" Mom cried. "We can make more! Slow down."

And then I realized that sometimes cupcakes are like friends . . . you can always make more!

Alexis

cool

as a

cupcake

CHAPTER 1

Partners? What Partners?

$\mathcal{B}$usiness first. That's one of my mottoes.

When my best friends and I get together to discuss our cupcake company, the Cupcake Club, I am all about business. My name is Alexis Becker, and I am the business planner of the group. This means I kind of take care of everything—pricing, scheduling, and ingredient inventory—the nuts and bolts of it all. So when we actually go to make the cupcakes and sell them, we're all set.

Mia Vélaz-Cruz is our fashion-forward, stylish person, who is great at presentation and coming up with really good ideas, and Katie Brown and Emma Taylor are real bakers, so they have lots of ideas on ingredients and how things should taste. Together we make a great team.

But today, when we were having our weekly meeting at Mia's house, they would not let me do my job. It was so frustrating!

I had out the leather-bound accounts ledger that Mia's mom gave me, and I was going through all our costs and all the money that's owed to us, when Mia interrupted.

"Ooh! I forgot to tell you I had an idea for your costume for the pep rally parade, Katie!" said Mia enthusiastically, as if I wasn't in the middle of reading out columns of numbers for the past two jobs we've had. The high school in our town holds a huge parade and pep rally right before school starts. It's a pretty big deal. One year some kids decided to dress up in costumes for the parade, and now everybody dresses up. The local newspaper sends reporters, and there are usually pictures of it on the first page of the paper the very next day.

"Oh good, what is it?" asked Katie, as if she was thrilled for the interruption.

"Ahem," I said. "Are we conducting business here or having a coffee klatch?" That's what our favorite science teacher, Ms. Biddle, said when we whispered in class. Apparently, a coffee klatch is something gossipy old ladies do: drink coffee and chatter mindlessly.

"Yeah, c'mon, guys. Let's get through this," said Emma. I know she was trying to be supportive of me, but "get through this"? As if they just had to listen to me before they got to the fun stuff? That was kind of insulting!

"I'm not reading this stuff for my own health, you know," I said. I knew I sounded really huffy, but I didn't care. I do way more behind-the-scenes work than anyone else in this club, and I don't think they have any idea how much time and effort it takes. Now, I *do* love it, but everyone has a limit, and I have almost reached mine.

"Sorry, Alexis! I just was spacing out and it crossed my mind," admitted Mia. It was kind of a lame apology, since she was admitting she was spacing out during my presentation.

"Whatever," I said. "Do you want to listen or should I just forget about it?"

"No, no, we're listening!" protested Katie. "Go on!" But I caught her winking and nodding at Mia as Mia nodded and gestured to her.

I shut the ledger. "Anyway, that's all," I said.

Mia and Katie were so engrossed in their sign language that they didn't even realize I'd cut it short. Emma seemed relieved and didn't protest.

So that's how it's going to be, I thought. *Then*

fine! I'd just do the books and buy the supplies and do all the scheduling and keep it to myself. No need to involve the whole club, anyway. I folded my arms across my chest and waited for someone to speak. But of course, it wasn't about business.

"Well?" asked Katie.

"Okay, I was thinking, what about a genie? And you can get George Martinez to be an astronaut. Then you can wear something really dreamy and floaty and magical, like on that old TV show *I Dream of Jeannie* that's on Boomerang?" Mia was smiling with pride at her idea.

"Ooooh! I love that idea!" squealed Katie. "But how do I get George to be an astronaut?" She propped her chin on her hand and frowned.

"Wait!" interrupted Emma. "Why would George Martinez need to be an astronaut?"

Mia looked at her like she was crazy. "Because a *boy* has to be your partner for the parade. You know that!"

Emma flushed a deep red. "No, I did not know that. Who told you that?"

I felt a pit growing in my stomach. Even though I was mad and trying to stay out of this annoying conversation, the news stunned me too, and I couldn't remain silent. "Yeah, who told you that?" I repeated.

Mia and Katie shrugged and looked at each other, then back at us.

"Um, I don't know," said Katie. "It's just common knowledge?"

I found this annoying since it was our first real pep rally and this was major news. "No, it is *not* common knowledge." I glared at Mia.

"Sorry," said Mia sheepishly.

I pressed my lips together. Then I said, "Well? Who are *you* going with?"

Mia looked away. "I haven't really made up my mind," she said.

"Do you have lots of choices?" I asked. I was half annoyed and half jealous. Mia is really pretty and stylish and not that nervous around boys.

She laughed a little. "Not exactly. But Katie does!"

Emma and I looked at each other, like, *How could we have been so clueless?*

"Stop!" Katie laughed, turning beet red again.

"Well, 'fess up! Who are they?" I asked.

Katie rolled her eyes. "Oh, I don't know."

Mia began ticking off names on her fingers. "George Martinez always teases her when he sees her, which we all know means he likes her. He even mentioned something about the parade and asked Katie what her costume was going to be, right?"

Katie nodded.

Mia continued, "And then there's Joe Fraser. Another possibility."

"Stop!" protested Katie. "That's all. This is too mortifying! Let's change the subject to something boring, like Cupcake revenue!"

"Thanks a lot!" I said. I was hurt that she said it because I don't find Cupcake revenue boring. I find it fascinating. I love to think of new ways to make money.

How do my best friends and I have such different interests? I wondered.

"Sorry, but you know what I mean," said Katie. "It stresses me out to talk about who likes whom."

Still.

"Well, no one likes me!" said Emma.

"That's not true. I'm sure people like you," said Mia. But I noticed she didn't try to list anyone.

"What do we do if we don't have a boy to go with?" I asked.

"Well, girls could go with their girl friends, but no one really does that. I think it's just kind of dorky. . . ."

I felt a flash of annoyance. Since when was Mia such a know-it-all about the pep rally and what was done and what wasn't and what was dorky and what wasn't?

"I guess I could go with Matt . . . ," said Emma, kind of thinking out loud.

"What?!" I couldn't contain my surprise. Emma knows I have a crush on her older brother, and in the back of my mind, throughout this whole conversation, I'd been trying to think if I'd have the nerve to ask him. Not that I'd ever ask if he'd do matchy-matchy costumes with me, but just to walk in the parade together. After all, he *had* asked me to dance at my sister's sweet sixteen party.

Emma looked at me. "What?"

I didn't want to admit I'd been thinking that *I'd* ask him, so I said the next thing I could think of. "You'd go with your brother? Isn't *that* kind of dorky?" I felt mean saying it, but I was annoyed.

Emma winced, and I felt a little bad.

But Mia shook her head. "No, not if your brother is older and is cool, like Matt; it's not dorky."

Oh great. Now she'd just given Emma free rein to ask Matt and I had no one! "You know what? I'm going to check with Dylan on all this," I said.

My older sister would certainly know all the details of how this should be done. And she was definitely not dorky.

There was an uncomfortable silence. Finally, I said, "Look, we don't have to worry about all this right now, so let's just get back to business, okay?" And at last they were eager to discuss my favorite subject, if only because the other topics had turned out to be so stressful for us.

I cleared my throat and read from my notebook. "We have Jake's best friend Max's party, and Max's mom wants something like what we did for Jake. . . ." We'd made Jake Cakes—dirt with worms cupcakes made out of crushed Oreos and gummy worms for Emma's little brother's party, and they were a huge hit.

"Right," said Emma, nodding. "I was thinking maybe we could do Mud Pies?"

"Excellent. Let's think about what we need for the ingredients. There's—"

"Sorry to interrupt, but . . ."

We all looked at Katie.

"Just one more tiny question? Do you think Joe Fraser is a little bit cooler than George Martinez?"

I stared at her coldly. "What does that have to do with Mud Pies?"

"Sorry," said Katie, shrugging. "I was just wondering."

"Anyway, Mud Pie ingredients are . . ."

We brainstormed, uninterrupted, for another five minutes and got a list of things kind of organized for a Mud Pie proposal and sample baking session. Then we turned to our next big job, baking cupcakes for a regional swim meet fund-raiser.

Mia had been absentmindedly sketching in her notebook, and now she looked up. "I have a great idea for what we could do for the cupcakes for the swim meet!"

"Oh, let's see!" I said, assuming she'd sketched it out. I peeked over her shoulder, expecting to see a cupcake drawing, and instead there was a drawing of a glamorous witch costume, like something out of *Wicked*.

"Oh," I said. Here I'd been thinking we were all engaged in the cupcake topic, and it turned out Mia had been still thinking about the pep rally parade all along.

"Sorry," she said. "But I was *thinking* about cupcakes."

"Whatever," I said. I tossed my pen down on the table and closed my notebook. "This meeting is adjourned."

"Come on, Alexis," said Mia. "It's not that big a deal."

"Yeah, all work and no play makes for a bad day, boss lady!" added Katie.

"I am *not* the boss lady!" I said. I was mad and hurt. "I don't want to be the boss lady. In fact, I am not any kind of boss. Not anymore! You guys can figure this all out on your own."

I stood up and quickly gathered my things into my bag.

"Hey, Alexis, please! We aren't trying to be mean, we're just distracted!" said Mia.

"You guys think this is all a joke! If I didn't hustle everything along and keep track, nothing would get done!" I said, swinging my bag up over my shoulder. "I feel like I do all the work, and then you guys don't even care!"

"Look, it's true you do all the work," agreed Emma. "But we thought you enjoyed it. If you're tired of it, we can divvy it up, right, girls?" she said, looking at Mia and Katie.

"Sure! Why not?" said Mia, flinging her hair behind her shoulders in the way she does when she's getting down to work.

"Fine," I said.

"I'll do the swim team project, okay?" said Mia.

Alexis Cool as a Cupcake

"And I'll do the Mud Pies," said Emma.

"And I'll do whatever the next big project is," said Katie.

I looked at them all. "What about invoicing, purchasing, and inventory?"

The girls each claimed one of the areas, and even though I was torn about giving up my responsibilities, I was glad to see them shouldering some of the work for a change. We agreed that they would e-mail or call me with questions when they needed my help.

"Great," I said. "Now I'm leaving." And I walked home from Mia's quickly, so fast I was almost jogging. My pace was fueled by anger about the Cupcake Club *and* the desire to get home to my sister, Dylan, as quickly as possible, so I could start asking questions about the pep rally parade and all that it would entail.

CHAPTER 2

The Quest for Cool Begins

*Y*es, it is dorky to go with a friend," said Dylan. "I mean, not totally dorky, like if you go in a group with some guys, too, but just you and another girl? Dor-ky!" she singsonged.

I had made it home from Mia's in record time and rushed up to Dylan's room. She and I get along pretty well, since it's just the two of us sisters and we're both pretty type A, according to my mom. This means we're both hard workers who never stop or compromise until a job is done perfectly. Anyway, it turned out Mia and Katie *were* right about everything. I couldn't decide who I was more annoyed at: them for knowing first about going with a boy to the parade, or Dylan for never mentioning it to me.

I flopped onto her bed, and then I rolled over and groaned. "So who am I going to go with?" I wailed.

Dylan was filing her nails. "Well," she began, pausing to blow at some imaginary piece of dust on her ring finger, "why not Matt?"

Dylan knows I like Matt Taylor because she helped me make myself over to win his attention a little while back. She also knew I wanted to dance with him at her sweet sixteen, which, as I mentioned earlier, I actually did.

"He'll never ask me," I whimpered.

"So? Ask *him*!" said Dylan.

Me? Ask *him* to march with *me* in the parade? Impossible! That was the same as asking him on a date, and there was just no way I'd ever do that!

"Yeah, as if!" I said.

"Why? You're best friends with his sister. You practically live at his house. You've worked on stuff together before. Look, don't forget boys are just as nervous about all this stuff as girls are, and he'd probably be grateful to not have to ask someone."

Ugh. The very idea gave me full-body shivers. "But I'm sure I'm *not* the someone he'd like to go with," I said.

"Why not?" she said, now slicking on clear nail

polish with an authoritative swipe. Dylan is nothing if not confident.

"Because I'm not . . . cool," I admitted.

Dylan narrowed her eyes and looked at me. "Well, I can help you with that," she said. "You know I love a challenge."

"Oh no," I said.

"Let me think about it, and I will get back to you with a plan of action tomorrow afternoon, okay?"

"Okay . . . ," I said hesitantly.

But she'd already turned to her computer and begun to type furiously. I guess I am quite the inspiring makeover candidate if she's always willing to take me on.

Double oh no!

That night I sent mini-overview e-mails of the Cupcake Club procedures to Mia, Katie, and Emma, explaining inventory, scheduling, purchasing, and invoicing, along with what we had coming up. I kept feeling like I'd forgotten something, but it was really just that I kept searching for Cupcake Club responsibilities and tasks and finding none. There were no columns of costs to doodle in my journal and no long-range schedules to sketch out. I hadn't realized quite how much time and energy—even my thoughts—the Cupcake Club consumed.

The next day I met up with the rest of the Cupcake Club at the school cafeteria. School hadn't started yet, but Mia had volunteered us to be on the decoration committee for the pep rally, much to my annoyance. (If she was going to volunteer us for something why not the refreshments committee, where we could at least promote our cupcakes?) But I held my tongue. I knew Mia loved anything having to do with design, so this was right up her alley.

On my way to the cafeteria, I met the math department head, Mr. Donnelly, in the hallway. He asked me if I had a few minutes to speak to him. I have an A+ average, so I figured he was just asking me to tutor some kid in the coming school year. Now that I had all this free time, I could say yes. But that wasn't it at all!

"Alexis, I have a great opportunity for you," he said. "I think you should join the Future Business Leaders of America, and I'd be happy to nominate you." He smiled at me happily.

Wow! That was not what I'd been expecting at all! "Oh, Mr. Donnelly! That's . . . that's just sooo great! Thank you! I can't believe I'd be eligible."

My stomach flipped over in excitement, and I got goose bumps up and down my arms.

The Future Business Leaders of America is part of a national organization, and we have a small chapter here at Park Street Middle School. The kids who are in it are by far the smartest kids in the school—the ones who are straight A+ students, honor roll all the way (well, like me, I guess). It's hard to get nominated. You can't ask anyone to nominate you—you have to be chosen, and it's a huge honor. They only choose four kids a year from each grade. And the best part is, the kids meet all the time with the faculty supervisor, who teaches them cool business stuff, like marketing and accounting theories, and then at the end of the year they go to a big convention in the city and meet with all kinds of famous businesspeople. It's supposed to be amazing!

Mr. Donnelly could tell I was thrilled. "I've heard so much about your wonderful Cupcake Club, and of course I sampled the goods at the school fund-raiser last year, and I think you've got a terrific business going. Your hands-on experience running it would bring a lot to the group."

"Well, my friends and I all run it together," I said modestly. But that really wasn't true. Except now, maybe it was. I kind of felt unsure of my role and didn't know what to say. I wondered if I'd be joining the FBLA under false pretenses if Mr. Donnelly thought I ran the whole Cupcake Club by myself.

"You'd be an asset either way. What do you think?"

I mentally scanned my other commitments and my time schedule. "Can I think about it for a day and discuss it with my parents? I have so much on my plate right now," I said. I was so flattered, I wanted to say yes immediately, but it's never good to agree to new responsibilities in a spontaneous fashion.

Mr. Donnelly smiled at me. "Spoken like a true professional," he said. "And absolutely. Let me know. The deadline is in about two weeks, so you have a little time to think about it, but it does look better if you submit early." He winked. "The early bird catches the worm."

"I know it!" I agreed. "Thanks, Mr. Donnelly!"

"Anytime. Just keep me posted!" he said as I sailed off to the cafeteria.

I could hardly wait to tell the others, but when I spotted them across the lunchroom, all sitting together and chatting excitedly, I knew they were not discussing Cupcake business but instead the pep rally parade and what they'd wear and who they'd walk with and all that. I felt myself deflate a little. I couldn't tell them about the FBLA. They wouldn't get it. And, anyway, there was something a tiny bit underhanded about only me getting nominated. After all, it's supposed to be all four of us in business together.

I trudged over to sit with them, dreading the discussion and wishing I could share my real news. It would just have to wait until I got home. My parents and Dylan would be ecstatic for me, I realized. Just picturing their reactions cheered me up a little and gave me the patience to listen to the pep rally chatter.

Dylan wasn't ready for my undorking when I got home, so I went to my room to start reading one more book before summer was over. I had decided to save my news for dinner.

At exactly seven o'clock, I skipped down the stairs to the kitchen table. My parents had come up to say hi when they'd gotten home from work a little earlier, but I'd restrained myself, even though I felt like I was going to burst. I wanted to see everyone's faces at the same time when I told them.

I sat down and waited until everyone had settled and we'd passed around the platter of stir-fried shrimp and veggies, and then I said, "Mom, Dad, Dylly, I have major news. Major *good* news!"

I looked with pleasure at the expectant faces of my family: Mom, Dad, and Dylan.

"Matt asked you to be his parade partner?" said Dylan excitedly.

My parents looked back at me with big smiles on their faces. I was irritated.

"No. Nothing to do with that." Now I wasn't sure how to make the transition. "It's about school," I said.

"Oh! I know! You're going to run for class president!" my dad said, grinning.

This was getting more and more irritating. "No. I am not running for class president," I said through gritted teeth. "This is not a guessing game. I am going to tell you."

"Oh! Sorry, dear," said my mother, blotting her mouth with a napkin. "Because I was going to guess that they put you on varsity tennis."

"Noooo! No more guesses!" I huffed. "Now my news isn't so great. I think I'm going to just keep it to myself," I said. Jeez, the nerve of these people.

"No, we're sorry, sweetheart. What is it? We'll

be thrilled for you no matter what, because if you're happy, we're happy!" said my mom, beaming.

I rolled my eyes.

My mom scolded me. "No pouting, now," she said. "Turn that frown upside down!"

Ugh. I hate when she uses her parenting-class voice on me. It's so humiliating.

"Fine. Mr. Donnelly asked me to join the Future Business Leaders of America. It's a really big deal. Only four kids from each grade are picked—"

"Oh, that's wonderful!" said my mom. "What an honor!"

But Dylan did not have the reaction I was expecting.

"No," she said. "Absolutely not." She folded her arms and leaned on the table, in direct defiance of my mom's strict mealtime-manners code, and she looked me in the eye. "You. Will. Not. Do. It. Do I make myself clear?"

"Wait, what?" I asked. I was confused.

"You have to say no. It's one thing to feel like a dork. It's another to take out a billboard announcing it. The FBLA is for *total* dorks. Complete, unredeemable, dorkorama! You cannot do it. Period." Dylan sat back in her chair and patted her mouth with a napkin. Having said her piece, she was confident I would obey.

"Dylan! That was absolutely inappropriate!" said my mom, in shock.

"Don't listen to your sister, sweetheart. Maybe she's just feeling a little . . . tiny, tiny bit envious," said my dad.

"Ha!" Dylan guffawed. If she'd been drinking her milk at the time, it would have come out of her nose. "That is one thing I am *not*."

I was stunned. Dylan was an overachiever, just like me. How could she not think this was a big, exciting deal?

"Dylan, you need to apologize to your sister. I'm counting to three. One, two . . ."

"Mom!" protested Dylan. "Stop! Alexis has hired me to help her undork herself in time to get a date for the pep rally. She has empowered me to advise her. And this is my first piece of advice: The FBLA is sudden social death. Do not join. If you take even one piece of advice from me, let it be that. I shall say no more on the topic." And she picked up her fork and began eating again.

I, on the other hand, had lost my appetite.

CHAPTER 3

The Commandments of Cool

*M*y parents banned the topics of dorkiness and the FBLA for the rest of dinner, but it didn't leave us much to talk about since that was all that was on my mind, anyway.

Afterward, I retreated to my room to continue reading my book while they cleaned the kitchen, and then I took a shower. A few moments after I closed my door, someone knocked.

"Come in," I said warily.

Dylan came in holding a file folder and sat on my bed, all serious. "Listen, you're the one who always says 'knowledge is power,'" she began.

I nodded and then shrugged.

"And you *asked* me to give you help and to share my wisdom."

Annoying but true. I nodded again.

"I've put together a report on the state of dorki-ness and how to convert it to coolness in six easy steps. It's all in here." She fanned the folder at me.

I rolled my eyes. I didn't want to play into her hands, but I really did have an urge to grab the folder and devour its contents. Instead, I waited.

"It's up to you which path you take, but I have illuminated the way to coolness for you, and I hope you will make the right choice. And just to reit-erate, the FBLA is *not* the right choice. Nothing personal."

Dylan moved to hand me the folder and I let it hang in the air for an extra second, then I took it from her and tossed it on my desk supercasually, like I didn't really care what it said.

"Thanks," I said finally, good manners winning out over my annoyance with her and her directives.

"Good luck" was all she said as she closed the door behind her.

I stared at the folder, knowing that once I opened it, my life would be forever changed, whether I acted on her advice or not. Maybe I didn't care if I was a dork. Maybe being cool would take up too much time and keep me from doing the things I really wanted to do, like joining the FBLA.

But knowledge is power; it's true that I always say that. And nothing tempts me like a well-done research project sitting inside a folder.

I sighed and picked it up, and then I began to read.

The report was long and involved. Dylan had really done her homework, as usual. There was a long list of "Don'ts" in the Dork section, as well as a list of individuals we both knew who were cited for their dorkiness (including my parents!). There was a filmography part, referencing movies I should see that would help to illuminate the differences between dorks and cool people, and there was a recommended reading list of magazines and blogs that would "cool me up," according to Dylan. It all looked like a lot of work.

But the main body of the report came down to the Six Commandments of Cool, as Dylan called them. They were:

(1)   Do well in school, but never mention it. Even deny it at times. (See Section A for examples of when and how to deny.)

(2)   Smile and be friendly, but not too friendly. (Do *not* encourage dorks by acting like they are your equals.)

(3)   In public, pretend that you do not care about the following: what you wear, how you look, who likes you. (But in private, DO pay close attention to these things.)

(4)   Do not be too accessible, either via e-mail, online social sites, IM, phone, etc. (and often say you have plans, even if you do not).

(5)   Go with the flow and just let things roll. (It's dorky to make a fuss.)

(6)   Always have a good guy friend. (See Section B for reasons why.)

I slumped in my desk chair and thought about all the advice.

This would be a lot of work. And some of it went against my better instincts. Like, why would I deny getting good grades? That was preposterous to me. And how could I not be friendly to people who were dorks? According to Dylan's list of dorks, many of them were my friends! Maybe not people I'd invite to sleep over, but certainly people I'd pick first as a lab partner in science class. I was suddenly supposed to not be too friendly to them? That would be impossible. And worse, I'd get stuck with a dumb lab partner and get a bad grade!

But the Cool Commandment that was the

hardest for me was number six. I really didn't have any guy friends, and I wasn't even sure who'd be a good candidate.

Section B said guy friends were good for stand-ins when you need a date but don't have one (Hellooo, pep rally parade!), and they can introduce you to other guys, one of whom might be boyfriend material. Guy friends also signal to other guys that a girl is okay. Like, if a girl is cool enough to be friends with this guy, then go ahead and like her because she's preapproved or something. Guy friends also give you a good perspective on what boys like in a girl and what's important to them. Also, talking with boys who you are not romantically interested in gives you practice for talking to the ones you *do* like. And so on and so on.

Section B wiped me out. I closed the folder, set it back on my desk, and then just sat there, stunned. I had an urge to do the only thing that would make me feel better: work on the Cupcake Club. But having resigned my duties, there was nothing for me to do.

There was another knock on the door, and this time it was my dad.

"Hi, sweetheart," he said from my doorway. "Can I come in?"

"Hi, Dad," I said. I was happy to see him, but I knew the lecture that was coming. I could have recited it myself.

He came in and sat on the corner of my bed so recently vacated by Dylan. "Alexis, your mom and I and all your friends and all your teachers think you are wonderful just as you are. You are talented, smart, ambitious, organized—"

I interrupted. "Thanks, Dad. But I'm okay. I don't need a pep talk. I really did ask Dylan for her help."

My dad pressed his lips together into a thin line and looked up at the ceiling while he gathered his thoughts. "I guess what your mom and I want you to know is . . . cool is temporary. It's a barometer kids use for a few years, when they are too unsure of themselves to be individuals. So they create this system that evaluates people based on criteria that literally have no bearing on the rest of your life. Trust me, once you are out of middle school and high school, there's no such thing as who's cool and who's not. So we suggest you forget about all that temporary stuff and just follow your passions. Those are what make a person great and attractive to others—being energized and excited about life! Not being boxed in by some rules or regulations . . ."

Boy, would his eyes pop out at Section A, I thought. I tried not to smile. It was just that his advice was such a contrast to Dylan's. I knew he was right when I really thought about it, but the truth was, I *did* have to get through these next few years worrying about the cool factor. That was just a fact of life. Following your passions, if they were dorky, did not exactly get you a partner for the pep rally parade.

"I know, Dad. You guys tell me this all the time," I said, trying to be kind but also wanting him to stop.

"We do?" My dad's face brightened. "Oh good! Then you're actually listening! That's great news!"

I smiled.

"Listen, honey, I just came up here to tell you that your mom and I think you should go for it with the Future Business Leaders of America. And don't listen to anything Dylan the Drama Queen tells you. Even if you did ask for her help. Okay?"

I nodded. "Thanks," I said, though I had every intention of doing the opposite of what he'd just told me.

He stood up and then planted a kiss on my head. "Get some sleep, now. It's late." And he walked out the door.

"Good night, Dad," I said.

I heard my dad enter Dylan's room and start lecturing her. I smiled with happiness, pushing aside the twinge of guilt I felt for bringing this all on Dylan. She really was just trying to help me, after all.

I picked up a pen and chewed on the cap, which is what I always do when I'm thinking. I was at a loss. I kept feeling anxious, like there was something I had to do. Then I'd realize it was the Cupcake Club and that, in fact, there *wasn't* anything for me to do now. I was so stressed about the other girls getting it all done, but at the same time I refused to chase them down with IMs and e-mails to make sure they were. It was just that one or two botched jobs could ruin our business for months, if not for good. When you run a business on word of mouth and good recommendations, your reputation is all you have. I chewed the pen harder.

Finally, I snapped. I decided to send an e-mail to the club to ask them for a Cupcake meeting at lunch tomorrow after our decorations committee discussion. With so many loose ends assigned to other people, we needed a meeting to catch up and to see how things were going, just for the good of the business. I vowed to myself that I would not take over or do any of the other girls' assignments. I just needed to put my mind at ease that the others were doing their jobs.

I hopped onto my e-mail account and sent the group the lunch meeting request. There was an e-mail in my in-box requesting that we do cupcakes for a book club meeting of a friend of Katie's mom. I forwarded it to Katie, since she was doing the scheduling now.

After pressing send, I packed my ledger and CC notebook in my backpack and then went to brush my teeth, wash my face, and get into my pj's. With my retainer in, I called downstairs to my mom that I was ready for her to come up to say good night.

While I waited I climbed into bed and grabbed the Cool folder from my desk. I just couldn't help myself. I flipped it open and then began to read it again.

CHAPTER 4

Go with the Flow

There were lots of kids at school the next day for various pep rally committees: the refreshments committee, the entertainment committee, and, of course, the decorations committee. I strained to hear if anyone was talking about who they'd march with, but I didn't hear any of the other girls mention boys' names. I hated to ask them directly; it would be rude. But I was dying to know if they were marching with boys.

I ran into Mr. Donnelly on the way to the cafeteria, and he immediately wanted to chat about the FBLA.

"Alexis! I haven't heard back from you about the Future Business Leaders of America! Are you interested? Did you discuss it with your parents?" He smiled expectantly at me.

I was a little taken aback. He had just asked me about it the day before! "Um. Oh, Mr. Donnelly. I'm so sorry to be slow on this. It's . . . uh . . . a big decision, and I just need a little more time to assess my workload. I'm sorry. I've just been so swamped with the Cupcake Club," I lied, crossing my toes inside my shoes and feeling guilty. I knew that if it were up to Dylan, I'd say that my parents and I had discussed it and I wasn't going to be able to fit it in for this year and thank you so much. But I still really wanted to do it. The battle raged inside my heart as I struggled not to let on one way or the other.

"Wonderful! Lots of big jobs coming up? All organized?" he asked enthusiastically.

"Uh-huh. You bet!" I said with false confidence. Little did he know, I had absolutely no idea whether things were under control or not, but I couldn't exactly explain that! I'm sure being cool and going with the flow are not quite part of the FBLA agenda.

"All righty then. Just let me know soon, because I don't want to wait until the last minute to propose you. And if you can't do it, I need a little time to find someone else, okay?" he said.

"Absolutely. I'm so sorry for the delay," I agreed. We said good-bye, and I practically ran away.

Being all cool and relaxed sure is stressful.

I met the Cupcakers at our usual table at lunch, my ledger and notebook secured in my bag. I wouldn't take them out unless I absolutely had to. I just couldn't imagine having a meeting without them, but we'd see.

Naturally, the conversation was about the parade as soon as we sat down.

"Mia! I think someone likes you!" said Katie mischievously as I put my tray onto the table.

Mia's face turned pink. "Who?" she asked.

Katie grinned. "Chris Howard! I saw him staring at you on the bus this morning, with his head propped on his hand, all dreamylike!"

Mia's face grew even redder. "Stop! No way, you're just imagining things!" she protested, but she had a little smile, like she was pleased by the idea.

"He'd be great to go with!" said Emma; a little wistfully, I thought. "He's cute and nice, and he's pretty tall!"

Mia nodded, but she seemed like she didn't want to commit.

Katie shrugged. "Anyway, I'm just saying . . ."

"We've still got some time to figure it all out," said Emma.

Mia nodded, happy, it seemed, to change the subject. "Yes. We should at the very least be working on our costumes. There's not that much time. I should organize a schedule, maybe."

"Yes! Please do!" said Katie.

Emma nodded vigorously. "That would be so helpful!" she agreed.

Have these people lost their minds? I wondered.

"Ahem," I said. "A schedule? For costume making?" I looked at each of them, but they didn't understand what I meant. "Hello? How about a schedule for cupcake baking?"

"Oh, Alexis! We're getting to that!" said Katie breezily. "Just let us have our fun first, before you start being a slave driver."

"I thought the *Cupcake Club* was supposed to be fun!" I said. I couldn't help myself.

Emma looked at me, all sympathetic. "It is fun, Alexis. Just . . . not as fun as pep rallies and parades! Come on. Be reasonable. You know that," she said.

"Hmph!" I said. I decided to just eat my lunch while they chattered on, talking about anything but our slowly shriveling business. My mind drifted back to Dylan's directives. *Go with the flow,* I told myself. *Stay cool.*

Fine.

After nearly an hour of costume and decorations chatter, the others finally decided to address the Cupcake Club agenda. I felt like I was about to burst from going with the flow!

"Sorry, Alexis." At least Emma had the decency to remember. "I know you wanted this to also be a Cupcake meeting," she said.

I shrugged, flowing (outwardly at least!).

"So when's the Mud Pie sample baking?" asked Emma.

"Let's do it this Friday at my house," offered Mia. I knew she was trying to make up for her previous lack of interest in the topic, but I wasn't going to be fooled.

"Okay. Have you finalized the order amount for the swim meet?" I asked her. I couldn't help myself. It had been keeping me up at night, worrying about it.

"No, not yet," said Mia casually. "But I will."

"When?" I asked.

Mia narrowed her eyes at me. "Later today. Is that okay, boss?"

I shrugged. "Whatever you want," I said.

"I'm just here to advise, not to boss." As much as I wanted to just let go and be cool, I couldn't. Instead I asked, "Do you know how much they'll be charging for the cupcakes at the fund-raiser?" That was the other thing that had been keeping me up at night.

"Why does that matter to us?" asked Mia, confused.

"Because that is a factor in where we set our wholesale price," I said. How could people not know something so obvious?

"Why?" asked Mia.

I sighed. *Stay cool, just stay cool,* I told myself. "Because if they are only going to charge a dollar and fifty cents for their cupcakes, we can't charge them a dollar and twenty-five cents wholesale. Then the margin is too small for them."

"What's a margin?" asked Katie.

"It's the difference between the buying and selling prices. The profit." I gritted my teeth, but I really wanted to scream. *Really, people? After all this time, you don't even know what a* margin *is?*

"Well, I don't know. But I do have a really cool idea for how to decorate them!" said Mia.

I sighed again. "How's the invoicing coming along?" I asked, turning to Emma. I didn't like to hear myself being such a taskmaster, but with all these loose ends that were driving me crazy, I had to carpe diem! (Seize the day! It's another one of my mottoes.)

Emma sat up straight in her chair. "Oh. Well, I started last night but . . . I felt really tired and went to sleep instead. I'll finish it tonight." She looked uncomfortable.

I was dying to ask if she'd even read my e-mail describing how to do it, but I restrained myself, thinking of Dylan's advice again.

Katie piped up. "I did do the ingredient inventory, though! We need to stock up on everything: eggs, flour, sugar—you name it. And I got your e-mail about the book club event. We're all set for that," she said, obviously proud of herself for being the only one who had actually done some work.

This made me relish bursting her bubble, cool or not.

"But, Katie, we have the swim meet to bake for that day, remember? And for inventory, I'm the one who has all the new stuff from BJ's. I have the new twenty-pound bags of flour and of sugar from last week. Remember? I said it in my e-mail."

Katie seemed to sink in her chair. "Oh."

I had to wonder if they ever read any of the

e-mail updates I sent out. It was starting to seem like they'd gotten in the habit of just ignoring them, knowing I'd take care of everything.

I didn't want my friends to hate me, but I was so incredibly frustrated. I knew it wasn't cool to care so much, but I couldn't help it. The three of them sat there, looking dejected and kind of lost.

"Well . . . anyone else heading home now?" I asked. But no one spoke up. "Then bye! See you later."

I was sure they'd be talking about me behind my back once I left, and I didn't feel so cool with that. Up ahead I spied Janelle Bernstein, my admittedly nerdy friend from science last year, who was also walking in the same direction. I was about to call out to her to wait up, but suddenly Dylan's words echoed in my mind. *Be friendly but not too friendly,* she had said. So I didn't call out. I walked out of the school alone, about twenty-five paces behind Janelle, and very, very lonely.

I decided I didn't want to walk home like I normally do, so I took the bus. Unfortunately, the dreaded girls of the PGC, the Popular Girls Club, decided that they were taking the bus that afternoon too. These girls are cool, and they sure didn't need a research report to tell them how to be that

442

way. They're also mean. Or at least their leader, Sydney Whitman, is. The rest of them are just followers, I guess. Not too bad if you meet up with them somewhere random, one on one, but they're very intimidating in a group.

Anyway, they were, of course, discussing the parade, and everyone else on the bus was all ears. The PGC girls knew they were, and it seemed like they were kind of onstage, hamming it up for the less cool girls who were hanging on their every word.

"I'm going to get fitted for my fairy costume this week!" announced Sydney, as if it was the most solemn and important news of the year. "My mom is taking me into the city to a costume designer she knows, who works on all the big Broadway shows. They're going to hand make the costume—masses of shimmery green tulle and floaty layers. It's going to be breathtaking!"

The PGC girls sighed with envy, all starry-eyed. It was annoying. *Go with the flow, go with the flow,* I reminded myself. Was I uncool for thinking Sydney was taking this all waaay too seriously? If I were cool, would I be more organized and psyched for it myself?

"Have you asked you know who?" Callie

Wilson asked Sydney. My ears perked up. I might learn something since the boy aspect was, of course, the most interesting and stressful part of the parade for me.

You could have heard a pin drop on the bus as everyone awaited Sydney's answer. And we didn't even know who "you know who" was! I was tempted to ask the boy behind me for the time, just to show I didn't care. Except that I did care. So I stayed quiet.

I glanced up to see Sydney grinning, faking modesty. "You'll never believe it, but *he* asked *me!*"

I looked away quickly.

As if Sydney would ever have to ask a boy out, not with her long, white-blond hair and fashion-forward clothes and chic little posse of friends. Not to mention her steamroller attitude. If the boy she wanted hadn't asked her, then I'm sure she would have engineered a way to march with him in the parade. Even if it meant poisoning his date.

I was dying to know who it was.

"How about you? Did lover boy call yet?" Sydney asked Callie.

Oh no! I felt a surge of adrenaline. Sydney must mean Matt Taylor!

Callie also has a crush on Matt Taylor, and she and Sydney have engineered lots of "coincidental" (not!) meetings between the two of them, sometimes when I'm actually there. I think it's mostly Sydney, really. It's like she's Callie's agent, the way she pushes Callie at Matt. Emma doesn't think Matt likes Callie, but it's not like it's exactly bad news if you're a guy and one of the coolest and prettiest girls in the school is after you.

"No," Callie said, all quiet.

WHEW! I wanted to yell. But I didn't (staying very cool!), and I had no excuse to stick around since the bus had arrived at my stop. I stood up to get off.

Sydney had a shocked look on her face. "Then *you'll* just have to ask *him!*" she said to Callie.

"Me? Call Matt? And ask him myself?"

Aha! So it was Matt. The idea sickened me. I started to walk down the bus aisle to leave.

I was happy to see that Callie clearly didn't like Sydney's idea.

"If you don't, I will. And that will look worse!" said Sydney.

I glanced at Callie one last time as I left the bus. She looked stricken, like Sydney had slapped her. Which I guess she kind of had.

Sydney is really just a bully who likes to push people around, I thought for the millionth time. Well, she wasn't going to push me around too. I needed to do something to get Matt to agree to be my date. But what?

CHAPTER 5

Half Cool

$\mathcal{F}$riday afternoon, after finishing up some more pep rally decorations at school, we went to Mia's house for a baking session. I was feeling really disconnected from the other girls because I hadn't been sending them Cupcake e-mails and, I noticed, none of them had been e-mailing me about anything. I was starting to wonder if we'd still be friends if we didn't have the Cupcake Club. I also wondered if we'd still have the Cupcake Club if I wasn't running it. These were both nerve-wracking thoughts.

As we walked to Mia's, Callie caught up with us on the sidewalk and walked a few blocks with us. I noticed her looking over her shoulder, as if to make sure Sydney didn't see her. Sometimes Callie is friends with us because she and Katie were best friends growing up, and their moms are still best friends. It's hard for them. It's like they're friends when they're alone together but not in public.

I tried to act cool, which meant basically not talking. I hoped some other kids like Janelle would see me walking with Callie and assume I was cool, maybe even in the PGC too. I looked around, but no one seemed to notice or care.

Anyway, as we walked, the others were discussing our eighth grade math placement test, which had been really hard. Even Emma, who usually gets really good grades, had thought she bombed it. I, on the other hand, was pretty sure I had aced it. We hadn't gotten our schedules yet, so we didn't know who made it into math honors.

"How do you think you did, Alexis?" asked Callie, trying to gauge how well she did.

I don't like to brag about grades, but I'm usually honest with my friends. Except this was Callie, who was not my friend. "Oh, I . . ." I was about to say I was sure I'd be scheduled for Mr. Donnelly's math honors class when I remembered Dylan's advice: Get good grades, but never mention it. So I clammed up. "I did okay," I said, and shrugged. It felt so weird to give the impression that I was less prepared or less smart than I really am. It felt like I was wearing a shirt that was three sizes too small.

Callie nodded, probably assuming I'd be in regular math like the rest of them. If one of the other girls had pressed me, I might have told the truth. But I didn't want Callie to think I was a dork, so I just left it like that.

Naturally, the conversation next turned to Topic Number One: the pep rally and the costume parade.

"Sydney's got us all organized," said Callie. "She says we each have to have a date and a particular kind of costume." She laughed it off, but her eyes weren't smiling along with her mouth. "What are you guys doing?"

Katie and Mia took the lead, discussing their costume plans and Katie's potential date with either Joe or George. Katie announced that Chris had asked Mia to go with him, but that she hadn't accepted yet because she was waiting to hear if a guy she liked in the city might come.

I was mortified. This was all news to me! I looked at Emma to see if she'd known any of this stuff, and it was clear that she was totally up-to-date. I was the only one in the dark! I wasn't about to look clueless in front of Callie by asking all sorts of questions, but as we walked on, I started to get really, really mad. After all, I work my butt off to include everyone in the Cupcake Club on every decision and every plan. And now they go making all sorts of plans without me!

Then the worst part came.

"What about you two?" Callie asked me and Emma.

"Oh, um . . ." I had nothing to say. No costume plan, no marching partner who was a boy. Should I have just announced that I'm a hopeless loser and got it over with? Put myself out of my misery?

But then Emma said, "I'm marching with my brother. We're going to be wizards together."

My stomach dropped and my heart lurched. *Really?* I looked quickly at Callie's face to see if it showed any emotion, but she must've been really good at "going with the flow" because she just nodded and looked away, saying, "Cool. Well, I'm heading off here." We all said good-bye to her and kept on walking to Mia's.

Now I was getting madder than I already was. I dropped back behind the others and brooded. Emma had known I was dying to go with Matt, and now she'd asked him and planned a matching costume with him. Talk about an opportunist!

Maybe I just wouldn't go after all!

I walked in silence while Mia and Katie chattered away. After about half a block, Emma dropped back and fell into step beside me. Then she turned to me and said, "You know I was just saying that so she wouldn't ask him, right?"

"What?" I was still blazing with anger, so I couldn't quite process what Emma had said.

"I'm not marching with Matt. I just didn't want Callie to!" said Emma.

The truth dawned on me, and I could feel my whole mood turn around, all my gripes forgotten. "What? *Really?*" I yelled, totally elated now. "Emma, you're the best!" I grabbed her in a big hug, even though I'm not much of a hugger, and Katie and Mia turned to look at us in confusion as I swung Emma around like a rag doll.

"Stop! Enough! Put me down!" yelled Emma, and finally, I did.

"What's all this about?" asked Mia.

"Emma is not marching with Matt."

"But you'd better ask him before someone else tries to," said Emma, wagging her finger at me.

"Do you think Callie would do that? Even though she knows you're marching with him? Or thinks you are?" I asked.

451

Emma shrugged. "Maybe not. But Sydney would."

"Hmm. Good point," I said. I guess I wasn't out of the woods yet. Plus, Emma had said I'd need to ask him.

Gulp. I had to figure this out fast!

Mia hadn't requested any ingredients from me, and I hadn't brought any, so we had to kind of scrounge around her house for our ingredients. Luckily, her mom had bought supplies for some cookies she was baking for her clients, so there was enough flour and sugar and butter to go around.

I was irritated, though. I almost wished Mia hadn't had the supplies, just so everyone could see the importance of planning ahead and being organized. Instead, Mia managed to slide by without doing any of the usual prep work that I had to coordinate for our baking sessions.

We had three batches going: one of Mud Pie samples, one of swim meet samples, and one for the book club Katie had double booked for us.

We usually have to bake mini cupcakes for Mona's bridal shop every Friday, but thank goodness Mona was on vacation and her shop was closed. I don't think we could have handled another order.

While we baked, we played one of our favorite games. It was easier than having a real conversation. Less stressful.

"Okay . . . orange cream cheese frosting, cinnamon pumpkin cake, a few candy corns on top, and orange wrappers . . . ," said Mia.

"Jack-o'-lanterns, of course!" said Katie. "That's too easy."

"Or you could call them Halloweenies!" said Emma with a laugh.

I wanted to be lighthearted and go with the flow, but I was stressing about the other girls' lack of plans for our upcoming events. I searched for a conversational opening in order to bring it up. Finally, when Katie had stumped the others with a request to name "marble cake, marble frosting, marbleized cupcake wrappers," I jumped in.

"Hey, um, I'm just wondering, speaking of marbles . . . Um, maybe I'm losing mine . . . but, Mia, what did you say the plan is for the swim meet cupcakes?"

Mia was making the Mud Pie frosting with cocoa powder, sugar, and butter. It was hard work to mix it, and she was almost panting with the effort. "Well . . . ," she huffed. "I was thinking we'd do white cake, with silver wrappers, and"—*huff, puff*—"swimming-pool blue frosting!" She paused to blow a lock of hair upward and out of her face. "And we'll lay them all out in the shape of a wave!" She smiled triumphantly at us.

"Cute!" said Emma.

I nodded. But Mia hadn't understood my question. I had to ask again.

"So, like, what are we charging them wholesale and how many cupcakes do we need and what's our unit cost? What's our timetable that day, now that we also have a book club to bake for?" I pressed, studiously avoiding looking at Katie, who was responsible for the double booking.

Mia stared up at the ceiling, like she was thinking. "Oh, I don't know. I'll confirm the cupcake count with them. For the wholesale price we can just kind of wing it, right?"

"Wing it?" I said. I felt like she wasn't speaking English. I just wasn't comprehending. I shook my head, as if I was clearing it.

"You know what I mean!" protested Mia. "They tell us the quantity and their retail price and then we can just back it out from there."

I shrugged. "I guess. That's not how we usually do it."

"But it will work, right?" said Mia.

Flow. Go with it. "Sure."

By the end of our baking session, we had reached a temporary truce, and I was feeling a little more included and up-to-date on everyone. We discussed Chris Howard. (Apparently Mia likes him but had been holding out to see if she could get a boy from her old school to come out for the pep rally. In the end she gave up because the travel logistics were too much.) So Mia said yes to Chris, and we joked that they could go as Angelina Jolie and Brad Pitt. We laughed really hard just thinking about it.

Katie told us she had decided to go with George because he had asked her first, and he was willing to dress up as an astronaut while she was a genie. They were just going as friends, even though "he'd like it to be more," according to Katie. We all whooped and hollered at that.

Emma and I looked at each other. "We'd better get cracking on this," she said quietly.

"I know. I guess I need Dylan's help," I said.

Emma knows Dylan almost as well as I do. "Oh no, it's come to that?" she joked.

"Unfortunately, yes," I said, and we laughed.

The first thing I did when I got home was attack Dylan and beg her to go to the Chamber Street

Mall with me the next day to work on my costume. I was surprised, but she readily agreed. It did make me wonder why she was so willing to help me. Was it because it looked bad for her to have a sister who was a dork? Was it because it was a fun hobby for her, making people over? Worst of all, was I such a dork that she felt sorry for me?

In any case, I was glad to have her help. I only hoped she wouldn't tire of the project and give up, leaving me only half cool. That was always a possibility.

Anyway, I decided to not ask too many questions but instead to just . . . you guessed it! Go with the flow!

But that night in bed, I tossed and turned, thinking about the pep rally parade and Matt, my costume, and the Cupcake Club jobs. At about one a.m., I decided that above all, I had to take charge of one thing: the costume. That way, even if I ended up marching with my grandma, at least I'd look good. Right?

CHAPTER 6

I Survived Shopping at Icon

$\mathcal{T}$he Chamber Street Mall is pretty big and pretty good. You have to have an idea of what you want before you go or you can waste lots of time going upstairs and down, back and forth.

Dylan had brainstormed a list of costume ideas, printed out a map of the mall at home, and made a plan of attack for all the shops we'd need to hit. My mom offered to take us, though I wasn't exactly psyched about that. First of all, it's not very cool to shop with your mom; even *I* know that. And second of all, whenever she and Dylan shop together, it turns into a war zone. They always fight about price, what's appropriate, how long it's taking to make a decision, and so on. The bottom line is: My mom hates to shop and Dylan loves it.

In the car, I looked over the list.

"Dylan, some of this is just . . . I mean, are you kidding me? Marilyn Monroe?"

"Oh, Dylly! No!" said my mom in alarm.

Dylan fumed. "Look, I was just brainstorming and trying to think of things that were kind of pretty and not too dorky."

"I'm all for dorky!" my mom said.

Dylan rolled her eyes at me from the front seat. (She always gets the front seat; it's not even a question.) "We know, Mom," she said.

"We'd better hear the rest of it," said my mom, skillfully piloting the car into the mall's parking lot.

"So . . . 'Marilyn Monroe, hippie chick, Pippi Longstocking'?" I read out. "Even *I* know that's dorky!"

"Oooh, I love that idea!" cried my mom "Braids and knee socks! With your red hair, it will be adorable!"

"Yuck!" I continued to read as we parked. "'Night sky' . . . What's that?"

"All black—leggings, long-sleeved T-shirt, socks, and shoes, and then silver or glow-in-the-dark star stickers all over," said Dylan.

"Hmm. That's kind of cool," I said. "'Cow girl, Gypsy, angel, cat'—kind of babyish, Dyl—'fairy . . .'

No can do," I said, thinking of Sydney.

"Fairy! That's it! That would be the best one!" said my mom enthusiastically. "Great idea, Dylly!" We all climbed out of the car, and my mom and Dylan collected their purses and my mom locked the car.

"I know," agreed Dylan. "Once I hit on that one, I almost just scrapped the rest of the list. It's pretty, it's current, and it has a lot of possible variations. . . ."

"And it is not happening," I said vehemently. "Sorry to burst your bubble."

They looked at me in shock. They'd been so engrossed in agreeing about this idea that they hadn't realized I wasn't on board.

"Why ever not?" asked my mom.

"Because," I said. It was too hard to explain, and also kind of humiliating.

"Don't write it off so quickly," said my mom. "We can look around at the other ideas, but keep this one in your back pocket. I'm sure we'll come back to it in the end."

Store number one was the costume store, and it was very picked over. There were a handful of interesting costumes left, but they'd obviously been tried on and shoved back into their plastic bags, so they looked kind of dirty and used. Plus, most of those store-bought costumes were kind of junky and uncomfortable. I wanted to make a bigger statement than just a little polyester and some funny glasses. My reputation might be riding on it.

We went to Big Blue, which is my favorite store. Dylan thought maybe we'd find some bell-bottom jeans and flowing tie-dyed shirts for a hippie look, but those styles were over, and everything was preppy.

"Ooh! How about a nerd?" said my mom, lifting up a plaid sweater vest.

Dylan and I looked at each other and then burst out laughing. "I don't need a *costume* for that, Mom!" I said.

"Don't be ridiculous, sweetheart," said my mom. But I knew from Dylan's silence that she agreed with me. She was just being polite because Mom was there.

We looked in the fabric store and in Claire's, just to get a feel for what they had. And finally we were at Icon, which is Dylan's favorite store in the world and my least favorite. The music is too loud, the aroma too strong, and the lighting too dark. It totally overloads my senses. Luckily, my mom feels the same way.

"Dylan, I think I'll just wait outside if you don't mind," said my mom.

Lucky!

"But, Mom!" Dylan pouted. I think she was hoping she'd hook my mom into buying her something, too, if she came in. I felt bad for Dylan, but I could totally relate to my mom.

"Why don't we do a preview scan, and then I'll get Mom to come look at our choices," I said. I always end up being the diplomat with these two.

They agreed, and in Dylan and I went.

Boom, boom went the music, and *blink, blink* went my eyes, and GAG went my throat, which was filled with tea-rose perfume and some other smoky scent I did not like.

"Isn't this great?" yelled Dylan. "Come over here where they keep the new stuff!"

Dylan and I turned a corner and almost crashed into Sydney and the rest of the PGC. Ugh.

I grabbed Dylan and tried to steer her down another aisle, but she was having none of it.

"Aren't those girls from your class?" she asked, rooted to the spot, refusing to budge.

I tried to drag her away. "Yes, but they're not my—"

"Hey, Alexis!" Callie called over the music.

"Hey," I said, suddenly feeling like a total dork to be shopping with my sister.

I saw Sydney shoot Callie a glare for saying hi to me, but then do a double take when she saw Dylan.

"Who have we here?" said Dylan, pouring on the charm all of a sudden. "Are you girls from Lexi's class?"

Oh gosh, why did she have to call me by my private family nickname in front of these girls?

Sydney narrowed her eyes and sized up Dylan. I could literally see her ticking things off a mental checklist. Cool outfit? Check. Pretty? Check. Good figure? Check. Only then did she put out her hand to introduce herself.

"Sydney Whitman," she said, tossing her blond hair in kind of a snotty, confident way.

Not to be outdone, Dylan took Sydney's hand and shook it, tossing her own hair. "Dylan Becker. You're the one who crashed my sweet sixteen," she said, regaining the upper hand. I saw Sydney cringe a little. *Yahoo! Score one for Dylan,* I thought. Maybe this wouldn't be all bad.

The other girls drew near, sensing their leader had respect for this new alpha female in their midst. I stuck close to Dylan's side, hoping some of the halo of her coolness would cast its protective light over me too.

Dylan and Sydney began a weird competitive shopping thing, where they'd each pull something out and show it to their little team (me and the PGC, respectively). They'd make comments about how you could accessorize it to make a total look. This was all well and good, but none of it was helping me find a costume.

"So, what are you girls dressing up as for the parade?" asked Dylan.

"Fairies," said Sydney breezily.

Dylan looked at me like *Gotcha!* "That's so funny! So is Lexi!"

But I shook my head emphatically. "No, actually. I'm not."

Sydney was staring at me like she'd just noticed me. She tilted her head to the side. "So what *are* you going as?" she asked. Everyone waited.

"Uhhhh . . . maybe . . . Marilyn Monroe?" I said.

"Cool!" said Callie. But Sydney shot her a look, and she shut up.

"But you have red hair!" said Sydney.

463

Suddenly there was someone standing beside me, saying, "Haven't you ever heard of a blond wig?" It was Mia!

I'd never been so happy to see someone in all my life, even if she did stink at scheduling and pricing. "Mia!" I cried, and I hugged her. Thank goodness she didn't act surprised by the hug, but instead hugged me back. I looked over her shoulder and saw her mom. "And Mrs. Valdes!" I cried. Another lifeline.

Mrs. Valdes said, "Alexis, *mi amor*," and double kissed my cheeks, European-style.

I turned to introduce Dylan and saw her and all of the PGC staring wide-eyed at Mrs. Valdes, who is gorgeous and probably the most chic person you'll ever meet in real life. She is a fashion stylist and always has on the latest styles, tweaked just so. Today she looked amazing in a riding outfit: black leggings, knee-high brown-and-black boots, and a longish fitted blazer with slanted pockets and a velvet collar. Her hair was in a bun, and she had on big gold knots for earrings.

"What are you up to?" I asked.

"Costumes, of course! I'm here to find a base for my witch dress that my mom can have Hector sew things onto," said Mia. Hector is Mrs. Valdes's kind of sewing wizard. He makes samples and stuff for her.

"Cool!" I said, remembering Mia's sketch from the Cupcake meeting.

"Do you need help too, *mi amor*?" asked Mrs. Valdes. "You know I love to dress gorgeous red-heads!" She always makes a big deal about loving my hair, even though I don't see at all why.

Dylan nudged me, looking at Mrs. Valdes

"Oh, duh! Sorry! Mrs. Valdes, this my sister, Dylan." I said.

"Of course, darling. Dylan, Mia just adores you, and I remember seeing photos from your fabulous party," she said, shaking Dylan's hand. "I love your outfit!"

Dylan actually blushed and smiled. "I've heard a lot about you, Mrs. Valdes. Alexis loved being in your wedding!"

I glanced at the PGC and saw they were hanging on their every word.

"Let's go look at the dresses in the back!" said Mia. She linked her arm through mine and pulled me away.

It looked like Mrs. Valdes thought we might introduce her to the PGC, but through unspoken agreement, Mia and I knew we would not.

"Bye!" we said, and we wiggled our fingers at them as we walked away. Dylan was now in an animated conversation with Mia's mom about hemlines and trends.

It wasn't long before Mrs. Valdes and Dylan had pulled a bunch of dresses for me and Mia to try. Mrs. Valdes was enthusiastic about one of them in particular for me. It was long and white and flowy in a fabric called jersey. I don't know if she was thinking Marilyn Monroe too or what she had in mind, but I wasn't about to second-guess a professional. Mia and I squeezed into the tiny, dark dressing room together and tried on the things.

Once I had on the white dress, I stepped outside. It was hard to see because it was so dark. I walked to the end of the hall and stood in front of a mirror under a lone spotlight.

"Oooh! *Yes!*" Mrs. Valdes clapped her hands and strode over to my side. Dylan followed.

Dylan was sizing me up. "It is very flattering," she agreed. "But not exactly Marilyn Monroe. Not at that length. Are you thinking we would shorten it?"

Meanwhile, the PGC had walked up and were waiting on a newly formed line for a fitting room. They too were sizing me up and whispering. I cringed. Then I thought of Commandment Three (since I've memorized them all): *In public, pretend that you do not care about the following: what you wear, how you look, who likes you. (But in private, DO pay close attention to these things.)* I tossed my hair and stood stock-still while Mrs. Valdes and Dylan brainstormed.

"I'm thinking maybe snow princess!" said Dylan.

"Love it!" said Mrs. Valdes She tapped her chin with her finger. "Or . . ." She gathered the fabric at my left and right shoulders and bunched it together, so it looked like thick straps. "Hector can gather and sew these, and we can pin on some vintage brooches and make her a Greek goddess!"

"Yes!" yelled Dylan.

I could tell the PGC was straining to hear what we were saying. I smiled smugly at them, like a real snow princess, or an ice princess for that matter, and let them wonder what we were discussing.

Then Mia came out, and I relinquished my spot and watched her get the Dylan-and–Mrs. Valdes treatment. By now the line had gotten shorter, and the PGC was within earshot.

"Hop back up, honey," Mrs. Valdes said to me, "and let's get another look, so Dylan and I can figure out the accessories." She began listing: strappy tie-up Roman sandals, a garland of greens for my hair, a gold lamé belt . . .

"Won't all that turn Matt's head!" said Dylan enthusiastically.

Wait, what?

"Matt who?" said Sydney while I was still standing there in shock.

Dylan turned to her. "Matt Taylor, of course! Lexi's marching with him in the parade!"

I turned every shade of red at that moment. I sneaked a peek at Callie, and she was red too.

"Wait, *the* Matt Taylor?" said Sydney, mad all of a sudden.

"The one and only!" singsonged Dylan. "You know he and Alexis have always been close."

I was speechless. *Oh gosh, Dylan. What have you done?* I thought. *Play it cool. Go with the flow.* But the flow had turned into a tidal wave!

Sydney turned to Callie and whispered furiously into Callie's ear.

"But I never had a chance!" protested Callie. And Sydney whispered again.

The only part I caught was "a dork like her!" I knew she meant me.

Callie eyed me guiltily.

"Tonight!" commanded Sydney, and Callie jumped.

Then their number was called, and they hustled into their fitting room, all four of them, like sardines in a can. I was left with my bubble totally burst, feeling like the least powerful goddess on Mount Olympus.

HUMBITE 100%!! my friends are cool!!

CHAPTER 7

Style Versus Substance

The rest of the Icon expedition was a blur. I hurried out of my costume and ran outside to tell Mom we found something. I wanted to go wait in the car, but Dylan said that would be rude to Mrs. Valdes, who was going to help us find the rest of the accessories, and my mom said it was dangerous for kids to stay in parking lots alone.

So I hid behind a planter.

I heard the PGC come out of the store, and I flattened myself, hoping they weren't coming my way. I was furious at Dylan! How could she have blurted out a lie like that about me and Matt? But worst of all was hearing Sydney call me a dork.

I mean, I know it's kind of true. Look, I like

school and don't mind homework. And I really don't care that much about things like school dances and pep rallies. It's just hard to hear it said out loud like that, plain as day. Especially from someone like Sydney. Especially when it's said with anger. I really wanted to cry. I wondered if Dylan heard Sydney say it. If she did, she ignored it.

Thank goodness the PGC went in the other direction, and then my mom and Mia and Dylan and Mrs. Valdes were soon upon me. Dylan and Mrs. Valdes were chattering happily and my mom and Mia were commiserating about Icon and how overwhelming it is.

I wanted to get Mia alone and ask her what I should do. I knew she would know. The truth about Mia is, she actually had a chance to be in the PGC. But she chose us, the Cupcake Club, instead. I always appreciated that about her, but it also gave her a social standing that was a little above the rest of us, which I sometimes liked and sometimes hated. On the plus side, it made her kind of our senior advisor when it came to social stuff. She was just good at it and a little more savvy. It's probably because she grew up in the city before she lived here.

In the shoe store, while Dylan scouted the sale

area for appropriate goddess sandals, Mia pulled me aside.

"Listen, I heard what happened in there. It's not your problem. You weren't the one who said it. No one could hold you to it."

I wondered if she'd heard Sydney call me a dork too. I could feel my eyes welling up with tears, but I didn't want to cry here. It was unprofessional. What if a client saw me? I sniffed and took a deep breath, then I touched my cuff to each eye to blot the tears.

Mia put her hands on my shoulders and looked at me carefully. "There is one radical thing you could do to make this all better," she said.

"What?" I croaked.

"Ask Matt to march with you."

"Oh, for goodness sake!" That wasn't the answer I wanted to hear.

"I'm serious, though. I know he'd say yes. He likes you, Alexis," she said.

No way. I shook my head. "I could never," I said. "What if he said no?"

"Even if he said no, which I doubt he would, I think he's smart enough and nice enough not to just say no, you know? He'd say something like, 'Oh man, I told Joe I'd march with him and be Tweedledee and Tweedledum' or something. . . ."

472

I had to laugh at that image and at Mia's imitation of him talking. Mia laughed too. "At the very least he's a good guy. He wouldn't embarrass you," she said. "And no one would have to know."

I thought about it. Would Matt tell Emma? Would he tell Callie? I pictured him saying, *Oh sure, Callie. You'll save me from going with that dork Alexis.*

"Alexis!" Mia said. "Come on! Just think about it. Anyway, you know you'll be looking great!"

With that we rejoined the shopping party and put together the rest of the things Mia and I needed for our costumes.

That night at the dinner table, Dylan could not stop raving about Mrs. Valdes and how cool she was.

"Would you like to trade moms?" asked my mom. "Because I'm going to start getting a complex!"

"But she's so chic! Imagine having someone so stylish living in your very own house! Imagine having access to her closet! I can't believe Mia doesn't just go hog wild every day!" said Dylan.

My mom and I rolled our eyes at each other, and my dad slurped his soup, oblivious.

"Mia is very cool too," said Dylan. "Not quite as cool as Sydney and her gang, but cool. Alexis, why don't you try to hang out more with those girls? They know what cool is."

"I *have* friends. And, anyway, the PGC are not nice. In fact, they're horrible, and they treat people badly. You know that," I said. Then I added, "Plus, I'd be friends with Mia even if she wasn't cool."

"That's your problem right there," said Dylan. "You have no standards. Don't sell yourself short. You and Mia could be friends with those girls. I don't know about Emma and Katie. You'd probably have to ditch them. They're kind of just luggage, but you two should go for it."

I winced. How could she say that about Emma and Katie?

My dad stopped slurping. "Dylan, you've got to be kidding me. Are we talking about Alexis's dearest friends as if they were slabs of beef?"

Dylan looked indignant. "I'm just trying to help," she said.

"You're not helping," said my dad. "Case closed."

"Whatever," said Dylan. And she finished her dinner in silence.

That night I heard my dad trudge up the stairs and give Dylan his old style-versus-substance lecture. We'd all heard it a few times, and it was about how to value the important things in life and how not to follow trends or overvalue superficial things. When he said it, it always made sense, but as soon as he walked away, you could feel yourself weakening and slipping back into bad habits almost immediately.

In my room, I sat there stressing, wondering whether Callie had called Matt yet to ask him out. Or if, in fact, she would. I couldn't stop thinking about it. Only one thing would distract me from all this, and I wasn't supposed to do it. But my fingers itched to get on the keyboard and organize. Finally, I couldn't resist doing a little research for the swim meet job. After all, Mia and her mom had been so nice and helpful to me today, the least I could do was repay the favor, right?

First, I went online to see if I could get a sense of how many people showed up for these regional swim meets. After some searching and doodling of numbers, I figured out an average of about one hundred and twenty attendees. That would mean about ten dozen cupcakes. We'd have to get up really early next Saturday to get that going, and we'd probably have to bake at Emma's because they have two ovens. I'd have to bring over the flour, sugar, eggs, and butter when I went, but it was worth it because baking at Emma's could mean a Matt sighting! My stomach clenched at the idea of him. Was Callie calling him right now? Would he find out what Dylan had told the PGC about us marching together? I decided I'd better warn Emma, in case it did get back to him, so she could defend my honor. I picked up the phone and dialed the Taylors', absentmindedly clicking through the regional swim meet photos on my computer.

Suddenly something occurred to me as I looked at all those photos of people in their bathing suits and the steamy windows in the big indoor pool rooms. It was going to be hot in there! And one thing that doesn't do well in the heat is buttercream frosting!

"Darn it!" I said out loud, just as someone picked up at the Taylors'.

"Uh, hello?"

It was Matt!

Oh no . . . I wanted to hang up! But caller ID! He would know it was me! What should I do?

"Hello? Alexis?"

Oh NO! He *did* know it was me!

"Uh, oh, hi. Matt?"

"Yup. What were you saying when I picked up?" he asked, sounding confused.

"Oh, nothing. Just . . . I just realized something bad on my computer right then, so . . ."

This was so awkward. My adrenaline surged. Should I just ask him? Right now? Should I do it? YES.

"Um, anyway, I was wondering—"

"Hello? Alexis?" It was Emma. She'd picked up on another phone!

"Oh, hey! Hi! There you are!" I said with relief. I felt like I was climbing down from the high dive, legs all shaky.

"Well, bye," said Matt.

"Oh, okay. Bye, Matt," I said.

"What's up?" asked Emma.

And then I started to laugh like a maniac, and I couldn't stop. It was giddy laughter, which was better than crying. I realized I couldn't tell Emma the story now—not over the phone. Not when there was a chance Matt might pick up and hear his name and stay on to listen. That's what I'd do, anyway, if it were me, whether or not it's cool.

"Okaaay . . . ," said Emma. "So why did you call, exactly?"

I didn't want to tell her about the cupcakes that would melt at the swim meet, and I didn't want to tell her about being called a dork at the mall,

477

and I didn't want to tell her how much I loved her brother and hated my sister, even though I *did* want to tell her all of that. So I just decided to go with the flow. I said, "No reason. Just called to say hi."

"Okay. Hi," she said. And then we both started laughing really hard. Emma really is my best friend.

Luggage. Hmph!

CHAPTER 8

A Flirting Failure

At our pep rally committee meeting on Monday, Mia and I filled the Cupcake Club in on what had happened at the mall. I apologized profusely to Emma for putting her and/or Matt in an awkward position, but she waved it off.

"Anyway, he'd probably think it was funny, girls fighting over him at Icon. Hard to imagine old Stink Foot generating that kind of adoration," she said with a laugh.

"So did, uh . . . did Callie call him?" I ventured.

"Nope. Not as far as I know. I can scroll through caller ID when I get home and find out for sure."

"Thanks," I gushed. I was relieved, but not totally relieved. I wouldn't be until I knew for sure. Now I had to think about whether I was going to ask him myself. And if so, how and when?

Just then Chris Howard walked by with his friends, and he and Mia waved and smiled at each other.

"I'm so jealous of your love life," said Emma sadly.

"Don't be. It's not love. It's just a little bit of like," said Mia, all cool.

"On your part," said Katie knowledgeably.

"Well, whatever."

"At least you have someone to march with. Alexis and I are going to be stuck marching together," said Emma.

"Well . . ." I actually wasn't planning on marching with Emma if I couldn't find anyone. I had promised myself that if it came to that, I just wouldn't go. Better to be thought a fool than to show up and prove it. That's another one of my mottoes.

"Wait, you *are* going to march with me, right? I mean, if these girls have dates, who else would I go with?" she asked, gesturing at Katie and Mia.

I decided to turn it into a joke. "It depends on your costume," I said.

"I'm being a hippie," said Emma.

I tapped my chin and acted like I was evaluating

her idea. She swatted me and said, "Shut up! You know we're marching together, so just stop!"

Not if I can help it, I thought, but I didn't say it aloud. Cool Commandment Four rolled through my mind: *Do not be too accessible . . . say you have plans, even if you do not.*

It was time to change the subject.

"Hey, so, um, getting back to my favorite topic . . ."

"Matt or the Cupcake Club?" said Mia wryly, and the others laughed.

I tossed my head and then sat up straight. "The club, of course. Jeez. Anyway, I know it's not my project or anything, but it's going to be pretty hot at the swim meet, you know? So I was wondering, is butter cream the best option?"

The others looked at me blankly.

"Because, you know, it will probably melt and then slide off," I added.

"Oh," said Mia. "Well. I already agreed on the recipe and the price with them."

"What price?" I asked. I couldn't help myself. She should have checked with me before she agreed to anything.

"One dollar a unit?" Mia didn't sound confident.

"One dollar a unit? But we never make

481

cupcakes for that price! It's always at least a dollar and twenty-five cents! We'd be losing money at one dollar a unit! This isn't a volunteer organization! What are they selling them for?" I tried not to lose my cool, but I felt like my head was going to pop off.

"Three dollars each?" said Mia sheepishly.

"So they make two dollars a cupcake and we lose money? That is a nightmare. We should be splitting the profit, which is standard in almost any industry, or at the very least taking twenty-five percent." I put my head in my hands. I knew something like this was going to happen!

I looked up, and the other three Cupcakers were glancing nervously at one another.

"Can you fix it?" Mia asked finally.

"Look. I'll figure something out. Just . . . next time, make sure you check first. Or, sorry—you should be making the decisions on your own, but at least consult the e-mails I sent you with the overview of how everything runs, okay?"

Mia nodded. "Sorry," she said.

"I liked it better when you were in charge, I think," said Emma.

"Yeah, well . . ." I wanted to say, *So did I*. But I didn't. It wouldn't have been cool.

❁

The rest of the week was a blur of doing but not doing Cupcake Club work, avoiding the FBLA decision and Mr. Donnelly, dodging the PGC, reading the articles Dylan clipped for me from magazines (if *Teen Magazine* tells me to "be a free spirit," which I'm totally not, but also to "always be true to yourself," then which is it?), and relentlessly checking in with Emma to make sure Callie hadn't called Matt. It was stressful, to say the least.

By the end of the week, all I wanted was to curl up in my room with a good Cupcake Club work-sheet in front of me and relax. But it was not to be.

On Friday afternoon we went to Emma's to bake for the book club job Katie had taken on. We decided we'd wake up early on Saturday to bake for the swim meet. Matt wasn't going to be home, according to Emma, so I felt a little more relaxed when we got there, but also a little less psyched than normal.

The book club order wasn't that big of a job, and they'd requested one of our old standbys, caramel cupcakes with bacon frosting, so it would be easy for us to make. The only problem was that Katie had forgotten to do the preshopping

483

for the ingredients, and there was no bacon at the Taylors'.

"Okay, well . . . I guess a quick bike ride to the Quickie Mart to buy some bacon is in order," I said. I wasn't going to volunteer. It wasn't me who had forgotten.

"I'll go. It's my fault," said Katie. "Could I have some Cupcake Club money, please?"

I looked at Emma. "Our account is empty. But Emma must have received the payments on those invoices she sent, right?"

Emma looked sheepish. "Um. I haven't had a chance to send them yet. Honestly, Alexis! I don't know how you do it! Between flute practice and baking and dog walking . . . there just isn't time!"

I shrugged. "You have to make time," I said.

Everyone sat there looking morose.

Finally, I sighed. I wanted to teach these people a lesson, but I also didn't want to run the Cupcake Club into the ground.

"Fine. Look, I always keep a cushion of cash for the business. It's called capital. You aren't supposed to use it except maybe, maybe in an emergency. I guess this is a small emergency." I reached into my book bag and pulled out a portfolio-style wallet.

Inside I had bank envelopes filled with bills of different denominations.

"Wow, Alexis, how much is in there?" asked Katie.

"We've saved a hundred dollars. I think we probably only need to take out ten right now, for the bacon, unless there's anything else you think we might need. What about tomorrow, Mia?" I asked. I didn't want to be the taskmaster, but this was getting ridiculous.

Mia bit her lip and looked at the ceiling, as if mentally reviewing her list. "Actually, we could use some silver foil cupcake papers," she said.

I sighed, then took another ten out of an envelope. I closed the wallet and then put it away. "Who's got a safe place to put this for the bike ride?" I asked.

Just then we heard the Taylors' back door open. My heart leaped! Matt! But it wasn't. It was Emma's oldest (and some say cutest, but not me) brother, Sam.

"Hey, Cupcakers," he said, throwing his backpack into his locker in the mudroom. (Yes, the Taylors have lockers, just like at school.) He took off his baseball cap, running his fingers through his wavy blond hair.

"Hi, Sam!" said Mia and Katie in unison, all perky. They love him. Mia batted her eyelashes at him, and Katie grinned a megawatt smile.

Emma's eyes narrowed with a plan. "Sammy? Could you take us to the Quickie Mart to get some bacon? Please, please, please? It would save us so much time!"

Sam was pulling food out of the fridge to make a salad or a huge hero or something. All the Taylor boys do is eat, I swear! He looked down at his ingredients, then he said, "I guess so. I could probably use some more mayo. Will you save me some cupcakes as payment?" he asked, his bright blue eyes twinkling.

Katie and Mia couldn't promise him fast enough. "Then let's go!" he said.

Being annoyed with everyone and having just arrived, I really didn't feel like going. Emma had to go, because it was her brother taking them. And Mia and Katie would not miss an opportunity to be seen driving anywhere with Sam Taylor, even if it was only on a bacon errand.

"I'll just stay here and start the batter," I said.

"Okay. Be right back!" called Emma.

I know the Taylors' kitchen as well as I know my own. I could reasonably show up and prepare a three-course meal there without anyone batting an eye, so I felt totally comfortable being left there by myself, especially knowing no one else was due back for a while. I turned on the TV to watch a rerun of my favorite dancing show, *Celebrity Ballroom*, and I quickly whipped up the batter in Emma's pride and joy: her pink KitchenAid stand mixer. I then ladled the batter into the cupcake liners that Emma had on hand. We were only making four dozen cupcakes today, so it was pretty fast and easy. When I'd finished, I put them in the oven and then began to wash the dishes, turning up the TV volume to hear over the water.

Between the hiss of the water from the faucet and the dance music blaring out of the TV, I didn't hear anyone come in. So when I heard someone call my name right beside me, I screamed and jumped about ten feet in the air.

"Sorry!" said Matt, hands in the air, backing away. "I didn't mean to scare you!"

I turned off the water and stood there shaking, my wet hands over my heart, which was pounding.

"TV's a little loud too, don't you think?" he asked, laughing as he turned down the volume.

"You scared me to death!" I said. I hate being scared. It always makes me feel cranky afterward. Somehow, today my annoyance negated my usual nervousness around Matt. I only felt mad.

"Smells good in here," said Matt, sniffing appreciatively.

I nodded. "Book club job," I said. "Caramel and bacon."

"Oh, those are one of my favorites! I love that bacon-caramel combo! Are you going to have any extras?" he asked hopefully.

Between the disorganized club members (not me) and the terrifying scare I'd just had, I was not in a nice mood. "Well, we already have to give some to Sam for driving to the Quickie Mart to buy bacon. I don't know how many they promised him, but we can't just keep giving away our profits like this . . . ," I said without thinking.

"Oh, hey, no problem. Sorry. I wouldn't want to eat up all your profits . . . ," said Matt, and he turned to leave the room.

Oh no. I suddenly realized I'd just been really mean. After all, there I was, taking over his kitchen, without his sister even being there, baking with his family's supplies, saying his brother could have some cupcakes but he couldn't. And worst of all, I was not being cool. I was caring way too much and being uptight and definitely not being a free spirit.

"Wait! Sorry! I'm sorry, Matt. That was really rude. I just . . . of course you can have some cupcakes. I love that you love them!" Ugh. Did I really just say that? Uncool!

"No, I get it. I totally understand. You guys are trying to run a business, so . . . that's chill. I'm just going to finish a design I've been working on. Later!" And he left the room.

I sat down heavily in a chair. *Why am I such a dork?* I thought, staring into space. *Why can I not know the right things to say or do at the right times?* Callie would have immediately turned that whole thing into a major flirt session. She would have said, *For you, Matt, anything! I'll save you the best ones, with extra bacon!* Then she would have flipped her hair and smiled a big sparkly smile at him. I, on the other hand, squashed all of Matt's friendliness and enthusiasm, turned him down, and barked at him in his own home.

I wanted to die.

CHAPTER 9

The CEO in the FBLA

$\mathcal{M}$att didn't come downstairs again before I left that Friday. I told the others sort of vaguely what had happened, and I set aside three cupcakes on a plate for Matt, kicking in three of my own dollars to make up for it. I felt awful.

The next morning, as I headed to Emma's to bake for the swim meet, I half hoped I'd see him and half feared it. Luckily, he was at cross-country practice when we arrived, and I was quickly swept up in all the work that needed to be done.

After thinking over the options on unit price, I'd decided we just needed to make the cupcakes a little smaller than usual. Instead of filling each wrapper three-quarters of the way with batter, we'd just fill them halfway, leaving us with cakes that were level with the tops of the wrappers once they were baked, rather than puffing into big, muffinlike crowns.

Mia was willing to agree to anything to redeem herself, and Emma and Katie were fine with the somewhat skimpy cupcakes.

"Never again, though!" I said as we filled the cupcake wrappers.

"Never!" promised the others.

Then Katie spoke up: "Alexis, um, we've been talking about it and . . . we think the Cupcake Club runs a lot better when you're in charge."

I looked up in surprise. Emma and Mia were nodding.

"We know it's a lot of work for you . . . ," Emma added.

"Actually, I don't know how you fit it all in!" said Mia.

"But we'd like to ask you to officially be our CEO," Katie finished.

"The boss!" said Emma, laughing.

"We really can't do it unless you run it," said Mia.

Of course I was thrilled to receive such acknowledgment. But I wasn't willing to accept so easily.

"Thanks," I said. "That's really nice. I do love it.

For me, it's as fun as . . . fashion design is for Mia! It's just, it does take a lot of time. And I hate always being the bad guy, the taskmaster."

The other girls were quiet while we filled cupcake wrappers and mixed frosting and thought about it.

"Maybe we need some flow charts or something. Like a company structure, where each of us has the same job all the time and we know how it needs to be done and when, and on a regular basis," suggested Mia.

"Yeah. It's too bad we can't send you to business school, Alexis!" Katie joked.

"I wish!" I said. But then suddenly, I thought of the FBLA. "Actually . . . Mr. Donnelly invited me to join the Future Business Leaders of America at school," I said. I felt like I was bragging by telling them. I was also nervous they'd think I was taking all the credit for the club or, worse, that it was too dorky to even consider doing. I regretted my words as soon as they left my mouth.

But I wasn't expecting the reactions I got!

Mia was so impressed. She said a high school girl who interned for her mom last summer had been a member of the FBLA in middle school, and that was where the girl learned everything she knew about business—and she knew a lot. Emma thought it was an honor to be asked. And Katie said, "I think I'm speaking for all of us when I say, first of all, congratulations. And second of all, it would be an honor to have you represent the Cupcake Club! You deserve it!"

We hadn't heard Matt come in (that guy sure is quiet). But suddenly he was there, saying, "Who's being congratulated? And who's representing the Cupcake Club in what?"

He sat at the kitchen table and began to pull off his sneakers, his light hair sweaty and matted, his dimples appearing in his cheeks as he grimaced. He looked gorgeous and strong and fit.

"Ew! Get out of here, Stinky!" said Emma.

"No, Emma, it's fine!" I said, quick to defend Matt.

"We were just congratulating Alexis," said Mia. "She's—"

"It's nothing," I interrupted. Dylan's words about social death floated through my mind. Could I join the FBLA and keep it a secret?

But Katie wouldn't be hushed. "Alexis was asked by Mr. Donnelly to join the Future Business Leaders of America at school! Isn't that great?"

I wanted to die. There was no flow to go with,

no way to act cool. Matt now knew for sure that I was a dork. It was curtains for me. I couldn't even look up.

"Wait, is that the thing where you get to go to the conference in the city at the end of the year?" asked Matt.

I looked at him and nodded miserably, bracing myself for a snide comment.

But instead Matt said, "Wow! That is so cool! Will you tell me if you learn anything I can use for my graphic design business?" Matt designs things on the computer for people (including the Cupcake Club), like flyers, signs, campaign posters—stuff like that.

At first I thought he might be teasing me, but he wasn't even smiling. He was dead serious. "Sure," I said.

"It's gonna be so interesting. You're lucky!" Matt got up and then walked into the mudroom. He flipped his sneakers into his locker, then went to wash his hands.

"And thanks for the cupcakes last night, Alexis. You didn't need to do that," he said, his back to me as he stood at the sink. I couldn't see his face.

I quickly looked at Emma. She shrugged and smiled. So she must've told him they were from me.

"Oh, no problem. I just . . . I know you like them so . . ." I tried to channel Callie and the other PGCs. It didn't feel right, but I went for it. "I made those especially for you, with extra bacon. I hope they were okay!" I blushed. I couldn't believe I'd been so flirty.

Matt turned around with a big smile on his face. "Thanks. Any more today?"

"No!" interrupted Mia. "Alexis is being very stern about our unit price and our markup. If we give any of the swim team's cupcakes away, the boss lady is going to dock our pay," she teased.

But I was mortified. "Oh, come on. Surely we could spare a couple of cupcakes for Matt!"

"Uh-uh. You said so!" said Katie. "Sorry, pal!"

But luckily Matt was laughing. "How much profit would I be eating if I had one?"

Everyone looked at me expectantly. I couldn't help myself. I quickly did the calculations in my head. "One dollar's worth. Or about three percent. It's fine, though," I insisted. "I'll cover it for the swim team."

"Nope! Every penny counts! Especially for future business leaders! Hey, maybe you should go as Donald Trump for the costume parade!" Matt cackled.

I froze. Matt had mentioned the parade. Here was my big opening! But could I really ask him on a date in front of all these people, including his own sister, my best friend? I thought of Dylan and all her advice. *Don't be too accessible* and *Have a good guy friend* were kind of canceling each other out right here. I knew she'd want me to march with Matt. But would it be cool if *I* asked *him*? Not so much.

While I stood there thinking, Emma piped up, "What are you doing for the parade, Matty?"

"Ah, you know I hate that stuff, I'm not going," he said, turning away to grab a bag by the door.

What?!

Luckily, Emma wasn't going to let him get away with that. "You can't hate it! It's a rite of passage! You've got to go!"

"Nah," he said. "Not for me. See ya!" And he left the room to go upstairs.

I looked at Emma after he left. I was aghast. "What do we do now?" I asked.

"I was waiting for you to ask him!" she said.

"Why should I ask him? You should have asked him! He's your brother!"

"Exactly! And if I do the asking, he'll say no. It's got to be you!"

"Why is this so hard?" I wailed, and covered my face.

Just then the timer went off for the first batches of cupcakes, and we had to get the next ones in. Time was ticking away. I snapped into action. Anything to distract myself from yet another missed opportunity. We flipped the cupcakes out onto the cooling racks and began filling the cupcake pans with new liners, being careful not to burn ourselves on the metal trays. It wasn't until I started ladling in the batter that something occurred to me.

"Emma," I said quietly. "If Matt isn't going to the pep rally parade, then Callie doesn't have a chance. Even if she does ask."

Emma looked at me like I was an idiot. "First of all, that doesn't solve any of our problems. We still have no one to march with. Second of all, don't you know he's just saying that? He's either too shy or too lazy to ask someone himself. But you can bet if someone asks him, he'll say yes."

Huh. "I guess you really do know boys," I said.

"Occupational hazard," Emma said with a shrug. "But I had another idea. I think you should ask him if he and Joe Fraser want to walk with you and me. Then it's like a group thing and not so date-y, which I know bothers you."

497

"It doesn't bother me. I just . . . I'm nervous, that's all."

"Well, the next time you see him, you have to ask him, okay?" she said. "It's only a week away, and I know for sure he doesn't have a costume of any sort. We can't let that become an excuse for him to not go. Okay? Pinkie promise?"

Ugh. I hate to pinkie promise, because then it means I have to do whatever dreaded thing I've promised to do. "Fine," I said, irritated. "Now let's focus on this swim team thing!"

CHAPTER 10

Take a Dive

ℐt felt good to be back in business, especially in the driver's seat. I ran the rest of our morning like a drill sergeant, but a nice drill sergeant. I tried not to be bossy, and the others tried not to mind when I was.

We got the bacon cupcakes assembled and delivered to the book club. Then we rushed back to the Taylors' to frost and pack the swim team cupcakes. At the last minute I grabbed the extra frosting and a bunch of plastic knives, and stuck them in my insulated tote bag. You never know.

Mia's stepbrother, Dan, picked us up in her mom's Mini Cooper, to give us a ride to the town's pool, where the meet was being held. It was pretty tricky fitting all us girls and all those cupcakes into the car. Suddenly (with visions of cupcakes splattered on the pavement) I called my dad and asked him to come in the Suburban. I sent the other three ahead with the first load and took three cupcake carriers and waited for my dad on the Taylors' driveway.

My dad pulled up quickly, and we loaded the Suburban and safely stowed the cupcakes, then headed out to the town's pool.

"Any extras?" my dad asked hopefully. My mom keeps us on a major health-food diet, so my dad is always looking for any little crumb of junk food he can get his hands on.

"Sorry, Dad, not today," I said. "It would be bad business. Our margins are too tight as it is. I'll make another batch soon, though, and save you some," I said, thinking of Matt.

"Hey, I meant to ask you, what did you ever decide to do about that business club at school?" he said, taking his eyes off the road to glance sideways at me.

I looked away, staring out the window. "Oh, I don't know. I'm not sure it's for me . . . ," I said. But I thought of Matt's reaction as I said it.

"Listen, sweetheart, I think you should go for

it. Don't listen to Dylan. It would be a wonderful experience for you," he said.

"It would officially make me a dork," I said. "With no hope of ever being considered cool."

"That's ridiculous. Being cool is a state of mind. As long as you're cool with who you are, you'll be fine," he said.

"Easy for you to say," I said.

"Well, you're right. But it's much more important to follow your passions and to be true to yourself. I mean look at all the people who didn't follow convention and who went on to do great things. Innovators, like Steve Jobs, Bill Gates, Jim Henson . . ."

"I know, I know," I said.

"The list of leaders is endless. And it's cool to lead. It's not cool to follow, to do what other people tell you to, or what you think other people think you should do. Does that make sense?"

"I guess. But Dylan . . ."

"Look at Dylan! A perfect example," said my dad. "Do you see her following anyone?"

I shook my head. "No. I guess not."

"So, there you go. Why should you follow her? Or anyone? Just follow your heart, follow your passions. Go for what excites you!" he said.

We pulled into the parking lot and then jumped out to get the cupcakes.

"Thanks for saving the day, Dad," I said, and I gave him a big hug.

"Anytime!" he said, kissing the top of my head.

Inside, it was hot and humid, just as I'd suspected. I reached the table where the other girls had been directed to set up the cupcakes, and I found them in a panic.

"Alexis! Thank goodness you're here! Look!" cried Mia.

She had arranged the cupcakes in a wave design, just as she'd planned. The pale blue frosting was pretty, and it did look kind of like a wave. Except for one thing. All the icing was sliding off the cupcakes from the heat.

"Oh," I said. "Okay. Well . . . let me think."

Emma stood there wringing her hands while Katie bit her lip and Mia hyperventilated. I looked around the room. It was starting to fill up. We didn't have time to go home and rethink this. I watched a kid dive off a diving board into the water, his hands slicing the surface, but his body leaving not a ripple on the water. Pretty amazing, those divers, headfirst . . .

"I've got it!" I said suddenly, snapping my fingers as it came to me. I began calling out orders.

"Emma, we have to get Matt to do a quick poster for us, in bright blues and greens. Just type. It needs to say, 'Take a Dive with the Swim Team's Cupcakes!' Okay? Can you call him and ask him to do that for us? He can put a credit and contact info for his company at the bottom of the sign. Tell him. He just needs to get it over here in the next . . . oh . . . half hour. Okay?"

Emma nodded, flipping open her phone.

"Mia and Katie, you're not going to like this, but bear with me . . ." I explained my plan.

Matt arrived, breathless, twenty-five minutes later, with three copies of an awesome poster for us to hang around the table. It said what we'd asked, but he'd figured out a way for the words to be splashing into water, with little droplets flinging off the letters, all green and blue.

"Oh, Matt, it's amazing! You're a genius!" I said. And I wasn't even hamming it up or flirting like Callie would have. I meant it! He actually blushed.

"No prob," he said.

He hung up the posters while I instructed the swim team cocaptains who were manning the table on what they'd do to sell the cupcakes.

"Okay, you're going to take the money—three dollars each—and put it into the cash box. Then you're going to pick up a cupcake . . ." We'd arranged them top down on the table, so they were resting on their frosted tops, with their bottoms in the air, still in Mia's original wave design. "Then you grab a knife and scrape the frosting off the platter, then get a little extra frosting from the bowl, and slather it all on top and hand it over. Okay?"

"Awesome!" one of them said.

"This is so cool! How did you ever think of this? It's so clever!" the other one asked.

"It was Mia's idea," I said, gesturing at her.

"No way. It was our boss, Alexis. She thought up the whole thing," protested Mia.

"Well, Matt Taylor did the signs!" I said. "You know what? It was a team effort!"

"A team effort for a team effort!" said Katie, and we all laughed.

"Let me be the first to buy a couple!" I said. I handed over six dollars and then gave the finished cupcakes to Matt.

"Thanks!" he said, surprised. "You didn't need to do that!"

"It's the least I could do after you saved the day like that for us."

"It sounds like you're the one who saved the day, actually. Here, I can't eat them both right now. Why don't you have one?"

I shrugged and took the cupcake from his hand. "Thanks."

"Cheers," he said, and he tapped his cupcake against mine.

"Cheers," I said back. I took a deep breath and decided to go for it. "Matt . . ."

I swear I was about to ask him to march with me right then when who should be walking up to us but Sydney, Callie, and Bella from the PGC. I didn't know Sydney and Callie were on the swim team, but they must've been. They were wearing bikini tops and short shorts with flip-flops, and Sydney was carrying pom-poms.

"Hey, Matt!" they singsonged as they walked up to him.

"Hey," he said, licking off frosting from his lip.

"Wow! Look at those cupcakes!" said Callie eagerly.

"Yeah, talk about fattening," said Sydney as I smushed my final, slightly too-large bite into my mouth. Whoops.

505

"Look at these cool posters," said Bella. "The letters are all drippy. It would be cool to do it in red, like vampire blood."

Sydney rolled her eyes. "Not everything in life comes back to vampires, Bella," she said.

I had finished chewing and was just standing there like an idiot, but I wasn't about to walk away from Matt and leave him to the wolves. I turned to Callie.

"I didn't know you guys are on the swim team," I said.

Callie looked at me, confused. "What?"

I gestured to her bathing suit and Sydney's. "I didn't realize you two were on the swim team."

Callie looked embarrassed. "Oh, we're not. We just . . . got dressed up to support the team, right, Sydney?" She kind of tried to laugh it off.

Sydney gave her a haughty look. "Yeah. The girls' swim team is for dorks. But we like coming to see the boys in their bathing suits. And we didn't want them to feel self-conscious, so we decided to turn it into a pool party! Right, girls?" She squealed and waved her pom-poms in the air.

"Buy a cupcake to support the team?" said one of the cocaptains, noting Sydney was a fan.

"Sure!" said Callie, reaching into her shorts pocket.

But Sydney stopped her by grabbing her arm. "No, thanks! Bikinis and cupcakes don't mix!"

Callie looked disappointed, but Sydney said, "We want to make sure we fit into our fairy outfits for the *pep rally parade*." She glared at Callie as she said it.

Callie blushed and then shook her head a tiny bit and looked down at the floor.

Sydney sighed in aggravation. "I have to do everything myself around here," she said.

I knew how she felt, but I wasn't exactly sympathetic. I knew things were about to spiral out of control. My control. I knew I should go with the flow, play it cool, be a free spirit, not be seen to care too much. But how do you get anything you want in life if you act like that? That's what I want to know. I steeled myself for what was coming next, and all the while my brain was racing to see if I could figure out how to get Matt away from the PGC and then invite him to march with me.

"What are you being for the parade, Matty?" asked Sydney, all flirty.

"Oh . . . I'm not . . ."

I knew what he was about to say, and I weighed

507

the risk of social ruin (the PGC finding out Dylan had lied about my parade plans) against mortification (inviting Matt in front of these girls), and I just blurted out the first thing that came to my mind.

"He's being a Greek god," I said. "He's marching with me." I couldn't even look at him as I said it. I just prayed he'd go along with it.

I could see him turn to me in surprise, and now I needed to cover for that. I looked at him. "You hadn't heard what our final costume plan was. Now I ruined the surprise! Silly me!" I said, and I laughed, all flirty. *Get me out of here, get me out of here,* I thought.

Matt was looking at me in confusion. Sydney looked mad, and Callie still looked embarrassed.

I pressed on. *If you're going to go down, at least go down in flames,* I thought. I said to Matt, "I know, I know, you didn't know what Emma and I had cooked up for you and Joe to wear when you marched with us. But failing to plan is planning to fail! That's one of my mottoes."

Finally, a big grin spread across Matt's face. "Whatever you say, boss," he said, chuckling.

Boss? I fake laughed. "Ha-ha. I'm not anyone's boss."

Luckily, the swim team coach chose that

moment to get on the bullhorn and announce the cupcake sale. The table was stormed, and Matt and I got jostled out of the way and separated from the PGC. As my adrenaline wore off, my knees started to shake when I realized what I'd done. *Oh my goodness!* I thought. I needed to cover my tracks.

I turned to Matt and said weakly, "Hey, so, I'm sorry about that back there. I just ..."

He was smiling, though. "Thanks. You saved me from looking like a major dork for not having any plans. I appreciate it. That was funny. Greek gods. Quick thinking!"

Wait, did he not realize I had actually just invited him? He thought that was just a joke? Like a bail out? What could I say? What should I do? If I told him I'd been serious, would I look like a major dork? I decided to go with the flow.

"Oh, yeah. Anytime. So ... I guess ... I mean, were you planning on going with them and I just messed it all up?" I asked. *Please say no, please say no,* I chanted in my head.

"No. Those girls are too much. I mean, Callie's fine, but Sydney is torture. She's so aggressive and bossy."

Bossy? "Is bossy bad?" I asked, thinking how he'd just called me "boss" and also seeing as how

I was the boss of the Cupcake Club.

"Well, yeah. Who wants to be bossed around?"

"Yeah. No one, I guess," I said. *Callie's fine* was floating in my head. *Is that a good "fine" or just an okay "fine"?* I wanted to ask, but that wouldn't be going with the flow, either.

Mia, Katie, and Emma appeared at our side. "Should we go?" asked Mia.

"I guess," said Emma. Turning to me, she asked, "What do you say, boss?"

"I am not the boss!" I said. It came out a little more forcefully than I had meant it to. Emma jumped and looked surprised.

"Okay! Sorry! I get it!" she said.

I rolled my eyes.

"Let's go," said Katie. "Alexis, is your dad coming back?"

I looked at my watch. "Yup. He should be here by now. He can drive us all. Let's get the cupcake carriers and head out."

"So, I guess you guys aren't staying for the meet . . . ," Matt said.

"Matt, thanks so much for your help," I said, all businesslike.

"No prob. Glad to be of service. Thanks for the cupcake," he said. Then he added, "And . . . for saving me." He hesitated a minute. It looked like he was going to say something else or ask me something. But then it seemed as if he changed his mind. "Anyway . . ."

I looked at him. "Okay, then," I said finally, going with the flow. "Thanks for the awesome posters."

"Bye."

"Bye," I said, and walked away.

CHAPTER 11

Greek Goddesses and Friends

That night, as I sat in my room—working on flow charts for the Cupcake Club, but actually thinking only about Matt and my bungling of the invitation today—there was a knock on my door.

"Come in," I said.

It was Dylan. "Dad says I have to tell you to stop worrying about being cool," she said with absolutely no animation or enthusiasm. Then she continued in a monotone voice as she took a seat on my bed. "I'm supposed to say it doesn't matter, follow your dreams."

I spun around in my desk chair to face her, put my fingertips together, and looked at Dylan. "Wow. You're doing a really convincing job," I said, echoing her monotone.

She smiled, then she sighed and began to speak normally. "Listen, just for the record, you're the one who wanted my help. It's not like I grabbed you and said, 'You're a dork. Let me help' or anything like that. Make sure Dad knows that, because it doesn't seem like he does."

"Okay," I said, nodding at her. "But just explain this to me: How is it that going with the flow makes such a mess of everything? It seems like it should be the opposite."

"I'm not answering any more questions. It only gets me into trouble," said Dylan, examining her nails.

"Come on, Dylly, just this last one!" I protested.

Dylan sighed heavily. "Look, I'm not an expert. I just know what I see. I'm starting to think maybe there are different kinds of cool. There's, like, 'leader cool,' where you do everything a little ahead of everyone else, and then there's, like, 'renegade cool,' where you just march to your own drummer. I guess I should have been a little clearer on that. I'm thinking you probably fall more into the renegade category, since you're not a cookie-cutter type of person."

"Oh great. I'm a weirdo," I said. "I knew it."

"No! Stop. You're not at all. You're just . . . You

have interests that are a little outside the norm for people your age. But that doesn't mean they're bad. It's just, if you're going to take a chance on them, you have to go for it, whole hog. Don't just do it halfway, you know? Like, if you're going to do the Cupcake Club, then go all out: run it, be a serious CEO, join the FBLA, read business books—whatever. Go for what you want. That's what is cool. Not doing it is dorky, and doing something only halfway . . . well, that's not really cool at all. It's just kind of lame. Do you get it?"

"I guess so," I said.

Dylan got mad then. "Don't tell Dad I gave you more advice on coolness, though, okay?"

"Okay! I won't! I already swore I wouldn't!"

Dylan stood up, satisfied with my answer.

First thing Sunday morning, Mia called me, all excited. "Come over! My mom got the costumes back from Hector! We need to try them on! The others are coming with their stuff too, and my mom's going to help us style them. Bring the sandals, okay?"

I had my mom drive me over to Mia's in a flash. Emma was already there, and Katie arrived soon after.

Mrs. Valdes took my dress and Mia's out of black garment bags and laid them out on the sofas in the living room.

"Wow!" Emma exclaimed breathlessly. "That's gorgeous, Alexis."

I leaned in to finger the soft material. Hector had added rectangular jeweled clasps to the shoulders, bunching the material so that it gathered in tiny pleats at the top, then draped down across the front in a graceful arc. I couldn't wait to try it on.

"Okay, *mis amores*, run and get into your costumes and then meet me in my room. We'll go through one by one and accessorize you!" Mrs. Valdes said.

We spent the next hour and a half playing fashion show, with Mrs. Valdes raiding her closet and trying things on us to enhance our outfits. Emma wound up looking amazing in her hippie costume. Mrs. Valdes added a hairpiece called a "fall" to her hair that made it look really long, then she lent Emma a suede fringed vest to go over the bell bottoms and tie-dyed shirt Emma had brought. Mia had a pair of platform boots that fit Emma perfectly, and they dug out a pair of round tinted glasses of Dan's to complete the look.

515

Next up was Katie, the genie. She had a pair of culottes and a long-sleeved shirt with a scarf to wrap around her head. Mrs. Valdes swapped out her shirt for this flowy, white one with billowy arms, and wrapped a gold lamé scarf around her middle as a belt. Then she took a little pillbox hat and attached Katie's head scarf to it, so it flowed down the back. Finally, she produced a pair of shoes from Tibet that curled up into pointy toes and looked magical. Mia gave Katie an anklet made up of tiny bells, which would jingle as she walked. She looked unbelievable!

I went next, and I was so psyched with how my dress came out. It was soft, it fit perfectly, and it was sooo comfortable, like liquid swirling around me. I strapped on my tie-up gold Roman sandals. Mrs. Valdes put my hair up into this loose bun and then pinned it, sticking little silk leaves all around my head. Then she put a garland of silk leaves around my waist, so it looked like a belt.

"And now for the finishing touch!" she said. I watched as she ran over to her jewelry box on her dressing table and pulled out the gold knot earrings she'd had on that day at Icon. She held them up and crossed back to clip them onto my ears.

"Oh, Mrs. Valdes. I can't wear these! What if I lose one?" I protested.

"I know you, Alexis, and you won't lose one. But even if you did, it's okay. I got them for fifteen dollars at H&M last year. They are temporary by nature. Now turn around, and let's see the full effect."

I spun in place, and everyone cheered. "Oh, I wish Dylan were here to see you!" Mrs. Valdes said as she clapped her hands.

"Me too!" I agreed. "She'll be so jealous when she finds out we raided your closet without her."

Mia went last, and her costume was the simplest but the best of all, just because it took kind of a standard idea (witch—black dress, black hat, black shoes) and made it so glamorous. Her dress had scraps of floaty black tulle sewn on that flitted and flicked as she moved. There were little sequins hidden here and there to catch your eye amid all the black. Her hat was very, very tall and very, very pointy—almost kind of kooky-looking, but chic. And her shoes were superhigh heels with super-pointy toes and bursts of tulle pointing off the toes and heels, like a little shoe Mohawk. Mia's mom gave her tons of silvery necklaces and jangly silver bracelets to wear, so she made a tinkly noise as she moved.

"Wow, Mia! You look beautiful!" I said. We all agreed. Her costume was fantastic!

Mrs. Valdes ran to get her camera, since she wasn't sure where we'd all be dressing for the parade next weekend.

"I'm so glad we're not fairies," said Katie.

"I know. Also, I think it's cooler that we're not all matchy, matchy. It's kind of babyish to go in a big group theme," said Emma.

"What are your partners being?" I asked Katie and Mia, thinking of Matt.

"Chris is a warlock," said Mia. "I helped him with the costume." She smiled. "It was fun."

Katie laughed. "I convinced George to be an astronaut like on the TV show, so he's going for it! His dad was going to help him make the costume. He's going to wear a bubble helmet and everything!"

"Fun!" I said. But I was feeling a little wistful. I wish I had had the guts to tell Matt I'd really been serious yesterday. I shouldn't have gone with the flow.

Emma and I avoided eye contact. We hadn't recently discussed going with Matt and Joe. But now that I had this great costume, I really wanted to march with Matt. I didn't want to waste it.

"Going with the flow doesn't get you what you want in life," I said out loud.

The others looked at me strangely.

"Of course not, silly!" said Katie. "Only limp noodles go with the flow!"

I giggled. "That sounds so appetizing. Like something a witch would make!"

Mia cackled. "Heh, heh, heh, my pretties! Who would like some limp noodle pie?"

We all started acting out our costume characters as Mrs. Valdes came back into the room with her camera. We hammed it up in all sorts of shots, and then reluctantly took everything off. It had been fun. And now I knew I had to get up the nerve to ask Matt. No more limp noodle pie for me!

CHAPTER 12

Carpe Diem—Seize the Day!

$\mathcal{I}$ knew all the teachers would be back at school Monday, getting everything ready for the new school year. So I called and left Mr. Donnelly a message. He called me back a few minutes later.

"Hi! Mr. Donnelly! Am I too late?" I asked.

"Hello, Alexis. I'm assuming you mean the Future Business Leaders of America? No, you're not too late. I was taking a calculated risk that you wouldn't take so long to think about it and then say no." He laughed. "So shall I write the letter?"

"Yes, please. And is there anything I need to do on my end?"

"You'll need to pull together a résumé. . . . I can e-mail you some samples. And then just write a one-paragraph essay on why you want to join and what your focus will be. Can you have it to me by Wednesday?" he asked.

I nodded. "I can have it to you by tomorrow."

"Even better! Great!"

That night, my mom helped me put together a really good résumé that listed all my business experience (babysitting, Cupcake Club, running bake sales at school, selling Girl Scout cookies when I was younger—stuff like that). I listed my areas of responsibility in the Cupcake Club, including the financial planning I do, along with the marketing ideas I'd had for Emma's dog-walking business, and a few other things.

Then it was time to write my paragraph. I sat at my desk and then cracked my knuckles. I'm better at math than writing, so I always have a hard time getting started. The clock ticked, and I shifted in my seat. Finally, I caved.

"Dad!" I yelled.

For the next fifteen minutes, my dad and I brainstormed, talking about what I enjoyed most in business and where I felt I needed to grow. I took notes and jotted down key words as we talked, and when he left, I felt energized. I knew what I wanted to say, and here's what I wrote:

My name is Alexis Becker. My business experience to date has been customer driven and marketing oriented, mainly in the food service industry, and now I'd like to take it to the next level. If I were accepted into the Future Business Leaders of America, my focus would be on innovations in leadership. I would like to learn how to better lead employees by inspiring them to be creative and by empowering them to work independently. I do not want to be a micromanager. I would also like to learn how to lead in my industry, developing new products before my competitors and finding new ways to reach customers through marketing. I would appreciate the opportunity to harness my enthusiasm and passions and turn them into action—to just go for it, to never hold back, and to learn how to lead by example. Thank you for your consideration of my application.

I thought it was pretty good, and my parents liked it too. Even Dylan, who was passing by as I read it aloud to them, gave me a thumbs-up. I felt great. I printed out the final copy and put it in an envelope to deliver to Mr. Donnelly the next day.

After finishing the letter, I wrapped up some Cupcake business, and it was still kind of early. There was something I needed to do, and it was on my mind. I just wouldn't feel settled until I did it. I thought of my own words from the FBLA paragraph. How I wanted to go for it and to never hold back. How I wanted to lead by example.

I can do this, I can do this, I told myself.

I took a deep breath, and I punched the familiar sequence of numbers into the phone.

"Hello?" asked a familiar voice.

"Emma, it's me, Alexis," I said.

"Oh hi! I was going to call you! When are we getting together to bake for the retirement party this weekend?"

"I just e-mailed everyone about that," I said. "It should be in your in-box. But we'll do it at Katie's first thing on Saturday, so we can get ready for the parade by three o'clock, okay?"

"Perfect. Anything else going on?" She was obviously looking to chat, but I didn't have time. I'd lose momentum.

I cringed. "Actually, I wonder if I could speak to Matt?"

There was a pause, then Emma said, "Oh. Right. Sure. Hang on. I'll get him."

The phone clunked on the table. I could just picture the upstairs hallway and Emma walking to Matt's room. I had kind of an unfair advantage in all this, in that I'd been to Matt's so many times and was so comfortable with his whole family. *Why should I be nervous, anyway?* I thought. *Why don't I just pretend I'm the CEO of a big company making a sales call. CEOs never take no for an answer!*

"Hello?" His scratchy, deepish voice startled me.

"Hey, Matt, it's Alexis." I gulped. I didn't feel so CEO-ish anymore. *Go with the flow,* I started to tell myself. But no! There's no flow anymore. *Carpe diem!* I reminded myself. *Seize the day!* That's better.

"Hey. How's it going?" he asked.

"Good. Listen, I'm just going to cut to the chase. . . ."

I could hear Dylan's advice in my head. *Go for what you want. That's what is cool. Not doing it is dorky.* I thought of making this into a big group invitation thing. I thought of inviting him and Joe to join me and Emma as a foursome. But then I thought about what I really wanted, what my own goal was: I wanted to march with Matt Taylor in the parade, darn it!

"Would you like to come march with me in the parade on Saturday?" I said it in one really quick rush. I guess it came out a little too fast, because Matt didn't catch it.

"What?" he asked.

I took another deep breath, dying that I had to say it all again. "The parade. Would you like to march with me on Saturday?"

There was a pause. I could hear the wheels turning in his mind as he struggled to find an answer, a gentle way to say no, to turn me down. I cringed and closed my eyes.

"Sure. Thanks," he said. "What do I need to wear?"

What?!

YAHOO!

Now I wasn't sure what to say, so I started to ramble a little. "Um, well, I actually am going as a Greek goddess. I wasn't kidding about that. You can wear whatever you want. Or you could be a Greek god and wear a toga. Like a white sheet, you know?"

"Oh yeah. Sam knows how to do that. His friend had a toga party last year. I could do that."

"Really? Oh, that's so great!" I said. I didn't want to sound dorky or overly enthusiastic, but this was turning out fantastically. Success made me generous. "Also, listen, Emma might need someone to walk with too. I don't know if she's talked to you about it or not, but . . ." I was just totally going for it now, covering all my bases.

Matt replied, "Well, I could bring Joe. I don't think he has a plan. We were just going to bail on the parade and go to the pep rally and bonfire, so . . . I'm sure he'd be happy to march. Should he wear a toga too?"

"Um, maybe he should be a hippie," I said. "That's what Emma's dressing up as, and she looks great."

"Cool. Okay. So we'll just meet you . . ."

"There. We'll meet at your house on Saturday, and we can all go over together. How's that?"

"Great. Sounds like a plan! Thanks," he said. I could tell by his voice that he really *was* happy about it. Maybe Emma knew her brother better than I gave her credit for. Maybe he was just too nervous—or too lazy—to ask anyone.

"It'll be fun," I said.

I hung up the phone and sat at my desk, staring at it with a huge, dorky smile on my face. I didn't care if I wasn't cool. I was sure I was the happiest girl in America right then. I'd gone for what I wanted and gotten it! And I'd hooked Emma up at the same time!

I went down the hall to Dylan's room in a trance. "You're fired," I said, walking in without knocking.

"What?" asked Dylan, looking up from her book in confusion.

"Your work is done," I said. "I'm cool."

Dylan rolled her eyes. "You can't fire me. I already quit," she said, and she turned back to her book.

"Either way," I said. "Mission accomplished."

CHAPTER 13

My Perfect Day

$\mathcal{S}$aturday was beautiful: a perfectly warm summer day, but there was a hint of fall in the air too. We were at Katie's bright and early, chatting about the parade route and whether we'd be cold in our costumes since the temperature was supposed to drop that night. Dylan had told me that kids in the past have gone to the stadium in advance to drop off bags with jackets and sweaters and stuff to save seats. I thought that was a pretty cool way to plan ahead, and I suggested we do that. Everyone loved the idea.

"How about the boys?" asked Emma. "Should we call and tell them too?"

"Well . . ." Not if I had to do the calling.

"Come on," said Emma. "It's not fair to them. They'll be freezing, and we'll be warm and toasty."

"Oh! I bet I could get Dan to lend me his jacket that would work great with Chris's costume. I'm going to call him and Chris right now!" said Mia.

"Alexis, you should call Matt," said Emma sternly.

"Fine," I said. And I did it too.

Lucky for me, he wasn't home, so I left a message with Mrs. Taylor. Phew!

We finished our cinnamon bun cupcakes with cream cheese frosting with plenty of time to spare. Katie's mom had Saturday morning hours at her office, but she was going to give us a ride, with our cupcakes, at twelve, so we had some time to kill.

"Hey, want to watch the last episode of *Celebrity Ballroom*? I DVRed it last night!" said Katie.

Emma and Mia were totally up for it, but I had to step in. "Ladies, let's do a quick meeting and then we can watch the show, okay? We just have some loose ends to tie up."

They moaned a little bit, but it was more for show, and I wasn't having any of it anymore. "If you want to stay in the club, pipe down. I'm toning down my management style, so you have to tone down your worker complaints, okay?" That shut them up fast.

I handed out flow charts that detailed the responsibilities of each person, the general time schedule we worked on, and an overview of the upcoming jobs we had for the next month. I also included a profit-and-loss statement that showed how much the cupcakes cost to bake and how much we could charge for them and how much we'd make. It was all organized by cupcake style, based on ingredients and unit cost.

"Wow, Alexis, this is awesome!" said Katie.

"You've been working really hard!" agreed Mia.

"I have. And the reason is so I don't have to be a nag anymore." I walked them through everything, and because it was laid out so cleanly and so simply, they understood it and were into it. It wasn't just some vague meeting with me nattering on about numbers. Mia had some good ideas about where we could innovate (display, supplying party goods) and where we might spend some of our profits (new platters, a new carrier to replace the one with the broken handle), and Emma made three suggestions for new recipes to try. Katie mentioned she'd seen the fancy vanilla extract we like for way cheaper at Williams-Sonoma, and we decided to take a field trip there the following week to stock up. All in all, it was a very productive meeting in which everyone felt heard and like they contributed.

"Okay? So we're all set," I said, closing my ledger and putting it away in my tote bag.

"Wait, that's it?" said Mia. "Usually we go way longer."

"Nope. Not anymore," I said. "Long, boring meetings are a thing of the past. Now let's go watch that show!"

At four o'clock, my mom dropped me off with my costume at the Taylors'. I was so nervous, I actually rang the doorbell. I felt like I wasn't sure who I was really going there to see.

Mrs. Taylor opened the door. "Alexis, honey! I'm so happy to see you! But why are you ringing the doorbell?"

"Um? I don't know. Practicing for Halloween, I guess!"

She laughed. "Come on in. They're upstairs."

"The Cupcakers? Who else is here already?"

"Oh, you're the first, honey. I meant Matt and Emma. Matt! Emma!" she called. "Alexis is here!"

"Okay! Hi, Alexis!" called Matt from upstairs.

I couldn't help it. I grinned from ear to ear.

"Come on up, Alexis!" yelled Emma.

I went upstairs with my bag, nervous and excited. My stomach was doing flip-flops and my palms were actually sweating. "Hello?" I called.

Matt cracked open his door. "We're in here, getting ready. Emma's in her room. We'll see you soon for the big reveal!" And then he shut the door again. I had to laugh.

"Emma?" I rapped on her door with my knuckles and then went in.

Pretty soon all four of us Cupcakers were there, laughing and playing music and getting ready. But I didn't want it to be too much about us four, so I hustled a little bit in order to get downstairs and meet up with Matt and Joe in the kitchen or TV room. I had heard them go down about ten minutes before we were ready.

"Let's go, girls," I said. They were all putting final dollops of makeup on and tweaking their belts and stuff as they looked in the mirror. Mia had done my hair, and I had dressed myself, carefully slipping on the glorious dress and adjusting my accessories. I had to admit, I looked great. I couldn't wait to see what Matt thought.

"You just want to get downstairs and see your date!" whispered Katie.

"So what if I do?" I laughed. I wasn't going to

hide my happiness or to play it cool. This was the best day of my life so far.

Just then there was a knock on the door. It was Mrs. Taylor. "Alexis, honey, your dad's on the phone."

"Okay, weird, but thanks." The Taylors were driving us over to the stadium in their minivan, so we could drop off our bag of sweaters and jackets, and then us to the start of the parade. I wondered why my dad could be calling.

"Hello?" I said, picking up the phone in the upstairs hallway. I smiled to think this was where Matt had been standing when I asked him out!

"Hi, sweetheart! I just couldn't wait to tell you. Mr. Donnelly called to say the head of the Future Business Leaders of America has accepted your application and that they were very excited about your essay and were looking forward to working with you. He said they don't usually call on the weekends, so he knew they were very impressed. Way to go, Lexi, my love!"

"Yahoo!" I squealed. "Thanks, Dad!"

I hung up the phone and went to tell the others. They were very happy for me, and we finally got downstairs, only moments before we were due to leave.

As I walked down the stairs, I thought about Dylan's advice on not being too friendly, acting like you don't care about stuff, playing it cool. I realized that's just no fun! Why hide your excitement?

As we rounded the corner and went into the kitchen, I saw Matt look up, his eyes searching for me. When they landed on me, they lit up. "Wow! Alexis, you look great!" he said.

"Thanks," I said, smiling. "So do you." And he did.

The parade was amazing, and the pep rally—with all our decorations—was even better. We stayed till the very end. The bonfire smoldered just at the end of the field, and the smell of the wood smoke, mixed with the smell of the popcorn and the hot dogs they were selling, created a delicious aroma I will never forget. It smelled like happiness. (I did make a mental note to approach the concession stand manager about selling cupcakes in the school's colors for the upcoming football games. Life's not all fun and games when there's money to be made!) We ate and cheered for our town's high school's fall sports teams. We had so much fun.

And of course we saw the PGC in their fairy costumes at the parade. Callie and Bella marched behind Sydney and her date. The outfits had actually turned out well. The girls looked beautiful, but they were clearly freezing to death. Their costumes were very light and sleeveless, and it was a bit chilly even for a summer night.

"Why do some girls think they need to wear so much makeup?" Matt asked as we walked by.

I shrugged. "I guess they think it makes them look cool," I said.

"It doesn't," said Matt, stating the obvious. Still, I was happy to hear it.

I felt Callie's eyes on us as we walked by, and I felt a little bad. But she did have a chance to invite Matt, after all, and she never went for it. Anyway, a part of me wondered if she really even liked him or if Sydney had just picked him out for her and bossed her into going for him. It was hard to tell. Either way, though, I was thrilled to be there—me, Matt, great costumes, fun night. It all worked out just right.

"Hey, Alexis!" I heard someone call. It was Janelle, who was dressed up as a nerd.

I cringed for a second at the thought of acknowledging her as a friend, right when the PGC was watching me, but then I pulled myself together and stopped to chat with her. After all, I had Matt by my side, so how uncool could I be?

By the end of the night, Chris and Mia were holding hands, and I saw George try to put his arm around Katie, but she swatted him away, laughing. I could feel Matt sneaking sideways glances at me, and it made me feel great. Emma and Joe had fun too, rating people's costumes and throwing popcorn at each other to see if they could catch it in their mouths. They were old friends after all, even though there was no romance there. By the end of the night, when Mr. Taylor came back to pick us up at our assigned meeting place, I didn't want to leave.

We dropped off Mia and then Katie. Chris and George had gotten their own rides home. Joe was sleeping at the Taylors', so he and Emma were still in the car—and Matt, of course—when Mr. Taylor pulled into my driveway.

Matt was sitting in one of the bucket seats next to the sliding door, so he hopped out to let me pass. Or so I thought.

"It's dark, so walk Alexis to the door," said Mr. Taylor.

"I was going to!" Matt said, and he walked me to my back door, which is kind of out of the way, on the other side of the garage.

"That was fun, Alexis. Thanks for inviting me.

I really had never planned on going. I thought it was . . . I don't know. Not such a cool thing to do. But you made it really cool, actually."

I smiled. "Thanks for coming with me. I had a great time too. I'm really glad we all went together too. Next time, I'll bring cupcakes," I said, laughing nervously.

We'd reached the door.

"Well, see you around school. Or, who knows, see you at my house tomorrow probably!" said Matt. And he leaned over and kissed me good-bye, really quickly, on my cheek.

I turned scarlet, but luckily he was already walking really fast down the path back to the car. "Bye!" I called, ecstatically happy. "Thanks!"

I sighed and just enjoyed the moment. Matt Taylor had kind of, sort of kissed me good night. It was absolutely, definitely the coolest thing ever.

Want another sweet cupcake?

Here's a sneak peek
of the next book in the

CUPCAKE DIARIES

series:

Katie
and the
cupcake war

Katie
and the
cupcake
war

You Are *Not* Going to Believe This!

"Mia! Is it really you? I haven't seen you in a gazillion years!" I cried, hugging my friend.

Mia laughed. "Katie, I was only gone for, like, four days," she said.

"That is four days, ninety-six hours, or five thousand, seven hundred, and sixty minutes," I said. Then I dramatically put my hand over my heart. "I know, because I counted them all."

"I missed you too," Mia said. "But you couldn't have missed me too much. You were trying out new recipes with the techniques you learned at cooking camp, weren't you?"

"Yes," I told her, "but it felt like you were gone forever. I almost didn't recognize you!"

Actually, I was kidding. Mia looked pretty much the same, with her straight black hair and dark eyes. She might have gotten a little bit tanner from her long weekend at the beach. She was wearing white shorts and a white tank top with a picture of a pink cupcake on it.

"Hey, I just noticed your shirt!" I said. "That's so cool!"

Mia smiled. "I made it at camp. One of the counselors there was totally into fashion, and she showed me how do this computer thing where you can turn your drawing into a T-shirt design."

I was definitely impressed. "You drew that? It's awesome."

"Thanks," Mia said. "I was thinking maybe I could make T-shirts for the Cupcake Club, for when we go on jobs. You know, so we could all dress alike."

Now it was my turn to laugh. We all like to bake cupcakes, but when it comes to fashion, the members of the Cupcake Club don't have much in common. "Well, I know we all wore matching sweatshirts when we won our first baking contest," I said. "But that was a special occasion. I don't know if you could create one T-shirt we would all be happy wearing on a semiregular basis."

Then the doorbell rang. It was Emma and Alexis, and what they were wearing proved my point. Emma is a real "girlie girl," although I don't mean that in a bad way, it just describes Emma really well. Pink is her favorite color, and I don't blame her, because pink looks really nice on you when you have blond hair and blue eyes like Emma does. She wore a pink sundress with tiny white flowers on it and pink flip-flops to match her dress.

Alexis had her curly red hair pulled back in a scrunchie, and she wore a light blue tennis shirt and jean shorts with white sneakers. And I might as well tell you what I was wearing: a yellow T-shirt from my cooking camp signed by all the kids who went there, ripped jeans with iron-on patches, and bare feet, because I was in my house, after all. Oh, and I painted each of my toenails a different color when I was bored.

"Mia! I missed you!" Emma cried, giving Mia a hug.

"So how was your first vacation with your mom, Eddie, and Dan?" Alexis asked. Eddie and Dan are Mia's stepdad and stepbrother, respectively.

"Pretty good," Mia replied. "The beach house was nice, and we got to play a lot of volleyball. And the boardwalk food was delicious."

"That reminds me," I said. "Follow me to the kitchen, guys."

My cooking camp experience had inspired me to surprise my friends for our Cupcake Club meeting. I had covered the kitchen table with my favorite tablecloth, a yellow one with orange and red flowers with green leaves. (Mom says she needs to wear sunglasses to eat when we use it, but I love the bright colors. Plus, they reminded me of the colors of Mexico, and it matched all the food I had made.)

Laid out on the table was a bowl of bright green guacamole, a platter of enchiladas with red sauce on top, homemade tortilla chips, a pitcher of fresh lemonade, and a plate of tiny cupcakes, each one topped with a dollop of whipped cream and sprinkled with cinnamon.

My friends gasped, and I felt really proud.

"Katie, this looks amazingly fantastic!" Mia said. "Did you make all this yourself?"

I nodded. "We had Mexican day in cooking camp, and I learned how to do all this stuff," I said. I pointed to the mini cupcakes. "Those are *tres leches* cupcakes."

"Three milks," Mia translated. "Those are

sweet and delicious. My *abuela* makes a *tres leches* cake when somebody has a birthday."

I nodded. "Emma, I thought they might be good for the bridal shop."

One of the Cupcake Club's biggest clients is the The Special Day bridal shop. We make mini cupcakes that they give to their customers, and the only requirement is that the frosting has to be white. Emma usually helps delivers them. She has even modeled the bridesmaids dresses at the bridal shop too. (I told you she was a girlie girl.)

"They look perfect!" Emma agreed. "So pretty. And I bet they taste as good as they look."

"Then let's start eating so you can find out," I suggested. "I think the enchiladas are getting cold."

Then my mom walked into the kitchen. She has brown hair, like me, but hers is curly, and today it was all messy. She looked tired, but I thought maybe it was because she had patients all morning. She's a dentist and has to work a lot.

"Oh, girls, you're here!" she said. "Alexis, how was your trip to the shore?"

"Actually, Mia's the one who went to beach," Alexis answered politely. "But thanks for asking."

Mom blushed. "Sorry, girls. I'm exhausted. My

head feels like it's full of spaghetti today."

"That's okay, Mrs. Brown," Mia said. "I had a good time."

Then the phone rang. "That's probably your grandmother," Mom said to me. "Come find me if you need anything, okay?"

"Shmpf," I replied. Actually, I was saying "sure," but my mouth was full of guacamole.

Alexis took a chip and dipped it in the guacamole.

"Wow, that's really good," she remarked when she was done chewing. (Unlike me, Alexis doesn't ever talk with her mouth full.)

"Thanks," I said. "Guacamole is my new favorite food. I could eat it all day. Guacamole on pancakes, guacamole pizza for dinner . . ."

"Guacamole-and-jelly sandwiches for lunch," Mia said, giggling.

"Gross!" Emma squealed.

"I think I'll stick to guacamole and chips," Alexis said matter-of-factly. Then she wiped her hands on a napkin and opened up her notebook. Alexis loves to get down to business at a Cupcake Club meeting.

"Okay. So, I was looking at our client list," she began. "The only thing on our schedule this fall is our usual gig at The Special Day. We need to drum up some new business. I was thinking that we could send out a postcard to everyone who's ever ordered cupcakes from us. You know, something like 'Summer's Over, and Cupcake Season Has Started.'"

"I like it," I said. Emma and Mia nodded in agreement.

"That reminds me," Mia said, pointing to her shirt. "I designed this. I could make a T-shirt for each of us. I thought we could wear them when we go on jobs."

"Oh, it's so cute!" Emma said. "Could my shirt be pink?"

Mia smiled. "I guess so. We could each have a different color shirt if we want. Unless you want it to be more like a uniform."

"Or we could expand our business and sell the T-shirts, too," Alexis said, sounding excited. "I bet we could find a site online where we could get the shirts made cheaply, and sell them for a profit."

Mia frowned a little bit. "I don't know, Alexis. I was thinking these should just be for us, you know? Special."

"But you want to be a fashion designer, don't you?" Alexis asked. "This could be the start of your business. Mia's Cupcake Clothing!"

Mia looked thoughtful, and I couldn't tell if she liked the idea or not. I decided to change the subject. If Mia decided she was interested, she'd bring up the idea again. Sometimes Alexis can get a little pushy when she wants the club to do something. Which is mostly good, because otherwise we'd never get anything done.

"Wow, I can't believe school is starting so soon." Then I said with a nod to Emma and Alexis, "Though what I really still can't believe is Sydney's singing routine at your day camp's talent show. It's in my nightmares."

When I first started middle school last year, Sydney Whitman made my life miserable. So I didn't feel bad about making fun of her—well, not *too* bad, anyway. My grandma Carole says that two wrongs don't make a right, and she's got a point. But Sydney really made my life miserable.

"Oh my gosh, I can't believe I forgot to tell you!" Emma said. "I have big news. *Huge!* You guys are *not* going to believe this!"

"Tell us what?" I asked.

"It's about Sydney," Emma said. "Sydney's mom returned a bunch of library books and told my mom that they were moving—to California!"

"No WAY!" I cried, jumping out of my chair. "Are you serious?"

Emma nodded. "I'm pretty sure they moved already. Sydney's dad got transferred to some company in San Diego or something. Sydney's mom said they had to move immediately for Sydney to start school there on time."

I started jumping up and down and waving my hands in the air.

"Look out, everyone. Katie's doing her happy dance," Mia said.

"This is awesome! Amazing! Stupendous! Wonderful! Did I say awesome?" I cried. "No more Sydney! No more Popular Girls Club to ruin our lives!"

"Well, actually, I'm sure the PGC will continue," Alexis replied. "They've still got Maggie and Bella and Callie. I bet Callie will become their new leader."

I felt like a balloon that somebody just popped. One of the reasons Sydney made my life miserable last year was because she took my best friend, Callie, away from me. Yes, I know that nobody forced Callie to dump me and become a member of the PGC. But it was always easier to blame

Sydney than to get mad at Callie. Callie and I have been friends since we were babies.

Oh, and the Popular Girls Club is just what it sounds like. It's a club Sydney started where they invite popular girls to join. They do everything together. I started to get so mad just thinking about it, then I realized Mia was talking to me.

"So Callie didn't mention any of this to you?" Mia asked.

"No!" I said, feeling a little exasperated. "I mean, I barely talk to her anymore."

I know I shouldn't get so freaked out about Callie. If she hadn't dumped me, I probably never would have become friends with Mia, Emma, and Alexis. There would be no Cupcake Club. But something happened to Callie when she got into middle school. Sometimes she could be not so nice. So it was probably for the best that we weren't friends. We saw each other when our families got together—our moms are best friends, and, yes, that gets really weird—but that was about it.

Anyway, I must admit, there was a little part of me that hoped, now that Sydney was gone, that Callie would be friends with me again. I imagined her showing up at the front door.

Oh, Katie, I have treated you so badly, she would

say. *Can I please join your Cupcake Club?*

Of course, I would say, trying to be the better person. *I forgive you, Callie.*

Then again, that would make things pretty confusing, because Mia was my best friend now, and I'm not sure how this would all work. Now *my* head felt like it was full of spaghetti. (Although I would never say that out loud, because that is such a weird mom thing to say.)

"Earth to Katie," Mia said. "You there?"

I snapped myself out of my fantasy. "Sorry. I must be in a guacamole haze," I said, taking my seat. "Okay. Enough about the PGC. Let's get down to business."

Maybe Alexis had the right idea after all.

What Was *That* All About?

(O)nce I stopped worrying about what Callie was going to do, I spent the next few days on a Sydney-free cloud of happiness. A world without Sydney was a world filled with rainbows, cotton candy, and sunshine every day. I didn't even get nervous about my first day of school.

Any normal person would have been nervous. Last year, the first day of middle school was one of the worst days of my life. I lost my best friend, got in trouble for using my cell phone, couldn't open my locker, and couldn't find my way around the school and was nearly late getting to every class.

But this year, things started out amazingly great. When I got on the bus, Mia was sitting in our usual seat in the sixth row from the front, saving it for me, just like always.

"Hey, you're wearing your lucky purple shirt," Mia said as I slid into my seat. She always notices what I'm wearing.

"Yeah, I need all the luck I can get," I said. "I do not want this year's first day of school to be like last year's."

Mia made a fake-hurt face. "Hey, you met me on the first day of school last year."

"That was the only good thing, believe me," I said. Then I remembered. "Besides meeting Alexis and Emma, too."

Then Mia noticed my hands. "Cool nails."

I wiggled my fingers. I had painted each fingernail in a different color this time. "For extra luck!"

"You don't need luck, Katie," Mia said. "You know how to do stuff this time. You'll be fine."

"I hope so," I said.

Then a boy with brown hair looked over the seat behind us. It was George Martinez, a kid I've known since elementary school. George always says a lot of funny stuff that makes me laugh. Sometimes he teases me, which is annoying, but he's still kind of funny. He was sitting next to his friend Ken Watanabe, as usual.

"Hi, Katie," he said. "How was the rest of your summer?"

George has never asked me a normal question like that before. For a second I didn't know what to say. I was trying to think of a funny reply, because I can usually make George laugh.

Then Mia nudged me, and I realized I was staring into space like a zombie again.

"Um, good," I finally answered.

"That's good," George said. Then he sat back down.

Mia leaned over to whisper into my ear. "He *so* likes you!"

"*Sshhh!*" I warned her. If George heard her, that would be so embarrassing. Mostly because I think I kind of like George, even though I'm not entirely sure what that's supposed to feel like. And if he liked me back, it might be awesome or it might be very weird.

Then the bus arrived at Park Street Middle School, a big U-shaped school made of bricks the color of sand. Before I climbed up the front steps with Mia, I stopped and got my schedule out of the front pocket of my backpack. I knew my homeroom class was in room number 322, but I wanted to make sure.

Just then Emma and Alexis walked up. They both live a few blocks away from the school, so they don't have to take the bus.

"Katie! Hooray! Now we can go to homeroom together," Emma said.

"Oh yeah! I forgot," I admitted. A few nights ago, we had all texted our schedules to one another to see if we were in the same classes together. Last year, I didn't have any friends in my homeroom class. I smiled. "Hey, I'm really lucky that you're in my homeroom. My good luck shirt must be working."

"*And* your good luck nail polish," Mia reminded me.

The front of the school was starting to get crowded, so I said good-bye to Alexis and Mia, and Emma and I headed to homeroom. We got to room 322 without getting lost, because we knew our way around the school already.

Inside the room we were greeted by these words written on the board: WELCOME, STUDENTS! GET READY FOR A MATH ADVENTURE! MR. KAZINSKI. The teacher sitting behind the desk at the front of the room was a tall man with sandy-blond hair and glasses. The walls around the room were decorated with posters that said stuff like "Believe

You Can Achieve," and others had math symbols on them.

Emma and I found seats in the row by the window before the bell rang. Mr. Kazinski stood up and smiled at us.

"Hey, it's good to see everyone today," he said. "I've got some announcements, but first, the news."

Right then Principal LaCosta's voice came over the PA speaker.

"Good morning, everyone, and welcome to the first day of school at Park Street," she said. "I can tell it's going to be a wonderful year. Let's start out by saying the Pledge of Allegiance together."

After the pledge, Mr. Kazinski started talking again. "By now you've guessed that my name is Mr. Kazinski, but you guys can call me Mr. K.," he said. "You'll see me for ten minutes every morning here in homeroom, and if you are taking my math class, you'll see me for forty minutes more."

I glanced at my schedule. I had math next, in this very room, with Mr. K. More good luck! I don't love math, but I already liked Mr. K. My math teacher last year, Mrs. Moore, was okay but she was pretty strict and not very friendly. She was a cloudy day compared to Mr. K.'s sunny day, if you know what I mean.

Another point for my lucky purple shirt, I thought happily.

And I got even luckier because even though I had to say good-bye to Emma after homeroom, Mia walked into the room. We had math together!

The morning just seemed to get better and better. My second-period class, Spanish, was just down the hall. Then I went to gym class, and I was so happy—Emma, Mia, and Alexis were there!

I should probably explain my history with gym, or "physical education," as teachers like to call it. I'm a pretty fast runner, but when it comes to most other sports stuff, I'm sort of a spaz. When we play volleyball and I hit the ball, I usually end up hitting the wall or the ceiling or a person. It's not pretty. And last year, I got teased pretty hard about it.

I *am* good at softball, though. I even made the school team. But I like playing for fun. I'm not competitive, and being on a team that always played to win stressed me out too much, so I gave it up.

This year, though, I would have my three best friends to back me up in gym class. And I knew I would need it, because I had the same gym teacher, Ms. Chen. She acts more like an army drill sergeant than a middle school teacher. Honestly, she scares me.

Since it was the first day of school, we didn't have to change into our gym clothes or anything. So before the bell rang, we were all just kind of hanging out on the bleachers. Some of the boys were running around and throwing basketballs at one another.

One of the balls bounced right up to where I was sitting with my friends. It rolled to my feet, so I picked it up, and George Martinez ran over to get it.

"Hey, Silly Arms! We're in the same class again," he said, smiling.

George started calling me Silly Arms last year, because of the way I play volleyball. I've never looked in a mirror while playing volleyball, but I guess I must look pretty silly. I never get mad because I know he's just teasing, like he always does. But then some other kids (like Sydney and her friends, for instance) started calling me that to be mean.

Before I could say anything to George, Eddie Rossi ran up behind him. Eddie is the tallest kid in our grade, and probably in our whole school. Last year he even grew a mustache. But I guess he shaved it over the summer, because his face looked clean-shaven again.

Anyway, this is what Eddie said: "Hey, leave her alone!"

"It's okay," George replied. "Katie's cool!"

Then he took the ball from me and tossed it to Eddie, and they both ran off.

My mouth was open so wide, you could probably have fit a whole cupcake into it.

"That was weird," I said.

"It's so obvious," Alexis said. "Eddie likes you."

"No way," I told her. "It makes no sense. Last year Eddie teased me just as bad as Sydney did. He used to call me Silly Arms all the time. Besides, he's a jock who likes popular girls, not girls like me."

"That doesn't mean he can't still like you," Alexis argued. "People change all the time. He doesn't even have a mustache anymore."

"Well, I think that Eddie and George *both* like Katie," Mia said.

I must have been blushing, because my face

felt hot. I am not the kind of girl who boys get a crush on, and especially not *two* boys at once.

Then Ms. Chen marched in, blowing her whistle, and for once I was glad to see her.

"Stand up and look alive, people! Just because it's the first day of school doesn't mean you can be slackers!"

I jumped to my feet pretty quickly. You definitely don't want Ms. Chen on your case. But I couldn't stop wondering about what happened with Eddie and George and if it meant I was still having good luck or not.

WORLD'S BIGGEST CUPCAKE!

This Means War!

$\mathcal{M}$s. Chen spent the whole gym period telling us the rules of gym and giving us advice about fitness. Finally, the bell rang.

"That was totally boring, but definitely better than being hit in the head by a volleyball," I told my friends as we left. Everyone laughed.

"Don't worry. I'm sure that will happen next week," Mia teased me.

"Hey, we can all go to lunch together," Emma realized.

"I'm going to stop at my locker first," I said. "This math book is pretty heavy. I don't want to carry it around all afternoon."

"No problem, we can all meet at our table, like always," Mia said.

I liked the sound of that. On the first day of school last year, I didn't know where to sit. Now I had three good friends to sit with. I would definitely call that lucky!

Last year I was convinced that my locker was an evil robot out to get me. It's one of those lockers where the lock is built into the door, and the school gives you the combination. I swear I always put in the right one, but that locker never wanted to open.

So I took a deep breath as I slowly turned the dial.

26 . . . 14 . . . 5 . . .

I pulled the handle, and the door wouldn't open.

Oh no! It's happening again! I thought. My heart began to beat faster. I took another deep breath and turned again.

26 . . . 14 . . . 5 . . .

Click! I pulled the handle, and the door opened up.

"Thank you, lucky fingernails," I whispered.

Then I noticed the two girls at the lockers next to me. They were talking pretty loudly.

"It's true! Sydney really moved!" one girl said.

"Does this mean no more PGC?" the other girl asked.

As I headed to the lunchroom, I heard more kids talking.

"I heard the PGC broke up."

"I heard that Sydney left Maggie in charge."

"I wonder if they'll let me join now."

I kind of couldn't believe how many people were talking about Sydney. She was miles away, and she was still the most popular person in school. In a way, that's kind of impressive.

Mia, Emma, Alexis, and I ended up in the cafeteria together at the same time. We made our way to our favorite table, near the back of the room. Alexis and Emma put down their backpacks and went to get on the lunch line. Mia and I always bring lunch from home, so we opened up our lunch bags.

"Did your mom pack you a back-to-school cupcake?" Mia asked.

"Probably," I said. There's been a special cupcake in my first school lunch ever since I could remember.

But when I opened up my bag, I found a turkey and guacamole wrap, an apple, a bag of carrot sticks, and my water bottle—but no cupcake.

"That's weird," I said. "Maybe she forgot to put it in." I felt pretty disappointed.

Suddenly a strange hush came over the noisy

cafeteria, and Mia and I both looked up to see what was going on.

My former best friend, Callie, was walking through the cafeteria with Maggie and Bella, the other two members of the PGC. Even though they all look different—Callie is tall with blond hair and blue eyes; Maggie is kind of short with crazy, curly brown hair; and Bella (her real name is Brenda) has dark hair and tries to look like that girl from those vampire movies—they were all dressed kind of the same. They each had on short-sleeved sweaters, plaid skirts, dark tights, and ankle boots.

"Those outfits are straight out of last month's *Teen Style*," Mia observed.

"Isn't it kind of warm for sweaters?" I wondered. "It's still officially summer, you know."

The three of them casually walked to the PGC's usual table, but you could tell they knew everyone was looking at them. Then Alexis and Emma came back to our table with their lunch trays.

"Well, I guess the PGC is still going strong," Alexis remarked.

"*Everyone's* talking about it," Emma said as she sat down.

"I know," I told them. "It's kind of crazy."

"Anyway, I have way more exciting news than

that," Alexis said. "We haven't even gotten our fly-ers out yet, but I booked a job today. Ms. Biddle stopped me in the hallway. She wants some cup-cakes for a birthday party in a couple of months."

Ms. Biddle was our science teacher last year, and one of our first customers. She's really cool.

"Awesome," I said. "I wonder what kind she wants?"

"Before we talk about that, we should talk about this year's school fund-raiser," Alexis said. "I so want to win again."

I took a bite of my turkey wrap and nodded. At the start of the year, the school has this big fair right before the first school dance, and school groups have booths and try to raise money for the school. Last year our cupcake booth raised the most money, and we won. The PGC did this awful makeover booth, and it felt kind of good to beat them.

"Last year we did the school colors and went with vanilla cupcakes," Alexis reminded us. "I'm thinking that we need to switch it up this year."

Mia nodded. "Yeah, we can do something really creative."

We all got excited thinking of what we could do.

"How about a big tower of cupcakes?" Emma suggested.

"Cool!" I cried. "Or maybe we could do the world's biggest cupcake and sell pieces of it."

"Then we would need the world's biggest oven," Alexis pointed out.

"Maybe we could think of a theme, and then we could decorate the booth in the theme and do cupcakes to match," Mia said.

We really liked that idea. "But what kind of theme?" I asked. "It should have something to do with school, right?"

We were so busy talking that I didn't notice when Callie walked up to the table, followed by Maggie and Bella.

"Hey, Katie," she said, and I jumped a little at the sound of my name.

"Oh hey, Callie," I said, although what I really wanted to say was, *What on Earth are you doing at our table?*

"So, I was just wondering if you guys are going to do cupcakes for the fund-raiser this year," she said.

Alexis looked straight at her. "Well," she said, "we're the Cupcake Club. It's kind of a given."

Callie ignored her. "Well, we were thinking of doing cupcakes this year."

I almost choked on my carrot stick. The PGC

could *not* do cupcakes! That was copying! I was about to start freaking out when Mia spoke up in her usual calm, cool way.

"I guess may the best cupcake win, then," she said.

Callie got a look on her face, like maybe she wasn't expecting that answer. Like maybe she *wanted* us to freak out. I was glad Mia spoke up first.

"Well, then, I guess it's on," she said, tossing her hair. (And when did she start doing that, anyway?)

Then she turned and walked away, and Maggie and Bella followed her, just like they used to follow Sydney.

"They can't even come up with their own idea!" Alexis fumed.

"'It's on'?" Emma repeated. "What is she even talking about? I thought Callie wasn't as bad as Sydney. She might be worse!"

Mia nodded. "I guess it's clear who the new leader of the PGC is."

I didn't say anything. I couldn't. I felt terrible. It wasn't just the PGC declaring war on the Cupcake Club. It was *Callie* declaring war on *me*. That's what it felt like, anyway. This was the girl I learned to ride bikes with, who I had a zillion sleepovers with, who knew my deepest secrets. I never did anything to make her stop being friends with me, and she dumped me. That was bad enough. But this . . . this really hurt.

I looked down at my rainbow-painted fingernails.

So much for my lucky day, I thought.

Still Hungry?
There's always room for another Cupcake!

Katie and the cupcake cure
CUPCAKE DIARIES
by coco simon

Mia in the mix
CUPCAKE DIARIES
by coco simon

Emma on thin icing
CUPCAKE DIARIES
by coco simon

Alexis and the perfect recipe
CUPCAKE DIARIES
by coco simon

Katie, batter up!
CUPCAKE DIARIES
by coco simon

Mia's baker's dozen
CUPCAKE DIARIES
by coco simon

Emma all stirred up!
CUPCAKE DIARIES
by coco simon

Alexis cool as a cupcake
CUPCAKE DIARIES
by coco simon

Katie and the cupcake war
CUPCAKE DIARIES

Mia's boiling point
CUPCAKE DIARIES

Emma, smile and say "cupcake!"
CUPCAKE DIARIES

Alexis gets frosted
CUPCAKE DIARIES

Designed by Mia

Mia is always sketching! She has dreams of being a world-famous fashion designer someday. In *Mia's Baker's Dozen*, she sketches a sleek winter coat, a birthday party dress for her friend Ava, and a Valentine's Day outfit.

Designed by . . .

Do you think you could be a fashion designer? Draw your sketches here. (If fashion isn't your thing, use the space to draw a picture of you with your BFFs!) (If you don't want to write in your book, make a copy of this page.)

A Little Sweet Talk! #1

There are 18 words in this puzzle, and they all have
something to do with your four favorite Cupcake girls!
Can you find them all?

(If you don't want to write in your book, make a copy of this page.)

WORD LIST: ALEXIS, BACON, BAKE, BATTER, CARAMEL, CHOCOLATE,
CINNAMON, COCONUT, CREAM, CUPCAKE, EGGS, EMMA, FLOUR, ICING,
KATIE, MIA, MILK, SUGAR

N	O	C	A	B	I	C	I	N	G
B	C	A	R	A	M	E	L	J	M
A	S	E	V	E	M	M	A	P	I
T	B	A	K	E	A	R	I	S	A
T	R	U	O	L	F	M	I	L	K
E	C	H	O	C	O	L	A	T	E
R	A	G	U	S	K	A	T	I	E
A	L	E	X	I	S	S	G	G	E
G	C	O	C	O	N	U	T	W	D
E	K	A	C	P	U	C	G	H	I
M	C	I	N	N	A	M	O	N	T

A Little Sweet Talk! #2

There are 22 words in this puzzle, and they all have something to do with your four favorite Cupcake girls! Can you find them all?

(If you don't want to write in your book, make a copy of this page.)

WORD LIST: AGENT, BROTHER, CAMP, CHARM, CONFIDENCE, CUPCAKE, DRESS, FRIENDSHIP, FLUTE, HIKE, JAKE, MODEL, PERFORM, POISE, POOL, SING, SISTER, STAR, STYLE, SWIM, TALENT, WEDDING

D	R	E	S	S	M	R	A	H	C
P	A	J	B	Y	O	J	A	K	E
O	D	G	H	M	D	P	M	A	C
I	R	S	E	F	E	L	Y	T	S
S	T	A	R	N	L	M	I	W	S
E	P	O	O	L	T	E	K	I	H
C	O	N	F	I	D	E	N	C	E
J	G	C	U	P	C	A	K	E	S
G	N	I	D	D	E	W	N	D	I
F	L	U	T	E	G	N	I	S	S
B	R	O	T	H	E	R	A	M	T
R	E	T	N	E	L	A	T	G	E
P	E	R	F	O	R	M	D	E	R
F	R	I	E	N	D	S	H	I	P

A Little Sweet Talk! #3

There are 16 words in this puzzle, and they all have something
to do with your four favorite Cupcake girls! Can you find them all?

(If you don't want to write in your book, make a copy of this page.)

WORD LIST: ACCESSORY, BLUSH, CAKE, FAIRY, FROSTING, GOOFY, HAIR,
INVOICE, LOCKER, MAKEUP, PARTY, PROFIT, PRICE, REPUTATION, STYLISH, WIG

```
R  E  P  U  T  A  T  I  O  N
C  O  E  C  I  O  V  N  I  K
F  Z  P  R  I  C  E  D  F  G
A  B  S  T  Y  L  I  S  H  Y
I  W  L  Y  T  R  A  P  N  C
R  Z  I  U  G  O  O  F  Y  P
Y  G  I  W  S  C  A  K  E  R
L  J  L  L  M  H  A  I  R  O
M  A  K  E  U  P  I  S  H  F
R  E  K  C  O  L  O  M  E  I
A  C  C  E  S  S  O  R  Y  T
G  N  I  T  S  O  R  F  A  B
```

All Mixed Up! #1

Mia gave Emma a shopping list, but Jake scrambled all the words. Can you figure out what the words are supposed to be? Write each word correctly on the lines. Then write the circled letters in order, on the lines on the bottom of the page. You'll have the answer to a cupcake riddle!

(If you don't want to write in your book, make a copy of this page.)

COCHOTELA _ _ _ ◯ _ _ _ _ _

AUSRG _ _ _ _ ◯

RACAMLE _ ◯ _ _ _ _ _

MAERC ◯ _ _ _ _

LIMK _ _ _ ◯

ESGG ◯ _ _ _

STARDUC _ _ _ _ _ _ ◯

NOMANNIC _ _ _ _ ◯ _ _ _

DANCY _ _ _ _ ◯

NOCCOUT _ ◯ _ _ _ _ _

LOUFR _ ◯ _ _ _

KEAC _ _ ◯ _

RIDDLE: Why did the cupcake laugh at the egg?

RIDDLE ANSWER:

Because the egg _ _ _ _ _ _ _ _ _ _ _ _ _!

All Mixed Up! #2

The words below were used in *Alexis Cool as a Cupcake*.
Unscramble each word, and write the correctly spelled
words on the lines. Then write the circled letters in order,
on the lines at the bottom of the page.
You'll have the answer to a silly cupcake riddle.

(If you don't want to write in your book, make a copy of this page.)

UBSESSIN Ⓞ _ _ _ _ _ _ _

KEACPUC _ _ _ _ _ _Ⓞ

YEALD _ _ _Ⓞ _

TORTU Ⓞ_ _ _ _

WEO _Ⓞ_

WHEENALLO Ⓞ_ _ _ _ _ _ _ _

PEICRE _ _ _Ⓞ _ _

DERAPA Ⓞ_ _ _ _ _

FESSPROION Ⓞ_ _ _ _ _ _ _ _ _

TUMECOS _ _ _ _ _Ⓞ

DIEINGRENT _ _ _ _ _Ⓞ_ _ _

RIDDLE: Why did the cupcakes think the cook was mean?
RIDDLE ANSWER: Because she _ _ _ _ the eggs
and _ _ _ _ _ _ _ _ the cream!

Two for the Price of One!

The Cupcake Club is having a sale: two cupcakes for the price of one! The only catch is that you have to find the two cupcakes in this dozen that are decorated exactly alike. Can you find and circle them?

(If you don't want to write in your book, make a copy of this page.)

ANSWER KEY:

A Little Sweet Talk! #1

```
D  R  E  S  S  m  R  A  H  C
P  A  J  B  Y  O  J  A  K  E
O  D  G  H  m  D  P  m  A  C
I  R  S  E  F  E  L  Y  T  S
S  T  A  R  N  L  m  I  W  S
E  P  O  O  L  T  E  K  I  H
C  O  N  F  I  D  E  N  C  E
J  G  C  U  P  C  A  K  E  S
G  N  I  D  D  E  W  N  D  I
F  L  U  T  E  G  N  I  S  S
B  R  O  T  H  E  R  A  m  T
R  E  T  N  E  L  A  T  G  E
P  E  R  F  O  R  m  D  E  R
F  R  I  E  N  D  S  H  I  P
```

A Little Sweet Talk! #2

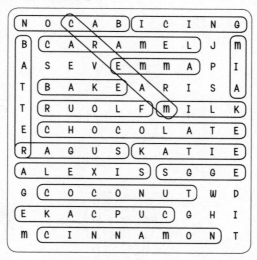

```
N  O  C  A  B  I  C  I  N  G
B  C  A  R  A  M  E  L  J  m
A  S  E  V  E  m  m  A  P  I
T  B  A  K  E  A  R  I  S  A
T  R  U  O  L  F  m  I  L  K
E  C  H  O  C  O  L  A  T  E
R  A  G  U  S  K  A  T  I  E
A  L  E  X  I  S  S  G  G  E
G  C  O  C  O  N  U  T  W  D
E  K  A  C  P  U  C  G  H  I
m  C  I  N  N  A  M  O  N  T
```

ANSWER KEY:

A Little Sweet Talk! #3

```
R  E  P  U  T  A  T  I  O  N
C  O  E  C  I  O  V  N  I  K
F  Z  P  R  I  C  E  D  F  G
A  B  S  T  Y  L  I  S  H  Y
I  W  L  Y  T  R  A  P  N  C
R  Z  I  U  G  O  O  F  Y  P
Y  G  I  W  S  C  A  K  E  R
L  J  L  L  m  H  A  I  R  O
m  A  K  E  U  P  I  S  H  F
R  E  K  C  O  L  O  m  E  I
A  C  C  E  S  S  O  R  Y  T
G  N  I  T  S  O  R  F  A  B
```

All Mixed Up! #1

COCHOTELA	C H O C O L A T E
AUSRG	S U G A R
RACAMLE	C A R A M E L
MAERC	C R E A M
LIMK	M I L K
ESGG	E G G S
STARDUC	C U S T A R D
NOMANNIC	C I N N A M O N
DANCY	C A N D Y
NOCCOUT	C O C O N U T
LOUFR	F L O U R
KEAC	C A K E

RIDDLE: Why did the cupcake laugh at the egg?
RIDDLE ANSWER: Because the egg CRACKED A YOLK!

ANSWER KEY:

All Mixed Up! #2

UBSESSIN   ⒷU S I N E S S

KEACPUC   C U P C A K Ⓔ

YEALD   D E L Ⓐ Y

TORTU   ⓉU T O R

WEO   O Ⓦ E

WHEENALLO   ⒽA L L O W E E N

PEICRE   R E C Ⓘ P E

DERAPA   ⒫A R A D E

FESSPROION   ⒫R O F E S S I O N

TUMECOS   C O S T U M Ⓔ

DIEINGRENT   I N G R E Ⓓ I E N T

RIDDLE: Why did the cupcakes think the cook was mean?
RIDDLE ANSWER: Because she B E A T the eggs
and W H I P P E D the cream!

Two for the Price of One!

Are you an
Emma, a *Mia*, a *Katie*, or an *Alexis*?
Take our quiz and find out!

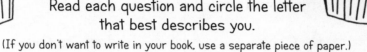

Read each question and circle the letter
that best describes you.

(If you don't want to write in your book, use a separate piece of paper.)

1. You've been invited to a party. What do you wear?

   A. Jeans and a cute T-shirt. You want to look nice, but you also want to be comfortable.

   B. You beg your parents to lend you money for the cool boots you saw online. If you're going to a party, you have to wear the latest fashion!

   C. Something pretty, but practical. If you're going to spend money on a new outfit, it better be one you'll be able to wear a lot.

   D. Something feminine—lacy and floral. And definitely pink if not floral—a girl can never go wrong wearing *pink*!

2. Your idea of a perfect Saturday afternoon is:

A. Seeing a movie with your BFFs and then going out for pizza afterward.

B. THE MALL! Hopefully one of the stores will be having a big sale!

 C. Creating a perfect budget to buy clothes, go out with friends, and save money for college—all at the same time—and then meeting your friends for lunch.

D. Going for a manicure and pedicure.

3. You have to study for a big test. What's your study style?

A. In your bedroom, with your favorite music playing.

B. At home, with help from your parents if necessary.

C. At the library, where you can take out some new books after you've finished studying, or anyplace else that's absolutely quiet.

D. Anyplace away from *home*—away from your messy, loud siblings!

4. There's a new girl at school. What's your first reaction?

A. You're a little cautious. You've been hurt before, so it takes you a while to warm up to new friends.

B. You think it's great. You welcome her with open arms. (Maybe you can share each other's clothes!)

C. If she's nice *and* smart, maybe you'll consider being friends with her.

D. You'll gladly welcome another friend—as long as she really wants to be friends with you—and not just meet your cute older brothers!

5. When it comes to boys . . .

A. They make you a little nervous. You want to be friends first—for a long time—until you'd consider someone a boyfriend.

B. He has to be tall, trustworthy, sweet—and of course, superstylish!

C. He has to be cute, funny, and smart—and he gets extra points if he likes to dance!

D. He has to be loyal and true as well as good-looking. You look sweet, but you're tough when you have to be.

6. When it comes to your family . . .

A. You come from a single-parent home. It's hard for you to imagine your parent dating, but you will try to get used to it.

B. You come from a mixed family with stepsiblings and a stepparent. At first it was overwhelming, but you're starting to get used to having everyone in the mix!

C. You get along okay with your parents, but your older sister thinks she's queen of the world. Still sometimes you ask her for advice anyway.

D. You live in a house with many brothers—dirty, sticky, smelly boys! You love them all, but sometimes would give anything for a sister!

7. Your dream vacation would be:

A. Anyplace beachy. You love to swim and also just relax on a beach blanket.

B. Paris—to see the latest fashions.

C. Egypt—you'd love to see the pyramids and try to figure out how they were constructed without any modern machinery.

D. Holland—you'd love to see the tulips in bloom!

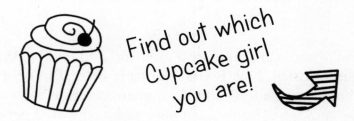

Find out which Cupcake girl you are!

Which Cupcake girl are you?
What your answers mean:

Mostly As:
You're a Katie! Your style is easy and comfortable.
You always look good, and you always feel good too.
You have a few very close friends (both girls and boys),
and you like it that way. You don't want to confide
in just anybody.

Mostly Bs:
You're a Mia! You're the girl everyone envies at school
because you can wear an old ratty sweatshirt and jeans
and somehow still look like a runway model. Your
sense of style is what everyone notices first, but you're
also a great friend.

Mostly Cs:
You're an Alexis! You are supersmart and not afraid to
show it! You get As in every subject, and like nothing
more than creating business plans and budgets. You love
your friends but have to remember sometimes that not
everyone in the world is as brilliant as you are.

Mostly Ds:
You're an Emma! You are a girly-girl and love to wear
pretty clothes. Pink is your signature color. But people
should not be fooled by your sweet exterior. You can
be as tough as nails when necessary and would never
let anyone push you around.

How well do you know the Cupcake girls?

Take our quiz and find out!

(If you don't want to write in your book,
use a separate piece of paper.)

1. Emma has three brothers. What are their names?

    A. Joe, Mark, and Sam

    B. Matt, Sam, and John

    C. Jake, Matt, and Sam

    D. Tom, Dick, and Harry

2. Who *loves* to dance?

    A. Mia

    B. Alexis

    C. Emma

    D. Katie

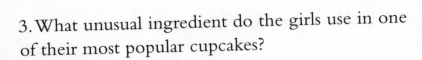

3. What unusual ingredient do the girls use in one of their most popular cupcakes?

   A. Salami

   B. French fries

    yum!

   C. Bacon

   D. Pizza

4. Where does Emma model?

   A. At the summer day camp

   B. At The Special Day wedding salon

   C. At the local swimming pool

   D. At school dances

5. Mia has a BFF in New York whose first name has three letters too. What is her friend's name?

   A. Amy

   B. Gia

   C. Ava

   D. Ivy

6. George teases Katie and calls her a funny nickname. (But it's okay though because Katie knows he likes her.) What is the nickname?

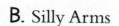
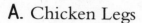

A. Chicken Legs

B. Silly Arms

C. Bigfoot

D. Man Hands

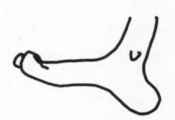

7. Which Cupcake girl has curly red hair?

A. Alexis

B. Mia

C. Katie

D. Emma

8. Who is the "mean girl" who loves to torture the Cupcake girls?

A. Sydney

B. Beth

C. Olivia

D. Both A and C

Did you get the right answers?

1. C   5. C
2. B   6. B
3. C   7. A
4. B   8. D

What your answers mean:

If you got all 8 answers right:
Wow! You know your Cupcake girls.
Four cupcakes for you!

If you got 6 to 7 answers right:
Pretty good! You just need to brush up a little bit on
your four Cupcake friends. Two cupcakes for you!

If you got 4 to 5 answers right:
You need to reread your favorite Cupcake books, but
you get one cupcake for your efforts!

If you got less than four answers right:
You're not paying attention. Reread this book (and all
your favorite Cupcake books) right now! No cupcake
for you—have a cookie!

Want more

CUPCAKE DIARIES?

Visit **CupcakeDiariesBooks.com** for the series trailer, excerpts, activities, and everything you need for throwing your own cupcake party!

Did you LOVE reading this book?

Visit the Whyville...

Where you can:

- Discover great books!
- Meet new friends!
- Read exclusive sneak peeks and more!

Log on to visit now!
bookhive.whyville.net

If you liked

CUPCAKE  DIARIES

be sure to check out these

other series from

Simon Spotlight

sew zoey

Great stories are like great accessories: You can never have too many! Collect all the books in the Sew Zoey series:

Ready to Wear

On Pins and Needles

Lights, Camera, Fashion!

Stitches and Stones

Cute as a Button

A Tangled Thread

Knot Too Shabby!

Swatch Out!

A Change of Lace

Bursting at the Seams

Clothes Minded

Dressed to Frill

Sewing in Circles

EVERY SECRET LEADS TO ANOTHER

SECRETS of the MANOR

Hidden passages, mysterious diaries, and centuries-old secrets abound in this spellbinding series. Join generations of girls from the same family tree as they uncover the secrets that lurk within their sumptuous family manor homes!

EBOOK EDITIONS ALSO AVAILABLE

SecretsoftheManorBooks.com • Published by Simon Spotlight • Kids.SimonandSchuster.com

If you like reading about the adventures of Katie, Mia, Emma, and Alexis, you'll love Alex and Ava, stars of the It Takes Two series!

A Whole New Ball Game
by Belle Payton

1

Two Cool For School
by Belle Payton

2

EBOOK EDITIONS ALSO AVAILABLE
ItTakesTwoBooks.com • Published by Simon Spotlight • Kids.SimonandSchuster.com